PRAISE F

SINNER'S CREED

"This may look like a classic Motorcycle Club tale, but Jones takes it to another level with a depth and realness that is absolutely refreshing."   —*New York Daily News*

"Unlike any MC romance you've ever read. Jones delivers an angsty, heart-wrenching and wholly unique story."
—*RT Book Reviews*

"Profane and raw."   —*Publishers Weekly*

"[Jones] takes the harshness of the MC lifestyle and breathes life into it . . . [*Sinner's Creed*] has every element that MC lovers crave and all the heart that romance lovers need."
—Mommy's a Book Whore

ALSO BY KIM JONES

Sinner's Creed

SINNER'S REVENGE

KIM JONES

B

BERKLEY BOOKS, NEW YORK

BERKLEY

An imprint of Penguin Random House LLC
375 Hudson Street, New York, New York 10014

Library of Congress Cataloging-in-Publication Data

Names: Jones, Kim, date– author.
Title: Sinner's revenge / Kim Jones.
Description: Berkley trade paperback edition. | New York : Berkley Books,
2016. | Series: A Sinner's Creed novel ; 2
Identifiers: LCCN 2015045536 (print) | LCCN 2015049996 (ebook) | ISBN
9781101987728 (softcover) | ISBN 9781101987711 (ebook)
Subjects: LCSH: Motorcyclists—Fiction. | Man-woman relationships—Fiction. |
BISAC: FICTION / Romance / Contemporary. | FICTION / Contemporary Women. |
FICTION / Romance / General. | GSAFD: Love stories. |
Romantic suspense fiction.
Classification: LCC PS3610.O6267 S58 2016 (print) | LCC PS3610.O6267 (ebook)
| DDC 813/.6—dc23
LC record available at http://lccn.loc.gov/2015045536

PUBLISHING HISTORY
Berkley trade paperback edition / July 2016

PRINTED IN THE UNITED STATES OF AMERICA

10 9 8 7 6 5 4 3 2 1

Cover photo by Claudio Marinesco.
Cover design by George Long.
Interior text design by Kelly Lipovich.

Penguin
Random
House

To *the true meaning of brotherhood, and those who* express it.

"I have only one job in this life—to be my brother's keeper."

—BHMS

ACKNOWLEDGMENTS

To God for giving me the gift of life, the courage to take a chance, and an eternal love.

The husband who loves me.

My family who believed in me.

My friends who bought me booze.

HNDW—my inspiration.

Amy Tannenbaum because I feel obligated.

The Berkley team who made this possible.

Everyone I forced to sit on my futon, so I could read to them.

Katy Evans—the woman who just gets me.

The BFF who has been with me since day one.

And every reader who makes my dreams come true every day.

PROLOGUE

PINK FLOYD'S "WISH You Were Here" is blasting on my stereo. I hear the low rumble of motorcycles, riding at a slow pace. Beneath my feet, the concrete shakes with the vibrations of pipes. Hundreds of bikes ride behind me in two straight lines. And in front of me, in a glass custom-built trailer, lies the body of my brother.

And my best friend.

I've tried to imagine I was honoring someone else while leading the pack in a final ride. My mind flashes with images of Dirk riding beside me. I can almost feel the hate radiating off him—his mind spinning in a hundred different ways on how to bring hell to those who just earned revenge by the hands of Sinner's Creed's finest. His presence is so powerful that I turn and look to my left, expecting to see him wearing that pissed-off look he perfected. But I see nothing.

The reality hits me again, and it hurts just as bad now as it did when I first found out.

One phone call.

Two words.

Dirk's dead.

He's gone.

Forever.

And all I have left are material things to remind me that he was real. His house. His money. What's left of his bike. And Saylor's diary—the most painful reminder of all.

He was her king.

She was his queen.

I hold the greatest love story of all time inside my cut—close to my heart. The story lives on, but their love will be buried today. Laid to rest with my brother, whose freshly dug grave lies next to the woman who saved him.

I wish this tragedy had ended differently. It should have been me they found dead on that highway. It should be Dirk riding behind my casket today. I pulled the trigger that night. But Dirk took the fall. If he were here, he'd tell me to quit feeling sorry for myself. He'd tell me he only had two reasons to live—Saylor and Sinner's Creed. One was already gone. The other he died for.

He'd give me that look that made me feel stupid. Then he'd ask, "Do you really think I'd just lay down and die? I went out the way I wanted. They didn't kill me, Shady. I was already dead."

And he was.

He is.

Tears fill my eyes, but I force them back. Dirk doesn't want my tears. He wants my wrath. My tribute will be paid by slaughtering those who did this. It's more meaningful, and a fuck of a lot bloodier.

Inside, I'm screaming in agony. But no one can hear me. My eyes are filled with sorrow and loss. But no one can see it. My chest aches with a thousand flames from the fiery sea of hell. But no one can feel it. No one but me.

Shady.

The man who was born with nothing, lost everything he'd gained, and has something he doesn't deserve. Life.

Whatever controls me, whether it is my instincts or my subconscious, leads me to a deep hole surrounded by men and a handful of shovels. These men are said to be my brothers, but the truth is, only one ever really earned that title. And I watch as they lower his body into the ground.

Every patch holder strives to make the club prosper. Many will die trying. Dirk did it by just existing. His life stood for what the patch really means. And his death proved that he was willing to give it all for Sinner's Creed.

He will be remembered as the greatest Nomad that ever rode.

A man of power.

A leader.

A ruthless enforcer.

A fucking legend.

He's the most loyal man I ever knew. I never understood respect until I gained his. He's the greatest loss I've ever suffered. And in this moment, I struggle to find the strength to let him go.

I want to crawl into the six-foot hole and breathe life back into his body. I want the man who was too fucking mean to die to rise from this grave. But death was peace for Dirk. And now I have to be at peace too.

I grab a handful of dirt, letting it slowly sift through my fingers and fall reverently on my brother. The granules of sand drop silently, but I swear I can hear every particle as they land on the wooden box.

The other patch holders follow suit, taking turns to bury one of our own. The process is slow and torturous, but I beg for it to go on forever. I know that once the hole is filled, then it's over. It will be the end. Just like the last page in Saylor's diary.

This is the end. The end to a beautiful life for me, Saylor Samson.

Now it's the end of Dirk's life. The only beauty of it came from his time with Saylor. With her he found happiness. And when he found it, it was like I found it too. But just like Dirk, that happiness is now buried.

After everyone leaves, I kneel at his grave. My fingers dig into the soft dirt as I bow my head. Two tears escape me. It's all I allow myself. A tear for Dirk, and a tear for me. A part of me did die out on that highway with him. And today, that Shady is laid to rest. As I stand, I leave what's left of who I was.

I'm no longer the lost little boy who nobody wanted. I'm not a young man searching for his place in the world. I'm not the same guy who ran his fingers over the threads of his new patch again and again.

My anger is fueled by all that's been lost. Fury blazes in my eyes. Rage consumes me. Revenge is my only thought. Killing is my ultimate goal. Death is the only justice.

Death Mob killed Dirk. Now they'll pay the price. Their blood will pour like rain from the sky. Their bodies will decompose in shallow graves. The smell of their fear will fill the air. Their days are limited. Their nights will be haunting. One by one, they'll die. Every death will send a message: I'm coming for them.

All of them.

But I'm not coming alone.

I'm bringing hell with me.

1

DIEM

WHEN I FIRST saw him, I knew he was the one who could make me happy. Even though he tried to conceal it, there was a playfulness about him. He wasn't trying to flirt with the waitress; it just seemed natural. I could tell the demons he carries haven't always been there.

I watched the way he narrowed his dark eyes at her, then countered the move with a small smirk. The way his middle finger tapped lightly on the table, drawing attention to his rough and calloused hands. The way he sipped his beer slow, making sure to lick his lips after his pull—teasing the waitress with thoughts of what he could do to her with his mouth.

What he could do to me.

He was no fool. He knew I was watching. When he stood, he made sure to walk around the side of the table that gave me a full view of him. He was shorter than six feet, but not by much. His body was lean, but muscular and toned. The white polo he wore contrasted perfectly with his tanned skin—the sleeves clinging tightly to his sculpted arms and across his broad chest. His jeans sat low on his waist and hung loose on his legs.

The tattoos on his arms formed a beautiful, intricate pattern that started at his wrists and disappeared under his shirt. They seemed to hold some type of meaning, one that couldn't be deciphered by anyone but him.

Even though he dressed the part, he seemed to be out of place. It was as if he was fighting to fit in, but really didn't belong. Unbeknownst to him, I felt the same way.

He disappeared inside without a single glance in my direction, but somehow, I felt like he was watching me—fully aware of every thought in my mind. I found myself longing for his return so I could find what it was about him that made me feel like I've never felt before.

Was there really such a thing as instant attraction? I'd read about it in books, watched it in movies and dreamt of it, but was it real? Or was I so obsessed with finding something to replace the monotony in my life that my subconscious had conjured up this feeling I had?

My thoughts shatter, my dreamy state lost as a guy at the bar approaches me. The light breeze blowing across the patio allows his scent to waft toward me, and I cringe from the expensive cologne overkill. Even his breath smells like Dolce & Gabbana.

"Can I buy you a drink?" the young, attractive guy asks. He's midtwenties, tall, muscular, and has the kind of hair that begs a girl to run her fingers through it. But even his silky locks can't get the image of short black hair hidden beneath a white ball cap out of my thoughts.

"No." I'm hoping my short answer is enough to persuade him to move the fuck along. Through my peripherals, I can see his stance is cocky, his smirk is confident, and his ego isn't suffering in the least. He's so sure of himself that he orders me a fruity cocktail, immediately stereotyping me to be the kind of girl who enjoys that shit. His boldness tells me one thing—he's looking to get laid.

On my left, another guy approaches. Maybe they're brothers. Maybe they're hoping for a little three-way action. Maybe there really are desperate women left in this world who fall for this type of bullshit. The new guy leans on the bar. Looking over the top of my head, he holds a conversation with the asshole on my right. He's telling him that what I need is a shot, not a cosmopolitan. His actions tell me that he is a certified schmuck. The kind that gets girls drunk and takes advantage of them. He's pretty sure I'm one of those girls.

"You on vacation, or you from around here?" I don't acknowledge him. He laughs with the other one, moves in closer and speaks again. "I like your legs."

I'm counting. I usually start back from ten, but I'm already past the point of pissed off, so I'm in the negatives. I'm trying to ignore them. But my body is buzzing. My strong desire to see them in pain is overpowering my control.

"You must have a boyfriend." He ducks his head and tries to meet my eyes. When I turn on my stool to face him, prepared to unleash my wrath, my eyes land on *him*.

He's standing next to us at the bar, his eyes on me. They're cold, unfeeling, and distant. I'm still staring, my mouth slightly parted, my breath a little heavier when his eyes leave me and focus on the bartender. With the slightest lift of his index finger, he gives the command for another beer. It's such a simple gesture. There's nothing worldly about his demand. But he makes it seem so powerful and lethal—like with just the lift of his finger, he could turn everybody in the bar to dust.

I've forgotten the other men, but they haven't forgotten me, and their eyes follow mine to the man standing there as if this is his world and we're just living in it.

"Who? This guy?" He claps the man hard on the shoulder, but he doesn't budge. His eyes drag ever so slowly and deadly to the hand that remains on him.

"Get your fucking hand off me."

One demand.

Six words.

It's all I need to know that he is the one who can protect me. His words are so dangerous and threatening that the air grows colder with their iciness.

The scent of cologne fades slightly as the men stand to attention, ready to fight. Even though they move to stand between us, the force I feel radiating from *him* is unwavering.

"Or what, Adam Levine?" They laugh, taunting him. He is outnumbered. Outsized. The odds are against him. But he's unaffected. He's not intimidated, afraid, or the least bit worried. And something tells me that his confidence isn't just a front.

When the fingers on his shoulder curl the slightest bit, my eyes widen, making sure to capture every moment of what I know is coming next.

The sound of a fist meeting flesh echoes around me, a second before a limp body falls at my feet. Then the face of the man that was beside him is met with the worn wood on the bar, splattering blood in every direction before sliding to the floor.

It took less than three seconds. Now it's over. And the silence is everywhere.

His eyes are locked on mine, his arms hanging loosely at his sides. His breathing is controlled but I can see the veins in his neck pulsing with the rush of adrenaline. He's not smiling. He's not angry or happy or proud. He's just as expressionless as I am.

He grabs his beer from the bar, stepping over the motionless bodies that lay unconscious on the floor. He throws some money down and nods to the bartender. Then, he turns to me, his narrowed, dark eyes holding me in place. Once again, his index finger extends slightly, this time in my direction.

"You're welcome."

I'm completely undone. Chaos surrounds me, but my focus is solely on him.

This man.

This being.

This force.

And as I watch him leave, I know, beyond a shadow of a doubt that he is the one . . .

The one who is going to break my heart.

2

SHADY

IT'S BEEN SIX months since Dirk's death. Six months since I buried him. Six months since I left Jackpot and everything else behind. Sinner's Creed is still my club. Still my life. But right now, my only priority is revenge.

My new home is located in Hillsborough, New Hampshire, which is within driving distance of eighteen Death Mob chapters. People here know me as Zeke Robinson, a website designer who moved here from Natchez, Mississippi, in hopes of finding a fresh start. Nobody really asks me a lot of questions, and I haven't drawn the attention of anyone until recently.

I'm sitting in Charlie's Pub, a local spot that has a patio overlooking the river. I come here almost every day I'm not working. For the past couple of weeks, I've noticed that *she's* been here too. She stares at me constantly, completely unashamed. Yesterday, she had an issue with a couple of guys who were from out of town. I was going to stay out of it, but one of them put his hands on me. I haven't been in a forgiving mood lately, so I reacted, even though I knew I shouldn't. Now I'm the local fucking hero.

And she's coming over.

I glare at her, my eyes warning her off, but she only smirks at me. Each step she takes is slow, deliberate. She's forcing me to look at her. Not just her face, but the sway of her narrow hips. The way her right foot crosses over her left like she's on a runway instead of an old wooden patio.

I'd say she looks like a fairy. A five-foot, one-hundred-pound fairy with a pixie cut and glittery shit on her eyes. But fairies are cute and childlike—she's not. She's fucking gorgeous, and all woman. There is a sense of power that surrounds her. She emits confidence. And every head in the bar turns when she crosses the floor. She's just that damn demanding.

"You," she says, taking a seat across from me—uninvited and not giving a shit. "Owe me a drink." She kicks at the chair between us, and places her feet in it. Making herself comfortable, she leans back and narrows her eyes on me. "My favorite shirt is now ruined with the blood of another man. A man I might have been considering taking home. You know, now that I think about it, you owe me two drinks."

I just stare at her, trying to hide the amusement in my eyes. I don't need a distraction right now. If she's selling, I'm buying, but I'm not in the mood for conversation. Someone once told me you don't pay a bitch to fuck you, you pay her to leave. I'm getting the feeling she's not the leaving type. She's the kind that wants more. She looks like a snake that won't let go of you until her fangs are empty of venom. Then she'll smile as she walks away while you just lay there and die.

"That mean death-glare shit you got going might work on some. But not on me." She levels me with a death glare of her own and my predictions are right. She's pure fucking poison.

I stand and walk to the bar. Clearly, I'm in the mood to entertain her. At least it will give me something to do. I've got two days before I can kill again. Sweating off my frustrations in the bathroom with her against the wall, begging me to let her come while I'm balls deep, seems like a good way to pass the time.

I return to the table with the drinks, and one of my eyebrows rise in question.

"Seven and Seven," I say, setting a glass in front of her. A flash of surprise crosses her face, but she quickly conceals it.

"Why a Seven and Seven?"

"It's what you want." I take my seat, noticing the curious looks we're getting from everyone here. Fucking small-town gossip.

"How do you know that's what I want?" she asks, amused.

I grab my beer from the table, taking a pull before leaning back and mirroring her position. "Well, you're not a fruity cocktail kind of girl and you're not much of a beer drinker either."

"Really." Defying me, she reaches over and grabs my beer, nearly emptying the whole bottle. I ignore her act of rebellion, and refuse to speak until she asks me for what she wants. I can be rebellious too.

We sit staring at one another, until eventually she caves. "You're smooth. But anyone could have simply looked over and guessed what I was drinking."

"I didn't guess."

"How do I know that? Maybe you just got lucky."

"Maybe." I shrug noncommittally. Her nostrils flare with anger at my indifference. When she grabs her drink, I'm sure she's going to throw it at me. But she simply sips it, then smiles. Challenge dances in her eyes.

"Okay, cowboy. I'll make you a deal. If you can give me the real reason behind my drink preference, I'll give you something. Something so hot and sweet, that even days from now, you'll still be thinking about it." She licks her lips slowly, her eyes growing heavy with lust and sparkling with promise. Her nipples harden at the thought, and my dick stands at attention when they bulge against the fabric of her thin T-shirt. Now she's speaking my kind of language.

Images of her tits bouncing as she rides my cock flash in my mind. I lick my lips at just the thought of her pussy that I'm sure is sweet to taste and hot to touch. Before I realize it, I'm telling her exactly what she wants to hear. "You strive to be different. You like to separate yourself from the normal. You don't like the idea of being stereotyped. Even if the drink is disgusting and you prefer a fruity cocktail or a light beer, you still get the unexpected. Because the enjoyment you get out of being unpredictable is greater than your preference for taste. So enjoyable that you realize the drink you chose really isn't that bad at all."

She sits silent. A little stunned and not afraid to show it. Eventually, she nods and raises her glass to me, drains it, then sets it back down.

"A deal is a deal. And I never go back on my word." She smiles, but the seriousness in her words ring loud and true. So much so that even though I don't even know her name, I believe her.

She walks around the table, leaning down until her face is level with mine. I'm suddenly surrounded by the scent of alcohol and something else. Cinnamon?

Without warning, she kisses me. When her tongue drags across my lips, I open to her. She explores my mouth for a moment before pushing something inside and pulling away.

Without another glance in my direction, she leaves. It's not until she's gone that I bite down on the hard candy in my mouth.

Hot and sweet.

An Atomic Fireball.

———

For eight years I've worn a Sinner's Creed patch. A patch that symbolized the unity of a brotherhood that shared the same beliefs—club first. I've always believed in our bylaws. I've always honored and upheld them to the highest degree. I swore that, for as long as I wore a patch, I would abide by the laws my brothers before me created.

But after Dirk died, I no longer felt like a brother. I'd betrayed my club and broken our laws. I carried pride in my heart. I put my own feelings before Sinner's Creed. I knew in my soul that my desire to kill was too hungry not to feed. I was going to make Death Mob suffer. But in the end, it would be my club that suffered the most. The debt was paid, and if I waged war, then Dirk's death would have been for nothing. And Sinner's Creed would fall.

I was aware of all these things. The knowledge was as familiar to me as breathing. Still, my determination and self-importance outweighed my need to carry on the Sinner's Creed legacy. I felt like I didn't deserve to wear the patch. Because somewhere along the way, I forgot its true meaning.

So I swallowed my pride. Hid my conceit. Stripped myself of honor. And bared my naked soul before my club.

I told them how much the brotherhood meant to me. How honored I was to wear our colors. How Sinner's Creed wasn't just a part of my life—it was the sole purpose of it.

I told them about the greed I was carrying—greed that overpowered me. That it had forced me to become selfish—not caring about how Dirk's death affected anyone but me. How heavy my heart was for revenge, and how I knew I'd risk everything to fulfill that need.

After my confession I just stood there, delighting in the feeling of heavy leather on my back. There was a great possibility it wouldn't be there for long. The decision to eighty-six me, or put me out bad, was a risk I took by going to them. And if they put me out, I'd have to carry that burden for the rest of my life—alone. I'd never ride with an MC again. My cut would be burned, my name forgotten, and my memory would be filed away alongside traitors, rats, and those who disgraced the patch.

But my club isn't just a group of men who ride motorcycles and live like outlaws. They are a band of brothers who have dedicated their life to protect, respect, and uphold the legacy of Sinner's Creed. And that includes everyone in it. Even Dirk.

Even me.

So the club agreed to turn their head and look the other way. They understood what I believed had to be done. And if any of my other brothers felt the same way I did, then they'd look the other way for them too.

The conditions were firm; there would be no negotiating their terms. I was responsible for my army. The club would allow me the time I needed to handle business, but they would come first. If they called, I'd come with no excuses, and perform my duties with no questions.

They didn't want to be aware of my plans. They wanted no knowledge of my intentions. And if Sinner's Creed was ever accused, they would deny it. And it would be me who would take the fall and give the ultimate sacrifice. It was a risk I was willing to take six months ago. And one I would continue until my job was done.

The first five months were spent creating the perfect plan. With the help of a few of my brothers, I'd done enough research to finally start the process of taking down Death Mob. And today marks the twenty-fifth day of their fall.

It's been two days since I've killed. Two days since I've slept. And two days since that crazy woman gave me that Atomic Fireball that I can't get out of my fucking head. But thoughts of her fade as

I pull my black hoodie over my eyes and stare at the creature in the mirror. My thirst for blood is unquenchable. My need for revenge is overpowering. And my desire to kill has my heart pumping venom through my veins.

This is for Sinner's Creed.

This is for brotherhood.

This is for Dirk.

I drive to Fitchburg, Massachusetts, to meet with Rookie and Tank. I was Rookie's sponsor during his Prospect period. I'd taught him everything I know, and what he didn't learn from me, he learned from Dirk. He's my closest brother and only friend, now that Dirk is gone.

Tank is the sergeant at arms for the Houston chapter. He completed our three-man army against Death Mob to avenge Dirk's death. He got his name from his size. He's built like a tank and about as indestructible as one. With my smarts, Rookie's heart and Tank's size—we had everything we needed to get the job done.

I meet them at an abandoned store less than three miles from the local Death Mob chapter's clubhouse. Every Tuesday night, several of the Death Mob members get together for a dice game. Tonight, there are eight playing, but only six will make it back home.

The plan is well thought out, but simple. It will seem as if they just disappeared. Once they pass the lookout point, Tank will set a Road Closed sign blocking all through traffic and any chance of witnesses, while Rookie and I do the same at the other end of the road. There will be no trace of their bodies, their bikes, or their cuts. There will be no witnesses, no clues, and no answers. But most importantly, there'll be no discussion, no other solution, and no fucking mercy. These men will die tonight in the same cowardly way they killed my brother.

If they survive long enough to ask why, I'll point to the tattoo on my forearm.

GFSD . . .

God Forgives Sinners Don't.

I'm calm. There is no rush of adrenaline or heavy breathing. My heart beats in a steady rhythm. The only sound is the crackle of burning paper as I take a pull from my cigarette. I'm more than ready. I look to Rookie and nod. He meets my dark glare and clenches his fist around the throttle of his bike—a silent gesture that tells me he's ready too. Headlights shine in the distance just as my phone vibrates.

It's time.

10:14 p.m.—Tank calls from his lookout.

10:15 p.m.—Two members of Death Mob roll through at a leisurely pace. Seconds later, Rookie and I fall in behind them.

10:16 p.m.—Twelve shots ring out into the night, hitting their targets directly in the back.

10:17 p.m.—Tank arrives with a truck and trailer. The bikes are loaded. The bodies are loaded. The broken motorcycle parts are gathered and loaded too.

10:22 p.m.—A truck with a trailer, two dead bodies, and two members of Sinner's Creed drive north.

10:22 p.m.—I ride south carrying two Death Mob patches with me.

Eight minutes. A foolproof plan. Twelve shots delivered from two revolvers that still contain the shell casings. Two signs that read Road Closed. Two bikes that will be disassembled and destroyed. Two bodies that will decompose in shallow, unmarked graves that will never be found. And two Death Mob patches that will burn with the same fire of hell that blazes in my soul.

3

AFTER EVERY KILL, I've made it tradition to drink a beer for Dirk while I burn Death Mob's patches. Tonight is no different. I lean back in my one and only lawn chair, listening to the crackle of the fire and watching the colors of Death Mob fade from red to black until there's nothing remaining but ashes.

The quiet here is deafening. Nothing surrounds me but woods and a dirt road that is almost always void of traffic. The place is nice, a one-story cabin with a big shed located on thirty acres. But even the serenity isn't enough to keep my demons at bay.

Nights are hard for me. Bad things seem to always happen in the dark. My fear stemmed from my childhood. Restless nights in group homes seemed to go hand in hand with being a child in the system. Every kid in my dorm suffered from insomnia. We were afraid that we couldn't be protected. Mostly because we never were.

Even after becoming a member in the club, I never felt safe against the darkness. I could kill in the night and stay in the shadows, but fear of what would come when I closed my eyes kept me from sleeping. The sun served as my safety net. And after all these years, it still does. So, I find myself driving back to town to sit in a noisy bar, avoiding the demons that lurk behind my eyelids.

It's after midnight and the only people left are a few regulars. Mick the bartender greets me with a chin tip before handing me a beer.

"Let me get a shot of Patrón too. Chilled."

"Make it three." *Her.* I'd recognize that damn voice anywhere.

"Three, huh?" I ask, not bothering to look her way.

"Yep." No explanation. Just a confirmation.

She takes a seat, adjusting her stool so that she's facing me. Then, her legs are thrown over my thighs. I look down to see a pair of black heels covering her feet. Slowly, I drag my eyes up her naked legs, her short, black skirt, to her white silk top, and finally to her face. Gone is the glittery eye shit from the other day. She looks . . . professional. Like a naughty schoolteacher. Only thing she's missing is the glasses.

"You wanna take a picture?" she asks, cocky as hell. She knows she looks good. Mick delivers the shots and she throws one back before turning to me. "Give me your hand." Without waiting for me, she grabs my hand from the bar and pulls it to her mouth, circling her tongue between my thumb and index finger. She then covers it in salt, licks it, shoots the tequila, then sucks the lime.

I'm annoyed that I'm letting her control me like this. But I'm more annoyed that I'm so turned on by it. She's so bold and sure of herself. Grabbing my beer, she chases the shot and then sticks her hand out to me. "Here, you try."

I'm not playing her game. Instead, I use the same hand she did. She throws her head back and laughs, pleased with herself. "I knew you'd do that. You couldn't resist my taste. Could you?"

"No." My sudden answer catches her off guard. I watch her cheeks turn the faintest shade of pink before she recovers.

"What's your name, mystery man?"

"Zeke." Shady, Sinner's Creed, Houston, Texas.

"I like it." She smiles, waiting for me to ask her name. She'll be waiting a while. I don't need her to tell me her name. I just want to hear how mine sounds when she screams it.

"Another round, Mick," I say, never taking my eyes off her. He puts two more shots on the bar. When she reaches for one, I catch her wrist in my hand. Rubbing my thumb over the soft flesh, I feel her skin prickle with goose bumps. Keeping one hand on her wrist, I pull her stool closer with the other until the backs of her thighs are pressed up against me.

"Now it's my turn to give you something. Something so salty and warm that even days from now you'll still be thinking about it."

Her eyes widen slightly at my words, and it's her only show of weakness. Her breathing is controlled. Her pulse is steady. And I wonder if she's trained herself to keep her composure, or if she's not affected by me at all. When I run my tongue up the side of her neck, and she shivers, I get my answer. Tilting her head, I shake the salt onto her velvety-smooth skin and lick. Then, I kiss her.

The tiniest of moans escapes her and I catch it with my mouth, moments before I pull away. I release her wrist and hand her the shot, then grab my own. And her fight for control is lost as her pulse beats heavily against the hollow of her throat.

I lift her legs before standing, then lay them back across the empty stool. I throw a bill down on the bar and give Mick a nod. Before I leave, I can't resist making her head spin one last time. She might be good, but I'm the best.

Rubbing my thumb across her bottom lip, I pull it from between her teeth. She's still breathless and reeling. I can only imagine what she'll be like when she's beneath me. "See you around, pretty girl." I walk away, and it takes only three steps for her to call my name.

I smile because she can't see me, but when I turn, my face is void of every emotion.

"You never asked me my name."

I want to smirk, but I hold it in. "That's because I already know it."

Her brows draw together in confusion. I watch as she fights hard to remember when it was she told me. Before she says anything else, I put her out of her misery.

"Good night," I say, finality in my tone. My voice drops slightly before I add, "Diem."

The last image I have of her is with her mouth slightly open, shock on her face and a flash of heat in her eyes.

And my newfound knowledge was worth every dime I paid Mick.

"There's not a fucking thing to eat in this house," Rookie told me the last time he was over. He and Tank had been slamming cabinet doors in my kitchen, looking for food. I guess they thought the more noise they made, the more likely they would find something. Dumb-asses.

"I mean you ain't even got a loaf of bread or a can of beans," he'd continued. "Beer and water. How do you survive off that shit?" It was late and there'd been nothing open within fifty miles. I'd felt guilty about my brothers going hungry. I'd been there before.

So today, I'm at the grocery store, shopping for what is probably only the fifth time in my entire life. I usually live off of takeout. Mostly because nothing makes a man feel more like a domesticated pussy than pushing a buggy alongside a shitload of soccer moms.

I'm in the cereal aisle, grabbing random boxes and tossing them in my cart, when my knees nearly buckle from the impact of a buggy hitting me at my ankles. Turning slowly, I expect to see some snaggletoothed, snot-nosed kid with a Kool-Aid ring around their mouth. What I see is Diem.

"Oops," she says, giving me an apologetic smile that I know is fake. "Didn't see you there."

"Really?" My eyes center on her blue mouth. Well, I got the Kool-Aid stain right. She's leaning on her elbows, holding a blue snowball in her hand. When she wraps her lips around the ice and sucks the juice from it, I suppress the urge to groan. A part of me wonders if she did that shit intentionally. "What you buying?" She walks up to me, leaning over and surveying the contents of my cart. "Cereal, bread, peanut butter, and canned beans. Hmm. Sounds delicious." She flashes me another blue smile and my lips twitch. Although she's annoying, I find her interesting.

Turning, I glance into her cart. "Juice boxes, nabs, NyQuil, frozen pizzas, and Popsicles. Well," I say, with a smile. "The kids will be happy."

She gives me a disgusted look. "No kids."

"What about a husband?" I ask, in my shitty attempt to pry into her personal life.

Shaking her head, she takes a bite of the blue ice before answering. "I killed him."

"With your cooking?" I smirk, and her eyes narrow on me.

"I'm actually a really good cook." Sure she is.

With challenge written all over her face, she smirks at me. "Let's make a bet. If you can guess what my favorite dinner is, I'll cook it for you."

Well, that's hardly fair. "Don't I get a hint?" I ask, wondering why in the hell I'm playing along with her silly game in a supermarket. Not to mention, I'm actually enjoying it.

"It's on that aisle," she offers, waving her hand toward the next aisle over. I look up and see the sign that reads "Pasta." Judging by the items in her cart, I'm sure her skills are limited—leaving only one possible answer. Well, that was a little too easy. She must really want to cook for me.

Before I can answer, my phone buzzes in my pocket, and Diem is forgotten as I push past her and take the call from Nationals.

"I need some information," Chaps, our national enforcer, tells me.

"And I'll get it," I respond, grabbing a pack of Gatorade as I round the corner.

"Ever heard of a guy named Fin?"

I search my brain, then remember Fin is the sergeant at arms for Death Mob. He'd given Rookie some shit once in Houston, but I haven't seen him since then.

"I know who he is," I growl, remembering how disrespectful he was and how badly I'd wanted to kill him.

"Get me everything you got on him. We've heard a rumor that he might be building an army." Stupid fucker. Did Death Mob really think they could fight us and win?

"I'll have it to you tonight." Hanging up, I see Diem at the end of the aisle bending over to grab something from the bottom shelf. Her round ass is barely concealed by her shorts and I'm practically salivating at the sight.

I usually like long legs, but there's something about her small, toned ones that send my dick into overdrive. They're petite, but perfectly proportional. Even her ankles are sexy. Damn. I need to get laid. I'd kissed her twice, so we were halfway there already. I had work to do tonight, so dinner was out of the question. But maybe she's up for a quick fuck in the parking lot.

Walking up behind her, I see her still struggling with whatever it is she's trying to get. All I would have to do is wrap my hands around her waist and lift her just a little to have her centered on my cock. Shaking the thoughts out of my head, I squat down beside her.

"Lose something?" I ask, and she jumps at the sound of my voice.

Glaring at me, I can see her pulse beating rapidly against her throat. "You scared the shit outta me," she hisses, grabbing her chest dramatically.

Rolling my eyes, I duck my head and peer into the bottom shelf. We're so close I can smell the blue raspberry on her breath. My cock becomes aware of her too, and I mentally tell him to back the fuck down.

"It's stuck on that thingy," she says, pointing to the last fifty-pound bag of sugar shoved all the way to the back of the shelf.

"What the fuck do you need with fifty pounds of sugar?" I mumble, attempting to grab the bag while she stays in my personal space. I turn to look at her, our lips a little too close for comfort. "Well, sweetheart, if you'll move, I'll unhook it from the thingy."

She backs away and I give the bag a jerk. It releases, and I effortlessly pull it from the shelf and set it in her cart. Dusting the granules from my hand, I brush them down the front of my jeans. I feel her eyes on me and glance up from beneath my cap to find her staring at my arms in appreciation. Maybe we'll be having parking lot sex after all.

Giving her my best panty-dropping smile, I pretend to wipe something from her lip that really isn't there. "Need anything else?" I ask, praying like hell she's picking up what I'm putting down.

Snapping back to reality, her back straightens. It's hard for her to look intimidating and like a Smurf at the same time, but I give her an *E* for effort. "No, I'm good." I bet she is.

"See you around, Diem." I start to walk away, but I want to remind her just how good I really am. And that I don't need to pay anyone for information. "Let me know how that spaghetti turns out." I wink, feeling a sense of satisfaction when I notice the look of shock on her face. And I'm pretty sure she's a little turned on too. She'll probably be moaning Zeke's name tonight while she touches herself.

"Sure will, Zack."

Or maybe she won't.

As soon as I'm home, I gather all the information on Fin I can find and send it to Cleft, who is heading up my job while I'm away. I instruct him to give it to Nationals and to call me if he has any questions. Then, I invite Rookie over for dinner. He declines because Carrie, his longtime girlfriend, is in town, so me and my Fruity Pebbles are left all alone.

My thoughts keep going to Diem, even though I try to think about anything else. She couldn't even remember my fucking name. When was the last time a woman had forgotten me? I must be losing my game. I'd have to fly back to Jackpot this week and visit the club. Surely the women there remembered who I was. If I couldn't fuck Diem, I might as well fuck her out of my system.

Things in the club were going smoothly. My help wasn't needed, so I spent the next two weeks living like a caveman—pouring over all my research to perfect my next kill. When the walls started to close in, I decided it was time for a break. So, I'm in Concord at some up-scale restaurant that promises me the best lobster on the East Coast, when I'm approached by a beautiful woman with skin the color of dark chocolate and legs longer than my own. I drag my eyes up her body, lingering longer on her cleavage than any gentleman ever would.

"May I?" she asks, already pulling the chair out and taking a seat. "I'm Ebony." She reaches her hand across the table, nearly blinding me with the diamonds that cover her fingers.

"I'm Ivory." My joke is funny to her. Too funny. I suddenly have flashbacks of the last time I visited Jackpot. The club whores laughed too hard at my jokes. Even when they weren't that funny. They'd do anything to get in my bed. I'm sure she's not a club whore, but I'll definitely have her in my bed if that's what she wants.

"I was sitting all alone at the bar when I saw you. Since you were all alone, I figured we could give each other some company." She winks at me, giving me her best seductive smile.

"Really," I say, bored beyond measure. "Can I buy you a drink?" My voice is lacking in enthusiasm, but she doesn't care. At my offer, her hand goes up and the house wine she's sipping on is forgotten. When the waiter appears, she asks for a cabernet that I know is the most expensive wine they offer. Oh, and two shots of Patrón—at twenty-six dollars a pop.

I was wrong. This lady is a whore. And by the looks of her, she's a damn good one.

"So, what brings you here to Concord? Business or pleasure?" she purrs, toying with the tiny, diamond-encrusted necklace at her throat.

"Both."

I engage in her forced conversation with lines of bullshit that I'm just making up as I go. She doesn't care. I could tell her I'm a serial killer and she would just smile and tell me how awesome that is. That's what whores are supposed to do. I'm sure she prefers the term *escort* over *whore*, but they're all the same to me.

My bill has probably exceeded three hundred dollars when the offer to get out of here nears. She's making advances, biting her finger and licking her lips. I almost want to lean over and tell her the overkill isn't necessary. I'd be happy to fuck her. There's no need to try and convince me further.

I summon the waiter, and she starts to get excited. She excuses herself to the restroom and I'd bet she's going to snort a line. That's fine too. I plan to smoke a blunt while she gives me head. Who am I to judge?

"Hot date tonight?" I look up from my bill that is a hell of a lot more than what I'd predicted to find Diem smirking at me. Ebony might be beautiful, but Diem is a vision. Her short, jet-black hair is perfectly smooth except for her bangs that are wildly untamed and lay over her left eye. The dress she wears is candy apple red, matching her heels that are at least six inches tall. All she needs is a pitchfork to complete her evil, demonic, sexy-as-fuck look.

Her skin seems to glisten like she bathed in baby oil, and I want to run my tongue and hands across every inch of her tiny body. People are staring. They are as captivated by this devil as I am. Damn, I want her.

"What do you want?" I ask, completely unaffected by her beauty. Or at least pretending to be. She raises her eyebrow inquisitively at me before turning her eyes to Ebony, who is walking toward us. The world seems to stand still a minute. The only thing happening is the unspoken conversation between the two women as they size each other up.

Jealousy flares in Ebony's eyes. It's not that she wants me; she just doesn't want to lose a client. Diem looks amused. Her gaze focuses back on me, her eyes dancing with laughter. She's definitely entertained by this and I don't know why.

"You know she's a whore, right?" Diem laughs, and now it's my turn to be amused.

"You jealous?" I challenge, enjoying the roll of emotions as they cross her face. She narrows her eyes, clearly pissed at my question. Then, as if the idea to fuck up the first possible piece of pussy I've had in weeks suddenly occurs to her, she takes a seat.

"I don't think your services are needed today, honey." She

plasters a fake smile on her face as she looks at Ebony, who's looking at me.

"Do you know her?" she asks, dabbing her nose with a napkin.

My eyes drift to Diem, who is completely relaxed. She feels like she's in control of the situation. I could prove her wrong, but if I had to pick one of them to occupy my bed tonight, it would definitely be Diem. So I play along.

Without a glance in her direction, I dismiss Ebony. "Sorry, doll. Looks like I have other plans."

The smile that lights up Diem's face is more genuine this time as she looks up at the tall woman. "Bye, now."

"Fucking bitch," Ebony mumbles under her breath.

Diem's smile is gone. The sparkle in her eyes is lost in the darkness that fills them. Her body straightens with lightning speed as she reaches out and grabs Ebony's wrist.

"Say it again," she demands, her voice low and threatening. The air seems to crackle around her and I shift uncomfortably. And maybe just a little turned on.

Ebony snatches her wrist away, narrowing her eyes on Diem. She tries to play it cool, but I can see the fear written all over her face. "Whatever." Then with haste, she leaves the restaurant.

I keep my focus on Diem, watching as she regains her composure. Grabbing my beer, she tosses it back, then snaps her finger for the waiter, who appears out of thin air. "Jack Daniel's. Double."

He nods and disappears, leaving me all alone with the confusing, infuriating, lethal woman sitting at my table. This bitch is eight kinds of crazy. And I'm so fucking intrigued that I can't leave, even though something inside my head is screaming that I need to.

"My mother was a whore. She was faithful to my father long enough to have me. After that, she fucked everything she could. Mostly his friends, family, business associates . . . It's not the act of sex for money that's so degrading. It's the disregard for all the hurt that is caused from it." She speaks like she's reading from a book. Like she rehearsed this line over and over. Hell, maybe she did.

"Did someone important say that?" I ask, raising an eyebrow.

"Yeah. Me." She's daring me to laugh. To ask her who she is. To feign shock at the possibility of her being someone of importance. Truth is, I don't really care who she is. "Do you have a wife, Zeke?" She's not judging, just curious. And she really does know my name.

I start to lie just to get a rise out of her, but there are way too many forks on the table. I'd hate to have my eye gouged out by a woman half my size. What would I tell people? So I answer truthfully. "No."

"So you came here looking for a whore?"

"I came here for the lobster."

She smiles a little and leans back, seemingly pleased with my answer. "So who are you, Zeke? You seem to know so much about me."

"I'm nobody important."

She laughs, her dark eyes sparkling once again. "I doubt that. You know, I'm pretty good at reading people too."

"Is that so?" I recline further in my seat, ready to hear what she's got. I already have my predictions as to what she'll say, but I'm anxious to hear it anyway.

The waiter shows up, bringing me a refill and the drink she ordered. He looks at me and I nod. Hell, what's another twenty bucks.

She raises her glass to me. "Thanks. Don't worry. It's cheap whiskey."

I smirk. So she thinks I'm poor.

"Let's make a deal." Great. Another fucking deal. "For every correct guess, I get a point. For every wrong one, you get a point.

Best three out of five. The loser has to do one thing the winner wants." She leans forward, dropping her voice. "Anything."

"What if I lie?"

"You won't." She's so sure that she offers her hand, wanting me to shake on it. Her trust in me is sweet. But not as sweet as she's going to look on her knees in the bathroom.

I take her small hand in mine. "Deal."

"You're hurting."

My brow draws in confusion at her words. Was that an assumption?

At my bewilderment, she smiles. "Point."

"Half a point. That could mean a lot of different things."

She shrugs. "Fine, pussy. Half a point." Taking a sip of her drink, she takes a moment to study me. I give her a lazy, challenging smile. She won't catch me again.

"You're hurting, because you just lost someone. Someone very close to you."

I swallow at the reminder, but keep my face expressionless as I manage, "Point."

"Hmm, let's see." Her eyes fall to my hands that are folded in my lap. "You're into fighting. Not MMA or anything, but like jiujitsu or martial arts."

"My point."

She frowns, clearly thinking she had that one in the bag. "Okay, I'm adding a clause. If it's something I really believe to be true, then you have to explain it to me if it's not."

I shake my head. "You can't just add a clause."

"You added the half-point rule," she argues. And she's right.

"I grew up in a rough neighborhood. I've been fighting all my life. But I'm not a trained fighter, just a street kid who learned to defend himself. You happy? Pussy?"

She ignores my throwback as she scans my body thoroughly,

then studies my eyes, my clothes, and finally my tattoos. Her confidence builds as the next theory forms in her mind. This one, I probably will have to lie about.

"You've done time. And I'll even go a step further and say it was for something you really didn't do." Her eyes soften with sympathy. I have to fight to control my laughter.

"My point."

"Shit!"

"One more and I win. But don't worry, I'll go easy on you." I smirk.

Throwing me a mock smirk of her own, she gives me the finger. So rude.

"Fine. You like whores. You like the idea of sex with no strings attached."

"You're cheating."

"Am I? Are you saying you don't like the idea of sex with no attachment? So, you're that kind of sap? The one that falls in love with every woman that lands in his bed?"

I glare at her. She glares back, daring me to say she's wrong. Fucking competitive woman.

"Point."

"That's what I thought. Now we're tied." She waits a minute before delivering the final blow. I guess she's hoping I'll become uneasy. Hope. It's such a dangerous thing.

"Deep down, Zeke, you're a good guy. On the surface you try to act bad and keep those walls up, but beneath all that, you're just a man who fights for what he believes in. A man whose loyalty knows no bounds. One of the few people left in this world that's willing to give his life for the people he truly loves." There is conviction in her words. She really believes them to be true. Some of them are.

I do fight for what I believe in. I am loyal and there is no limit to my dedication. I would give my life for the people I love. Just like life has been given for me. But what she sees isn't an act. I'm not a good guy. I'm a murderer. A cold-blooded killer. And if that's not enough to make me a bad guy, not feeling the least bit of remorse for my actions is.

I stand and reach my hand out for hers. She takes it without hesitation. I pull a handful of money from my pocket and drop it on the table. Then leaning in close, I take her earlobe in my mouth, biting softly before whispering, "My point."

4

"IT'S SO PEACEFUL here." Diem closes her eyes and inhales the night air that is crisp and cool even in the summer. I'd driven us back to my place, stopping to grab some beer and a bottle of wine for her. Not that she needs it. She's been drinking out of my bottle since we got back.

"I like it," I say, focusing more on getting this blunt rolled than I am on her. Cheap-ass cigars.

"Here, let me." In true Diem fashion, she pulls the work in progress from my lap without asking and sets it on the porch railing. She's standing in front of me, her fingers working quickly and efficiently. In record time, she's sealing it with her wet tongue and handing it to me.

"You a hippie or something?"

"Something." Well that's evasive.

She leans over the railing, looking out across the field. "I grew up in Chicago. The lights and noise have always been home to me. But seeing this makes me wish sometimes that I grew up somewhere else."

I get the feeling she's not just talking about the place she lived. From the melancholy in her voice, it sounds like she wishes she had a different life altogether.

I light the blunt, not surprised at how tightly it's wrapped or how well it burns. I move to stand next to her, leaning down on my elbows and offering her a drag.

She shakes her head. "No thanks. I gave it up a long time ago. My job doesn't allow me to indulge in such reckless behavior." Her shoulder nudges mine as she smiles.

"And what kind of job is that?" I ask, enjoying the burn in the back of my throat and the feeling of relaxation as it swims through me.

"I'm a pharmaceutical sales rep."

I smile at the irony. Or the weed. "So you sell drugs."

She laughs. "Pretty much. I moved here to Hillsborough because it's a central location for my clients. And it's nice to have a quiet escape from the city. There's nothing like coming home to silence after you've worked all day." I can relate to everything she's saying.

"And you? What do you do, mystery man? Or am I going to have to guess?" Her smile is lazy and her eyes heavy. She might not be smoking it, but she's too close to not be affected. And I'm sure she knows that too.

"I'm a website designer."

She isn't surprised. "Nerd. And here I was thinking you were an ex-con struggling on your path to rehabilitation. Figures you'd be a computer geek."

"I wouldn't be so cocky, Diem." I narrow my eyes on her, knocking the cherry off the tip of the cigar. "You're the one that lost a bet to that nerd. What does that say about you?"

She rolls her eyes. "Who said I lost?"

"You're here. And you're at my mercy." The threat in my tone doesn't faze her. She isn't scared of me, and I don't know if I should be offended or turned on. Or a little bit of both.

"I'm here because I want to be. Not because I lost. The truth is I let you win."

"Bullshit. You're not the kind to let anyone win."

Pride sparkles in her eyes. "I know what I want. And I get what I want. Tonight, I wanted you. And guess what?" She got me. But I refuse to say the words. "I wasn't lying when I said I could read people. I can figure you out, Zeke. I can unveil all your little secrets right here and now. And I gained this knowledge by just watching you." She leans closer, running her finger down the front of my shirt. "I didn't even have to pay a bartender to get it."

Fucking Mick. He ratted me out. Although she seems smart enough to have figured it out on her own.

"Tell me." My voice is low and gruff. Partly from the smoke and partly from desire. I want her. So fucking bad. But I won't have her because she lost a bet. I'll wait until she begs me.

"What do I get in return?"

"Nothing. No deal. No bet. Just you, me, and the truth. If you know so much, tell me."

"That's not how the game is played, Zeke."

"I'm not playing games, Diem."

Her eyes are heavy with lust. She wants me too. Every time I speak, her resolve crumbles a little bit more. "You first. What do you see when you look at me?"

Everything. She's an open book. And she doesn't even know it. But she's fixing to.

"You did want me to win. You spend the majority of your life being the one in control, but you knew I wouldn't let you control me. That's why you're attracted to me. You want to let go. Let someone else take the reins and let you be the submissive one for once."

She doesn't deny or confirm it. Her face is impassive. Her eyes cold and unreadable. That's sign enough that everything I'm saying is the truth. "Go on," she encourages. Who am I to deny the lady in red what she wants?

"You also wanted me to win so you wouldn't feel like a whore. Even though you're nothing compared to your mother, the similarity of the situation was there. The difference is you do have a regard for people's feelings. That's why you asked if I was married."

"That's enough." She cuts me off, using that tone of authority she uses on everyone else. But this is the first time she's used it on me.

"Don't ask me for the truth if you don't want it, Diem."

"And don't underestimate me, Zeke. I never offer anything without getting something in return. That's just bad business." The hunger in her eyes is long gone. Whatever chance I had of her begging for me tonight has been lost.

"So, what do you want?" I ask, wondering what's going on in that guarded mind of hers.

She smiles, shaking her head slightly. Everything about her is back to the fun, playful Diem she was earlier tonight. Everything but her cold, unforgiving eyes.

"A beer."

My guard is up when I walk inside. My buzz is fading. I take a piss and splash cold water on my face, sobering me completely. Grabbing two beers from the fridge, I walk back outside, ready to end whatever this is. She can drink her beer on the way home.

But she isn't on the porch. She's not leaning on the railing where I left her. She's not sitting in the chair or on the steps either. I look behind me, but I would have known if she walked in.

When I turn the corner to look out into the yard, I know for sure she is gone. She didn't leave a note. She didn't draw a message in the dirt. There's not a forgotten shoe or a bread crumb trail to inform me of her leaving. It's the absence of something that makes me realize she really is not here. Regardless of the situation and how much it should piss me off, I find myself smiling. *"I never offer anything without getting something in return."*

She's a woman of her word.

I'm a fool.

I underestimated her.

Now she's gone.

And she took my fucking truck.

I didn't expect her to return it, so I wasn't surprised when she didn't. I stayed home the next day, making sure there was nothing inside or outside of my house that might link me to Sinner's Creed. This included emptying my safe—forcing me to carry an extra bag filled with its contents on my trip. Well, everything but the untraceable guns, which I left behind. There was a bike in my shed, but it along with everything else was registered in Zeke's name. Even the brand-new, sixty-thousand-dollar truck she took.

Stole.

Bitch.

There was nothing in my truck other than the registration and insurance papers. And my favorite fucking T-shirt. I knew exactly where the truck was from the GPS tracker that was on it. But I figured she knew that too and was waiting for me to come get it. I just hope she isn't holding her breath.

On second thought, I hope she is.

A cab takes me to the airport, and by Monday afternoon, I'm back in Jackpot, Nevada, where I'll be spending the next couple of weeks. Rookie and a Prospect meet me at the gates. I'm happy to see my brother. I'm happy to see my bike waiting for me. But it's the sight of my cut Rookie pulls from his saddle bag that has me completely elated.

"Welcome home, Shady." *Shady. My fucking name.*

The smell of leather engulfs me. The weight of it hangs heavy on my shoulders. With it surrounding me, I feel complete. My *1%* patch is worn over my heart. The number thirteen is across from it. My side rocker states that I am Night Crew. My back patch says I'm Sinner's Creed. The heart in my chest awakens, making me feel more alive than I have in months. The heavy beats pound out a message— *I'm home.*

I ride for hours, only stopping for gas. Rookie rides on my right, the Prospect directly behind me. Sometimes we ride hard— speeding at a pace that exceeds a hundred miles per hour. Sometimes we ride slower—taking the time to enjoy the view. There is no music, only the sound of pipes and the rush of wind.

By the time we make it to the bar with Nationals, it's the early hours of the next morning, but the party is still in full swing.

"Heyyyyy, Shady," the girls at the bar greet me with a smile. I've known them for years. They're always here, always willing, and always ready. There's no challenge. No bets or deals or games to play. If I want it, I get it.

"Heyyyyy, ladies," I drawl, thickening my accent.

"We missed you." Monica pouts, poking her lips out and reminding me of why I like them so much.

"It just hasn't been the same without you here," Jennifer adds, lining up shots on the bar.

"I missed y'all too." I toast with them and, keeping to tradition, I announce to the entire bar, "Rally rules!" The girls squeal. The men cheer. And I sit back and watch as the women stand on the bar and start peeling off what little clothes they had on. Damn, it's good to be back.

Before I indulge too much in the premium liquor and the easy pussy, I make my way to the porch, where I know Nationals are waiting. They all stand to greet me, taking turns to shake my hand

and clap me on the back. Everyone else is dismissed and I find myself inside the circle of men who call the shots for Sinner's Creed.

With the pleasantries out of the way, they get right down to business.

"We got an offer for you, Shady," Jimbo, Nationals president, says. "We want you as a Nomad." My back stiffens at his words.

"Why me?"

"You're the best man for the job." He shrugs as if it's just that simple. But it's not. Being a Nomad comes with a huge responsibility and one of the highest levels of respect. There are many other men in our club who are more worthy of the title than I am.

Being a Nomad was never really something I wanted. I liked being behind the scenes. But only because Dirk needed me there. Nobody could do what he did. Not even me.

"I appreciate the offer, but I don't think I have what it takes," I answer honestly. I didn't want to disappoint my club. I didn't want to disappoint Dirk.

"Yes you do," Chaps, Nationals enforcer, says. "People respect you. They listen to you. You have more knowledge about the field than anyone else. You were Dirk's right-hand man. The two of you were a team. Together, y'all made a difference. You deserve it. And we all agree that Dirk would have wanted you to have that rocker." The men around me all nod in agreement.

Jimbo leans forward in his seat, wrapping his hand around my shoulder. "Dirk set the bar high. He'd been a Nomad for years. He earned everything he ever got and then some. You'll do the same. It'll take time, but I know you can earn that same level of respect from your brothers as Dirk did. Don't doubt yourself, Shady. If I didn't think you could do it, I wouldn't ask you to." He drops his hand and leans back, lighting a cigarette.

"Take six months and think about it." Jimbo levels me with a look. He's giving me the time I need to finish my current job before taking on this one. "In the meantime, enjoy yourself while you're here. I need you in Texas next week. Got a big shipment coming in."

I'm dismissed, but the meeting is still in order. I'm sure they're discussing whether or not I'll take it. If they know me like they should, then they won't have very much to discuss. I don't care about being a Nomad. The title don't mean shit to me. But I'd just been asked to fill the biggest shoes of the best man I'd ever known. So I'll say yes.

Because it's a fucking honor.

5

"HOW'S CARRIE?" I ask Rookie, passing him the joint. We're on my porch, Dirk's porch, where we've seemed to end up every night since I got here.

"She's good. Took a job travel nursing. I see her when I can." The sadness in his voice doesn't go unnoticed.

I nod, not really knowing what to say. "You ready for tomorrow?" We would be heading down to Texas to work our asses off for a week. It wouldn't be an easy task considering we hadn't done shit since I got here.

"I guess. I just hate dealing with those Spanish-speaking motherfuckers. I know they speak English. I think they just like making us feel stupid." He passes the joint back to me, and I take a drag before knocking the cherry off and sticking the roach in my cut.

"Well lucky for you, I speak Spanish fluently."

"Bullshit."

"I swear, man. Ask me anything."

"How the fuck I'm supposed to know if you tellin' the truth or not? I don't speak Spanish."

I laugh, giving his shoulder a push that nearly knocks him off the porch. Making me laugh harder. "Seriously, man. I ain't ever lied to you. Come on. Ask me something."

He shakes his head, clearly annoyed with me. "You're fucking high, Shady. Too high. You need to take your ass to bed."

I am high. Maybe even too high. I've been doing that a lot lately. It's easier to try and stay here when I'm under the influence. I tried to do it sober. That shit didn't work. The depression seems to worsen when the reality that Dirk's body is buried in the backyard hits me. It slams me right in the chest. Every fucking time.

I watch Rookie walk to his bike, the white threads of his cut no longer new. They are dirty and worn—a sign that he'd been doing his job.

"Hey, man, don't leave," I yell out. He'd stayed with me every night. And every night we did this. But we always wound up back at the clubhouse. This time I was hoping to finally confront my fears and actually walk through the door. Having Rookie here would help. And with him around, I managed to get some sleep even before the sun rose. Tonight I really need him, or else I'll never make that ride tomorrow.

"I'm not fucking leaving. But if you call me 'man' one more time, I'm breaking your jaw." He's serious, but I still smile. "I got some company coming to the clubhouse tonight. I figured she might help you sleep," he calls over his shoulder.

"Who?" Like it matters. They are all the same. They all feel the same, smell the same, and when I dare, they taste the same.

"Monica. So try to sober the fuck up. You're getting on my nerves." Even though he acts pissed, he gets me. He doesn't take my shit, but he knows how hard it is for me to walk through the door of Dirk's house. That's probably why he told Monica to meet us at the clubhouse. And why he hasn't rearranged my face yet. I've seen him fight. He's good.

Rookie pulls me up from the porch—the bag he'd retrieved from his bike slung over his shoulder. I'm glad that nighttime is finally here. I hate looking at everything that reminds me of Dirk and Saylor. But the guilt of seeing it when I'm fucked up would be even worse. I didn't want to disgrace this place. The first time Saylor walked through the door, she made it a sanctuary for her and Dirk. I wanted to keep it that way. But if I went in like this, I'd be failing. Miserably.

I stop at the threshold just as Rookie opens the door. The smell of citrus hits me in the face—the scent of Saylor. For a moment, I feel like I can do it. But it disappears just as quickly when I see that nothing has changed. The evidence of the last night Dirk and Saylor spent in this house still remains. Even after we'd buried Saylor, I'd sat silent on the couch next to Dirk while he stared blankly around the room—reliving her last moments over and over.

I sober slightly at the reminder of that night. Dirk's last words echo inside my head. *"She'd want you to have this."* My hand moves to Saylor's diary I keep inside my cut—close to my heart. The wound is still fresh. The pain is still too real. I swallow back the tears that threaten and shake my head at Rookie.

"I can't." He shuts the door without a word, looking at me with understanding in his eyes. He knew I couldn't do it. But he knew I had to try.

"You know you gotta do this one day, Shady. You can't hide from it forever."

I look around the porch, unable to stop the memories of me and Dirk standing in this very spot from resurfacing. My chest aches and my eyes burn as I think about Christmas here. Thanksgiving. Saylor's sleepover. How at home they made me feel and how easy it was to think of it as mine. I'd never had a real home of my own. Now I do. And I can't even walk inside.

The frustration with myself begins to take its toll, just like it did every other time I did this. I pull a cigarette out and light it. When I look up at Rookie, he's already nodding his head. He knows what's coming, and like the good brother he is, he doesn't ask questions. He just accepts it.

"Let's ride."

The ride to the clubhouse is short, but I'm almost sober by the time we get there. My thoughts have a way of doing that to me. After a cold shower, my buzz has completely faded and I'm wide awake.

Instead of going to a room, Rookie sprawls out on the couch while I take a seat in the recliner. He says he likes being close to the door. But I know it's because he doesn't want to leave me alone. And keeping good on his word, Monica walks through the door minutes later.

Like she isn't already high enough, she stops at the bar to down a shot and snort a line of Sinner's Creed's finest. Walking toward me in a halter top and cutoff shorts, she smiles. Monica is pretty with plenty of curves, thick legs, and long brown hair. She's in her early thirties, but looks over forty. She's always been good to me and my brothers, and every time I've had her, she never disappoints.

"Hey, baby," she purrs, crawling onto my lap. My hand slides up her thigh, but there's no reaction to my touch. I'm just another cock to her. "Long night?"

"Something like that." I smirk, knowing she doesn't really care about my night.

"Well, you just relax and let me take care of you. Tell Monica what you want." Fuck. Even her voice is fake. And she's speaking in third person. But my dick doesn't seem to mind. He's already hard with just the weight of her ass on him.

"I want your pretty lips wrapped around my cock."

She beams. Probably because now she won't have to fake an

orgasm. She lowers herself between my legs, slowly unbuckling my belt as she stares at me with her big, sultry eyes. That look is fake too. She's probably wondering what time her next appointment is. Or if she turned the coffeepot off.

I glance over at Rookie, who lays motionless with his hat over his face. How did he do it? Was Carrie worth resisting temptation?

"Quit looking at me, Shady. It's fucking weird. You're getting your dick sucked. Look at her." I laugh at his words, and Monica takes the time to laugh too. She probably thought I was talking to her. I guess that confirms that she might physically be here, but her mind is somewhere else.

When she eases my cock to the back of her throat, I don't give a fuck what she thinks. Or who she is. Or where I am. Or who's watching. This bitch is a whore for this very reason. She pauses a moment, gagging slightly, before pulling me out of her mouth and smiling. Her eyes are watery and she's breathing heavily, but she doesn't let it slow her down.

I lean back, closing my eyes and letting the sound of her gurgling fill the room. Everyone can hear it, but nobody says a thing. She pulls my jeans to my ankles so she can cradle my balls in her hand while she sucks. She must be in a hurry.

My phone vibrates in my cut, and I frown in confusion when I realize it's Zeke's phone that's ringing. I start to silence it, figuring it's a wrong number. Nobody even knows I have this cell. But the caller is persistent and I pull the phone out to see a New Hampshire number flashing across the screen.

"Yeah?"

Loud music blares in the background. Several people are talking. When the caller realizes I'm actually on the other end, the music is turned down.

"This truck is fucking awesome." I still at the words. My eyes widening as I recognize the voice.

That *bitch*.

"I mean, seriously awesome. This backup camera is so high-tech that I haven't even taken it out of reverse." My hand fists in Monica's hair. I'd forgotten I was holding it.

"You crazy bitch. Get out—" Monica takes that exact moment to swallow my cock and I groan. I open my mouth to continue, but nothing comes out. I pull back on Monica's hair until she releases me. "One minute, baby."

"Wait, are you *fucking* right now?" Diem's voice is loud enough for Rookie to hear, and he lowers his cap to narrow his eyes on me. If Monica can hear, I wouldn't know it. She's too busy texting.

"If I was, I wouldn't have answered the phone," I say, keeping my voice low and even.

"So what are you doing?"

"You don't want to know." Tires screech. People yell. The radio is cut off. "If I didn't want to know, I wouldn't have asked." She sounds pissed. Good. That makes two of us.

"How about we talk about what the fuck you're doing in my truck. The truck you stole." I can feel Rookie's eyes on me, but I refuse to look his way.

"I didn't steal it. You gave it to me. Don't you remember?"

"I didn't give you shit," I growl, wishing I was there to shake the shit out of her. Or fuck her. Either would work.

"Believe what you want. Where are you anyway?" She asks the question like she's deserving of an answer. Meanwhile, my blood is rushing through my veins. I'm so pissed I could tear the roof off this fucking building.

"Diem, I swear if you put one scratch on that truck there will be hell to pay. So get your shit, your friends, and your ass out of it." My voice shakes with fury, and I wonder what my hands around her throat would feel like.

"I'll make you a deal," she starts, then pauses, waiting for my reaction. I'd give her one, but I'm too pissed to speak.

Instead, I close my eyes and try to think of shit that might calm me down. When I can't, I lower Monica's head back onto my still-hard cock. Not because she did anything special, but to send a message to Diem, I let out a groan. The moment I do, I can feel the anger radiating from Diem through the phone.

"You're doing it again," she says, deadpan.

"Doing what?" I sound bored. Like it's an inconvenience to talk to her. Right now it is, but on the inside I'm smiling.

"That. I'm guessing you're getting your dick sucked. Actually, I'm pretty sure of it." I don't answer her, and I imagine her reason for silence is because it's her mouth that's filled with my cock. Not Monica's.

"You know, it's a pity you never asked for the favor I owed you. Maybe you should've asked for that." I can hear her smile through the phone. I shouldn't take the bait, but I can't help it. I want to hear this great punch line she thinks she has.

"Why's that?"

Bringing her lips closer to the phone, she whispers in that sexy, submissive voice that I'm sure few people have ever heard. "Because then, it would've been your dick I sucked in your truck. Not someone else's."

I'm sure Monica's cheeks are killing her. But after Diem hung up, I couldn't get her last words out of my head. Now my dick was having some trouble with release. Every time I'd near the edge, images of her sucking some dude's cock in my truck would surface, and I was back at my starting point.

After a while, I pull Monica from the floor, offering her an apologetic smile. "Maybe another time, babe. I got a lot on my mind tonight."

She shrugs it off, just happy for the opportunity. "No problem. Call me?"

"Definitely." I stand, pulling my jeans up before kissing her cheek and giving her ass a squeeze.

"Your money's on the bar, sugar," Rookie announces, still on his back on the couch. Figures he'd be awake.

"You know, Rookie," Monica says, dragging her finger up his leg. "My services aren't limited to just Shady. I'd offer you the same." When she reaches his crotch, he grabs her wrist in his hand. Removing the cap from his face, he kisses the back of her hand, giving her a lazy smile.

"I appreciate that. But I'm good."

"No, you're pussy-whooped," I say, falling back down in the recliner.

"Says the man who let a bitch steal his truck. And his balls."

"She don't have my balls, asshole."

"So why couldn't you bust a nut?" Smart-ass. But he's right.

Diem had me by the balls. And that's exactly where she wanted me. But after next week, that shit was gonna change. I'd let her play her games long enough. Now she was gonna play mine.

6

I ALWAYS DO my best to avoid worst case scenarios. But when you add the blistering heat of El Paso, Texas, a tired, pissed-off Rookie, two Mexicans who refuse to speak English, and an eighteen-wheeler trailer missing half of our shit, worst case scenario is exactly what you get.

"Where's the rest of the shipment?" I ask, speaking slower this time in hopes they understand. My patience is running thin, but somehow, I'm keeping my shit together. I can't say the same for Rookie.

The two drivers standing in front of us, just off the deserted, dusty back road we'd met them at over an hour ago, once again start speaking at a rate I can't follow. Every now and then, I catch a word I understand, but I'm still clueless as to what the fuck they're trying to say. These aren't our normal drivers. They're new, but have clearance from our contact across the border. We were told we could trust them. I'm not so sure anymore.

"Shady," Rookie warns. I hold my hand up to silence him. He rolls his neck, and flexes his hands—never a good sign.

"Ricardo! English!" Even my raised tone isn't enough to persuade him. I catch a glimmer of humor in his eyes, and the moment I hear Rookie mutter, "fuck it," I know he saw it too.

Pulling a gun from his back, he points it between Ricardo's eyes. I pull mine too. Not to be outdone, I fire—grazing the flesh on his partner Eddie's right arm. He screams like a girl, but closes his mouth when I cock my head to the side in warning.

"I'm not as good of a shot as Shady." The calmness in Rookie's voice is more frightening than his anger. "If I pull this trigger, I'm gonna fuck something up. Permanently. Now, where is our shit?"

"It's coming. Tomorrow. I swear on mi m-madre," Ricardo stutters, swallowing loudly. His eyes cross as he looks at Rookie's gun positioned between them.

"Why tomorrow?"

"Problem at the border."

"Why the fuck didn't you just say that?" Gone is the calmness in Rookie's voice. Now, he's pissed.

Ricardo gives him a sheepish grin and shrugs. "Just fuckin' around, mano."

"I'm not your fuckin' brother," Rookie sneers, lowering his gun. I shoot him an amused look. "I didn't know you spoke Spanish."

"And I thought you did."

"I do," I say, sticking my gun back in my pants. "Fluently."

"Do you even know what fluent means?"

"Of course, papi." He glares at me a moment before shaking his head in disgust and walking away. I turn to Ricardo, and my smile falters when I see the shit-eating grin on his face. "What?"

"You called him daddy."

Of course I did.

The job in Texas kicked my ass. By the time I make it back to Hillsborough, I'm exhausted. But I find the energy to check the house and make sure it's still in one piece. I also look in the closets and under the bed. It would be just like Diem to find a way past my security system, to hide somewhere and then kill me in my sleep.

I haven't heard from her since that one night. She never called back, and hell would freeze over before I called her. Tonight I would be getting my truck back. Once I had it, I would start planning my revenge. Diem had more than earned my wrath. Now she was about to get it.

It's almost three in the afternoon when I roll my sorry ass out of bed. After a quick workout, I shower, then pull up the GPS on my truck that's linked through my computer. I write down the coordinates, then program them into the navigation on the rental car I'd picked up at the airport.

The address leads me to a small house at the end of a dirt road. A black BMW sits next to a truck that looks like mine. But, it couldn't be mine. Because this one was completely totaled. Chunks of grass and dirt hang from the busted grill. The front tire is completely missing, and the others are damaged beyond repair.

Long scratches run the length of the truck, deep enough for the metal to be shining through. What isn't scratched is dented or dirty. It's not even black anymore. It's gray. The windshield is busted, the headlights are busted, the driver's side door is caved in, and I can't help but hope her face looks the exact same way.

Without hesitation, I walk to the front door. Not bothering to knock, I turn the knob. It opens easily into a large den. My eyes scan the room. There is a leather sectional that takes up the majority of the space, a coffee table, a flat-screen, and a mural of a woman wearing a red dress. But my focus is on the woman who has a gun trained on me.

"I don't know if you're brave or just stupid." Diem lowers the gun back into the side of the couch where she is laying. I should feel good about what I see, but I don't. I wanted her to look as bad as my truck did. But she doesn't. She looks worse.

I survey my surroundings a little more and notice how messy the place is. Empty water bottles, old pizza, bloody gauzes, bandages and about twenty NyQuil bottles litter the coffee table and floor. I step closer, shoving my hands in my pockets to keep from reaching out to her. But I still don't know if it's to hurt her or help her.

"As you can see, I'm not in the mood to entertain today. So, if you don't mind, you can see yourself out." She doesn't look at me, but the side of her face I can see is swollen and bruised. A blanket covers her from the waist down, and she cradles her left hand like it's broken. Her hair is everywhere and she looks like she hasn't showered in days. That might be what I smell too.

"You wanna tell me what happened?" I ask, grit in my tone.

She lifts her hand and gives me the finger. Figuring the worst she can do is shoot me, I stand between her and the TV. Now I have her attention. And she has mine. She's cut up, banged up, and clearly in pain. She tries to hide it, but I can see it written all over her face. But those eyes, still cold as ice.

"I'll take care of your truck. Give me a couple of weeks. But right now, you need to leave." Her voice is strong. If I wasn't looking at her, I'd never know she was hurt.

"Looks like you can't even take care of yourself." I cross my arms, nodding my head toward the endless pile of shit next to her.

"I'm fine," she says between her teeth. Her nostrils flare wide, and I don't know if it's from pain or anger.

"Why didn't you go to the hospital?" I ask, narrowing my eyes on her.

"I did. I got a DUI too. Does that make you happy?"

"They didn't keep you?"

She rolls her eyes. When she lets out an exasperated breath, she flinches, then speaks again through her teeth. "They did. I left. Nothing they could do for me there. I didn't want to humiliate myself any more than I already had. I work with hospitals, remember?" Leaning over, she fumbles for a bottle of water. It falls from the table, rolling just out of her reach. Instinctively, I move in to grab it. But when I look up, her gun is once again trained on my face. This time, it's an inch from my head.

"Zeke, you need to leave. I won't tell you again." The threat is real. She doesn't want to shoot me, but for some reason, she feels like she has to. But I've taken enough shit off of her to last me a lifetime. So, just when she thinks I'm retreating, and she starts to let down her guard, I easily bend her wrist and grab the gun from her fingers.

For a split second, she looks relieved. But her walls come back up and she glares at me. Her eyes shine with unshed tears. Her lip trembles slightly. But she pulls it between her teeth, biting hard enough to bring blood. It's then I notice she hasn't moved her hand.

Placing the gun in the back of my jeans, I gently take her hand in mine to examine it. I expect her to pull back, but she doesn't. She just lays there, letting me run my thumbs over the small bones. Tears leak out the corners of her eyes, but she doesn't blink. This is someone who's endured pain before.

"It's not broken," I say, now caressing the inside of her wrist.

"I know that. I know all of my injuries. And I'm fine. I just need some time to heal." She's so determined. So independent. So fucking stubborn.

"Where else you hurting?"

"Leave," she snaps, ignoring me.

I look around again. It's clear that she's the only one who's been here. "Have your friends not come by to check on you?" I ask, feeling my anger shift from her to the motherfuckers who left her here to suffer.

"I don't have friends."

"You had a shitload of them the night you called me." At the reminder of her stealing my truck, her friends are forgotten and my anger is focused solely on her once again.

She rolls her eyes. "I don't even know those people. I met them in a bar. Just like I met you. Which reminds me, I don't really know you either. And I don't want you here. Seriously," she adds, giving me a lethal look.

"I didn't want you to steal my truck, but you did. I guess that makes us even." But we're not even. Even would be me leaving her here to suffer on her own. And for some reason I just can't do that. I'd never physically harm a woman. I guess I can't stand to see one hurt either.

"That's right, Zeke. So hate me. Hate me for stealing your truck. For mind fucking you. Hate me. Just leave." I catch a hint of fear in her voice. My suspicions rise immediately. If this girl is in trouble, I don't need to get involved. I have enough shit going on in my life. But if I left and something happened to her, I would never be able to forgive myself. I'm struggling enough with that as it is.

I don't allow myself time to really think about what I'm doing. I just go with my gut. I do need to leave. But I'm taking her with me.

I walk down the hall, ignoring the protests she screams at my back. I open doors until I find a room that looks like hers. In the closet, I grab a handful of clothes and move shit until I find a duffel bag. I stuff it with more clothes from her dresser until it's full. When I get back out into the hallway, she's made it off the couch, leaning heavily on the wall.

Bypassing her, I rummage through the shit on the table, but can't find any medication. Only prescriptions that haven't been filled. Shoving them in my pocket, I walk out to the car, trying to block out her voice. She's calling me every motherfucker in the book. I come back empty-handed, and walk directly up to her. She's too pissed to let the pain stop her from trying to fight back.

Easily, I avoid her fists and cradle her in my arms. The movement silences her. When I look down, she's taking short, shallow breaths. Shit. I hurt her. I ignore the feeling of regret, and keep moving until she is sitting in the front seat of my car. She's not fighting anymore, and she's pale—white as a ghost. By the time I'm back from shutting the door, she's passed out.

The drive back home seems to take forever. I should take her to the hospital, but she said she'd already been. And she claimed she left on her own free will. I wasn't sure if that was the truth, or if she was kicked out for pulling a gun on someone. Either way, I was going to have to play doctor for a little while. At least until I could figure something else out. Not sure who else to call, I phone Rookie. Hoping like hell he can shed some light on this shitstorm I've gotten myself into.

"I got a problem," I say as a form of greeting.

"A big one or a little one?"

I think about that a moment before answering. "An unusual one."

"Aw, shit. Would this have anything to do with the carjacker?" My silence is answer enough. "I can come, but I got Carrie."

"Perfect."

I carry Diem's unconscious body into the house. Unsure of where else to put her, I lay her in my bed. Then I just stand over her wondering what the hell to do. She's wearing a button-up shirt and a loose pair of drawstring shorts. My eyes scan her body looking for injuries, but other than bruises, I don't see any. I unfasten the buttons of her shirt, and just below her bra is the most sickening swirl of blue and purple circles I've ever seen. Her whole abdomen looks bruised and battered.

"I didn't peg you to be a kidnapper." I turn my head to find her watching me. She's eerily calm, but that evil glare is in her eyes. The look she's giving me makes me think if she had that gun, I'd be a dead man.

"There's a lot you don't know about me." I sit next to her on the bed, her eyes following my every move. "Tell me what happened."

Between shallow breaths, she lays out the events like she's reading them from a book. Something she's done before. "I was on my way home when I wrecked. I flipped the truck, managed to crawl to the road, but I didn't see a car for almost two hours. So, I laid there, in a fucking ditch, until someone passed by. They called the cops, I went to the hospital, they drew blood work, found out I was over the limit, gave me a ticket while I was laying in the ER, then the doctors wheeled me up to my room. The next day, I asked how long I'd be staying and they said until I could get up and walk out. So I did. Now here I am. Except this time, I didn't go voluntarily. You took me." Every detail is said matter-of-fact. She never faltered. I wonder if she's lying.

"Why didn't you fill the scripts?" I ask, pulling them from my pocket. Lortab 10s. The good shit.

"I don't take pain meds."

"But you drink NyQuil like it's water."

"It helps me sleep." Damn she's exasperating. I take a deep breath, trying to hold tight to my growing temper. I don't know if I'm more pissed because she's ungrateful for my help, or because I'm actually helping her.

"Just stop, Diem," I say, the words rushing from my mouth.

"Stop what, Zeke?" she snaps.

"Stop being so evasive. Stop pushing me away. Stop being

such a fucking bitch." Her eyes roll to the ceiling. When she doesn't speak, I push forward.

"What hurts?" Such a simple question, yet she seems to struggle to find a way to tell me. "The truth, Diem," I add, probably a little too harshly.

"Several ribs are broken. One bruised lung. Both my wrists are fucked up, but my left one is worse. They're not broken, but need a brace. My ankle is sprained, and my neck hurts. Probably from whiplash. Other than that, I've just got some bruises and cuts. I have a pretty bad one on my back. They stapled it, but I think I pulled one out." Her eyes finally meet mine. If she's searching for pity, she won't find any. I'm not going to feel sorry for her, because she doesn't want me to. And she brought this on herself.

"You eat today?"

"No. Yesterday either. And I'm starving. So, if you want to play Nurse Betty, then waddle your ass in the kitchen and fix me something." I can't do anything but stare at her. She's like a pit bull that needs rescuing. I have a softness inside me for dogs. But for impossible, self-righteous, hateful women like her? Not so much.

"Let's make a deal," I say, throwing the offer she's always suggesting back in her face. "I'll help you when you ask for it. Until then, you're on your own." I don't bother looking at her as I get up and walk out.

"I don't even want to be here!" She yells, her words laced in malice. With words just as angry and powerful, I spit them back at her as I slam the door.

"Then get to fuckin' walkin'."

7

WHEN I MOVED to Hillsborough, Rookie moved too. He now lives fifty miles west of me. I feel guilty for invading on his time with Carrie, but she was a nurse and while he was helping me sort my shit out, maybe she could help with Diem.

I'm on the porch when they arrive. Pulling Carrie to me, I hold her a while. I haven't seen her since the funeral. Rookie gives me a nod and I fill them in on what happened. I'm not sure what all Carrie knows, but if Rookie trusts her, then I do too. She was his ol' lady. That made her my family.

She offered to take a look at Diem without me even asking. I appreciated the gesture, but I wasn't sure how Diem would react. Where she was hard and mean, Carrie was soft and nice. The two together might turn into a disaster.

"I appreciate that, Carrie. Really, I do. But she's a little . . . fucked up. Not just physically but mentally too." Carrie just nods and flashes me a reassuring smile.

"I can handle myself, Zeke." She winks at Rookie and adds,

"Joe." Rookie must have told her about our change in identities. I follow her inside and to my room. Not sure of what will be waiting on the other side of the door, I pull Carrie back to open it and walk in first.

Diem is still lying in bed, her eyes focused on the ceiling. For a minute, I wonder if she's dead. When she speaks, I hear myself and Rookie sigh in relief. "You know, if you're going to talk about someone, then maybe you shouldn't do it so they can hear you. But don't worry, Carrie." She turns her head, giving Carrie an evil smile. "I don't bite."

I was a dumb-ass. Of course she could hear us. We were just outside the window. I replay everything in my mind, but nothing about our conversation pertained to anything but her and the accident. Oh, and me calling her fucked up.

"Pity," Carrie says, moving to the other side of the bed. Leaning close, she whispers, "I like to get bit." My eyebrows shoot to my hairline as my gaze slides to Rookie. His nostrils flare and he shifts, his eyes burning with passion—for his woman. The one who was good enough to keep him from temptation.

"Guys?" Carrie asks, looking at us expectantly. I refuse to leave her and with just a shake of my head, she nods and focuses her attention back on Diem. Her fingers move down her body, applying pressure, asking questions and rotating her slowly. Diem acts the good patient, answering all her questions and succumbing to her every demand. I've never been more thankful to have Carrie here. Chances are, Diem wouldn't have been so yielding to me.

"That hurt?" Diem whimpers in pain at Carrie's question. She's on her side facing me, but she doesn't look at me. "I can stitch you up, but I don't have anything to numb it."

"It's fine. Just do it," Diem snaps, her hand shaky as she brings it to her face. With her thumb and finger, she squeezes her eyes, drying the tears. Digging in her bag, Carrie gets to work. With every stitch, I feel Diem's pain. And when her eyes narrow and her lip goes between her teeth, she seeks me out.

I meet her gaze, never taking my eyes off hers. It only takes Carrie a few minutes, but when she's finished, it seems like a lifetime has passed. "All done," she announces, helping Diem roll to her back.

"Do you have any pain meds?"

"She does." I answer Carrie's question, knowing Diem will refuse them.

"Good. That and a lot of rest will help. Zeke can wrap your wrists later. I'll leave him some bandages. You might want to get a bath first. That back wound is pretty messy." Diem doesn't answer and Carrie looks at me. I shrug and she smiles, following us out.

"Hey, Carrie," Diem calls, her voice weak. "I owe you one." Carrie just nods, but I personally know the depth of truth in Diem's words. She's indebted to Carrie, and I know she'll keep her word.

After Rookie and Carrie are gone, I find myself going back to check on Diem. I don't know why. I'm just gonna say that it's my duty because she's my houseguest. I find her in the same position, still staring at the ceiling.

"I thought you weren't going to help me anymore. But you did, and I didn't ask you to." Even exhausted, she finds a way to be an ass.

"I wasn't going to, but Carrie offered," I say, shoving my hands in my pockets and propping up in the doorway.

"Well, for whatever it's worth, thanks." I'm shocked at her gratitude, but don't let her see it.

"You're welcome." I let the silence sit until it becomes uncomfortable. "Well, good night."

"Zeke," she chokes out. A sob? "I can't do this alone." Her admission is sobering. The amount of pride a woman like her has to swallow to say those words is unfathomable.

I walk over, looking down at the broken woman lying in my

bed. Tears pool in her eyes that seem almost lifeless. My chest tightens at the sight. "I've got money. I'll pay you."

"Diem," I start, but she shakes her head.

"Just until I can get on my feet."

"Whatever you need," I cut in, before she says anything else to make her feel worse. Or me. "Tell me what I can do."

Attempting to sit up, she leans on her elbow, pausing to close her eyes and grit her teeth in pain. Her bottom lip trembles as she holds her breath. After a moment, her chest begins to rise and fall while she struggles to control her breathing. "I'm not sure what I need," she whispers.

She gazes up at me with dark brown pools of aching need. They plead with me to just help her in whatever way I can. Because right now, she can't help herself. And although she's hurting, she's not desperate enough to ask.

My lips pressed in a thin line, I give her a nod. "I got you."

I walk to the bathroom, remembering that Carrie insisted she bathe and clean the wound on her back. As I fill the tub, I make a mental list of the things within my power I can do for her. She needs food, clean clothes, plenty of liquids, and something to help the pain—even if it's NyQuil.

Grabbing some clean towels from the dryer, I rummage through my laundry basket until I find a clean shirt. I return to the room to find her sitting on the side of the bed. "Can you walk?" I ask, knowing good and damn well she can, but testing her to see how far she plans to go. Even though I feel sorry for her, and I'm willing to help her, doesn't mean I trust one strand of hair on her pretty little head.

"Yeah," she says softly, standing slowly. I admire the fight in her as she shuffles to the bathroom, using the walls as a crutch. "No bubbles?" She smirks. Well, at least she hasn't lost her sense of humor.

"I like to save the romantics for women I like." I give her a playful smile that she returns. "Sit," I say, pointing to the toilet.

She obeys, and my dick twitches at the thought. *Fucking pervert.* Kneeling in front of her, I unbutton her top, keeping my eyes on her face as I do. Pushing it from her shoulders, I look down at the sports bra, wondering how in the hell I'm supposed to get that damn thing off without hurting her.

"Cut it," she tells me, keeping that bruised and cut, yet still beautiful, face impassive.

Pulling my knife from my jeans, I flip it open. She turns her head slightly to the side, appraising me as I place it between her breasts. She doesn't blink or look the least bit concerned. Either she trusts me not to kill her, or she doesn't give a shit if I do.

Gripping the material in my hand, I pull it tight and feel the back of my fingers brush against her breasts that I'm sure taste just as delicious as her mouth. Sliding the blade down the material, it cuts easily, and soon it's splayed open and barely covering her nipples.

"Don't worry," she says, the corner of her lips turning up. "I'm not very modest."

Unsure of how that makes me feel, I give her a cold look. "I figured as much," I mumble. Ridding her of the bra completely, I focus on her collarbone, refusing to look at the two perfect tits I know are begging for my attention.

Helping her to stand, I turn her around to avoid temptation, and force a shield over my mind, my thoughts, and my cock. I've thought about what Diem would look like naked plenty of times, but this isn't how I want my first experience to be. I'm here to help her, not fuck her. If this were Carrie or Saylor, there would be no lustful thoughts running through my brain. So I pretend she's my sister. That she belongs to one of my brothers, so I show her and her body the same respect I would show them.

Pushing her shorts to her feet, I grab her hand as she steps out of them and lead her to the bathtub. Keeping a firm grip on her waist, I hold tight to her tiny body until she is seated. "Close your eyes," I instruct, grabbing a plastic cup and filling it before pouring water over her head.

She sits silent and motionless, allowing me to wash her hair. When I'm finished, I focus on her back, carefully cleaning around the wound. I keep in mind that this is probably a lot harder for her than it is for me. Diem is not the type to be waited on, bathed, or pampered. I'm sure this is a first.

"You okay?" I ask, pushing the wet strands of hair back from her face as I mentally try to prepare myself for bathing the rest of her. *She's your sister. She's your sister.*

She avoids my gaze, looking down at her crippled hands in her lap. "I can't do this," she says, shaking her head. "Get out."

I frown, not sure if I heard her right. "Diem, I don't mind—"

"I said get out." Her voice is firm as she turns those eyes of steel on me. She's disappointed in herself and determined to do this on her own. And I get it.

I leave, closing the door behind me but making sure not to lock it. If she calls for me, I want to be able to get to her. But something tells me she probably won't.

Lighting a smoke in the hall, I wait for her to finish. Standing right outside the door, I listen as the water splashes. Every once in a while, I hear a sharp intake of breath, a growl of frustration, and sometimes even a whimper. I allow her the space she needs, but I'm not happy about it. I wish her stubborn ass would just let me help.

When the bathroom grows quiet for longer than I think it should, I knock on the door. "Everything okay in there?" I ask, my hand already on the doorknob.

"I'm fine," she snaps, and I smirk at the vision I have in my head of her glaring at me.

Figuring if she's pissed, she really is fine, I make myself useful in the bedroom. I rip the sheets off the bed that are already stained with her blood. Throwing them in the washer, I dig through the closet until I find another set before remaking the bed.

There's never shit to eat here, but I find a pack of nabs in my duffel and pour her a tall glass of water. Searching my pitiful medicine cabinet, I locate some over-the-counter pain meds. Then I roll a blunt, thinking it will help her sleep. If she refuses it, I'll just smoke it myself. I'll probably need it to sleep tonight too.

Just as I'm passing the bathroom, the door opens and Diem appears in a towel looking like she's just run a marathon rather than take a bath. She's out of breath. Her shoulders sag and her legs struggle to hold her up. She's proved her point. Now I'm taking over, whether she likes it or not.

"Put your arm around my neck," I say, bending my knees so I shrink to her level.

Without argument, she slides her arm across my shoulder, and my skin ignites at the touch. Cradling her knees under one arm, I move the other around her waist and lift her. Her head falls to my shoulder, clearly not having the energy to hold itself up any longer.

Gently, I set her on the bed before grabbing the bandages and wrapping both her wrists. Finished, I crawl behind her and rub ointment on the cut centered in her back before covering it with the gauze Carrie had left for her.

I slip my T-shirt over her head, and the moment it's on, she practically falls to her side. "I'll rot before I do that again," she breathes, her hair disheveled all over her pale face.

Reaching my hand under her shirt, she stills. "Just getting the towel, baby. Don't get excited." I give her a wink, and her hand lifts. I know she's attempting to give me the finger but it's impossible with her hands wrapped. Throwing the towel to the floor,

I stand and tuck her legs under the covers before pulling them up to her shoulders.

"I got you some stuff," I say, standing beside the bed as I look down at her. Now that she's tucked in and there's nothing left for me to do, I feel helpless.

She starts to speak, but has to close her mouth and swallow before she can. "I can't sit back up. Just let me lay here."

"You hurting?" I ask, even though I already know the answer.

"I'm dying."

I smirk. She's so dramatic. "I got something that will help you relax. You trust me?"

She gives me an uneasy look before her eyes settle on the blunt I hold between my fingers. Lighting it, I take a few drags. Her eyes close a moment as she inhales the smoke from a distance. When it fades, she looks up at me and nods, wanting more.

Kneeling beside the bed, I take a pull from the cigar. Holding the smoke in my mouth, I lean in, keeping my lips just a hairsbreadth away from hers. She draws in a breath, inhaling the smoke as it floats out of my mouth and between her lips. She takes only what her lungs can handle—closing her mouth when she's had enough, then parting her lips when she's ready for more.

Before the blunt is finished, her eyes are heavy and her body relaxed. On the last drag she pulls from me, she whispers against my lips, "Kiss me."

I don't know if it's the weed talking, or if she's as worked up about being this close to me as I am about her. But I don't question it. I simply give the lady what she asks for. I kiss her softly, teasing her with my tongue as she lazily kisses me back. My dick hardens at the contact. This is the most delicious she's ever tasted. Two of my favorite flavors combined.

Before she becomes breathless and I lose control, I pull back slowly. "Sleep, pretty girl," I whisper. And with one final nod, she does just as I ask.

Diem sleeps all night and most of the next day. I checked in on her from time to time, but she never stirred. She still hasn't eaten, but she did drink some water sometime during the night. When she finally wakes up, she doesn't say much. She just names off some things she needs, then asks for her bag. I'm hesitant to leave her, but I do and head into town for everything she listed.

By the time I'm back, she's showered and is standing in the kitchen. I freeze at what I see. She's wearing one of my shirts. Even though I'd dressed her in it, I'd yet to notice. Now that I am, I realize I like what I see.

"You can't pack for shit. What did you think, I was gonna sleep naked?" She's leaning over the sink, peeling boiled eggs with one hand while she holds the other near her stomach.

"What are you doing?"

"I'm eating boiled eggs. It's the only damn thing you have here." She looks better—like she feels better too.

"Well, I wasn't expecting company," I say, setting the bags on the counter. I grab a beer, then lean against the fridge watching her. She's all legs in my workout T-shirt that has the arms and neck cut out, giving me a view of her sides and hips. There isn't any underwear in sight and I shift at the thought. *Fucking pervert.* The woman can barely get around.

"I changed your sheets. I didn't feel comfortable sleeping on something that might be infested with some STD." Popping an entire egg in her mouth, she starts the process of peeling another one.

I don't bother telling her I'd already changed them. I'll just let her think what she wants. "You shouldn't have. Really. 'Cause you're sleeping on the couch." I might be nice, but I'm not that nice. Clearly, she can take care of herself. And this Diem isn't the one I saw yesterday.

"The fuck I am," she says, her mouth full. "You forced me here, so I'm taking the bedroom. *You* can sleep on the couch."

I shake my head. "Not happening. And you can leave anytime you want. What happened to 'Please help me, Zeke'?" I say, imitating a whiny voice that sounds nothing like her.

"I had a moment of weakness. Starvation and dehydration will do that to you." For emphasis, she downs a glass of water, then puts another egg in her mouth.

"You're such a pig." I smirk.

She just shrugs. "Call me whatever you want. I'm still sleeping in the bed. I don't give a shit if you're in it or not." Images of Diem in my bed wearing nothing but my shirt are something I don't want flashing in my mind. "Did you get the stuff?" she asks, and suddenly I feel like it's my balls she's chewing on. Not eggs. And I don't like the feeling.

I don't answer as I walk out of the house, slamming the door behind me. Taking my frustrations out on my punching bag in the shed, I try to find the answer to the one question probing my brain. What the hell am I doing? Not only do I not know her, there is something about her I don't trust. And I'm letting her sleep in my house? What the fuck?

Two hours later, I'm exhausted from my workout and have to drag myself inside and to the shower, completely ignoring Diem on the couch. I let the water beat down on me until it runs cold, then I wrap a towel around my waist before walking to my room. And there she is, sprawled out on my bed with her arms and her legs stretched in every direction.

"Get out of my bed, Diem," I growl, rummaging through my drawers in search of some clean underwear.

"Put some damn clothes on. There's a lady in the house."

There's laughter in her voice, and when I turn she is smiling. It's a sight I hadn't realized I missed. With the thought of making her blush, I remove the towel and stand in the middle of the room, bare-ass naked.

She scans my body, and it's all I can do not to shake my dick at her. Her eyes widen as she stares at me, not breathing and unmoving. I smirk. "Wanna take a picture?" She jerks her eyes away, her lips pressing in a thin line. I don't know if she's mad because she got caught or mad because she likes what she sees. I don't really give a shit either way.

"You don't wanna play that game with me, Zeke. Trust me." She's right. I don't. I can barely stand the thought of her in my shirt. Much less out of it. I pull on some jogging pants, then set the house alarms from my phone. "I need my wrists wrapped." I raise an eyebrow at her. "Please," she adds, saying the word like it tastes bad in her mouth.

I wrap her wrists quickly, noticing how she watches my face as I work. I hate how she looks at me. I like it too. It's like she's trying to tell me something with her eyes. But when she speaks, she's just a bitch. I like her better mute.

"There," I say, throwing the tape on the dresser. "Now get out of my bed."

"No."

"Diem."

"Zeke."

"You're starting to piss me off," I snap, but the truth is, I enjoy our bullshit banter.

"This," she says, circling her face with her finger. "Look at it. Does it look the slightest bit like I give a shit about your feelings?" I lied. I don't enjoy this. Not even a little bit. I hate her. I really do.

"That," I say, mirroring her finger-waving shit. "Is fixing to look a helluva lot worse. I'm not playing with you, Diem. I'm fixing to fuck you up." She laughs. *Bitch.*

"Seriously, Zeke? You expect me to believe that? You'd never hit a woman. Trust me. I know the men capable of it. You're not one of them." Anger ignites inside me at the thought of her even knowing people like that. Much less being their victim. Although I don't think I could blame them. They just didn't have the tolerance I did. The before-Saylor Dirk, would've done choked her ass out.

"You're pushing my fucking limits." I sit on the bed, forcing her to move over before I crush the rest of her ribs. She does, but she's not happy about it.

I turn the TV on and she looks at me like I've just committed some act of treason. "I'm tired."

"Go to sleep," I say, leaning back on my arm and flipping to the Western Channel.

"I can't. The TV bothers me."

"Then get your ass on the couch."

I feel her eyes burning into me. I don't want to look, but that force she has pulls my eyes to hers. Then, the most wicked smile I've ever seen crosses her face. "You know, it's kinda hot in here." With that, she slips her arms inside her shirt, my shirt, and pulls it over her head. And this time, I was going to look.

The two most perfect tits I've ever seen in my entire life stare back at me. They're bigger than a handful, but not by much. I can tell by just looking at them that they're not fake either. I have a thing for natural, beautiful tits with small, light brown nipples that look better in my mouth than on her chest. Feeling my cock stiffen, I remember he does too.

Before I start thinking with the wrong head, and she has a chance to push the covers off the rest of her body, I'm on my feet. I'm frustrated because I can't have her, and even more so because I actually want her. She isn't even my type.

Grabbing my pillow, I walk out, taking the remote with me.

"The T—," she starts, but I cut her off.

"Turn it off your fucking self."

"I'm gonna kill her, Rookie. I swear I'm gonna do it." I'm in the shed, considering flying back to Jackpot for the night. I'd have to be back by tomorrow, but it would be worth it.

"Dude, it's three o'clock in the morning. My ol' lady I ain't seen in three months is naked and in my bed, and I'm outside on the phone with you. So next time, kill her first. Then call me and I'll come help bury the body. Until then, throw the bitch out, or sleep on the couch."

The phone disconnects. So much for fucking brotherly love. I light a cigarette, thinking about taking my bike out, when I hear her calling my name. I run full speed inside, panic filling me. How can I care about someone's well-being so much and hate them at the same time?

I bust through my bedroom door, flipping the light on and scanning the room for intruders or ghosts or spiders. Fucking something. But what I find is an amused Diem, alone and safe in my bed. Back in my shirt.

"Where's the fire?" she asks, fighting a smile.

"Diem," I say in warning.

"I was just going to see if you would turn the air on. It's seriously hot in here." She fans herself dramatically. And it's my breaking point.

"That's it. I can't do this." She looks a little worried, as she should. Careful not to kill her, I grab under her knees and around her back. She hisses at the movement, and not one fucking inch of me feels sorry for her. Lifting her from the bed, I take her to the living room, and deposit her gently on the couch—fighting the urge to throw her through a window.

"If you come back in my room, I'm gonna break your legs. You don't believe me, then try me." My voice is hard, cold, and so harsh that she presses further into the couch.

When I'm alone, in my bed that smells just like her, I finally settle in for a peaceful night of sleep. And I don't get a wink of it.

8

THE NEXT MORNING, I'm in kill mode. Not because of the woman staying in my house, or the fact that I've had no sleep in two days, but because today is the day I get to settle a score. I've waited weeks for this day—giving Death Mob enough time to let their guard down again after my last kill. There are several mutual MCs who said Death Mob claimed their "missing members" were due to a change in National hierarchy. Apparently, some members didn't agree and decided to cut their losses and get out. It was a perfect assumption—eliminating Sinner's Creed as a suspect. This knowledge is what I've been waiting for to put my plan back in full swing.

Tonight I'll be travelling three hours away to Bristol, Vermont, where Death Mob is throwing a birthday party for a local chapter member. The need to kill and get away from here is so desperate that I'm already packed and ready. And I still have twelve hours before I can leave.

"Going somewhere?" Diem asks from the couch as I throw my bag on the floor and take a seat in the recliner.

"Yeah."

My short answer doesn't appease her and she looks at me expectantly. When I don't say more, she pushes further. "Well, where you going?"

"Away. I'll be back tomorrow." I flip through the channels, then realize I'm starving and walk to the kitchen to dig for some food. I can feel her as she follows behind me.

"You leaving now?"

"No. Tonight." I rummage through the fridge. Not finding anything, I move to the cabinet.

"That sucks," she murmurs mostly to herself.

"I said I'd be back tomorrow," I find myself saying, and I feel a hint of regret for leaving her. She's only been here a couple of days.

"Oh no, don't get it twisted, Zeke." I turn to see what she finds so amusing. "It sucks because you don't leave until tonight. You have my permission to leave now if you want." She looks at the floor, fighting her smile.

I slam the cabinet and she jumps. Then grabs her side and winces, taking short, shallow breaths. I close the distance between us until I can feel her breath on my face as she looks up to meet my eyes. I'm sure mine are cold and lifeless, just how I feel right before a kill. No sympathy, no understanding, and no tolerance for bullshit.

"I don't ask for permission, Diem. If I want something, I take it." Before she says something that will make me do something I regret, I grab my bag and leave.

Claudette's is a shitty little strip joint discreetly located in an old, rundown building just inside the Bristol city limit. The strippers are homely and thin—preferring a line of coke over a decent meal. The main room is dimly lit, illuminated only by strands of randomly hung Christmas lights. The stench of the building is old and musty, even though they try to cover up the smell with vanilla scented candles. It's the kind of place most people avoid. Good thing the man I'm fixing to kill doesn't fall under the category of "most people."

I've been watching him for nearly an hour, hiding in the shadows, which isn't hard to do considering the poor lighting. Rookie is in my peripherals, but like me, he's hidden from view. It's just the two of us tonight—more than enough to handle this one-man job.

I'm on my third beer when the man finally stands and makes his way toward the door. His bike is parked near the back of the building, which made the task of disabling his ignition that much simpler. I wait a full minute before I follow him out, giving Rookie a thirty second head start on me. As I round the side of the building, I come face-to-face with Rookie. The morose look on his face causes an uneasy feeling to settle over me, even before he speaks.

"We've got a problem."

Every part of my plan has been flawless, but tonight, Death Mob threw a kink in it. At the back of the building, standing next to the patch holder, are two Prospects. Two young, innocent Prospects who don't deserve to die for a brotherhood they aren't even a part of yet. Their innocence is due to ignorance—they have no idea what Death Mob has done. Knowledge is privilege. It has to be earned. These men are still trying to prove themselves. Club business isn't shared with anyone who isn't a brother. And killing a third-generation member of the biggest one-percent MC in the nation is definitely club business.

I want to call it off. I want to walk away and wait for another opportunity to present itself. I'm willing to let a man more than deserving of death live, just so these Prospects can live too. But things don't quite work out that way. Before we can leave unseen, they see us. Immediately, I'm made. The patch holder knows something is wrong, and reaches for his gun—leaving me no choice but to put a bullet in his head. And without hesitation, I kill the Prospects too. It has to be done. Now, their bodies will rot next to a man who was more than deserving of death. All because they chose to ride on the wrong night with the wrong club.

Sickness fills my gut. And even the knowledge that I did this for Dirk isn't enough to justify what I've done.

I pull my bike into the shed a little after midnight. Too troubled by the thought, I don't perform my usual ritual. Instead, I torch the patches in my shed until they turn to dust. I make the call to Rookie and he confirms that everything has been handled. He sounds bothered too, and I hate that I dragged him into this.

"Shady, you did what had to be done. That's what we do. It's not their fault. But it's not yours either. They chose to ride with outlaws. They knew it was a possibility." His words do little to comfort me, but I thank him anyway.

I disconnect the call, my eyes drawn to the dried blood caked around my fingernails. I'd delivered perfect kill shots on all my targets—ending their lives quickly and with minimal blood. But somehow, what little bit of blood there was managed to find me. It's as if it was placed there by some higher power to serve as a reminder of what I was feeling for the first time in my life—remorse.

I keep my hoodie pulled tight over my face and body to hide the bloodstained evidence when I walk inside the dark house. I don't give the couch a second glance as I head straight to the shower. Watching the blood swirl around the drain as it fades to pink and then disappears, I wash the proof from my body—proof which reminds me once again that I killed two young, innocent men tonight. Six months ago, that could've been Rookie.

I lean my head against the wall, letting the water rain down and wash away my sins. But there's no cleansing for my soul. It's tarnished beyond repair. Even though I feel remorse, it doesn't count. Because now, I'm thinking of an even worse death for the ones who forced me to do this.

I close the door to my bedroom before turning on the light. I hear a groan from the bed and close my eyes. I'm really not in the mood.

"Seriously? Go away. It took forever to get your stench out of these sheets. Don't come in here and fuck it up now." I ignore her, keeping my back turned as I pull some shorts on. I turn out the light and climb into bed, anxious to fall asleep and escape from reality. "What the hell are—"

"Not tonight, Diem," I say, cutting her off. There's no fight in my voice, because I just don't have the energy. "Please," I add, hoping she gets the message. She lays silent for a little while.

When she speaks, her tone isn't bitchy, and there's the slightest hint of concern. "You okay?"

I think about her question before answering. I could choose to say nothing, but I find myself telling her the truth. "Not this time."

She doesn't know what I mean, but minutes later she shifts slowly to her side. Then her small, bandaged hand comes to rest on my stomach. And when I wake up the next morning, it's still there—giving me the courage I need to push the shit from last night to the back of my mind.

I'm starving. Diem has to be starving, but she has yet to demand anything since she sent me to the store the last time. She's getting better, but it's only been four days and her movements are still slow.

Standing in the living room, freshly showered with her short, wet, black hair brushed off her face and still wearing my shirt, she finally makes a confession. "I've eaten everything in the house. We're completely out of food. So, are you gonna go shopping or do I need to hunt for some wildlife in the backyard?" Considering she didn't snap at me and demand I do it, I feel like she's making progress.

"Yeah, I'll go. You wanna make a list?" Pulling her hand from behind her back, she hands me two pages of shit she thinks we need. I scan the list, frowning when I come to the part that mentions what *she* needs. "I have razors," I say, then continue with the other things. "And shampoo, and soap, and lotion, deodorant . . . Eye cream? What is this shit?"

"You have the shittiest razors ever invented. You must have got them on sale. Five hundred for five bucks. And the shampoo smells like a man. So does the soap, and lotion, and deodorant. And I need the eye cream because I don't want to look thirty."

"You're thirty?" I ask, completely shocked. I thought she was in her early twenties.

She smiles. "Hence the eye cream." Then she adds, "Oh, and I don't have any money on me. So, I'll have to pay you back."

I roll my eyes. No shit she didn't have any money. She must not have any clothes either. "You gonna cook?" I ask, looking at the list again.

"Yes. But don't expect me to become your personal chef. I'll cook and you can eat it or fix your own." That sounded fair enough to me. It was nice to see Diem finally coming around. Who knows? I might actually let her stay longer than necessary. "And while you're at it, pick yourself up a new toothbrush." My brow draws in confusion. I'd just bought a new toothbrush.

"I used yours to clean the toilet yesterday." On second thought, she couldn't leave soon enough.

———

Six hundred dollars and three hours later, I'm standing in the kitchen while Diem and I argue over what goes where.

"Nobody puts spices in the same cabinet as everything else. You have a special place dedicated for spices only," she says, speaking slowly like I'm a small child.

"It's my fucking house. I'll put the shit where I want to."

"Well, as long as I'm staying here and cooking, I need it to be organized." I glare at her, holding a bottle of cinnamon in one hand and a bag of sugar in the other. I start to just let her win and put it where she wants me to, but then she snaps her fingers at me. I drop the sugar and cinnamon on the floor, and walk out, leaving her cussing at my retreating back.

That night, I eat my first home-cooked meal since Thanksgiving at Dirk's last year. The meatloaf was dry, the potatoes clumpy. and the peas tasted like rubber. But I didn't complain. Diem managed to eat as much if not more than me. Because she seemed to be moving slower than normal, I offered to do the dishes.

"Damn right you're doing the dishes. I cooked."

Tomorrow, I would be cooking. And I plan to poison her food.

When I see her walking toward my room, I know she's going to get in my bed. I let her go, hoping she'll be asleep by the time I'm finished. But when I walk in, she's not there. I glance across the hall to see the bathroom door shut. Good. I'll just lock her ass out.

I spread out in the bed, relaxing into the double-sized mattress. I hear her turn the doorknob, and smile when she can't get it open. "Your pillow's on the couch."

No sooner are the words out of my mouth than the door is opened and she's walking in, flipping on the light switch as she does. "I know. I got it." She smiles, holding it in her arms along with the steak knife she used to break in. Her smile is an act though. I can tell she's hurting.

"What's wrong?"

"Nothing," she says, easing down on the bed and laying on her side. Her back is to me, but I can see the rise and fall of her body as she struggles to breathe. She flips to her stomach, and I notice her hand fist into the pillow.

"Diem, you're not here for my amusement. If something's wrong, tell me so I can help you." I wait patiently for her answer that never comes. "Fine. You could have at least cut the light off," I mumble, getting out of bed and flipping the switch.

I lay there in the darkness, waiting for her breathing to slow. When it finally does and I feel like she's asleep, I allow my own eyes to close. And I find myself wondering once again why I even care.

9

"ZEKE."

"Zeke."

"Zeke!" I wake up, wondering if she was calling my name or if I was dreaming. "Wake up." Her voice fills the room, and I know I wasn't dreaming.

"What?" I ask, my words thick with sleep.

"I need a favor." I finally open my eyes to see her standing next to my side of the bed. She looks like shit. "I need you to put this on my back and then cover it with this." She holds up some kind of ointment in one hand and some gauze in the other.

"Could you not have told me this when I asked earlier?" I grumble, sitting up.

"Well, I wouldn't ask you at all, but I'm not a contortionist and can't do it myself."

I motion with my finger for her to turn around. When she does, she carefully removes my T-shirt and I'm left looking at her ass, barely covered by a pair of gray satin panties that don't entirely cover her cheeks. I swallow at the sight. Her ass is toned, but not muscular. Her skin is flawless, and I want to touch it to see if it feels that way too. She shifts, and it jiggles slightly. My dick surges and I bite back a groan.

"Stop looking at my ass, Zeke," she snaps. Reluctantly, I drag my eyes north until I land on the big cut that is centered in her back. It looks a little red and swollen, but other than that, it's healing. Carrie did a good job of stitching her up.

"It looks good," I say, squirting the ointment on her back.

"Squats." I smile at her response.

"I meant the cut, babe. But your ass is nice too."

"Don't call me 'babe.' I'm not a pig." I tape the gauze over the cut, and just 'cause I'm an asshole, I smack her ass when I'm finished. The joke's on me though because my dick hardens further at the feel of it against my hand. *Damn.* It *feels* like satin. "I'm gonna let that one go. I'll consider it payback for waking you." Always playing games.

I lay back down and moments later hear her as she crawls in the bed. Then shifts. Then groans. Then shifts again. "Fucking ribs and back and hands," she mumbles. She ends up on her side facing me. I look over at her, the moonlight casting a glow across the room. I frown; she really does look uncomfortable.

Knowing I'll never get any sleep as long as she keeps wiggling, I flip to my back. "Come here," I command, but my voice is off. It sounds like a tone I'd use when I wanted to do more to her than hold her.

She just stares at me, one eyebrow raised in suspicion. Moving closer to her, I wrap my arm around her shoulders until her head is on my chest. Grabbing her knee, I pull it across my legs. She shifts slightly until half of her body is laying on mine. It doesn't take her long to relax further into me.

"Better?" *Yes.*

"Mmm." And moments later, she's asleep.

"You can't do it like that," Diem tells me the next evening, from her very comfortable position on the porch. Meanwhile, I'm in the yard cutting back the hedges that have nearly overtaken the front of my house. I thought it would be better than being locked inside with her. I was wrong. She was just as annoying outside.

"Why don't you get your ass down here and do it?" I ask, leaning over to glare at her—sipping her fucking lemonade like a queen.

"Well, I would, but I'm not quite ready for manual labor, boss."

"Yeah, and whose fault is that?" She doesn't answer, and I'm glad for the break from her nagging.

"You should get a dog."

"I already have one mutt around here. No need for another one." I'm sure she's giving me the finger, but she should have known better than to say some shit like that.

"I cannot wait to get the hell away from here," she mumbles. Like she's some kind of prisoner.

I stab the trimmers in the ground, then walk over and snatch the lemonade out of her hand. "Nothing between you and anywhere but here except air and opportunity."

She gives me a disgusted look as she eyes the glass in my hand. Then she smiles. "Why, when I could stay here and make your life miserable too?"

"You're doing a good fucking job at that." I light a smoke, fighting the urge to stab her in the eye with it.

"Whatever. Admit it. You like having me around."

I laugh. "Yeah, about as much as I like being told what to do. And what not to do. And how to eat, sleep, sit, and trim hedges. You can't leave soon enough in my eyes, sweetheart."

Her lips curl into a snarl at my words. "Stop it with the pet names. They weird me out."

Handing her back the now-empty glass, I shoot her a wink. "Whatever you say, pretty girl." As I get back to my yard work, I realize that not once had she asked me not to call her that.

Diem cooks again and it's just as bad tonight as it was last night. It's some kind of casserole that has the consistency of Jell-O and tastes like cardboard. I manage to eat three bites before I make a sandwich. The next meal we share will be pizza.

Per my usual ritual, I'm sitting in my recliner watching the Western Channel waiting for my eyes to get heavy enough to sleep. Since Diem has been here, I haven't had a problem falling asleep at night as long as she is in bed with me. I don't dwell on it though. The thought of me feeling safe around her makes me feel like a pussy.

"Move over," she says, already acting like she's fixing to sit in the chair with me.

"What? No. Get your ass on the couch. This is a one-person chair. Tonight and every other night, that one person is me." She ignores me, easing her ass down on the arm of the recliner and leaning against my shoulder. In her hands she holds a big bowl. "What's that?"

"This? This is a one-person bowl of ice cream," she says, giving me a sardonic smile.

"Is there any more?"

"Nope," she answers shortly, keeping her eyes on the TV.

"Give me a bite." I'm practically whining.

"Move over."

Letting out a loud breath, I pull out the recliner, noticing her pleased smile as I do. Smart-ass thinks she knows everything. Sliding over, I give her an inch of space that she manages to wiggle her little ass in.

"Now give me a bite." She passes the bowl over, already absorbed in the show. I look down, and there's a fourth of a spoonful left. Just enough to piss me off.

"Go fix us some more," she demands.

I close my eyes, trying to calm down the beast inside me that begs to bite her face off. "You said there wasn't any more," I grit through my teeth.

"I lied. Hurry up while the commercials are on." She grins up at me, her eyes flashing with mischief.

I slam the recliner shut with my feet, and the jerk of the chair causes her to wince and hold her side. I match her evil grin with my own. "Oops."

"I hate you," she calls as I make my way to the kitchen.

"I hate you more," I yell over my shoulder. And really, I do.

By the third episode of *Gunsmoke*, Diem is laying across my chest. My arm is around her waist, her legs are tangled with mine, and we're both finally comfortable. She looks up at me, her eyes shining with curiosity beneath her long, dark lashes.

"Kiss me." My eyebrows raise in question. "Kiss me. Like you did that night in the bar."

"Why?" I ask, feeling my blood rush faster to my cock.

"Because I want you to."

I smirk. "No."

She leans her head back further against my shoulder, her lips nearly touching my cheek. "Please?" Did she seriously just say please? Or was I hearing shit?

"I like when you beg," I say, my gaze drifting from her lips to her eyes and back.

"Please, Zeke. Just kiss me." She's serious. And I'm hardening. Maybe she'll beg for that too.

Cradling her face with my hand, my thumb runs over the fading bruise under her eye. Sliding my hand down her neck, I hold it, my mouth barely grazing over hers. "Like this?" I ask, planting a soft kiss on her parted lips.

"More," she whispers, trying to move her mouth closer. But I move my hand to her throat, applying a little pressure to keep her where I want her.

My mouth covers hers, kissing her a little harder. When she parts her lips, I pull back. "Like that?"

"A little more," she breathes, and I can feel her pulse quickening. Drawing a lazy circle around her lips with my tongue, she moans. As soon as it escapes her, I give her the kiss I know she wants. She tastes like ice cream and Diem. I never knew chocolate and watermelon were such a delicious combination.

She becomes limp in my arms, all but her hand that fists in my shirt. I grab her knee, moving it over my cock. When she feels it beneath my jeans, her moan deepens. Trailing my fingers up her thigh, I guide them beneath her shirt, caressing the smooth skin with my fingertips. Keeping my mouth on hers, I slip my hand into her panties, and she pushes against me, begging me to touch her.

The feel of her bare pussy against my fingers isn't enough. So I part her lips, feeling the wet heat on my middle finger as I drag it up to her clit. Rubbing it in slow circles, I look down at her as her head falls back, breaking our kiss completely.

A guttural moan rips from her, and it's the sexiest fucking thing I've ever heard. Her mouth is open, her eyes squeezed shut, and every few seconds, her breath catches in her throat. She is the epitome of sexy. Slowly, I drop my finger lower, shoving it inside her—groaning when I feel how wet and satiny her walls feel around me.

I can smell the sweet scent of her arousal from beneath her panties. If it's intoxicating from here, I can only imagine what it must be like with my nose buried in her pussy. My tongue thrusting in and out of her—tasting her . . . drinking her . . . fucking devouring her.

I can't fuck her. She's too hurt and I'm too anxious to trust myself to take it slow. I know that watching her come will give me the worst case of blue balls I've ever had. But I can't deny her. Not now. So I work my magic with my hands, and soon, she's coming in my arms. She doesn't jerk or spasm like I expect, she simply goes limp—her entire body relaxing as she lets out a slow moan on a breath.

It's like I've just lifted the weight of the world off her shoulders. Like I'm the world's greatest drug—guaranteed to escape her from reality. Or, at least my fingers are. I cup her pussy in my hand, leaning down to kiss the hollow of her throat before sliding it out of her panties, up her stomach, and finally to her tits.

Fuck, they feel so good. I squeeze them gently, rubbing my thumb across her nipple as I wait for her to break through the fog. She's still breathing slowly, every once in a while letting out a soft moan. She's limp, spent, and sated. I still my hand, but the little moans continue and it doesn't take me long to realize she's asleep.

"You're welcome," I mutter, easing the recliner shut and standing with her in my arms. Figures I'd get the shitty end of this deal. Not only will I have to jerk off, but now I have to carry her ass to bed too. If I could put her to sleep this fast with my fingers, she'd be fucking comatose if I showed her what I could do with my tongue. I smirk at the thought.

Tomorrow, I just might have to try that.

My plan with Death Mob needs some rethinking. So Rookie and Carrie are coming over for what Diem thinks is a barbeque. She's been here over a week, and even though she tries to hide it, she looks a little excited at the thought of company. I'm excited about not having to eat her cooking. I think the bitch is trying to kill me.

"I have a problem," she announces, busting through the bathroom door while I'm in the shower.

"No shit you have problems, but which one are you talking about."

She ignores my comment, and I hear her flip the lid down on the toilet and take a seat. "I don't have any shoes."

"And?" I ask, washing the soap from my hair.

"And I don't want to look like a hillbilly." I smile. Even with overalls and a piece of straw hanging out of her mouth, there was no way Diem could look like a hillbilly.

"You look fine."

"I need you to go shoe shopping."

My hands still in my hair. She did not just tell me to go shoe shopping. "Yeah, that shit's gonna happen."

There's a long silence before she speaks. "If I don't have shoes, then you don't have shoes."

Even as I say the words, I begin to doubt them. "But I do have shoes. Lots of 'em."

"Yes, you do. But you'll never find them unless you get me some." That sneaky, conniving, *bitch*.

"Diem," I growl in warning.

"Zeke," she says, in a terrible attempt to mock me.

I turn the water off and jerk the curtain open. She looks up at me innocently. Glaring at her, I snatch my towel from the rack, wrapping it around my waist as I go look in my closet. They're gone. All of them. Even the ones I never wear. I walk to the living room and even my tennis shoes are gone. I open the front door, and my boots that usually sit covered in mud on the porch are gone.

I slam the door, stomping through the house to find her still sitting on the toilet with a pleased smile on her face. "So, do we have a deal?" she asks, raising her eyebrows in question.

Any man who has ever owned a decent pair of riding boots knows how long it takes to break them in. I could buy a hundred more pairs, but none will fit as well as my favorite ones do. That goes for my running shoes, my rain boots, and even my fucking flip-flops that I wear on really rare occasions.

"Diem," I start, moving closer to her. My eyes narrow on hers as the rage inside me begins to build. It's not just about the shoes—it's the whole fucking situation. And because she'd just come all over my fingers less than twenty-four hours ago and I couldn't beat my dick enough to get the memory out of my head.

"I will torture you. I will make you wish you left a long time ago. You've played your little games long enough. If you don't have my shit waiting for me, in the exact condition you found them in, by the time I get dressed, I'm going to put your ass in the trunk of my car and drive you so far into the middle of nowhere that you'll never find your way back home."

When I'm finished talking, or shouting, or growling, her head is shoved back against the wall. Fear dances in her eyes. It's something I've never seen from her, and I sure as fuck hope she heeds my warning. Because just like her, I'm a man of my word.

When I emerge from my bedroom minutes later, my shoes are laid out in a perfect line down the wall. At the end of them is a note.

Sorry –D.

10

I DON'T SEE Diem for the rest of the day. And every minute that passes without her presence, I feel shittier. I shouldn't; she brought this on herself. But all she wanted was some shoes. I was the one who brought her here. I was the one who packed her bag. And she knew what I would say, so she did what she had to do to try and convince me to do what she asked.

By the time Rookie and Carrie show up, I feel like I've hit my all-time low. What kind of fucked-up monster was I that I felt more remorse over not buying shoes than I did when I took someone's life? I needed some serious help. I was losing my mind.

"Where's Diem?" Carrie asks, holding a department store bag. "I brought her something." You've got to be shitting me.

"I don't know. She's somewhere around here," I say, noticing Rookie narrowing his eyes on me. Just then, Diem appears in the doorway of the house, looking like someone who'd been drug behind a truck.

Her shirt is torn and hangs off her shoulder. Her shorts are big and baggy, nearly falling off her waist. And because I'm an asshole, she's barefooted. Then I notice that it's my clothes she's wearing. I hadn't seen her in anything but my T-shirt. Could she not have found anything in that bag of hers to wear?

"Hey," she says, giving them a small, embarrassed smile. "I didn't really have anything to wear."

Carrie shoots me a look of hate before turning to Diem and smiling. "You look fine." She walks in and I finally turn to Rookie, who's giving me the same disgusted look.

"You're a real piece of shit, you know that?" During my fit of rage, I'd called to tell him about her latest stunt. He just laughed and called her spoiled. But seeing her like this, I guess he felt differently. He walks past me, following Carrie inside. What the fuck just happened? He was my brother. It was in the bylaws that he was supposed to have my back—always. Right or wrong.

Diem is standing in the doorway, holding open the screen for our guests. At the pitiful sight of her, I decide that my company can wait. First I'm going shoe shopping. But when she looks over at me, an evil smile spreads across her face. In that moment, I realize Rookie, Carrie, and I had been played. She had shit to wear; she was just doing this to get back at me. Before shutting the door, she gives me the finger and mouths, "I always win."

And dammit if the bitch don't.

"She's good," Rookie says, clearly amused at my situation with Diem. We're grilling outside while the girls are inside, probably deciding how to kill me.

"No, she's fucking evil. I'm telling you she's going to be the death of me." I grab a beer, passing one to him before getting my own.

"Then take her back home," Rookie suggests with a shrug. "She's better now. Looks like she can take care of herself."

I shake my head. "I can't. If I do that, it's like she wins."

"Bullshit. You're just making excuses because you want her here. Admit it."

My eyes narrow. "I don't want her here." The finality in my tone only makes him smirk.

"I'm not judging, I'm just saying that if she really gets under your skin that much, let her go. There are plenty of whores around these parts. You don't need her." I remain silent, and can almost see the lightbulb when it goes off in his head. "Holy shit . . . you haven't fucked her." He looks at me in disbelief and I light a cigarette, avoiding his eyes. "You're falling for this broad."

"No I'm not," I say defensively. "She's practically fucking handicapped. I may be coldhearted, but I ain't that big of an asshole."

"Yeah, but you ain't no saint either."

"Did you come over here to play Oprah, or can we actually try and get some work done?" I snap, ready to get off this topic and onto anything else other than mine and Diem's fucked-up . . . whatever the hell this is.

"Whatever you say, boss," he says, wearing that shit-eating grin that makes me sick.

"Good. Now how the hell are we gonna pull this off? I don't want a repeat of last time."

"We'll just have to target them at church. Prospects aren't invited in."

"But they're still around," I say, cutting him off.

He thinks a minute. "Then maybe we need to start targeting them from the inside."

"You mean during church?"

He shrugs. "Why not? Maybe they went in and never came out." My wheels start spinning immediately. This could be done.

"Rookie, you're a fucking genius."

Taking the cigarette from between my fingers, he nods. "I know."

———

We're seated around the table, and I can't avoid the glares Carrie keeps giving me. I look to Rookie for help and he shrugs, but gives Carrie a look that tells her to chill the fuck out.

"This chicken is great," Diem announces, and everyone mumbles in agreement.

"What did you cook, Diem?" I ask, making sure not to taste the potato salad or the baked beans until I know for sure she didn't cook them.

Carrie gives me a warning look before smiling and glancing over at Diem. "The potato salad, and I'm sure it's delicious." Shoveling a heaping spoonful in her mouth, she pauses, fighting the urge to vomit before forcing it down.

"I'm sure it is," I say, smiling. Moving it over to the other side of my plate, I make sure not to touch it.

Rookie covers his mouth to hide his smile, and I feel the table move when Carrie kicks him. "Diem," she says, looking over at the oblivious woman who is somehow managing to eat the rancid potato salad. I'm sure it's just to prove a point. "How much longer you plan on staying?"

"You know," Diem says, wiping her mouth before placing her napkin in her lap. "I was thinking that since Zeke and I are both single, that maybe we should just move in together and share rent."

"I think that's a great idea!" Carrie beams, and I level her with a look.

"Well," I start, pushing my plate back and lighting a cigarette. "I was thinking that maybe I could just kill myself and save the misery of seeing your face another day."

Rookie bites his lip. Carrie's face grows red with anger. And Diem, well she simply smiles. "Or you could just ask me to leave."

All eyes are on me, waiting for my comeback. I don't really

want her to leave, but I don't want her to know that either. She has me by the balls, and she knows it. "Well?" she asks, looking at me expectantly. "What's it gonna be, Zeke?"

Carrie crosses her arms over her chest, leaning back in her chair, challenging me with a look. Knowing I have to win her heart back, I prepare myself for the act of my life. I could give a shit less what Diem thinks, but I can't stand the thought of Carrie hating me. I have to make this right, and to get a woman on your side, you have to think like one. And if Diem was going to play on Carrie's emotions, then I was too. So I go in for the kill.

Reaching out, I take Diem's hand in mine. She narrows her eyes in suspicion, glancing down at our joined hands. I let out a deep breath, drawing my brows together and frowning. "I'm sorry," I start, hearing Carrie's intake of breath at my words—knowing it is something we never say.

Softening my tone, I continue. "I know sometimes I'm not a good man. I say things I don't mean and do things I shouldn't, but the most important thing right now is for you to get better. And I promise to try harder. Forgive me? Please?"

If Diem's look could kill, I'd be a dead motherfucker. But there are tears in Carrie's eyes at my words. She knows the kind of man I really am. And she knows having Diem here is challenging for me. What she doesn't know, is that I'm full of shit. But it doesn't matter. I'm forgiven in her eyes, and now it's Diem's turn to be on the chopping block.

"Well? What's it gonna be, Diem?" I ask, throwing her words back in her face.

Clenching her jaw, she speaks through her teeth. "Fine."

I hear Carrie sigh before clapping her hands together. "Okay," she says standing. "Who's ready for dessert?"

When she's out of earshot, Diem grips my hand and leans forward. "I hate you."

Jerking my hand from hers, I give her a smirk. "Don't worry, doll. The feeling is fucking mutual."

After Rookie and Carrie leave, I fall back in my recliner. My mind is too occupied with Rookie's idea for Death Mob to pay much attention to what's going on around me. Before I realize it, my fingers are drawing circles on Diem's waist while she lays across my lap in her usual position.

"I'm still mad at you," I say, but I damn sure don't sound like it.

"No you're not."

"You made me look like an ass in front of my friends."

"Yeah, well I looked like an idiot, so I guess that makes us even. And the whole apology scene? That was a little much." She yawns, and I consider shoving the remote down her throat until she chokes to death.

"I packed you some clothes, Diem," I say, getting back to the topic that initiated the fight. "And if there wasn't enough, you could have asked me to go back and get some more."

"First, I don't want you creeping around my house. Second, yes, you did pack me some clothes. Two pairs of underwear, a shitload of sweaters and a scarf. Next time, pull from the other side of the closet. That's where I keep all my summer clothes."

"Oh, forgive me. It's hard to think when there's a gun pointed at your head." She looks up at me and rolls her eyes.

"You're so dramatic. I've been walking around here for over a week wearing your T-shirt and nothing else. Surely you noticed I didn't have any clothes." I keep my face impassive. I guess I haven't noticed. Maybe I really am a piece of shit.

Clearing my throat, my eyes focus on the TV. "I'll make it up to you."

She sits up in my lap. "Good. I was hoping you'd say that. I know just how you can do it." Aw, shit. Here we go. Maybe she'll want me to finger her again. I get excited at just the thought. But this time, I won't let her come.

"How's that?" There's a little too much hope in my tone and she notices.

Tentatively, she tells me what she wants. "Take me out for ice cream."

Well, shit. "Fine," I say, the disappointment evident in my voice. She stares at me until I finally give in and look at her. "What?"

"Now, Zeke. I want to go now." Of course she does.

"Yeah, let me get a vanilla ice cream cone and a hot fudge sundae."

"Extra nuts."

"With extra nuts and a—"

"Oreo McFlurry."

"An Oreo McFlurry,"

"Extra Oreos."

"Would you shut the fuck up?" I snap at Diem, who's leaning over me to look at the McDonald's drive-through menu.

"Sir?"

"Not you, I was talking to my . . ." My eyes move over Diem, who shrugs. "My dog." She drops her elbow on my nuts and I groan.

"Will that be all, sir?"

"Mmm-hmm."

"First window, please."

"When we get home, I'm putting you on a leash," I say, pulling the car around to the window.

"Ooh fun!" she says, clapping her hands together. "How about you put a ball gag in my mouth and some beads up my ass too? I think it's time we shake things up a bit." Her big, fake, clown smile appears and she gives me the finger.

"Oh, I can put something in your ass if that's what you want." Heat flashes in her eyes for a split second before she looks away.

"You're disgusting," she mumbles and I catch a glimpse of pink in her cheeks.

Amused, I raise my eyebrows at her. "You've never had it in the ass?"

"I am not discussing my sex life with you." She crosses her arms and stares out the windshield.

"Come on," I tease, squeezing her shoulder.

She shrugs me off. "No. I'm not telling you shit."

I pay for our ice cream, then hand her the tray—taking my ice cream cone and leaving the rest for her. She occupies herself with the sundae, trying to ignore me. "Tell me how you like it."

"Stop talking." She shovels a spoonful in her mouth, still refusing to look in my direction.

"Let's make a deal," I offer.

Unable to refuse the challenge, she agrees. "Fine."

"I'll tell you something, and you tell me."

"So what's the prize?" she asks, a little more interested now that it's a competition.

"The knowledge."

She laughs. "But I don't care to know. It's not like we're ever gonna have sex."

"This is true, but in the event I get really shitty and don't find you repulsive, I'd like to know what pleases you," I say, images of her riding my cock already flashing in my head.

"One thing. You tell me one thing, and I'll tell you one. That's it. After that, no more talk about it. Deal?"

"Deal." I grab my ice cream cone, noticing how she watches me as I drag my tongue across it. "My favorite part of fucking is eating pussy." I pause, waiting for my words to sink in. "I love the taste of a woman's arousal. Just knowing that it's me who made her so wet, makes it that much sweeter." Her sundae is forgotten as she stares at me, swirling my tongue over my cone. I even throw in a moan or two.

"Your turn, pretty girl." I can feel the heat emanating from her at my words. I know she's thinking about the other night. But hell, I can't lie—I am too.

When she doesn't answer, I look over to find her still staring at me. "Cat got your tongue?" I ask, dipping my tongue into the ice cream. It's a little overkill.

She seems to snap out of her trance like someone flipped on a light switch. Trouble is written all over her face, and I know I'm gonna pay dearly for my actions. My cock already starts to harden at her admission that I'm sure is coming.

"I like to deep throat." I nearly wreck us when she purrs the words. "I like taking it all the way in the back of my mouth until my eyes water and I can't breathe." She licks her spoon, pulling it deeper in her mouth than necessary. "There's just something about the way a man's eyes roll back in his head when you swallow his cock, looking up at him from your knees. It just makes it that much sweeter." Her tongue pushes against the corner of her cheek while her hand makes a fist around an imaginary dick.

I'm tempted to replace it with something real. So tempted, that I start to wonder what she would actually do if I asked her to. She'd probably bite my dick off. Just the thought has me in pain.

"Wanna play again?" she asks innocently. Knowing she won't shut up, I make sure to say something that will give me the last word.

"Sure, but let's change it up a little bit."

"I like change."

"Good," I give her a sardonic smile that widens when that smart-ass look she's wearing begins to fade. "This time, how about you show me?" And just like I predicted, peace and fucking quiet.

11

"**I NEED YOU** back in Houston." Nationals' orders the next evening come as a surprise to me. I had plans for Death Mob tonight, but the club comes first.

"When?"

"Yesterday." The phone disconnects and I'm on my feet. Diem looks at me from the couch, and I feel her eyes on me until I disappear into my room. Locking the door behind me, I pull the duffel that's already packed from under my bed. Unlocking my safe in the closet, I grab a few stacks of cash, a couple of guns, and a cell phone.

When I open the bedroom door, Diem is standing on the other side, her eyes narrowed on me. "I have to leave. I'll be back in a few days." I notice how her face falls a little at my words. I hope she don't start asking questions. "Do you have a phone?" I ask, knowing she would need a way to call if something happened. And because I want her to call me.

"That thing that connects you to the outside world? Oh yeah, I've been using it for days. Haven't you noticed?" Smart-ass.

"Have fun on your super-fucking-weird, late-night business trip."
She throws me a fake smile. "Who knew website designing was
so exciting?"

"It's my family. They need me." My answer wipes the arro-
gance right off her face. I almost feel guilty for how sympathetic
she looks. "See ya around, pretty girl." I give her a wink, and the
slight tremble in her knees at my words doesn't go unnoticed.

I drive my rental to the airport, calling Cleft on my way, who
tells me there is a ticket waiting for me. "Your things are already
here in Houston," he says, and I feel my chest swell with pride.
My things are my bike and my cut.

"Good. I need you to ship a cell phone to my house. Get it
through a local carrier and put it in Zeke's name. Nothing fancy,
just something with text and calling."

"Done. Anything else?"

"Yeah," I say, wondering if it's a mistake. "Send some flowers
too. A bunch of 'em."

"That all?"

"And some of those Atomic Fireball candies."

"Are you trying to get laid?" Am I? That would be better than
saying I'm doing it because I feel like shit for leaving her all alone
for a while.

"Maybe."

"Well she must be some woman. I've never known you to have
to work for pussy." I start to snap his head off and tell him it
ain't like that. Instead, I just hang up before I say anything.

Houston is a clusterfuck. San Antonio is a shitstorm. Production
is behind. Officers aren't enforcing the bylaws. And I know my
time here is gonna be a helluva lot longer than a few days.

Without Dirk, the chapters are starting to fall apart. With

him in mind, everyone knew that if they fucked up, he would be paying them a visit. Until I officially take over Dirk's role in the club, I can't demand anything of them. But Nationals wants me to sit in and listen. Observe what's happening in church and report back to them. It makes me feel like a rat.

Rocks has been the president for the Houston chapter for years. But you're only as good as your team. And his team was failing him. Miserably. There were too many club parties and not enough business. Half the members weren't even riding. They were a disgrace to all one percent clubs. But most of all, they were a disgrace to Sinner's Creed.

So I called Nationals and told them the situation. I was more than surprised when they told me to handle it. Jimbo put in the call to Rocks himself, and told him to invite me to church. And that I was stepping in as a National and would be making decisions on their behalf. Rocks wasn't happy about it. Neither was I. Houston was my home chapter. I didn't want to be an asshole, but I didn't want to see my brothers eighty-sixed either.

It's the second night I've been here and I'm anxious as church begins. I'm even more anxious that I haven't heard from Diem, even though Cleft assured me all my packages had been delivered. As we crowd around the table, every eye is on me. Rocks told them why I was here. And like him and me, they aren't happy about it.

"Okay, Shady," Rocks says from the VP seat while I'm sitting in his. "The floor is yours." Pissed about the situation and pissed about Diem, I go straight to business. Letting my anger overpower the uneasiness I'm feeling.

"You're not doing your job. Just because the money is good, don't mean it's easy. The work is hard. The risk is high. You knew that shit when you signed up. Ever since Dirk's been gone, you've gotten lazy. Production in Houston is two weeks behind everyone else. Other chapters are complaining, saying that y'all are receiving special privileges because of me. I don't like that." Just saying the words pisses me off further. If anything, they should be working harder than anyone because of me. They should be picking up my slack while I'm gone. That's the job of a good brother.

"I'm pulling your bottom rockers." The air in the room grows thick with tension at my words. Every brother at the table looks at me with a different emotion—hate, betrayal, envy . . . but some look at me with respect. "I'll give you two weeks. If you're not ahead of everyone else, I'll pull back patches. After that, you'll be sewing on Prospect rockers. I don't think I have to tell y'all what happens if you fail then."

Cuts are laid across the table as I use my knife to remove the *Texas* patches one by one. The bottom rocker represents your state—what charter you belong to. Having it removed is a way of branding those that aren't living up to the expectations of the club. It's a blow to a man's pride. He's no longer worthy of a full patch. And to get it back, he'll have to earn it.

Before I leave, I call Nationals and inform them of my decision. They're not surprised by my actions, they're proud. "You'll make a fine Nomad, Shady. Now go to San Antonio and do the same."

The news of what happened in Houston spread like wildfire. By the time I left, they were working harder than any chapter in the country. When I finally make it San Antonio, they're throwing a party in my honor. I'm sure it's in hopes to avoid having their patches pulled. But just to show them I'm not impressed, I called a meeting as soon as I walked in the door. Now the only man wearing a bottom rocker at my party is me. And just like I saw in Houston, respect is in the eyes of some of my brothers.

I've been gone for two weeks.

Two long fucking weeks.

I've thought of Diem every day since I left. Not one moment has gone by that I haven't wondered what she was doing. If she was wearing my shirt. How she was feeling. If she was thinking of me . . .

But my pride was too big for me to text or call. She must have been suffering from the same prideful issues. Because in two weeks, I haven't heard from her either.

I'm nervous when I pull up to my house. I'm not sure what to expect. When I hear a glass shatter against something inside, I grab my piece from my bag and nearly knock the door off the hinges trying to get in. My mind races with thoughts of what I'm up against. An intruder? Has Death Mob figured me out? Has the club found out about Diem? Is there a raccoon in the kitchen . . . again?

Shards of glass litter the living room floor. The broken pieces were once a plate. Other than the hundreds of tiny, sharp objects, everything else seems to be in place. My boots crunch across the glass as I keep my gun up and make my way to the back of the house. Kicking open my bedroom door, the barrel of my automatic comes face-to-face with the strikingly beautiful Diem.

"Get that fucking thing outta my face," she greets, slapping the barrel of my gun out of her way before pushing past me.

"Well, hello to you too." I turn to follow her, but she stomps back into the room before I can take a step—attempting to slam the door in my face. I catch it with my hand, unable to hide my smile. Damn I've missed her cocky ass.

Speaking of ass, she looks perfect. No bruises. No slow movements. She's all sexy and pissed dressed in an outfit that I've never seen her in. Thinking back, I remember Rookie telling me that Carrie had brought her some clothes after our last incident. And I'll have to remember to thank Carrie for her choice.

Tight jeans, an even tighter top, and lo and behold . . . fucking shoes.

"What are you smiling at?" she snaps, filling her duffel bag with clothes. She's leaving?

My smile fades as I realize that's exactly what she's doing. "Where you goin'?"

"Where you goin'?" Her shitty attempt to impersonate me has me smirking once again. "You wanna know where I'm *goin'*? None of your fucking business. That's where." She's so pissed her voice is shaky, and for the life of me I can't figure out why.

"Diem," I start, but she whirls around on me and pokes her tiny finger in my chest, managing to push me back a step.

"Don't you 'Diem' me. You've been off for two weeks doing who knows what with who knows who." She stomps across the room, then comes back, knocking shit over on the dresser as she does. And all I can do is stand and watch in amusement. "I've been here, Zeke. Stuck in this fucking house eating carbs and watching westerns and counting the blades of grass in the yard. I've drove myself crazy while you've been partying and playing and probably eating steaks and drinking premium liquor and fucking random whores in some shitty southern brothel."

"Diem," I try again, but the look she shoots me has me shutting my mouth.

"I will kill you, Zeke. I'll take your gun and put a bullet in your head. Both of them," she adds, her eyes dropping to my crotch. My dick starts to swell at just the sight of her looking at it.

"Calm down. I told you, I was with my family."

"You think I give a shit what you've been doing?" she yells, and my eyes widen at her outburst. "Well I don't. I'm leaving."

"No, you're not."

The silence is deadly. But her look is even more lethal. "Excuse me?" she whispers, and it's so threatening, I swallow. Then I check to make sure my gun is still securely in my hand.

"I said, you're not leaving." The words aren't out of my mouth before I'm ducking. Something hard hits the wall behind me and I turn to see my iPod laying on the floor—the screen cracked and busted. Before she can throw the other object, a lamp, I move. Knocking it from her hands, I pull her to me, forcing her to look up at me.

"I've been with my family," I snarl, noticing how my glare does nothing to intimidate her. "I didn't think I would be gone that long, but I was. So get the fuck over it."

"Fuck. You," she whispers, her breath blowing over my face. It's intoxicating and I want nothing more than to kiss her. And something in her eyes tells me that she wants me to. So I don't. Instead, I let her go.

I'm nearly to the door when her words hit me in the back, and pierce straight through to my heart. "I needed you." I freeze, keeping my back to her so she can't see the regret in my eyes. She continues to kill me with her words, completely unrelenting in true Diem fashion. "I asked you for help and your exact words were *anything.*"

I hear the sound of a bag zipping, and I know she's really leaving. And she's hurt. Not physically, but in the worst kind of way. I'd given her my word, and then like always, I'd put the club before everything else. Because the club is what's most important in my life. But the truth is, she's important to me too.

"Don't leave," I say, turning to face her. She stands tall and proud, her head lifted high. Her eyes are cold, lifeless, and narrowed at the corners. She looks right through me, like I'm not here demanding her to stay.

"I'll make you a deal," she offers, a sardonic smirk playing on her lips.

Anything.

"Move aside, or I'll rip this whole fucking house to shreds. It's your choice." Her voice is harsh. Her expression hard. Her words promising. And I don't doubt her. But I haven't wanted to do anything but kiss her since I first saw her moments ago. I thought I could deny her, but I can't. And I'll be damned if she tries to stop me. In this moment, no one could.

Closing the distance between us, I toss my gun on the bed then reach for her throat. When I tighten my hold, her eyes widen in shock, but it's her parted lips that let me know she wants this just as much as I do. My mouth crashes to hers. Her body fights me, but her tongue submits, letting me suck on it and taste her. She kisses me back with passion, while her hands fist in my hair, pulling tight like she's trying to pry my head away from hers.

But it only lasts a second. Then she's pulling me to her. She can't get enough of me. Her fingers claw at my neck—forcing my mouth to crash harder against hers. She tastes like fucking sunshine.

"I missed you . . . ," I say, not fully breaking the kiss. "So fucking much . . ." She moans into me, and I know in this moment that everything we've been denying each other is finally over.

Pushing the duffel off her shoulder, my fingers curl around her perfect ass, lifting her around my waist effortlessly. Her legs circle my hips and I walk forward, pushing her into the wall and kissing her harder when she groans with pleasure at the roughness. I kiss her neck, sucking hard on the sweet, watermelon-scented flesh that I've missed.

Impatient, my fingers curl around the V at the collar of her shirt and rip the fabric open. Then I rip her pretty lace bra that's also new to my eyes. Two perfect fucking tits stare back at me, and I lift her higher so I can take the light brown peaks into my mouth. Loosening her legs from around me, I hear the sound of her jeans as they hit the floor, then her fingers are on the buttons of mine. I step back long enough to push them to my knees, grab a condom from the dresser next to us and keep my eyes on hers as I sheath my dick.

They're burning with desire. With raw fucking need to have me inside her. There's no love or passion, just a primal craving that demands I fuck her on the same level of insanity that she drives me to. Lifting her again, I drop my head and watch as my cock goes inside her—needing no guidance or direction. Out of pure instinct, I find her swollen, wet pussy and drive deep, burying everything inside her but my balls.

She feels like fucking satin. She's smooth, wet, warm, and I have to pause to keep from coming—and I haven't even gotten started. I distract myself with her mouth—kissing her softly at first, then building it up until we're both breathless. Her hips jerk. Her legs tighten. She pulls my hair so hard it hurts. She's doing everything in her power to get me to fuck her. And when I finally get my shit together, fuck her is exactly what I do.

When she screams, I match it with a growl and slam her small body on top of me, over and over. I'm hurting her . . . but it's the good hurt. The kind that has her hissing in pain and begging for more in the same breath. My fingers dig into her sweet ass that fits perfectly in my hands. Her fingers claw into my back, tearing deeper into my flesh with every pump of my hips.

We're scarring each other.

Hurting each other.

Torturing each other.

And it's never felt so fucking good.

"I fucking hate you," she says through her teeth, moving her hips to meet me.

"Not as much as I hate you," I growl, and like the fucked-up creatures we are, our words are our undoing.

She screams as her pussy clenches around me. Her orgasm

wracks through her body violently. I bury myself deep, stilling so she can feel the way my cock pulses as I come inside her. I don't cover her in sweet kisses or tell her how awesome she was. Because she already knows. Instead, I bury my face in her neck, nipping at her skin with my teeth, then licking it with my tongue. She rubs her hands across the swollen scratches on my back. It's as intimate as we get, and neither of us would have it any other way.

Slowly, her legs untangle from my waist. I hold her by her hips until she can stand on her own. But even then, I don't want to let her go. Not just yet. I keep her pressed against the wall, sympathizing with my cock that softens the instant the cool air of the room hits it—no doubt in shock after leaving the hottest, sweetest pussy it's ever been inside of.

"I'm still leaving," she says, breathless and beautiful and impossibly fucking infuriating.

"You can try." I place my forehead against hers, trying to find the strength to take my hands off her hips.

"What if I do?" I hear the smile in her tone and can't keep from smiling myself.

"Then you do." I lean closer, biting her ear before whispering, "And I'll just fuck the urge out of you again."

12

DIEM STAYED. SHE tried to leave twice. Keeping good on my word, I fucked it out of her both times. But when I woke up this morning, she was gone. All that was left was a note.

Shithead,

Playtime is over for me. I have to get back to work. Maybe I'll call. Maybe I won't.

—D

She'll call. I'm sure of it.

I spend the day trying to get my house back in order. When she left, she made sure to leave me with the mess she created. I think it was her way of punishing me. But a part of me is glad she's gone. I need the time to get my head back in the game. I have plans this week. Plans for death. I drive north to Tamworth, New Hampshire, calling Rookie when I'm fifteen minutes out. We meet up at a motel with Tank to go over the plan once again.

The chapter has ten patch holders that would be present at church. They don't have a clubhouse, so instead they meet up in the president's shop located just outside his house. As is tradition in their chapter, the ol' ladies gather inside the house, which is about forty feet from the shop. And most of the time, the Prospects stay under the porch, completely out of view of the shop, until the meeting is over.

So not only are we putting Prospects at risk, but now the ol' ladies are a potential threat too. Rookie has been staking out the site for quite some time and assures me the women never come outside. To take out ten patch holders in one night would be worth the risk. But I know if I had to kill a woman, it would be a hard pill to swallow.

The house is located on a river, providing us with an escape route just through the woods. The issue there is getting all the bodies out of the shop, drug through the woods, and into the boat that will take us to the truck. And we couldn't leave a blood trail. I was beginning to think the job was impossible, but leave it to Rookie to come up with something in that crooked-ass mind of his.

"Let's drug 'em," he says, shrugging at the suggestion like it was just that simple.

"And how the hell do you suppose we do that?"

"They end every meeting with a shot. We go in tonight, slip something in every bottle of liquor they have, and after they toast, it shouldn't take but about five minutes. We wait, and if they don't come out, we go in."

"So how do we get them out of the shop? We'd have to make at least four trips. It's too risky."

He smiles. "Good thing we got a lot of brothers with a lot of muscle. And I know a chapter that's on probation. This would give them a chance to get their bottom rocker back." It sucked having a brother smarter than me.

I call Nationals, unsure of my decision only after I have them on the line. "San Antonio is on probation. Rookie and I could use their help with something. I'll make sure it's beneficial for the club too. It'll also give them a chance to prove themselves. It's nothing they haven't done before."

"How beneficial to the club will it be?" Jimbo asks, and Rookie passes me a piece of paper.

"Two keys. At least. And about twenty or thirty stacks." I wait while the call is muted and they discuss. A few minutes later Jimbo comes back on the line.

"You got the green light. Just don't fuck up."

Great. No pressure.

That night, Rookie and Tank stand guard as I pick the lock and enter the shop. There are only two bottles of liquor in the building, and I empty the contents of the package Rookie gave me inside them. Looking around the shop, my eyes search for the hidden stash of dope and money. Rookie assures me it's in here somewhere, he just doesn't know where.

After fifteen minutes of searching, I still can't find it. Time is up and I walk back into the woods to meet Rookie and Tank. "I couldn't find it," I whisper, knowing that if we didn't, then we would be indebted to Nationals. It wasn't about the money, it was the promise of getting them something and not delivering.

"Did you check the floors?" Rookie asks, completely calm.

"Concrete."

"What about the walls?"

"Nothing." I wasn't an amateur, for fuck's sake.

"What about the deer?" My eyes move to Tank, who hasn't said a word the entire trip. Hell, he never says anything.

"The what?"

"The deer. There's a deer mount on the wall. Look in the hollow of its neck." I look to Rookie and he shrugs, again. I guess that's his answer for everything.

We walk back to the shop, and I start searching the mounts. There are four of them, and the first three have come up empty. Taking a deep breath, I pull the fourth from the wall, noticing how easily it came down. Where the wooden plaque was solid on the others, this one was hollow, leading into the neck of the deer. Inside lay my word to Nationals. And now I have two brothers that are smarter than me.

Six probationary members from San Antonio arrive the next day. I hardly recognize them in normal clothes, and I even laugh at how awkward it is having all of us together with no patches on. We go over the plan until it's perfected, then split up into three boats that sit waiting at the riverbank.

We're silent as we walk through the woods. At ten minutes past ten, Rookie eases up to the window of the shop. Moments later, he waves us over. We enter with pistols drawn, silencers intact. With a wave of my finger, the unconscious bodies are lifted one by one and removed from the room. I grab the last of them, throwing him over my shoulder, and silently thanking my brothers for leaving the smallest one for me.

Slowly but surely, we cross the hundred yards back through the woods and throw the bodies in the boats. Fifteen minutes later, we're throwing them into the back of the covered trailer attached to the truck Tank is driving. We strip the men of everything but their underwear, before locking the door and driving to the location that is becoming a Death Mob cemetery.

I don't let myself relax until we're miles away from any threat to our plan. Now the fun begins. Unlocking the door, we find the men in all different states. Some are pissed. Some are confused. Some have their hands up in surrender. But they all wear a look of fear when their eyes focus on the ten men surrounding the trailer with automatics pointed at them. Just to make them even more uncomfortable, I drag out their impending doom.

"You know what I love about you boys?" Of course they don't answer, but I give them time just in case. "Y'all are so predictable. I mean a shot after church? Really? What the fuck are y'all toasting to?"

I look around at my brothers, who are itching with the desire to kill. I am too, but the sadist inside me wants a little more. I don't just want their blood, I want their fucking souls.

"Who are you?" one of the men asks. He's so brave, I consider letting him live.

"Me?" I ask, feigning shock. "And here I was thinking I was some kind of celebrity." I move suddenly, propping my leg up on the bumper of the trailer and the man flinches. Well, that sealed his fate. He wasn't as brave as I thought he was. Now I guess he'll die too.

"Who I am is not important," I start, feeling my desire to kill overpower my desire to play games. I'd let them live long enough. "So I'll cut the shit. Sinner's Creed is using you to send a message," I say, adrenaline rushing through me. My trigger finger twitches in anticipation. "And Dirk sends his condolences."

Standing next to my brothers, I point my gun between the eyes of the first man I see. It only takes one shot for the others to follow suit. I watch as one by one they fall. All I can see is death. All I can hear are the sounds of gunshots ringing loudly in my ears. All I can smell is the scent of spilled blood. And it is fucking divine.

Because I was the one who pulled San Antonio's bottom rockers, I have to be the one to give them back. I fly down on Friday, and by Sunday I'm back in my house, which feels empty. The smell is too manly. The silence is annoying. And I realize what's missing is Diem.

I can't get her out of my head.

The scent of her pussy.

The shape of her ass.

The taste of her flesh.

I hate that she is under my skin. I'd rather have her clawing at it. Fuck, I want her. Again and again until I can't move and she doesn't want to leave. I consider calling her, but I refuse. I'm not that desperate.

To keep from going crazy, I drive to the bar, where Mick greets me with a beer and a shot. The place is crawling with people, busy even for a Friday night. I scan the room, hoping to find her. Wanting her to show up and order a shot and put it on my tab. But she doesn't show.

Four drinks in, my pride has taken a nosedive and I text her.

Hey pretty girl.

Almost immediately, my phone buzzes with a response.

Bout time.

I smile.

You miss me or something?

Or something . . .

Come have a drink with me.

Can't.

I feel a frown forming and knock back a shot, hoping to find my balls at the bottom of the glass. I wasn't expecting that response. Something along the lines of *on my way* or *of course* with one of those little fucking emojis I can never understand. Not just *can't*.

My phone buzzes again and I nearly drop the bastard trying to read the message. I'm such a pussy.

You're such a pussy. Look at you . . . frowning and shit.
☹

I can sense her staring at me, and reluctantly, I drag my eyes up to find her smirking at me from across the room—phone in hand. I flip her the finger and she strolls over, stopping conversations and making every head turn as she walks. Pride swells in my chest and I shove it back down. I shouldn't feel it because she doesn't belong to me.

She's dressed to kill in tight white pants, a low-cut red top that shows off her tits, and tall red high heels to match. Her short black hair is perfectly messy. Her lips are a deep red, her olive skin seems to glow, and those dark eyes are big and bright, shining with pure fucking evil. She's mouthwatering. But of course, I appear unaffected. To add to my façade, I drag my eyes down her body and smirk. She stops and does a once-over, making sure her pants aren't unzipped and there isn't toilet paper on her shoe.

I laugh and she smacks me with the red wallet she'd been carrying under her arm. "I haven't missed you at all," she says, snapping her fingers at Mick, who happily obliges her with a shot. She throws it back and motions for him to keep them coming.

"I haven't missed you either," I lie, wanting to kiss that lipstick right off her juicy lips. I want to fuck her in those heels. And tonight I will.

"Says the boy who pouts when I say I can't drink with him tonight."

"But, you're here. So what does that say about you? Oh, I know." I grab her drink, smiling at her. "It says you want me."

"You're right."

She floors me again. Dammit. How does she do that?

"So are you gonna give the lady what she asks for, or are you gonna make me beg? Either way, I'm getting what I want."

I throw Mick some money and take her hand. Damn right she's getting what she wants. And what she wants is me.

Diem is on her knees in front of me. Her ass is high in the air, giving me a full view of the prettiest pink pussy my cock has ever had the pleasure of being inside of. I tease her with the head of my dick, listening to her beg when I place the tip inside her. Then I listen to the sound of her breath catching in her throat when I drag the wetness up to her ass, noticing how she tenses, but does nothing to stop me.

I drive into her pussy, letting the sound of my name filling the room fuel me until I'm fucking her unmercifully, watching the remnants of her releases glisten on my cock as she comes over and over. She's perfect. And those red high heels are perfect. And her ass is perfect . . . her hair . . . her scent . . . her moans . . . fucking everything.

When I feel the urge to come, I slow down. I've been doing this for over an hour, and now, Diem can hardly stay up on her knees. My legs hurt. My throat burns with dehydration. The scent of sex and tequila that seeps through my pores fills the room.

My shins are bruised from the constant banging against the

bed frame. My arms ache from pulling her back to me time after time when I fuck her so hard her body slides forward. And every time I bring her back, her ass slaps against me and she moans. I roar. And the sound vibrates the windows in my bedroom.

"You're killing me," she pants, but her next words are "give me more." So I do. I have. I will. Until I can't go any longer. I could fuck her all day and all night, but my balls are stretched to the point of pain. They ache with every slap against her tiny swollen clit. And when I finally do come, it's the greatest release I've ever felt. She's the greatest thing I've ever felt. Her response to me is overwhelming. The way she shudders, sweats, moans, and comes is a new experience for me. And it's fucking epic.

I still inside her, leaning over her back and kissing a trail down her spine. I rain tender kisses all over her neck, shoulders, back, and ass until I'm too exhausted to stand. Then I collapse in the bed beside her. She is frozen in position, unable to move her limbs that still quiver. "You okay?"

"I think I'm dead."

I smirk. "You're not dead."

"I can't move. I'm numb."

Wrapping my arm under her stomach, I pull her to me, curling her into my side. Burying my face in her hair, I inhale the flowery scent of her hair products. Liking the scent of her skin better, I move my nose to her neck, which is slick with sweat. Watermelon. Much better.

"I think we're spooning." I want to vomit at my admission, but instead find myself pulling her closer.

"I think you're right. How lame does that make us?" Her breathing growing deeper by the moment.

"Who the fuck cares?" I grumble, feeling sleep taking over my body. She mumbles something, but I'm already too lost in the darkness to comprehend.

13

"GET THE YELLOW one."

"I don't like yellow."

"Well, I do. So, get the yellow one."

I fight the urge to choke Diem in the middle of the department store that I'm sure I'll be damned to hell for even entering. There is no doubt in my mind that somewhere in the Sinner's Creed bylaws, there is a rule that forbids us to go shopping for comforters at any store. But especially this ritzy fucking one Diem dragged me to. All because she said my covers were outdated.

They're covers.

Blankets.

Quilts.

Whatever you want to call them.

But still, they're just fucking covers.

"I'm not getting a fluffy, pansy-ass, yellow comforter for my bed. We'll get this one. It's on sale," I tell her, grabbing the big plastic bag and pulling it down from the shelf.

"That's hideous." She snatches it from my hand, chucking it down the aisle and scaring the shit out of two little old ladies.

"That was a little uncalled for, don't you think?"

"Here, what about this one?" She ignores me and points to a white down comforter that cost more than my whole bed did.

"If I buy that, when I walk out the door with it, something is going to hit me in the ass. Do you know what that is?"

Glaring up at me, she seems annoyed, but asks, "What?"

"My fucking change. I'm not paying five hundred dollars for something that's just gonna end up on the floor by the morning anyway."

I've taken a seat on one of the model beds. Now Diem and I are at eye level, and I can feel every dagger she shoots at me. She looks fierce in tiny blue jean shorts, T-shirt, and flip-flops, and wearing yesterday's makeup. She still smells like me, and I get hard at the thought of what's between her smooth, tanned legs.

She catches me eyeing her and smiles her mischievous grin. "Make you a deal?" Aw, shit.

"What?" I ask cautiously.

Standing in front of the display like she's Vanna White, she starts modeling the products. "Buy this comforter, these sheets, and throw in these two accent pillows, and I'll let you go where no man has gone before." Just in case her words weren't clear enough, she drops her sunglasses and bends over to pick them up, sticking her glorious little virgin ass in the air for me to see.

"Do we have a deal?" she purrs, and I'm already on my feet grabbing shit off the shelf and barking out commands.

"Get the fucking pillows."

Of course Diem found a way to torture me before making good on her promise. She claimed I'd never taken her out on a real date. She's right. So she wants to get all dressed up and go somewhere fancy. After the thousand dollars I just dropped on linens, I can't afford fancy.

Well . . .

I can, I just don't want to.

But I've decided that I like having sex with her, so I want to keep her happy. Now, at her demand, I'm picking her up. I almost stop and pick some weeds out of the ditch to give her just to be an ass, but decide against it. When I pull in her driveway, the first thing I notice is my totaled-out truck. Sickness fills my gut and I hate her all over again. I'm disgusted by the time I knock on the door.

"Come in!" she yells from somewhere inside, and I stomp in, debating on killing her. The last time I was here, I hadn't paid much attention to the place. But without a gun trained on my head or the sight of a banged-up woman laying helplessly on the couch, I finally get the chance to fully take in my surroundings. Her house is cleaner than before, smells like a home should, and seems a lot less feminine than what I would expect Diem to have. I never gave it much thought before, but it doesn't seem like a place she would live.

The furniture is expensive, but the house is old and outdated. The TV and sound system are state of the art, but the floors are worn and the carpet is thin. I move to the kitchen and all the appliances are brand new, and look completely out of place in the small, shabby room.

I glance around for mail or a landline but come up empty-handed. Following the sound of her shuffling around down the hall, I find her in a bathroom that should be fit for a queen—considering how vain she is. Instead, it too is old and outdated.

"How long have you lived here?" I ask, and the tone in my voice has her raising an eyebrow at me.

"Is there a reason you want to know?"

"Curiosity." I shrug.

"Not long. I lived in a nicer place in Concord, but I wanted out of the city so I moved here. This was the only place available." Well, that explains it. Sort of.

"Ever thought about updating?" I pry, narrowing my eyes on her. She's hiding something. I can feel it.

Taking a seat on the edge of the bathtub, she matches my glare and explains. "No. I don't plan to be here forever. I want to build a house somewhere. I just haven't had the time. There's no sense in me updating a house that I'm going to lose my ass on when I decide to move. Why all the questions?"

"Like I said." I hold my hand out to her. "Curiosity."

She takes my hand and stands. "No, you're just being fucking nosy. You're wondering why I have all this nice shit in this not-so-nice house. Well, here's an answer for you. Mind your own fucking business." She flashes me a fake smile and walks past me. Only someone who would have wondered the same thing would have guessed the true meaning behind my questions. I guess great minds think alike.

In the car, I finally notice what Diem is wearing. I was too busy digging for information to even bother looking before. Now I wonder how I could have missed it. She's in a short black skirt that molds to her skin. It sits high on her waist, starting just below her breasts, which are nearly bulging out of her white, sleeveless top.

Diamond bracelets cover her wrists, and a diamond pendant rests at the hollow of her throat. Even from a distance, I can tell they're real. And you can't buy diamonds on a salary like hers.

"Nice bracelet," I say, raising my eyebrows in question. She turns to look at me, her bangs falling over her eyes. Pushing them back, she glares at me, but doesn't say anything. I love how those big, red lips poke out on a pout when she's pissed. "Did your daddy buy that for you?"

Rolling her eyes, she twists her body so that she's looking out the window, giving her back to me. "Are you insinuating that I'm privileged?" she asks, and I hate that I can't see her. I trust her expressions more than her words.

"Maybe." There's no point in lying about it.

"Well, the answer is no. My *daddy* didn't buy me these. They're gifts from my ex-lovers. And I'm still waiting on yours."

I laugh. "Don't hold your breath, sweetheart. We're not lovers and I don't buy diamonds."

Twisting back, she puts her elbow on the console, leaning close to me. "Not even for your mama?" I don't have to look at her this time. I can hear the evil in her words and they cut me back down to size. I shouldn't talk shit about her upbringing. Especially with one like my own.

"Nope," I answer, keeping my eyes on the road. "Not even for her." At the tone of my voice, she becomes piqued with interest. Great. I could have played that a little better. Good job, Shady. Good fucking job.

"You should be ashamed," she chastises. "I'm sure your mother is more than deserving of diamonds." I feel another rip in my heart at her words. If she was deserving of anything, I didn't know it. Hell, I didn't even know her name.

Not wanting to visit that dark place again, I decide to shut her up. "My mother is dead." This time, I level her with a look. Her face falls and I almost feel guilty.

She clears her throat, but doesn't apologize. Instead, she changes the subject. "So, where we going?"

"McDonalds," I say, feeling my dark mood lift at her expression.

"Funny. Real fucking funny."

"I'm not lying. And since you took the time to get so pretty for me, I'm thinking I might even take you inside." I look over at her smiling, surprised to find her blushing.

"You think I'm pretty?" Is she serious? This is a girl whose ego got more strokes than my cock. Trying to keep from killing us, I glance back to the road for a split second before looking at her again. The blush is still there. And she looks shy. What the fuck? I didn't call her "pretty girl" to be a dick. I meant it.

"Diem, come on. Really?"

"What? You've never told me. And you've seen me at my worst, so I can't imagine how bad that vision scarred you." She's so vain. Maybe that's why she didn't call anyone to help her. She didn't want them to see her at less than her best. I guess she's past caring if I see her that way. The thought is unsettling, but for some reason I kinda like it.

"Yes," I say on a sigh. "I think you're pretty." There. I'd said it.

"Thanks, Zeke." Her voice is barely audible, and there is true appreciation in her tone. It softens me. Maybe she did need to hear it a little more. But I know that the truth is she really just needed to hear it from me. And from now on, she will.

I'm a steak and potato kind of man. Diem is probably more of a duck and lamb kind of woman. So I made sure to find somewhere that wasn't too ritzy, but still classy with a good menu. The Granite Restaurant in Concord had both of these things, and a bar. There was no use in searching for anything else.

Diem straightens her skirt as she gets out. I'm glad she didn't expect me to open her door, but I do hold it open as we walk in, then put my hand on the small of her back and guide her to the bar. She doesn't complain about us not getting a table, and I'm starting to think that maybe this date might not be so shitty after all.

When I order a glass of wine, she gives me a strange look. "What?

It's good with steak," I argue in my defense. But I feel like I might have just become a little less manly in her eyes. Not that I give a shit. I've defended her honor before by knocking out two guys. If that wasn't enough to prove I wasn't a pussy, I don't know what is.

"I'll take a Seven and Seven," she tells the bartender, shooting me another unsure look. "I don't even know who you are anymore."

Grabbing her chair, I slide her closer to me before whispering "I'm the man who fucked you until you couldn't move." I feel her body ignite at my response and smile. "Do you need a reminder?"

Taking a long pull from her drink, she shakes her head. Well I'll be damned. I've rendered her speechless. That's a first.

"What are you eating?" I ask, sliding the menu over to her.

"Do they have burgers?"

My face falls at her question. "Are you fucking serious?"

She winks, letting me know she isn't. "I think I'm going to get the filet. And maybe the salmon. Oooh," she says, getting excited. "And maybe the trout."

"All of it?" She must be joking.

Glaring at me, I know she's not. I really can't believe a thing she says. I have to wait and look at her face to know if she's telling the truth. "Yes, all of it," she snaps. "Don't worry. If you can't afford it, I'll just pawn one of my flashy diamond bracelets or put it on my daddy's card." Here we go. "Or maybe I'll sell these six-thousand-dollar heels."

I stop her there, holding my hand up to shush her. "Did you say six-thousand-dollar heels?"

She nods. "Yeah. I have a thing for shoes."

I groan. I'd definitely be fucking her in them tonight. Something about knowing how much money it cost her just to dig them into my ass makes it a little more erotic. "Look," I say, defeated. I can't take any more. The shoes have just floored me. "Order anything you want. Hell, order everything. I don't give a shit. But whatever you do . . ." I give her a look of warning before dropping my voice. "Don't take off them heels."

"See?" She smiles. "It feels good to appreciate the finer things in life. But seriously, I'll just bang the busboy if you can't afford the bill."

Like she summoned him, the young busboy appears and I have to fight the urge to kill him. This woman will be the death of me. I'm still shooting daggers at him when the bartender asks for our order. Finally, Diem has to kick me—with those six-thousand-dollar shoes—to get my attention.

"The filet. Medium. Baked potato."

He walks away and I focus my attention back on my lovely date. "So, you come here often?" I wiggle my eyebrows and she slaps at my chest, playing along.

"Sir, I have a boyfriend."

"Pity. I have a dick like a rocket."

Laughing, she rolls her eyes. I can't stop looking at her. She really is a beautiful sight. "You're growing on me, Zeke," she says, and I'm not sure if she meant to say it out loud. But I'm looking at her. I know the meaning behind her words. She's telling the truth. And it feels too fucking good to hear it.

"You're growing on me too, Diem," I admit. She starts to turn cold, ready to crash the feelings I think might be developing for me. In an effort to not ruin the night, I lighten the conversation and bring it back to something that's more our pace. "I mean, it's kinda like a fungus that's itchy and festering, but it's there."

"You're disgusting." She narrows her eyes and I smile. The banter is normal for us. This we both can handle. "Let's play a game." She grows excited just at the mention of a challenge, and now it's my turn to roll my eyes.

"Fine." I might as well give in. She already thinks I'm a pussy. And to drive the final nail in my coffin, I take a sip of my wine.

"Let's see who can pick up the hottest date."

"Fuck no," I snap, already getting pissed at just the thought of her picking up some other guy.

"Oh, come on," she whines. "It'll be fun!"

"Somehow, I don't believe that to be true," I mumble, downing my wine and trading it in for a shot of whiskey.

She holds her fingers up to the bartender, adding another five shots to my order. "All you have to do is get a phone number. The first person to do that wins."

"Excuse me," I say to the bartender. "Can I borrow your phone?"

"That doesn't count," she says, waving off the bartender, who looks at us both like we're crazy. Hell, she is and she's driving me that way too.

"So what do we win?" Might as well find out the consolation prize. It might actually be worth playing this stupid game.

"What do you want?"

"I get to pick?" Can't believe that shit.

"No." I knew I couldn't believe it. "I'm just asking."

I shake my head at her. Does she ever listen to herself? "You already owe me one thing, if I remember correctly." At the reminder, her cheeks heat. "I can't think of anything else I really want."

"What about a time? I never said when." Shit. She had me there.

"Okay." I smirk, a little more interested now that I have a goal to work toward. "If I get the number first, then you let me go where no other man has gone before." I throw her exact words back at her before adding, "Tonight."

She shrugs. "Done." That was too easy. I wait for the double-edged sword to strike. When she gives me that evil smile, I know I'm fixing to get it. "And if I win, you get nothing."

Handing her a shot, I grab one for myself, then clink my glass to hers. "Game on, pretty girl."

I waste no time getting to work. I'm sure I'll be back at the bar before my steak comes. Although I doubt I'll be able to eat it with her precious little ass in mind. I scan the other side of the bar, making sure to find someone that can't see Diem and me from where we sit. My eyes land on a very attractive girl who looks to be in her early twenties. She's holding her cell phone in her lap texting. The glass of wine in front of her looks untouched.

She's dressed up like she's expecting a date, but no one showed. Poor thing. Tonight, I'm going to become her tattooed hero. And if Diem's into it, maybe even a little three-way action. But I don't get my hopes up.

Grabbing the busboy I'd wanted to kill moments ago by the shirt, I pull him out of sight. He looks at me like he might shit his pants, so I offer him a kind smile while I smooth his shirt back down. "Hey kid, I ain't gonna hurt you."

"O-okay," he stutters. I must be on my man period, because I suddenly feel sorry for him. He'll never get laid with a face like that. I hope he has a good personality. Or at least some good acting skills.

"I need a favor." I pull two hundred-dollar bills from my pocket, fanning them in his face. His eyes grow wide at the sight. It probably takes him all week to earn that much. "You see that girl over there sitting alone?" I ask, and he peeks around my shoulder before nodding. "I need you to spill her glass of wine on her. And be a dick about it. Can you do that?"

"Why?" he asks, confused, looking back at the woman. Rolling my eyes, I pull him back to look at me.

"So I can step in and save her. You follow me?"

"Yeah, but why? You have the hottest chick in here." Observant little shit, isn't he.

"It's complicated," I say in an attempt to explain. He just raises an eyebrow at me. "You want the money or not?"

He nods. "Hell yeah I want the money."

I smile. "Good. Now earn it." This kid might not be handsome, but his acting skills are spot-on. Bumping the table, he spills the girl's wine into her lap. She gasps in shock as he smirks at her, and says something that has her cheeks turning red with embarrassment. Before management can intervene, I step in to save the damsel in distress.

"Watch it, kid," I snap, warning him off with a look.

Putting his hands up in surrender, he backs away. "All right, man. My bad."

"You okay, babe?" I ask the girl who is looking up at me with wide, hopeful eyes. *Yes, honey. I'm real.*

"I'm fine," she says, all breathy.

Giving her a smirk, I turn those bedroom eyes on her. "Yes, ma'am, you are." The southern accent—it gets 'em every time. "Can I buy you a drink?" I ask, my eyes moving to her lips. They're pretty damn nice.

"I'd like that."

"I'll be right back, beautiful." I leave her with a wink, and she blushes a deep red.

Walking to the bar, I notice Diem is watching me from her seat. A man sits next to her, but she pays him no attention. She narrows her eyes on me—a look I return when she smiles at the man next to her. If she's trying to make me jealous, it isn't going to work.

Drinks in hand, I walk back over to my potential phone number girl, who beams at the sight of me. If she noticed the look Diem gave me, she doesn't care.

"I'm going to run to the ladies' room and see if I can get this out," she says full of regret. "Just two minutes."

"Take all the time you need. I'll be right here," I promise. She blushes again and hurries off to the bathroom. This dating shit is kinda fun. I should do it more often.

Reluctantly, I look over my shoulder to see how Diem is doing but she isn't in her seat. An uneasy feeling comes over me when I think about where she might be. It's not that I'm worried about someone hurting her, I'm more worried about her hurting someone. In particular, my damsel in distress.

Hoping that I'm wrong, I walk to the women's bathroom and push the door open a little. I can see the girl scrubbing away at her dress with a towel while Diem looks on in silence. From where they stand, they can't see me.

"Who's that guy with all the tattoos?" Diem asks, pretending to be nice.

I can't see her face, but I hear the girl sigh. "I don't know, but fuck he's hot." I smile at the compliment. And silently thank her.

"Yes he is," Diem agrees, defeat already in her tone. "He didn't call you pretty girl, did he?"

"No," the girl answers, and I breathe a sigh of relief. Diem is turning to leave and I start to shut the door when the girl says something that stops Diem in her tracks.

"What did you say?" Oh shit.

"I said he called me beautiful." Motherfuck me.

"Did he?" Diem's voice is cold.

Please don't say anything else. Please don't say anything else. "Yes, and he had the cutest smirk when he said it." *Shit. Shit. Shit.*

"I bet he did." I know that tone. She's going to make me pay for this. Dearly.

Before she can walk out, I leave and find her potential date at the bar. Grabbing him on the shoulder, I flash him a look of death. "You're fucking with my girl. Leave right now, or I'll splatter your brains all over this fucking bar." With a deer-in-the-headlights look, he leaves the bar with haste and I reclaim my seat just as Diem walks up.

She glances at her date's empty chair, then back at me. "What did you do?" she asks cautiously.

I start to answer, when the girl rushes past us and out the door without a glance in our direction. Seeing her, I change my answer from a lie to the truth. "Probably the same thing you did." And with a smirk, I add an endearment that has her smiling, letting me know I'm forgiven. "Pretty girl."

"Now where are we going?" I ask after dinner. I'm full and sleepy and horny because Diem is still in the dress that barely covers the ass I'm going to fuck tonight.

"It's a surprise."

"I don't like surprises."

"Shut up."

Fucking woman. I continue down the road until we finally come to a large port just off the river filled with shipment containers.

"Find number 8794." I find the eights and drive nearly to the end of the lane. This is the perfect place to kill someone and I make sure to keep Diem in my peripherals at all times.

"Here," I say, pulling up next to the container and shutting off the car. Unlike all the others, this one looks brand new. She gets out and I follow her to the locked container. Fishing a key from her cleavage, she unlocks the container and pushes the door up.

"Go ahead." She motions for me to go in and I shake my head.

"You first."

Rolling her eyes, she calls me a baby and walks in. Inside the dimly lit container is a truck. An exact replica of my truck before she wrecked it. I run my fingers down the cool metal door and peer into the blacked-out windows.

"How did you get this? My insurance?" I question, still not believing that my baby is here in front of my very eyes.

"I owe you a truck. And eight hundred and seventy-three dollars. It's in the glove box." I stare at her over the hood. She's not bullshitting me.

"My insurance would have bought me a new truck."

"I know that. But my insurance is better." She smiles. "I come from money. This is nothing."

"Spoiled little rich girl." I smirk, but she finds no humor in my words.

"I've earned every penny I've ever spent and then some." The ice is in her eyes. The steel is in her voice. The conviction she so often conveys is in her words. She means what she says, and I believe her.

"I would say thank you, but you owed it to me, so I won't."

"I don't need your thanks, Zeke. All I need is for you to know that I always keep good on my word." Diem didn't have to buy a truck to prove that to me. I already knew it. But, since she's being so generous, I know something else she promised that I'm still waiting on. Neither of us had won the bet, so she doesn't have to give it to me tonight, but I'm hoping like hell she will.

She notices the flash of heat in my eyes, and it feels like someone dashed it with cold water when I watch that wicked smile creep across her face. I already know what's coming, and I start shaking my head in protest.

"Welcome to locker 8794," she says, holding her arms out and looking around for emphasis. "Where no other man has gone before."

My phone rings in the early hours of the morning waking me. I untangle myself from Diem and reach over to the nightstand, hitting things until I find it.

"Yeah?" I say gruffly.

"Get up. Meet me at my house. I have something for you." Rookie hangs up in my ear and I slide quietly out of bed. I make minimal noise getting dressed and grabbing my duffel, but Diem speaks to me before I can make a clean getaway.

"You coming back?" she asks sleepily. She's most beautiful and vulnerable this time of day—sleepy and naked and tangled in my sheets. My very expensive sheets.

"Not sure, pretty girl. Stay though. Be here when I get home." She nods, submitting to my demand before turning over on her stomach. I leave the bedroom quickly, and I don't look back.

Rookie lives about an hour from me. I drive my new truck to his house, getting there as fast as possible. He's standing outside when I arrive, smoking a cigarette. Rookie is always calm and controlled, so there is no way of knowing if what I'm walking into is bad or really bad. To him, it's all the same.

He motions for me to follow him and leads me to his shed. Flipping on a light switch, two dead Death Mob members, riddled in bullet holes, lay on the floor. Next to a woman.

"Who's she?" I ask, pointing to the half-naked woman.

"Collateral damage," he says, lighting another cigarette.

"I don't like collateral damage." My temper is rising as I look at the young woman who Rookie has been kind enough to turn faceup and cover with a sheet.

"Yeah? Me neither. But they killed her, so I killed them. I figured I better take them all."

"Why did they kill her?"

"Don't think they meant to. She was standing across the street when they shot. They missed me. But they got her. Right in the heart."

"Fuuuuckkk." I run my hands through my hair. "What happened?"

"Said they recognized me. From Houston. They're from the town just up the road, Shady. I was out getting shit for Carrie and they just confronted me. You think they're onto us?"

I shake my head, but I'm still unsure. "Nah. Just coincidence. You know her name?" He hands me her purse and I find a driver's license with her address and name. "Anyone else see you?"

"Nobody that I know of. But I was wearing black and it was dark so even if they did, they wouldn't be able to make me out."

I nod, putting my hand on his shoulder and giving it a squeeze. "It's all right." He just shrugs. Unaffected on the outside, but something tells me he's struggling on the inside. "Get rid of them. I'll call Tank to take care of her. She deserves a proper burial and her family deserves some kind of explanation." It wouldn't be the truth, but it would give them closure.

I put in the call to Tank, who shows up an hour later. He assures me he can handle it with no problems. I trust that he will. We burn the cuts at Rookie's house, and the sun is up when I finally make my way back home. My phone flashes with a text from Diem.

See you around.

And just like that, my day got even shittier.

14

"I'M GOING TO be staying the next few weeks with you," Diem informs me the next weekend. We're in my recliner, watching westerns, and she's wearing my shirt.

"You are?" I ask, unable to drown the happiness that is bubbling in my gut. I hate the feeling.

"I'm getting some home improvements done. Someone told me a couple of weeks ago that my house pretty much looks like shit."

"Whoever they are sounds like a real douche bag."

"Yeah, he is."

This is how all conversations seem to go between me and Diem. There is no normal everyday talk. No *how are you*s, or *was your day good*s or *can I get you anything*s. We argue over everything. We call each other names. I hate her and she hates me. We fuck like wild rabbits and each time is better than the last. I like it this way. So does she.

This week will be no different. I'm sure of it.

"I need Carrie's number," she tells me on Monday. I'm at the table, pretending to work on my laptop. When what I'm really doing is playing a game of Solitaire—that she just rudely interrupted.

"For what?"

"Because I want to ask her something."

"She's not your friend, you know. You have no friends. Nobody likes you."

"Give me the number," she demands, but I don't give out *my* friend's numbers. So I call and give Carrie hers.

Thirty minutes later, Diem informs me that we are going to see a band in Concord tonight. She's already confirmed it with Rookie, or Joe as she knows him, and Carrie and I don't like being the fourth fucking wheel. So I call Rookie and chew his ass for making plans without me. He blames Carrie, like the pussy he is, because he knows I could never be mad at her.

We meet up at the club and I'm surprised to see Carrie in something other than scrubs. No wonder Rookie keeps her hidden beneath those shapeless clothes—the woman is built like a brick shithouse. She's got a body like Kate Upton—big natural tits, thick legs, and long brown hair. I feel so guilty about checking out my brother's woman that I tell him just how hot I think she is.

"Damn, Rookie. Carrie is fine. No wonder you don't bring her around that often." My eyes trail up her long body. She's wearing a short black dress with heels so high they make her almost as tall as Rookie.

Pride sparkles in his eyes as he takes her in himself. "I'm gonna marry her," he says, as nonchalantly as if he was telling me he had to go take a piss.

"What? Why?" I ask, shocked at his admission.

He just shrugs. "It's important to her, so it's important to me.

Speaking of ol' ladies, yours is pretty fine herself." I follow the direction of his chin tip, and Carrie seems to blur out of the picture when I look at Diem.

Motherfucker . . .

She's wearing a turquoise blue dress that ties around her neck. It dips down low in the front, exposing the sides of each of her perfect tits and dips even lower in the back—a hairsbreadth from the crack of her ass. Her olive skin looks darker against the material, and the silver straps of her shoes climb all the way up her calf. How the fuck had I not noticed her before now? The truck was dark. We were arguing when we left, so I was avoiding her. But was I really that blind?

"We're going to dance," she tells me, and all I can do is stand here and gape as she sashays onto the dance floor with Carrie in tow. Rookie claps me on the back, finally snapping me back to reality.

"Come on, brother. I'll buy you a drink."

Rookie and I are at the bar having a drink with Mick, who coincidently happened to be here too. I'm introduced to his friend, Joel, who I know now is his lover. Fine by me. I should introduce them to Saylor's friends Donnawayne and Jeffery. Everyone is having a good time. The guys are drinking, the girls are dancing, the night is perfect.

But then I hear them.

The unmistakable sound of Harley-Davidson motorcycles. It could be a bunch of guys just out on the town. But my gut tells me it's not. By the way Rookie is looking at me, his is saying the same thing. My whole world changes in the blink of an eye when six Death Mob members walk in, scanning the crowd. I grow tense, knowing that Rookie had killed two of their guys out in the open just a few days ago. They look at us but don't concentrate too long, and I let out a sigh of relief. It's time to go.

But the band decides to cover The Pretty Reckless's "Heaven Knows" and it just so happens to be Diem's favorite fucking song. So I'm forced to stay a little bit longer.

Death Mob is loud and obnoxious, speaking crudely to a group of women near the bar and shouting their demands to the bartenders. I don't like it. The hate I have for them grows as I watch them disgrace all MCs with their behavior. Sure I'd done my fair share of hell-raising, but only in places that belonged to Sinner's Creed. This is not their usual spot, but they're letting everyone know that this is their territory. Concord is their town. And they can act however the fuck they want.

Don't get involved.

Don't get involved.

I'm chanting to myself. I'm trying to find anything to watch other than the scene in front of me. I look at Diem as she moves her ass on the dance floor, her eyes trained on me. I'm counting the beats of the song, and it seems never ending. Then my eyes fall back to Mick and his friend as they sit minding their own business and share a moment. And I'm not the only one who notices.

One of Death Mob's members says something to his brothers, and soon all their eyes are on Mick and Joel. I turn to Rookie to see the vein that appears on his forehead as his anger rises. It tells me that he can't distance himself from what's happening much longer. He hates Death Mob as much as I do. It's hard when you're within spitting distance of men worthy of a slow death and you can't do anything about it.

When one of them puts their hands roughly on Mick's shoulder, I'm on my feet. As I walk over, I know I'm making a mistake. I'll raise the suspicions of everyone here and draw the attention of Death Mob chapters from near and far. But I don't care. When

I see Rookie stand and walk behind me, I know he don't give a shit either.

Mick sees me approaching and the relief is evident on his face. He looks like he's fighting to contain a smile too. He thinks his new friend Zeke is coming to his rescue. But he's wrong. Tonight, I'm not his friend, and I'm not Zeke.

Tonight, I'm a one-percenter.

I'm Sinner's Creed.

I'm fucking Shady.

15

DIEM

BAD BOYS. THERE'S something about them. It's almost like they possess some magical power that controls your mind . . . and your heart.

I've always been drawn to them. I like the way their appearance screams confidence. I like the way they make me feel safe. I like that even though everything inside me tells me to stay away, I can't. The goose bumps, the butterflies, the thrill and the fear always win against original, ordinary, and safe.

I guess it's the rebel in me. The bitch that claws at my skin, forcing me to adhere to something I know is no good for me. The lady dressed in red that cheers for the evil that's buried deep within me. The Diem that longs to let the man take control. Whichever one it is telling me that Zeke is who I want is throwing one hell of a celebration right now. Because what I'm witnessing in this moment, is the fucking epitome of a bad boy.

I've been watching him and Joe for the last five minutes. His transformation isn't instant, but changes by the second. One minute he's calm and collected, and then his eyes narrow on something. I can almost hear the rush of blood in his veins as it flows faster and faster toward his quickening pulse.

The steady rhythm of his heart has intensified to a hard punch that vibrates his shirt with every beat. His nostrils flare with every new idea of pain he wants to deliver. The knuckles on his once-relaxed hands are now bone white, stretching his skin to the point of breaking. He taps his foot as if he's counting, trying to calm himself. But the rage is too intense, and when he finally has enough, he stands.

I feel like the world shifts on its axis. The floor seems to shake with his every step—not from the weight of his body, but out of fear. He exudes the power of a god. So much so that I stand expectantly, waiting for him to summon lightning from the sky. I've never been so captivated by anyone in all of my life. Just the mere thought of his presence makes me feel like I'm safe from everything.

Joe flanks him, and although he's significantly bigger, he seems small compared to Zeke. He's angry too, but can't hold a candle to the evil that's radiating off the man beside him.

I move closer, although I'm sure he can be heard from anywhere in the bar. Even though his voice is low, the strength and conviction in it allows his words to carry far beyond normal reach.

"Get out." His demand leaves no room for negotiation—no conversation, no options, and no fucking excuses. My whole body just melted, and he's done nothing but speak.

The men he's confronting are the notorious Death Mob one-percenters. They're big, mean, and look down at him as if he's nothing more than a smear of dog shit on the bottom of their shoes. Once again, he's outnumbered, outsized, and doesn't care.

Instead of getting nervous for him, I become excited. Everything around me blurs, as my eyes focus on the only man in the room. He's not intimidated. If anything, he's confident in his ability to take on the six bikers, without the least little bit of doubt. It's almost like he has a personal vendetta against them, and has been looking forward to this opportunity for quite some time.

Everything seems to happen too fast for my eyes to see, and too quick for my brain to register. It's not your typical barroom brawl—this is a one-man show. Joe is caught up in the mix, but it's clear he's only there to prevent them all from jumping in at the same time.

If Steven Seagal and Jean-Claude Van Damme had a baby, I'm sure Zeke would be the result. His moves are quick, precise, and he seems to be one step ahead of the men he's fighting. The blows he lands are always in the right places, dropping the men completely or at the very least bringing them to their knees. If I wasn't seeing it with my own eyes, I wouldn't believe he was capable of doing so much damage.

Even though he's good, he's not a ninja. I flinch every time he gets hit, but he doesn't seem to feel it. He's in the zone. Or he's immortal. Or he spikes his drinks with a liquid form of kryptonite. That would explain why his beer tastes so good. Why *he* tastes so good.

After what seems like forever, but is really only a couple minutes, security shows up and breaks up the fight. The bikers are escorted from the bar. Surprisingly, they leave without argument, carrying the ones out that are still unconscious. They're screaming "fuck you" and "you'll be seeing us again" all the way to their bikes.

The smell of whiskey, blood, and leather hangs heavy in the air. But it can't mask the scent of male sweat mixed with a little smoke, a hint of cologne, and a whole lot of Zeke.

He's standing in front of me, his breath heavy and his eyes blazing. They're focused solely on me, and I can feel the intensity of their heat in places I want his mouth. He has a small cut on his lip, and a slight swell in his jaw. The cut wells with blood and I'm tempted to lick it. And the beads of sweat above his lips. And everything else I can put my tongue on.

He's under my skin. He's in my head. He gives me everything I never knew I wanted and then some. If I thought I was falling before, I'm sure of it now. There is no place in this world I'd rather be than in his arms, on his nerves, and at his house. He makes me feel like there is something magical inside me. He brings out my worst, then contradicts it with my best.

I never want to be where he isn't. He wants the same thing. And like me, he just can't admit it. But this man would kill for me. I know it. He's holding in a secret that I haven't figured out, and frankly I don't care to. Everything that's bad about him and unknown to me only makes me want him more. And by the look he's giving me, he wants me too.

"You okay?" he asks, and a small hint of regret flashes in his eyes.

"Yes." I had a smart-ass comeback, but I couldn't manage to find the air to say it. I'm just as breathless as he is and I haven't done a damn thing.

I'm waiting for him to give me a smirk, or for his concentration to break. But his fierce gaze never falters. It's like he's trying to tell me something with his eyes—something I don't want to hear. He's giving me a warning. He's telling me that this is who he is. That he's a bad guy. That he's no good for me, blah, blah, blah.

So I match his glare with a glare of my own. I'm giving him a warning. I'm telling him this is who *I* am. That bad guys don't scare me. And that I don't care if he's no good for me, because the reality is, I'm really not that good for him either.

16

SHADY

"YOU ARE SO fucking hot!" Diem says for the hundredth time since we left the bar. She's buzzed. And horny. And that's fine by me. I need the distraction.

We're in the truck and she has my dick in her hands, her mouth on my neck, and my new shiny truck isn't new and shiny anymore because I keep hitting ditches. Finally, I pull over.

No sooner is the truck in park than I'm in her mouth. And just like she promised—I'm all the way at the back of her throat.

"Motherfucker . . . ," I groan, fisting my hand into her hair. Her mouth is like a vacuum suctioned around my cock. Her tongue is practicing magic on my shaft. She's gripping me with muscles I never knew existed inside a woman's mouth. Her lips are pinched tight, forcing all the blood to the head of my cock as she pulls back. Then they part—and the feeling of release is so overwhelming, I almost come in her mouth.

"Come here," I growl, lifting her onto my lap—knowing I won't last one more second if I stay inside her mouth any longer. With a slip of my fingers, her panties are pushed to the side and I'm sinking inside her—bareback and not giving one ounce of fuck. My hands tighten around her waist as I move her body up and down on my cock.

"Ohmigod you feel so good," she breathes, her head thrown back so her neck is exposed to me. I bite her, lick her, suck her sweaty flesh, and my dick grows harder with her every moan. She feels like heaven. We're flesh on flesh, skin on skin, my cock is soaked in her wetness, and I've never felt anything like it.

Her hips move in sync with me. She dances on my cock, her bare thighs bouncing on mine every time I lift her, then slam her back down. I flip up the console, then move us until she's laying on her back and I'm driving into her. Pushing her dress up her body, I run my hands over her smooth stomach, knowing that in moments I'll be coming on the flawless, tanned flesh.

I look down and she is splayed open before me, and I can't fucking help it. I have to taste her. Pulling out, I bury my face between her thighs, licking and sucking her until she's coming in my mouth. Then I'm filling her again—pounding into her quivering pussy.

I flip her to her knees, pushing her skirt up over her back so I have a full view of her ass that calls my name—begging me to be inside it. She's so turned on at this point, I know she is as ready as she'll ever be. I put my hand on her back, pushing her further down in the seat. Her ass raises slightly and I flex my hips to hit that sweet spot inside her. With every stroke, she moans, her body jerks, and she becomes more relaxed—opening herself up to me.

My finger circles her ass—moistening it with her own arousal. I slip the tip inside and she doesn't even flinch. Taking it further, I continue the slow, torturous strokes while my finger slides in and out of her—widening the one thing on her body that has never been touched. The one thing that will solely belong to me. The one thing that I've wanted, dreamed about, and went to extensive lengths to gain. Now she was going to give it to me.

When I place the tip of my cock in her ass, she flinches and my fingers find her pussy. She loosens up, and I slide inside her one painstakingly slow centimeter at a time. My eyes roll back in my head at the feel of her. She's so tight it almost hurts—but it's so fucking good.

"Relax, baby." My words are a strangled whisper, but at my command her body relaxes. Something about dominating a woman as independent and self-righteous as her makes the feeling of being inside her that much sweeter.

After what could have been hours, I pull out and slide easily back inside. I don't even try to suppress the guttural sounds coming out of my mouth. And with my response, she relaxes further—completely submitting her body to me. Knowing that I have it at my disposal and she's completely at my mercy makes me want her that much more.

"Does this sweet ass belong to me, Diem?" I ask, my tone low and throaty.

"Yes," she breathes, and I feel her pussy tighten around my fingers at the sound of my voice. She likes when I talk dirty. And I like to give my girl everything she wants.

"You should fuckin' see how good you look from behind."

Her answer is a moan that comes from so deep inside her, I can feel the hum on my cock. "Your ass in the air . . . my cock going in and out of you . . . your sweet, perfect pussy coming all over my fingers . . . It's fucking beautiful, baby." And damn if it ain't.

I love fucking her like this. I've claimed her ass. I finally got what I've been wanting. And I know how not to fuck up a good thing. I don't want to hurt her or be the reason she can't walk tomorrow, so I refrain from fucking her like I want to—hard and fast and raw. But she has no regard for her own well-being and demands I give it to her just like she likes it.

Just like I like it.

Hard and *fast* and *raw.* My grip on her waist tightens, and with the jerk of my arms, I'm pulling her back against me. Before the sound of her ass hitting my stomach can fill the air, I'm driving inside her again until the sound of her screams overpower the sound of flesh on flesh. Her fingers find her clit, and almost instantly, she's coming on my cock.

When I feel my balls tighten, I pull out and flip her on her back. I want to look at her when I come. Seconds later, I'm coming on her stomach. Her hands slide over her skin, rubbing my come over her stomach and the top of her pussy. She's panting. Her eyes are wide and captivating. I can't do anything but look at her. She's fucking beautiful.

I don't know why, but I can't wait to hold her. I want to kiss her soft and slow and hold her so close to me that our bodies mold together into one. I don't want to just fuck her. I don't want to fight or argue or make deals . . . I don't want to think about Death Mob, or the consequences of my actions or Sinner's Creed. I only want one thing.

Pulling her dress down, I grab her hand and tuck her into my side. She rides there, her head on my shoulder until we get home. She's asleep when we arrive so I carry her in. Then I strip her down, clean her up, and finally give myself what I've really been waiting for all night.

It's not a quick fuck. It's not her ass that she'd never given to anyone else. It's the simplest thing that I never thought I'd ever want. Now it's all I can think about. The one thing I've been waiting for since I woke up this morning is the one thing I can't get soon enough . . . just me and Diem in my bed.

———

We're eating cereal, in bed, naked, the next morning when she asks, "You wanna tell me what happened last night?"

I shovel another spoonful of cereal in my mouth, not meeting her eyes. "I don't like bullies," I mumble.

"Well you don't have a problem bullying me."

Nudging her shoulder with mine, I give her a wink. "That's because I don't like you, gorgeous. But Mick I consider a friend."

Taking her bowl from her hand, I turn it up, finishing off the milk before getting out of bed. Something, a shoe I think, hits me in the back as I make my way to the kitchen.

"The milk is the best part, you bully," she says, but I can hear the smile in her voice. And I'm thankful that she doesn't push the issue further. I don't know what I'd tell her. And I don't want to lie.

Standing at the sink, I look out into my backyard, wishing I wouldn't have taken all of the beauty of this place for granted. I never know when it's going to end. I was playing with fire last night. Chances are, I was fixing to get burned. As if they could sense my uneasiness, I hear my phone ringing and find Nationals' number flashing across the screen.

"Yeah?"

"Jackpot. Tomorrow. Check your calendar." Jimbo hangs up in my ear, and my brain goes into overdrive wondering what event is happening tomorrow. And how in the hell I forgot. If I had it on my calendar, it must be important.

Diem is in the shower, so I lock my bedroom door and dig the small notebook out of the back of my safe. Sinner's Creed lives by many codes. If the feds were to ever raid my home, they would find plenty linking me to the club. But the information they found could not be decoded by anyone other than a brother. Not even ol' ladies know the codes. It's in the bylaws.

The month is June, which is July for Sinner's Creed. Tomorrow is the sixteenth, but to us it's the second. I hold my breath while I open the small datebook. It could be anything—a hit, a benefit, a delivery . . . Whatever it is, isn't what has me nervous. It's how long I'm gonna be gone.

Diem flashes in my mind. I can hear her on the other side of the wall. Her body naked and wet and in my shower. I don't want to leave her for long periods of time. But, if the club tells me to, I will. And there will be no regrets, no doubt, and not a second thought if what we have has to end. My club comes first. Always and forever.

I scan the pages, running my finger down the dates until I come to tomorrow's. A slow smile creeps across my face as relief floods through my veins.

Chaps. B.

It's Chaps's birthday. A hell of a reason to celebrate. Two days of partying. Two days with my brothers. Two days where nothing else matters but commemorating the life of one of our own. Two days and I would be back here with her. And I haven't even left, but already, I miss her.

"What you so pissed off about?" Tanner, the San Antonio sergeant at arms, asks me the next night. I'd given them back their rockers, and now I guess he feels like we were pals.

We aren't.

I'm not in the mood to make new friends. I'm not even in the mood for the couple I have. My mind is clouded with thoughts of Diem. I want to be with her. I want to be Zeke—the man that allowed a woman to invade his home and try to control his life. For some reason, I actually like being that man.

"Another," I tell the slut behind the bar. A few months ago,

I'd be banging the shit outta her. But right now, I find her almost repulsive. Too easy. Too fake. Too cheap. Too not like Diem.

"It's really none of my business, but I know a thing or two about relationships if you wanna talk." I glare at Tanner, hoping he gets the message. He doesn't. "I got three baby mamas, and a wife. Trust me, I know what I'm doing."

I want to kill him. But I can't. He's my brother. So I just get up and walk away, mumbling my opinion of him on the way out. "Yeah, Tanner. Sounds like you're a real fucking hero."

I move to the patio, trying to escape my thoughts of Diem. But, even here with the booze, naked women and blunts, I still can't get her out of my head. It goes back to when I told her I was leaving. I'd forgotten that we'd made plans to go out. I'd asked her on a date during a moment of weakness yesterday. I can't seem to shake the conversation or the vision of her holding a pair of the sexiest black heels I'd ever seen in her hand.

"So you won't be here tonight?" she'd asked, wearing nothing but a towel. She looked pissed.

"No."

"And tomorrow?" Yeah, definitely pissed.

I swallowed hard, shaking my head as I told her the truth. "I don't know."

"You know, Zeke," she snapped, losing her temper. "It's not that you're leaving, it's the fact that you made plans with me first. I don't like being lied to."

"Diem, I didn't lie. Something came up." Liar. Well, something did come up, but it damn sure wasn't the "family issue" excuse I'd been claiming for months now.

"I'm going out tomorrow." Her voice was more controlled, but cold and threatening. "And I'm wearing these heels. And if your ass isn't there, then I'll be digging them into someone else's." She stomped out, and I just stood there.

It's not like we're monogamous. She can fuck whoever she wants. That feeling of jealousy she had, I've never experienced. I wasn't going to start now. I'm miles away . . . surrounded by women begging for my cock. I don't need her. Let her fuck some other guy. I don't care.

I Don't Care.

I DON'T CARE.

But for some reason, I can't resist the urge to put my fist through something.

It's night two of Chaps's birthday celebration. I'm hungover, tired, and feeling more dangerous and lethal than I can ever remember. I want to kill that motherfucker Diem dug those heels into last night. I want to crush his skull with my bare hands. Then I want to let her dig them heels into me, and dare her to tell me she liked *him* more.

Zeke's phone buzzes in my pocket and I deliberate opening the message. Knowing Diem, it's probably a selfie of her riding some random guy's cock. With the idea of killing them both, adrenaline bolts through my veins as I open the message, already preparing her slow death like I have so many times before. But the message I see has me melting all over my barstool like a lovestruck fucking pussy.

I didn't go out last night. Me and my heels made a decision . . .
We'd rather just wait on you.

I nearly knock Cynthia, the naked woman who's been trying to get my attention all day, off the stool next to me when I stand and hit the call button.

"Diem," I say, my voice low and thick and laced with need. I'm walking outside and away from the noise. But apparently, I don't escape fast enough.

"Are you at a party?"

"Yes." I don't lie. I don't have any reason to.

"Well, that's just perfect, Zeke." She sounds pissed.

"Are you mad?"

"Mad? No. Mad would be me frolicking through a field of flowers. Pissed off would have me burning your fucking house down."

"So . . . you're not mad?"

"Not mad."

"But you're pissed off."

"Very much." Shit.

"What are you so pissed about, Diem?" Silence. "Diem?" More silence. I check my phone to see if I lost connection. I didn't. "Hello?"

"I'm losing my mind," she whispers, and I can hear her as she paces the floor.

"Are you okay?" A long pause.

"No. I don't think I am." She hangs up, and I ignore the women who beg for my attention as I walk back in. The guys call to me from across the room, but I ignore them too. I'm removing my cut as I find Cleft, who has a whore in his lap. I fold my patch, holding it out to him. He stands, knocking the whore on her ass in the process.

"I need to go home, Cleft. Tonight."

I was a fucking idiot. I *am* a fucking idiot. I'd let thoughts of Diem being with another man boil my blood. The rage was so intense, I wanted to kill. Then, she told me she was home. At *my* home. Waiting on *me*. Not once did I consider how it would make her feel if she thought I might have done something with someone else. Now she had suspicions that I might have.

It takes me almost eight hours, but finally, I'm pulling into the driveway. The house is completely dark, but it's not that late. I pull my gun from my back as I quietly walk up the steps on the porch. It's a precaution when I've been away, but always a precaution when it comes to Diem. She'd pointed a gun at me once. This time, I believe she's mad enough to use it.

I walk in and hear music coming from my bedroom. My eyes scan the living room and kitchen. Everything still seems to be intact. I sniff the air, searching for the scent of gasoline, but I don't smell any. Thank fuck. Maybe the house will survive after all.

I ease open the door to my bedroom and the smell of weed is thick in the air. She must have found my stash of pot and emergency candles. Every one of them is lit, casting a glow across the room.

My shadow dances across the far wall and on the floor, facing it, sits Diem with her back against the bed. I drop my gun in my underwear drawer just as the song starts up again. It's bluesy, slow and the woman singing sounds almost desperate. She must have it on repeat. I look over at my iPod and see *Girl Crush—Lady Antebellum* displayed on the screen—definitely not one of mine.

I approach Diem like I would a frightened animal. She's dressed in shorts and a T-shirt, but her hair is styled and those heels are on her feet. Between her fingers, she holds a blunt.

"Diem?" She doesn't acknowledge me, and her head dips further, preventing me from seeing her. "Are you crying?"

"No," she sniffs.

I ease down on the floor next to her. Taking her chin in my hand, I turn her head to see black streaks running down her pretty face—her mascara staining her cheeks. "What's wrong?"

She doesn't meet my gaze when she answers. "I've got a girl crush." She frowns as two more tears fall freely from her eyes.

"A what?" I ask, confused as fuck as to what she's talking about.

"A girl crush, Zeke. I got a girl crush on the woman who had you . . ." That must be some good weed.

"What woman?"

"That woman you were with earlier." She wipes her nose with

her hand. Damn she looks pitiful. Who knew with a little bit of pot, Diem could transform into a normal girl who has feelings and shit.

"I wasn't with a woman," I say, forcing her to look at me. "I wasn't with a woman, Diem." I tell her again when her eyes finally land on mine. At my admission, she cries harder.

"I'm crazy, Zeke. I'm totally losing my fucking mind. I've never been jealous in all of my life, but you . . ." She pokes her finger in my chest, her lips quivering. "You make me want to feel that way. You make me want to possess something that's not even mine." I take the blunt from her fingers, taking a much-needed drag before stubbing out the fire in the ashtray.

"You're not crazy, Diem."

"Why would you want me to hear the sound of some bitch choking on your cock?"

"That was a long time ago," I say in my defense.

"What about today? Was that a long time ago too?" She's hurt. I'm an asshole. And I'm feeling every bit of the side effects from that title too.

"I didn't want that girl, Diem. Not then and not today."

She searches my eyes, looking for truth. She'll find it. Monica was convenient, but I never really wanted her. And I never gave those bitches today a second glance.

"Prove it," she challenges, finding her backbone.

"I will."

"Now, Zeke. Prove it now."

Bringing her hand to my lips, I kiss her fingers. "I never kissed her . . . I couldn't kiss her," I admit, a little ashamed. For a man like me, kissing a woman was more intimate than fucking one.

"Why?" she whispers, just as the song starts over again.

I run my thumb across her bottom lip. "Because these are the only lips I want." She closes her eyes, and my knuckles graze the tear streaks on her cheeks. "I didn't touch her either."

She leans into my touch. "Tell me why."

"Because I knew she wouldn't feel like you." My words are directed toward her, but it's like as I say them out loud, the truth of them is registering for the first time with me too. "She didn't smell like you. She didn't taste like you." I pause, narrowing my eyes at my own confession. "She wasn't you, Diem." Dropping my voice, I place my forehead against hers. "None of them were you."

"You mean that?" she whispers, still sniffling.

"Yes."

"But you don't even like me."

I smile. "You don't like me either."

She laughs, and I didn't realize how much I missed the sound. We just sit a minute, both of us looking down at our intertwined fingers in her lap. "I can feel my control slipping, Zeke," she says, her head leaning a little heavier against mine at the admission.

"What are you so afraid of?"

After a long pause, she finally answers. "Weakness."

"You don't have to be strong all the time, Diem. You can let go. With me." She raises her head to look at me, her eyes guarded as she studies the sincerity in my expression for a long time.

"Don't treat me like your whores, Zeke," she says, and the warning can be heard loud and clear. "You told me I was different from them. I was different from my mother. Make me feel that way."

Unsure of how else to prove it, I kiss her. Not a fast kiss to hurry up and get the ball rolling, but a slow, torturous kiss that has her melting in my arms. She doesn't taste like cinnamon or tequila or ice cream. It's just her mixed with a hint of smoke—the perfect concoction.

I wrap my arm around her waist, flipping her until she's beneath me—not on her knees in front of me or between my legs, but to where I'll have a full view of her face when she falls apart. Her hands fist in my hair, and I easily grasp them both in one of mine and hold them over her head. She struggles with the loss of control, and I drag my lips to her ear.

"I got you." I run my hand under her shirt, lazily dragging my fingers up her side until she relaxes. I squeeze her hands, letting her know to keep them there, then release them and fist her shirt in my hands. I pull it over her head, to find her not wearing a bra. It's only been two days since I've seen her tits, but they're better than I remember. Her nipples harden with the intensity of my gaze. "They're fucking perfect," I say, watching them pucker further when my breath blows over them.

Her back bows off the floor when I take one in my mouth. She whimpers in need and I massage her other breast with one hand, using the other to unsnap the button on her shorts. My tongue trails down her stomach, where the bruises have almost completely faded. I kiss along the hem of her shorts and in the wake of my lips, I leave a path of goose bumps.

My fingers curl around her shorts and she lifts her hips. I drag my eyes back up her body—she's naked and shaking in anticipation for me. For *Zeke*. Fuck, she's beautiful. Breathtaking, gorgeous, submissive, vulnerable, needy . . . all the things I've never seen her be. Like this, she's a stranger to me. And I don't know what way I like her better. Maybe because I like them all.

I stand over her, watching her eyes grow hungry as I remove my boots, my shirt, then my jeans. Her breath catches at the sight of my cock, hard and ready for her.

Only her.

Diem.

I sheath it with a condom, torturing her further by prolonging the process. When she presses her thighs together and grinds her hips looking for release, I finally show her mercy. Laying back across her body, I support my weight with my arms. Her knees separate, inviting me in. Slowly, her warm, wet pussy surrounds my cock, and I groan at the feel of her tight walls as they clench around me, pulling me further inside.

I fuck her slow, not letting one moment of her response to me go unnoticed. I don't fuck her hard and fast, even though her heels dig into my ass, urging me deeper. I don't want to fuck her like before. I don't want to fuck her like I have any other woman. Because they were all whores. So I give her a side of me I've never given to them.

My mouth finds hers and we kiss; the intimacy is foreign to me, but it feels so right. I couldn't imagine fucking her any other way. I want to kiss her. I want to take my time. I want to explore every part of her body with my mouth, my hands, and my cock.

When I feel her tighten around me, her eyes close, but I want to see her when she lets go. "Open your eyes, Diem. Look at me." Surprisingly she does. And I'm thankful. I was prepared to stop and force her to look at me. But she's letting me control her. And when her eyes lock on mine, there is no doubt—no fear, no walls, no ice, and no indifference. They tell me everything. They burn with desire and trust. The impact of what I see on her face is more powerful than the way her pussy squeezes my cock as she comes.

Her moans fill the room, drowning out the song completely. The sound alone is enough to have me coming too. With her, my feelings are heightened, and the fight for control is the hardest battle I've ever faced.

I lean down and kiss her, feeling her body shake as I rock my hips inside her a few more times. I move to lay beside her, and she folds her body into mine. Her head rests on my chest, her leg is tangled with mine. My arm goes around her waist and I hold her. Just like I hold her when we sleep. And when she sits in my recliner. Just like I should. And just like I've never held anyone else.

17

"**WHAT'S YOUR LAST** name, Diem?" The thought that I don't know it suddenly coming to mind. We're in the kitchen and she is cooking me breakfast. One I'm sure will be just as disgusting as everything else she has ever cooked.

She turns to look at me, leaning against the counter. Her eyes survey me in nothing but a pair of basketball shorts and I can't help but smirk when she blinks a couple of times to gather her bearings. "What's yours?"

"Would it make a difference if I told you?" I ask, grabbing the OJ from the fridge and drinking straight from the carton.

"Well that depends." She turns her back to me as she asks, "What if it's Dahmer? Or Bundy or Sells? Then I might think you were a serial killer. That would make a difference." She finally turns around so I can see her face. I study it to see if she's serious. Thank fuck she's not.

"You caught me." I smile. She's knows I'm joking. What she

doesn't know is that I'm worse than any serial killer she's ever Googled.

"Unless you plan to marry me, why do you want to know?" I laugh at the thought of marrying her crazy ass. That would never happen. A lifetime with a nut like her wasn't in my future plans. But my eyes move to her ring finger and I imagine how it would make me feel seeing her wear one. One that I gave her.

I really can't imagine spending the rest of my life with her. It seems unreal. But the thought of not having her in my life hurts in places I don't like feeling pain. Dead in my chest. In the center of my fucking heart. I don't want her to think about anyone else. I don't want her to be with anyone else.

"You and me," I start, narrowing my eyes on hers. "We're something. I don't know what it is, but when you said you were going to wear those heels for another man, it drove me fucking crazy. Those shoes, and every other pair you own, they belong to me. Those tiny little feet of yours, belong to me too. All ten of your toes, your fingers, your smile, your laugh, and that sweet pussy . . . it all belongs to me."

She smiles, trying to appear unaffected, but her eyes widen at my admission. "Getting attached, are we?" My silence speaks for itself and the moment she realizes her assumption is true, all humor is lost and her cheeks turn pink with embarrassment. "Oh," she says, busying herself with the burnt eggs in the skillet.

"I'm gonna go out on a limb here and say that the feeling is mutual." I walk up behind her—noticing how she stills when she feels my presence.

"Hardly." She attempts to scoff, but it comes out as a whisper. A very unbelievable whisper.

"Then why can't you look at me?" My pulse is beating faster than it should. I feel like I'm on a high. I'm fucking giddy when I let the realization settle inside me that she is in my kitchen, half naked, recently fucked, and cooking me breakfast. Then I feel murderous when I think about her in someone else's house doing the same. Is this what infatuation feels like? If so, I'm fucking crazy about her.

She finally turns around, and a hint of fear is in her eyes. Along with that same burning need I feel inside my chest. "Because this is something. And the feeling is mutual . . . and it scares the shit outta me."

Even though everything inside of me is screaming to make this a special moment, the seriousness of it is just too much. So I smirk. And she pushes me. And the moment is lost, but the truth is out—something that had to be said has finally surfaced. Now she knows that I'm hers. And she sure as fuck is mine.

The breakfast is worse than I ever could have imagined. I've never eaten dog shit, but I think if it was scrambled in eggs, her cooking is exactly what it would taste like. So I offer to buy breakfast instead. Diem agrees only after telling me that hell would freeze over before she cooked me eggs again. I believe her. I thank her too.

Now we're at the Hillsborough Diner and are waiting patiently for our food, which just so happens to be nearly every damn thing on the menu. The silence between us isn't uncomfortable at all. If we have nothing to argue about, conversation seems awkward. But I want to know everything about Diem. I know it's selfish to not tell her much about me, but I can't stand not knowing shit about her.

"Tell me about your job," I say. Her eyes drag up from the coffee cup in her hands. She continues to blow on it, looking at me annoyed.

"Why?" She takes a sip, makes a face, adds more sugar, then looks at me over the top of her cup.

"Because, regardless of how much we are unlike normal people, I think we should at least attempt to try and get to know each other." *Or me just get to know you*, I think.

"I already know everything about you. Just like you know everything about me. Or at least the important stuff."

"The only thing I know about you is that you're exasperating, infuriating, and completely fucking crazy."

"You forgot thief." She beams proudly.

I decide to let it go. If I pushed any further, I'd sound like one of those housewives off them reality TV shows. Diem would have a damn field day with that.

Our food comes and we eat in silence. It's only when we're down to the chocolate chip waffle we agreed to share that she speaks.

"I love chocolate," she says, scraping all my chocolate chips to her side. The fact that I let her is a milestone. If Rookie would have tried that, I'd stab him with my fork. "I like flowers. My favorite season is spring, and I hate the beach."

"No girl hates the beach," I say, figuring long walks on the beach with the sun setting in the background and all that romantic shit is on every girl's fantasy list.

"I'm not your ordinary girl, Zeke. Haven't you figured that out?" True. "So there are a few things about me. Not that I give a shit, but please, enlighten me with a little bit about yourself."

I smirk. She wants to know. If she didn't, she wouldn't be looking at me so expectantly. "I love chocolate too. I hate flowers because they smell like funeral homes. I've never been to a beach." With that, her eyes grow wide with shock.

"Are you serious?" I nod. "Who the hell don't like flowers?" I stare at her in confusion, thinking the beach was a much bigger deal than flowers. Then she smiles. "The beach really is overrated, but you should go. I'll take you."

Now I really am confused. "But you said you hate the beach."

"I do," she says, shrugging. "But I'll go for you." She stares at the table, her brows drawing together in confusion at her words. Then, she mumbles something and excuses herself. While she's gone, I pay the ticket. And for some fucking reason, I can't keep the smile off my face.

"What's Diem's favorite color?" Carrie asks me. It's been two days since I've heard from Diem. After breakfast, she'd left and has yet to call or text. To escape the feeling of loneliness in my house, I'd come to Rookie's.

"Hell, I don't know," I tell her, flipping through a magazine on the couch. She's sitting in the floor folding clothes while Rookie washes dishes—domesticated pussy.

"How do you not know? I mean if y'all are official, then you should know these things."

"We're not official. It's . . . complicated." Really complicated.

"Are you having sex with other people?" she asks, and I shift uncomfortably at her question.

"No. But just because we're monogamous doesn't mean we're official."

"Yes it does," Rookie calls from the kitchen.

"Well, do you know her favorite movie? Or what makes her laugh? Or her favorite food? I mean . . . anything?" I don't meet Carrie's eyes. I don't know if it's because I feel ashamed or because I feel like it's none of her business. Either way, I become aggravated at the situation.

"I know who she is. I know what kind of person she is. And

I know that she loves chocolate and flowers. I think that's enough," I say, unable to keep the grit out of my tone.

"It is enough," Rookie snaps, suddenly appearing in my line of sight. There is no mistaking the warning in his tone. I'm not pissed at Carrie. I'm pissed at myself for not knowing these things. But I damn sure didn't make it sound like that.

"It's fine." Carrie pushes at Rookie's leg, trying to remove him from between us. When it doesn't work, she peers around him. "As long as you know that, that's all that matters. You'll figure the other stuff out along the way." She gives me a smile that could melt an iceberg, and it makes me feel like shit.

I stand, figuring my time here is up considering Rookie is still looking at me like he wants to kill me. "Take care of that woman," I say, pointing down at Carrie. "She's too damn good for you."

In my truck, I'm calling Diem before I hit the highway.

"Hello," she says breathless, her voice echoing through the sound system.

"What are you doing?" I ask, my blood turning cold and my voice deadpan. Now I know what she felt like when she called while I was getting head.

"I'm running. What do you want?" I nearly wreck with relief, and when I let out a breath, she laughs. "Damn, I should have played that better."

"Not a good time for that," I growl, trying to calm myself down.

"What's wrong?" She's serious now, genuinely concerned. I'd play on *that*, but I'm too worked up.

"I need your favorite color. Carrie wants to know," I half lie. I want to know too.

"Red. Bright red." I listen to the sound of her feet on the pavement . . . a steady, fast-paced jog.

"What makes you laugh?" I ask, my voice lower. Damn, I

wish I was with her. Running right beside her and watching her tits bounce up and down.

"I'm not much of a laugher," she pants, then only the sound of her breathing fills the truck. She's stopped running and is trying to catch her breath. "You," she starts, still struggling. "You make me laugh. That's why I do shit to piss you off. It makes me happy."

I make her happy.

Sure, it's in a fucked-up kind of way, but still . . .

I make her happy.

"Why all the questions, Zeke?"

I think about that a minute before finally telling her the truth. "I just want to know . . . I want to know everything about you."

Time seems to stand still while I wait for her to answer. Forever seems to pass before she finally does. "If I tell you something, will you stop asking questions?"

"Yes," I agree without hesitation.

I hear the sound of her feet moving once again. Slower this time. "I'm still figuring myself out. But when I'm with you, I feel like I'm finding me. All my favorite things are determined by who makes me happy. So ask me that. Ask me who makes me happy."

"I already did," I say, starting to wonder if I heard her wrong the first time. But when she answers, my chest fills with pride and I know what I heard was right.

"Then you already know everything about me."

The phone disconnects before I have time to tell her that if what she says is true, then she already knows everything about me too.

18

"**DO YOU HAVE** an answer yet?" I look out across the patio at all the leaders of Sinner's Creed, who are anxiously awaiting my decision about their offer. They want me to become a Nomad. They want me to pick up where Dirk left off. Houston and San Antonio were a trial run, now they want me to go nationwide. They'd offered to give me six months to think about it. I didn't need that long. I'm ready.

"Yes. I'd be honored." Shaking hands with all of them, I stand and let them cut my bottom rocker off. The *Texas* patch is folded and put away, and one that reads "Nomad" is handed to me in return.

Pulling the small sewing kit from my inside pocket, I remove my cut and take a seat. The lighting out here is shitty. It would benefit me better to go inside. But there's something about the struggle that makes me feel like I'm more worthy.

Eight years ago, I sewed on my Prospect rocker, sitting in a field, in the middle of the night. The only lighting I had came from matches that I'd light and hold between my teeth until it burned my lips. It took four hundred and seventy-three stitches, six hours, and twelve needles, but I finally finished.

A year after that, I sewed my top rocker, bottom rocker, side rocker, full back piece, one-percenter patch, and number thirteen on while a whore named Gabby held a flashlight. That one took all night, and as soon as the sun rose, I was ordered inside back to the darkness again.

They say anything worth having is worth working for. I say, anything worth having is worth earning. Tonight, for the first time ever, I have my Nomad rocker. And I'm sure as fuck gonna earn it.

With every prick of my finger, I bleed love for Sinner's Creed. Pride swells in my chest with every stitch. My hands are numb. My eyes hurt. The pain in my back from my hunched-over state is almost unbearable—and I love every second of it.

Two hours later I'm finished. My patch is perfectly aligned, stitched to perfection. The tip of a knife can't fit between the threads. To cut it off, they'll have to pull it from my back and even then, it will be a struggle.

My cut feels heavier when I slide it over my shoulders. The weight is warm, welcome, and comforting. I'll wear it with honor. I'll wear it for Dirk. I'll do it justice. I'll make him proud.

The club is gathered around me. The feeling is overwhelming. I'm no longer just a patch holder. I'm not just another brother. I am the greatest thing I've ever been. I'll never be more than I am in this moment.

I am proud.

I am powerful.

I am his legacy.

I am Sinner's Creed Nomad National, Shady.

I hadn't given much thought to how being a Nomad would affect my time with Diem. I like her—a lot. But I love my club. There will never be a time I put her first. This is my life. If she wants a place in it, she'll have to settle for second.

Even though she's not my top priority, she's never far from my mind. I think about her every day. I miss her more than I should. I haven't been apart from her long enough for my absence to be questioned, but I know that's all fixing to change.

It's time for me to start making my presence known. Today, I'm in Los Angeles, where things are different. The brothers here are different too. They don't trust easily, and they don't take well to change. Dirk didn't care about their trust. It was his respect they had to earn, not the other way around. But I'm not Dirk. And they're not letting me forget it. I start to call Jimbo and ask him for a little advice on how to bring them down to size. But it's Diem's number that I dial instead.

"Well hello, stranger," she greets, and I smile.

"Where are you?" My first job as a Nomad isn't going as well as planned. Because of this, I find myself wishing I was at home and she was on her way over.

"I'm out of town on a business trip. Won't be back for a couple of days. Where are you?"

"Same. Meeting with some clients out west." I light a cigarette, listening to her vent about some work colleagues that can't seem to do their job, which means that she is called out to pick up their slack. Then about how she doesn't get the respect she deserves because everyone thinks they are in charge.

"I know the feeling. Sometimes, there are too many chiefs and not enough Indians," I say, stubbing out my cigarette and digging deep to find the courage to go back inside the Los Angeles chapter's clubhouse.

"True, but what they don't know is that I'm not a chief or an Indian. I'm a wolf . . . the one everybody should fear." She doesn't know it, but her words were just the kick in the ass I needed. It sounds just like something Dirk would say.

"Go be a wolf, pretty girl, and call me when you get home." I hang up and walk inside with a newfound confidence. This place is swarming with chiefs, but just like Diem, today I'm a motherfucking wolf.

"You did what?" Jimbo is pissed. The president of the Los Angeles chapter is in the hospital. And I'm at a gas station on my way back home.

"With all due respect, Jimbo, what the hell did you expect me to do? They didn't want to listen to me, and if I'm here to represent you and Sinner's Creed, then that means they disrespected all of us. Me, the patch, and Nationals. Now, if you want me to go back, apologize, and renege on everything I did, I will. But if what you want is an army you can trust and soldiers that know their place, then I suggest you back the fuck up off me."

I'm breathing hard. I'm beyond pissed. With every word, I became angrier. I didn't mean any disrespect toward Nationals, but they sent me to do a job and I did it. If my methods were too harsh for their sensitive little Los Angeles chapter, then next time they could send someone else to do it.

Jimbo's breathing is all I can hear on the line. I don't know if he's trying to calm down or preparing to tell me to come back so he can kill me. What I do know is that I'm in the right on this one. And I ain't backing down.

"If I didn't witness his burial with my own eyes, I'd swear I was talking to Dirk," he murmurs, more to himself than to me. "Get on down to Phoenix. And this time, try not to break any bones."

I don't make any promises.

"When are you coming home?" Diem asks a week later. She sounds like she's tired. And lonely. And missing me.

"Soon, pretty girl. Real soon," I lie. The truth is, I don't know when I'll be home. I'm starting to like the feeling of power that courses its way through my veins with every chapter I visit. I like the way my brothers look at me with a twinkle of respect in their eyes. I like it more than pussy, but I can't deny that I miss Diem.

"Well hurry the hell up. I'm starting to rethink this whole 'I'm yours' and 'you're mine' monogamous talk we had."

"So, if you're that desperate, then why are you still waiting on me?" I know her answer will probably be something about her giving her word. But what I want her to say is that I'm the only man she wants. That with me, it's different than it is with anyone else. That she has feelings for me that run deeper than sex. But, as always, she surprises me with words of truth.

"Because I know you'd kill them."

Damn right I would.

I'd been gone for twelve days. Not one day had passed that I didn't talk to Diem. It was nice to hear her voice, but it was never enough. I wanted to see her. Touch her. Sleep with her. At this point, I don't even care about the sex—I just miss her.

My club wanted me to start making my presence known all around the country. First was Los Angeles, then Phoenix and Albuquerque. The days were exhausting, the nights long, and by the time I make it back, I'm so tired mentally and physically that all I want to do is sleep. I'm sunburned, my ass hurts, and my nuts are still vibrating from the endless hours on my bike. But I'm home, and she's here—waiting on me naked and in my bed. It's a welcome-home present I didn't realize I needed until this moment.

Her olive skin seems to glow against the million-dollar white comforter. Her black hair is messy and matches the thick, black eyeliner she wears. Long, red nails match her perfectly painted toes, and she looks like sin just laying here waiting for me.

I take my time crawling on the bed between her thighs. I drag my hand slowly up her smooth calf, trailing it up her stomach, her chest, her neck, until I'm holding her face and kissing her like I missed her. Like I can't get enough. Because I did. I can't.

We don't speak, we just fuck—soft and slow, hard and fast, in every position until we both collapse from exhaustion. Then I hold her. And I realize that sleep has never come as easy as it does with her in my arms.

We're still in bed. It's sometime in the middle of the night and we're eating crackers and drinking beer. Naked. She's telling me about how being a wolf worked out in her favor. I tell her the same, only a little more evasively.

"I didn't realize being a pharmaceutical sales rep could be so challenging." I smirk. She narrows her eyes on me, clearly pissed with my choice of words.

"And being a website designer, for a company that you run is?" She shakes her head. "You know I don't buy that bullshit. I just go along with it because I know that whatever it is you're hiding must be pretty important." I just smile, not letting my eyes give anything away.

"Actually, I run a large company. It's worldwide. I have a lot of people who work under me. Most have never even met me before. So, when a guy like me shows up and demands respect, you can imagine why they're a little hesitant." I snatch a cracker from the pack lying on her belly. "But you . . . you just sell drugs."

"Actually," she says, coming to a sitting position. "I sell drugs to a number of companies. And unlike you, I work for a corporation where there are lots of employees who are on the same level as me. The difference between me and them is that I want to make my way to the top. They want to stay exactly where they are, so they throw their workload on me because they have nothing to lose."

"Maybe you shouldn't be so ambitious."

"Or maybe I should just become barefoot and pregnant and let some man take care of me like my mother did." She offers me a sardonic smile, and even though I didn't mean to, I somehow struck a nerve. The mood seems to shift at the mention of her mother, but she wouldn't have brought her up if she didn't want to talk about it.

"Do you really hate her?" I ask, wiping a crumb from the corner of her lip.

She frowns. "No. Not at all. But I've always been a daddy's girl." Her eyes seem to brighten as she continues. "When I was little, he used to take me to all his business meetings. I became obsessed with the company. He was so powerful and demanding. I used to practice his facial expressions in the mirror. Eventually, I perfected them."

"Where is he now?"

Her eyes narrow as she peels the label from the beer bottle in her hands. "He's still around. I'm just not his little girl anymore."

"Do y'all still speak?"

She nods. "When we can. It's complicated."

"Doesn't seem complicated," I counter, letting her know her excuses don't pacify me.

"Well, when you're surrounded by guards and guns and people telling you what you can and can't do, it is. You want another beer?" she asks, changing the subject.

"Sure." I watch her naked hips sway as she walks out. *Prison* must have been too hard of a word for her to say. I guess having a father locked up was about as bad as not having one at all.

She comes back with the beer, and my eyes zoom in on her tits as they bounce when she literally jumps back on the bed. "What about your parents?" she asks, twisting the top off and handing the bottle to me.

"I don't have any." I turn up the beer, helping it wash away the reminder. When I look at her, she sits expectantly, waiting for me to elaborate. "I was born a ward of the state. You know those movies where people drop their babies off on the doorsteps of an orphanage? Well that shit happens in real life too."

"But you have a family," she says, and I remember I told her my family was the reason I was away for so long.

"Adoptive family. They took me in, when I was older. Helped me get on the right path." I look down at my beer bottle, unable to meet her eyes. I'm not lying to her, I'm just not telling the whole truth. In my book, that's the same damn thing.

"Family is family. And at the end of the day, your family is all you have." Like she's done so many times before, her words are rehearsed—like she's been told that her whole life.

"That's some Mafia shit right there," I say, tilting my beer to her.

She laughs. "I guess I've been watching too much *Scarface*. What can I say? I love Al Pacino."

"Want to shay 'ello to my lil' friend?" I ask in my best Tony Montana voice.

She pulls her lip between her teeth, crawling seductively across the bed and straddling my lap. "I thought you'd never ask."

19

IT'S MIDNIGHT. DIEM is laying in my bed, the covers tangled at her feet. And I'm just standing in the doorway watching her sleep. There's something about it that's peaceful—a peace I've never experienced.

My duffel is slung over my shoulder. I'm dressed in black. Rookie is waiting just down the road for me. After the fight with Death Mob in the nightclub, I made the decision to step away for a while. It gave me time to handle shit with the club, but now, it's time to focus on my ultimate goal. And tonight, we're going to make a kill.

Take a life.

Seek revenge.

Bring hell to those that wronged my brother and my best friend.

But tonight, it feels different. Because for the first time, I don't want to kill. I don't want revenge. I don't care about Death Mob. I love Dirk, but I'm tired of fighting this battle.

I just want to crawl back in bed with Diem. I want to spend my nights with her wrapped around me. I want to spend my days laughing with her. I'd rather argue with her over something as simple as who left the light on than avenge the death of my brother. I was fucked up, and I was falling hard.

Pulling the door closed behind me, I ease out of the house, then jog down the road toward Rookie's waiting truck. Midstride, I let my emotions get the best of me. I let all the feelings I've been shoving to the back of my brain finally surface.

I don't just like Diem.

I'm not just infatuated with her.

This isn't just a fling or a lay.

This is something bigger . . . something better . . . something I just can't shake . . .

I'm not just falling hard, fast, deeply and madly for Diem . . .

I'm falling in love with her.

"You look different," Rookie says, eyeing me warily when I get in the truck.

"I just had a revelation." Admitting it should be hard, but if anybody gets it, Rookie will. "I'm in love with Diem."

"No shit you are," he says, acting like the news is old to him. "But you know it will never work."

I jerk my head to look at him. "What the fuck? What kind of shit is that? I just told you I was in love with a woman. You . . . the most pussy-whooped man I know, and you have the balls to tell me it won't work?"

"That's what I said. You're too selfish, Shady. And you have no remorse for your actions. You're a cold-blooded killer whose only mission in life is to avenge the death of a brother who would tell you the same thing if he were alive."

I shake my head. "No, Dirk wouldn't say that. He'd be happy for me. See, that's the difference between you and him." I turn away from him, gritting my teeth. "What makes you think you deserve love and I don't?"

"Because my woman knows nothing about what I do. She only sees the good side of me, because that's all I let her see. But Diem?" he says, letting out a loud breath. "She won't be that easy to pacify. She'll dig until she finds something, then she'll rip your heart out and ruin you and the club. It can't happen."

As much as I want to deny it, Rookie is right. It didn't matter how coldhearted Diem seemed to be. If she ever figured out the monster I really was, she'd ruin us all. Carrie and Saylor had something in common—they were both innocent and naïve. Diem was nothing like that. She'd get to the bottom of it. She might not care right now, but months or years from now, she would.

"You're playing with fire. You better end it while you still can." Rookie's advice hits me right in the heart—that one organ that I'd finally decided to listen to only moments ago. But as much as I want to, I know I can't. I have the power to do a lot of things, but letting Diem go isn't one of them. I was playing with fire.

But getting burned never felt so good.

We killed six men that night. It was a bloody, fucked-up battle that turned south because my head wasn't in the game. Too anxious to get back to Diem, I started shooting the moment I laid eyes on Death Mob. Somehow, Sinner's Creed managed to walk away unscathed. Lucky for us, Tank and Cleft were in town and helped clean up the mess before anyone witnessed anything. It was after noon when I got home and Diem had already left.

I exhausted myself with exercise. I butchered the punching bag in my shed until my fists were bloody and I nearly had to crawl inside. My mind was in overdrive. My heart felt like it had already been ripped to shreds. Now I'm on the phone with

Nationals and the news they're giving me is worse than any feeling I could have ever imagined.

"They know."

Two little words had just ruined my whole life. I knew who "they" were—Death Mob. Sinner's Creed wanted me in Jackpot in the morning. It might very well be my last time there. Rookie comes over to tell me that he was called in too. I assured him he had nothing to worry about. This blood was on my hands. I knew getting into this that my life would be the penalty if I ever got found out.

Now I had.

My life was at stake.

And I was ready to give it.

I believed in my mission, and for the most part I accomplished it. Over sixty members of Death Mob had been killed. It didn't destroy their club, but it damn sure made them bleed. I'd won. Dirk had won. Sinner's Creed had won. The price to pay was worth it all.

My only regret was Diem. This wasn't fair to her. She hasn't said it, but I know she loves me. I should break her heart so that her memory of me won't hurt her. But I can't do that. Instead, I call and invite her over like nothing is wrong.

I'm anxious by the time she arrives. I haven't seen her in days and when she walks in, I feel the full impact of the saying, "Absence makes the heart grow fonder." She's all business in a white pantsuit and matching heels. She looks stunning, but tired and overworked.

"Rough day at the office?" I smirk, grabbing her duffel from off her shoulder. Pulling her down with me, we sit in our usual position in the recliner. She kicks her heels off, rubbing her feet up and down my jean-clad leg.

"Something like that . . . You?" She nods her head toward my laptop and the scattered papers around it I'd planted just for her to see.

"Nah . . . just being a nerd." We watch a couple of westerns, enjoying the silent company. But after a while, I know I can't postpone it any longer.

"I'm leaving tomorrow," I tell her, feeling her head nod into my chest. "I'm not coming back." Slowly, she drags her head up until she is looking at me—searching my eyes for humor, or doubt, or any other emotion that's not truth.

"Where are you going?" she whispers. I close my eyes, memorizing the sound of her voice—something Dirk did when he knew Saylor was soon going to leave him.

I cradle my hand around her face, whispering back to her. "I just have to go."

She shakes her head. "But I don't want you to go."

Fuck.

"I live a really messed-up life, Diem. There is a lot of darkness and pain. I cause a lot of that. But I've never regretted it. Never felt bad about the people I hurt." I swallow, letting Rookie's definition of me resurface in my brain. "I'm not a forgiving guy. I don't have remorse for my actions. I'm selfish and reckless and tarnished."

"But you're not like that with me," she cuts in, her body curling deeper into my side.

I smile. "No. I'm not."

"Why?"

At first, I'm not sure what to say. But something is happening inside me. I'm overwhelmed with a feeling. A feeling so intense that it stretches my heart to the point of bursting. My chest expands with pride as the knowledge registers in my brain. *I love her.* I already knew this, but for the first time, I really believe it. Love is a feeling that cannot just be felt, it has to be expressed—it has to be said, and my throat burns with the desire to tell her. So, I do. Without hesitation.

"Because I love you, Diem."

She melts in my arms from relief. It's like she's been waiting for me to tell her this—like she needed to hear me say it to reassure her that this is the same feeling she has too. Her eyes become shiny with unshed tears as she gazes up at me with a look of longing. This is a Diem I don't know. This is the first time I've ever seen her like this. And it will be the last.

"I love you too," she breathes, and I can relate to her feeling of relief. She'd just changed my whole fucking life with three little words.

She loves me.

And suddenly, that's all that matters.

I made love to Diem after that. We were the picture-perfect, Hallmark-card couple for the remainder of the night. But now it's morning and I have to leave. And that sweet couple from last night is long gone.

"I'm not cooking shit. I've done told you that."

"Babe," I coo, grabbing her around the waist in the kitchen.

She stomps my foot, causing me to release her before unleashing her wrath on me once again. "What did I tell you about those pet names? If you're hungry, eat some cereal."

"We don't have any milk," I spit through my teeth, hopping around the kitchen on one foot.

"Well then take us out for breakfast."

"Fine, I will," I snap. And I do.

"So," she starts, picking at her eggs. We're in the Hillsborough Diner, in our same booth, and she has barely touched any of her food. "You're really leaving." I nod, staring at her, but she avoids my gaze. "I meant it when I said I didn't want you to leave."

"I meant it when I said I love you," I tell her, offering her a smile when she raises her big dark eyes to mine.

"I know. I just don't understand. Is this really good-bye?" I look away, watching as Rookie pulls into the parking lot. He's here . . . ready to take me to my doom.

I reach across the table, taking her hand in mine. She looks at our fingers, entwined together. "Look at me, Diem." She does and I can see the hurt and confusion there, and I hate it has to be this way. I hate that I hurt her. And that I lied. "If things were different, I'd spend the rest of my life arguing with you. I'd let you cook me shitty eggs every morning."

She smiles, shaking her head. "You know that will never happen."

My smile dies when I realize that it won't. "In another life, I could have made you happy. Really happy. I'd have done things different. I'd have made you my queen." Rookie's horn sounds and I know if I don't leave now, we'll miss our flight.

I stand and grab my bag. Handing her the keys to my truck, I shoot her a wink. Then, I leave her with my signature good-bye . . . the last one she will ever hear from me. "See ya around, pretty girl."

20

DIEM

HE WALKED OUT the door and I realized he really was the one . . .

The one who'd just broke my heart.

21

SHADY

AT THE BAR in Jackpot, we're all gathered for the meeting. There is no round table with our emblem in the center or thick, wooden doors separating us from the outside world. Instead, we're on a patio sitting on coolers and broken chairs, smoking blunts and cigarettes and drinking beer. This concrete slab is where all important National matters have been handled since the beginning of time. Today, it feels no different.

"Dorian wants a meet," Jimbo says, still unable to look me in the eyes. "Death Mob contacted them, said they had proof that Sinner's Creed was killing their guys. They want to wage a war, but Dorian wants to hear everyone out first. Says he has an announcement to make and we all need to be there."

Dorian is the king. Not just of the Underground Mafia, but of every organized crime gang in the States. Everybody answers to him. But Sinner's Creed and Death Mob are the two biggest affiliates and produce the most revenue. If he's calling a meet with us, something big is about to go down.

"I suspect that Death Mob is going to present their case. They're gonna want you, Shady, just like they wanted Dirk." For the first time, he looks at me. His eyes are dull and lifeless.

This is a part of his job that we all hate. But I'm a soldier. So I ease my leader's mind by telling him, "I'm ready." And I am.

"Rookie," Jimbo calls, and Rookie appears from the back corner of the patio. "I need to know where you stand."

"I stand with Sinner's Creed." The words are hard for him to say. He's just admitted that he won't take the fall. That even if I go down, he will stand and say nothing. Because the club needs him alive. It proves his loyalty to the club, and to me. I would expect no less of him. This is one of those trying moments I trained him for.

"Good. Meet's tomorrow. Stay the fuck outta sight."

Rookie and I ride to Dirk's house. I still haven't had the courage to go inside, but now I have no choice. Pushing open the door, the scent of citrus surrounds me, and one step over the threshold, I stop and take it all in. Covers still litter the floor from our last night in this house together. It was a sleepover that sounds absolutely ridiculous, but was exactly what Saylor wanted, so it's what we did.

I walk through the living room, glancing into the kitchen and small dining area before walking down the hall. Their room is untouched. Fuck, I miss him. The pain seemed to dissipate somewhat when I was with Diem. She filled the void in my life when Dirk left. Now she was gone too. Soon, so would I. There was no need to dwell on the ache in my chest from Dirk leaving. Because tomorrow, I'd be joining him.

Silence—it's deafening.

And I feel like I'm the only one that hears it. It's like someone has hit the pause button on my life, and I'm having an out-of-body experience, watching the scene unfold before me. Eight black, steel horses ride six inches apart in two straight lines down an open highway. Their riders are dressed in black. Full face helmets hide their identities. There is no way of knowing who we are, until the dark blur of our posse passes. Then the colors of Sinner's Creed patches that cover our backs are shown proudly.

We are earth's hell. If there are those that don't fear us, they damn well should. We're the outcasts. The forgotten. The bad guys. The one percent of those who don't give a fuck. We are evil. We appear to stand still, while everyone else rushes away from us, out of fear, praying that we'll hurry and pass them by. That's how much power Sinner's Creed exudes.

This is why we do this. This is why we chose this life. We are superior. We feel immortal. And we are lethal. Everybody wants to feel important, and we're the motherfuckers that you have to prove something to.

And on what could be my final ride, I look at myself as I ride free and open down the highway surrounded by my brothers, and ask one question. Was it worth it? And behind my helmet, I nod. And I tell myself, "You damn right it was."

In the small town of Taylor, Nebraska, just off the North Loup River, is a warehouse. It belongs to the Underground Mafia and is used for storage of products until they're ready for distribution. Dorian pays well for the piece of private property that can't be located on any map. Few people know about its location, and they won't say anything in fear of dying or not getting paid.

Two unmarked, black SUVs sit at the gate when we arrive. A man who could give Tank a run for his money steps out and waves us through. When we pull inside the warehouse, I take full count of all the guns including the men standing guard on the second level.

The sound of our pipes reverberates off the metal walls of the large, empty building. We're directed to the right and straight across from us, within spitting distance, stands ten very proud Death Mob members. Front and center is Cyrus, the very soon to be dead killer of my brother.

Silence descends as one by one we shut off our bikes. My fingers twitch to put a bullet between the eyes of Cyrus, but I refrain. If I don't, I'll have to watch as my brothers die too. I'll have my chance very soon. I might die today, but that motherfucker is going with me.

We stand in front of our bikes, glaring at our enemies across from us. Everyone wears the same pissed-off look—all but Cyrus, who smiles like he knows some fucking secret the rest of us don't.

I hear the sound of tires on gravel moments before a black stretch limousine pulls into view. Several of the guards rush to surround the car and I can tell by their actions that this is the infamous Dorian none of us have ever seen. One of the goons opens the door and he steps out. He looks familiar, but I can't quite place him. He's tall, Greek, wears a suit worth more than my Harley, and has an air about him that informs us all that he is the man in charge. The only thing he's missing is a cigar and a beer gut.

His black eyes quickly scan the room, warning us all with his pissed-off look. Men fear him, now I see why. He's intimidating as fuck. His back straightens as he buttons he suit jacket, then he reaches his hand back into the car. I watch with curiosity as an olive-toned leg wearing a red high heel steps out moments before the woman becomes visible.

She's beautiful.

She's powerful.

She's sexy.

Intimidating.

Cold.

Lethal . . .

She's Diem.

My heart stops. The world stills. I try to swallow the lump in my throat, but I can't force it back down. My instincts tell me to go to her. To protect her. Although, she doesn't look like she needs protecting. She exudes as much power and authority as Dorian. I don't know what she's doing here, but judging by the determination on her face, she's here to prove something. And just when I think shit can't get any worse, Dorian speaks.

"My new second in command," he announces, his voice low and raspy and more threatening than I could have imagined. "My daughter, Diem."

I can feel Rookie burning holes in my back. I turn to look at him, giving him a small shake of my head before looking away. I can tell he's confused as fuck, and so am I. I'm fighting to keep my shit in check. I don't know if I should feel heartbroken, betrayed, or horny. She'd once told me she was someone important. She sure as fuck wasn't lying about that.

She looks exquisite in a long dress with a slit that travels all the way up her thigh. And it's blood red—her favorite color. Her eyes are cold, her expression unreadable, and she scans the crowd but has yet to notice me. When she finally does, she lingers on my face a second longer than anyone else. The only thing she gives away is the slight rise of her right eyebrow, then her gaze moves on. That one moment is all I need to know that she is just as surprised to see me here as I am to see her.

"My friends," Dorian starts, clasping his hands in front of him. Diem stands to his right, keeping her attention focused on anyone who isn't me, but not being obvious about it. Following her lead, I focus my attention on Dorian and try to regain control over my wandering mind. But her words keep flashing through my head.

"I'm not his little girl anymore . . ."

Not because he was in prison. Because he was her boss.

"I called you all here today for a few different reasons," Dorian continues, the powerful sound of his voice forcing me to forget my thoughts and pay attention. "First of all, it seems that the two of you are having some issues."

His eyes move to Cyrus, who gives him a nod of confirmation. Then, like the fool he is, Cyrus speaks. "That's right. We have some big issues." He looks over at me, then spits, and I roll my neck, feeling my blood rush faster and faster to my head. Now I have Dorian's attention.

"Him?" Dorian asks, pointing a finger at me. Diem looks in my direction, but her gaze seems to go straight through me. "Would you like me to go ahead and kill him now?" he asks Cyrus. I don't flinch, and neither does Diem. She remains impassive and completely detached. Either what we had was never real, or she's a damn good actress. I'm hoping like hell it's her acting skills.

"I'd like to do the honors," Cyrus says, and it's enough to break my concentration with Diem and smirk at him. But I'm smart enough to keep my mouth shut.

"Business first." Dorian walks forward, leaving Diem next to the car as he takes center stage. "I didn't get where I am by making fast, irrational decisions. I think everything through. And I'm a very patient man." He places his hands behind his back, walking in large circles and gliding through the thick tension in the room as if it's nothing but clouds.

"Some people believe I'm immortal. But of course, that isn't true. I won't live forever, but my empire will. So I decided that the best way for what I have spent my whole life preserving to survive is to implement some change. My change begins with my daughter, Diem." He offers Diem a smile that doesn't reach his eyes. I'm surprised he even knows how. "From now on, you will answer to her.

And you will do well to remember that she holds as much power as I do. I will only warn you once. Underestimating her will be a very deadly mistake." No shit it would. Hell, I could have told them that.

On cue, Diem walks forward. I'm still reeling, unable to pry my eyes off the woman I love. The woman I held in my arms. The woman who made me laugh. The woman who I never thought I'd see again. All her softness is gone. Her vulnerability lost. She can't show weakness here, and neither can I. Even if she is standing in those high heels looking more fuckable than I remember.

I inhale and try to focus. Forcing myself to look away from her, I notice the men in the room. Every eye is trained on her body. The lust and want is evident in all of them—even my brothers. I want to tell them all to keep their fucking eyes off what belongs to me. I want to tell them that she is *my* woman, and I'll kill any motherfucker who tries to cross me. But there's something in the back of my head that's telling me I might be wrong—she might not be mine at all.

"Cyrus," she says, and I nearly groan at the sound of the ice in her voice. I want to throw her in the back of that limo and stick my fingers and tongue and cock in her until she speaks in that breathy tone I love.

"Yes ma'am," he drawls, already underestimating her. I want to kill him more for showing her disrespect than for murdering my brother. The thought is unsettling, but I dismiss it—knowing if anybody can cut him down to size, my girl can. That is, if she's still my girl.

She turns to walk back to the center of the floor, her lips pursed while she nods her head. I know that look. Something bad is fixing to happen. "I know that the transition for all of you will be difficult. But, I don't care. I'm not sympathetic to your egos. If anyone has a problem with a woman being in charge, the door is open for you to leave."

She gives us about three seconds to make up our minds, then continues. "That's what I thought. Cyrus, you claim that Sinner's Creed has been murdering your men. Do you have proof?"

I level Cyrus with a look, and can tell by his expression that he don't have shit. "I don't have any physical proof, no. But I do know that Shady has been MIA here lately and the days he wasn't accounted for coincide with the dates my brothers went missing."

"Shady?" she asks, and I remember that she only knows me as Zeke.

"Him." Cyrus points to me, and when she turns, a flash of fear is in her eyes, but she quickly conceals it with a smile. Being a gentlemen and all, I smile back.

"Shady, huh?" Diem asks, her voice low but loud enough for everyone to hear. "Do you have any specific dates?" She keeps her eyes on me as Cyrus rattles off a bunch of dates. She quirks an eyebrow and I realize she's doing the math in her head. Unable to verbally defend myself, I straighten and clench my jaw, trying to remind myself to keep my mouth shut.

"I can find people to vouch for that if you need me to," Cyrus offers, digging my grave a little deeper.

"No need. I'm sure those dates are accurate." She gives me her most threatening look and I have to bite my cheek to keep from smirking.

"So, you know I'm right," Cyrus boasts, and I'm surprised he doesn't give his VP a high fucking five.

Diem ignores him, then spits out another question. "Why would Shady want to kill your men?" She's pissed now, although I think it's more toward me than anyone.

"Because I killed his brother," Cyrus answers, his voice deadpan as he looks at me over the top of Diem's head.

"So turnabout isn't fair play?"

"No. His brother and him killed twelve of my men. We offered a deal, but they refused. They sacrificed one of their own for money. They were warned."

My hands fist and I feel Jimbo's hand come to rest on my shoulder. It's not to hold me back, because a bulldozer couldn't do that. It's a gesture of comfort or warning, I'm just not sure which.

"I see. And what was the name of this brother you killed?" Diem asks.

"Dirk." I close my eyes at the sound of my brother's name on that motherfucker's lips.

"Dirk Dixon, right?"

He nods, and I feel the air shift in the room. The tension between Death Mob and Sinner's Creed is unfathomable. But there's something else too. I look around and notice that the guards seem to stand a little taller. Dorian seems to get a little colder, and Diem's fingers twitch behind her back.

"Enough," Dorian barks, and we watch as he walks across the floor, grabs a member of Death Mob, and pushes him to his knees. Pulling a gun from his back, he walks behind him and puts a bullet behind his right shoulder. The man's screams echo off the walls as he falls to his side in pain. Then Dorian points the gun at the man's head and pulls the trigger. The only sound is the ringing in everyone's ears.

"Is that how you killed him?" Dorian asks, the sound of his voice wavering slightly. Before Cyrus can speak, the man next to him is shot and falls dead at his feet.

"Yes!" Cyrus yells, his own voice breaking at the sight of his two dead brothers.

Dorian tucks the gun behind his jacket before turning and addressing the whole room. "Do any of you know what happens when a man with as much power as me has a son?" Nobody answers, or even breathes, but you can hear the wheels spinning in everyone's head. "He doesn't get to live. My brothers, they all died before they could step in for me because they were murdered. Killed by my enemies and by my own. People don't like change. They are scared of it. So they do what they feel like they have to, to survive."

"My children were the light of my life. I prayed every day that my wife would give me a daughter so that my son wouldn't suffer the same fate as so many others. My prayers were answered, and on the same day my worst fear came true. My wife had twins, a boy and a girl. So I developed a plan. A plan that would change the face of my business. A plan that would allow my daughter to carry on my legacy, because she wouldn't be seen as a threat and would be allowed to live to an age where she could protect herself. A plan that would give my son life—life provided by a family who took care of their own. A family like yours." He points to us, and I feel like my heart has been ripped from my chest all over again.

"My plan worked for so many years. But you," he says, pointing to Cyrus. "You destroyed that. You didn't take the life of a member of Sinner's Creed. You didn't take the life of Dirk Dixon. You took the life of Dirk Demopolous—my son."

My heart hammers against my chest at his admission. I can't believe my ears. *Holy fucking shit.* Dirk was Dorian's son. Diem was Dorian's daughter. Dirk was Diem's brother. And I'd been fucking his sister. If he were alive, he'd kill me.

Dirk's life was doomed from the beginning. His family couldn't protect him. And neither could his club.

A wave of emotions seems to crash through the warehouse. Sinner's Creed—guilt and heartache. Death Mob—fear and regret. Dorian—grief and failure. I look at Diem, and her eyes hold the same emotion I felt in my heart at Dirk's death—pain. "Please, hear me out," Cyrus begs, his hands folding before his chest like the coward he is. "We gave them a choice. Dirk's death isn't on my hands. It's on theirs." I start toward him, but Jimbo grabs one arm and Chaps grabs the other when I reach for my pistol. Dorian turns toward me, his look unreadable.

"He killed twelve of my men," Cyrus continues. "They did nothing to warrant death, but he killed them in cold blood."

"You initiated the fight by finding his weakness," Diem adds. I can hear the grit in her tone, but Dorian's gaze paralyzes me and I can't look at her.

"But we gave them a choice."

Dorian holds his hand up, silencing Cyrus, and speaks to me. "Tell me he's lying."

I shove my brother's hands from my shoulders, and reluctantly they let me go. "The choice was Texas or Dirk's life. Dirk knew that if Sinner's Creed lost Texas that the club would fold. As a Sinner's Creed National he had a say in the decision. He knew the woman he loved was dying and he couldn't live in a world where she didn't exist or the club didn't exist. So he sacrificed himself." I pause, fighting to control my anger and emotions. I didn't like speaking about Dirk's death like it was nothing more than a means to an end. He was a fucking human being. He was my brother. My friend.

"We couldn't stop him. And we wouldn't have tried, because he had more pride and honor than any man I've ever met. And what he did was the same thing you've done. He protected his family, his empire, and did what he had to do to ensure that his legacy lived on."

Dorian's eyes narrow, his expression more thoughtful, and I'm sure it's because I've said words about his son that make him proud. The regret in his face shows, and I know that's because I know more about his own son than he did.

"Why did you take on this battle, knowing that you would lose? That you would die?" His question catches me off guard, but I don't have to struggle to find an answer. The truth comes as easy as breathing.

"Because he's my family." He nods, but I'm not finished yet.

"I'm not like you. I'm not a coward." Jimbo grows still next to me, as Dorian's eyes narrow further, making them seem colder and deadlier. Chaps calls my name in warning, but I ignore him.

My next words will either kill me or save my life. But the outcome doesn't matter. I've got something to say and I'm fucking saying it.

"I don't send my family away out of fear. I fight for them. I honor them. I keep my word to them. And either I'll succeed, or I'll fucking die trying."

I stand tall as he walks toward me. I'm not intimidated by him. If anything, I feel peace. The same peace I felt with Diem. Dorian looks like Dirk. He walks like Dirk. Talks like Dirk. And Diem, she's Dirk in a woman's form. This is his blood. His father and his sister. I'd show Dorian respect if he deserved it, but I stand firm behind my words. I'd called him out, and if he kills me, then it will prove that not only is he a coward, but that he is too weak to handle the truth.

"You're ballsy. You know that?" he asks, a lethal gleam in his eyes, but I see a hint of respect there too. "But you're right. I am a coward. I took the easy way out. But one day you will have children of your own, and you will find that sometimes being a coward is worth more than your pride." He looks at my brothers, taking a moment to stare each of them in the eyes. "I thank you for what you did. And it gives me great honor to know that my son was so well loved and respected. If he was the man you say he was, then I couldn't be more proud of him than I am in this moment."

With a lift of his chin, several men surround the members of Death Mob, knocking them all to their knees. He looks down at Cyrus, who's fighting hard to keep his shit together. "I've waited months to do this. But now that everything is in place, I want you to know what is fixing to happen," Dorian starts, drawing the words out painfully slow. "You are going to die. Your club will cease to exist. Sinner's Creed will take over your territory and Death Mob will not even be a memory. Killing your men will not bring my son back, but it will bring me great joy."

"Dorian," Jimbo calls, and I take a deep breath as I prepare for what he is fixing to say. "With all due respect, I believe that

Cyrus's life should be taken by us. I believe I'm standing next to a brother who deserves this honor." As my eyes meet Dorian's, I think about Dirk. About what this means for his death. But more than that, I think about Diem. She'd just found out who I was. She knows that I'm a killer. That I'm a monster. That I have an incurable disease that blackens my soul. But she's never watched me pull the trigger. And more than anything, I'm afraid that once she witnesses what I'm capable of, she will never be able to remember me as the man I was with her—only as a monster.

I drag my gaze to Diem, whose face is completely unreadable. I try to ask her with my eyes what she will think of me, but she gives nothing away. I've never seen her so distant. It's as if she's trying to remain unattached, especially in this moment.

"I understand that, Jimbo. But you see, I've already promised this to someone else. And I never make a promise that I don't keep." Dorian hands the gun to Diem, who offers him a nod. She's not nervous or shaky and there is no fear in her eyes, only a burning desire for the same thing I've been wanting for months—revenge.

She steps in front of Cyrus without hesitation, then lifts her arm. And just like that—boom, the bullet hits him right between his eyes.

His body falls limply to the floor. A weight seems to lift off me at the sight. But it's replaced by a feeling of remorse for Diem. Moments pass before she looks away, and her eyes seek me out. She holds my gaze, telling me everything she can't say in words. I see her past. I feel her pain. And my soul rejoices with hers.

I know who she is. I see myself in her eyes. I realize that in this moment, I have nothing to worry about. Diem will not look at me any different. She can't. Because just like me, my woman, my love, my Diem, is a cold-blooded killer too.

22

THE RIDE BACK to Jackpot is silent—and I appreciate the hell out of it. My thoughts come clearer at a hundred miles per hour down an open highway than anywhere else. The first one, I'm still trying to wrap my head around.

I'm alive.

I'd woke up this morning thinking it would be my last day on earth. Part of me was relieved. I would finally get that sense of peace I'd always longed for. But fate had different plans. Which reminds me of the second thought that's in my head and weighs heavy on my heart.

Diem.

The *Mafiusa*.

She's not a pharmaceutical sales rep—she's a fucking drug dealer. Her daddy's not in prison—he's the don of the Underground Mafia. She's not powerful and persuasive and conniving because she's a bitch—it's because her life made her that way.

And even though she's not who I thought she was, I still love her. Maybe even more now than I did then.

She gets me. She understands my lifestyle. I'll never have to hide anything from her. But in the back of my subconscious, I know that she isn't like me. She's more than me. She's my fucking boss.

I wait for the blow to my ego that never comes. If anything, I'm turned on by her authority. I was in love with the most powerful woman in organized crime. Yesterday, she was in love with me too. I just hope like hell that doesn't change.

The club is still in shock over the turn of events. Relieved, thankful, nervous, and skeptical. But above all, we're proud that justice has finally been served. We're in Jackpot, at the clubhouse, on the patio. We're not finished smoking our first welcome home cigarette when Chaps finally asks what's on everybody's mind.

"So, what's up with you and Dorian's daughter?"

All eyes turn to me, waiting for the juicy gossip like a bunch of women in a beauty shop. I feel a heaviness in my chest at the mention of her. Truth is, I don't know what's up. After she pulled that trigger, I wanted nothing more than to go to her. But, she'd warned me off with a look, then left with Dorian.

"I saw those looks she was giving you. You hit that or something?" Chaps pushes, and I level him with a look.

"Mind your own fucking business," I warn before stomping back inside. At the bar, I can't seem to do anything to calm my nerves. I become more restless by the minute. Downing some shots, I wait impatiently for the liquor to help numb my brain, but nothing is working. Rookie takes a seat next to me, offering his silence as comfort and surprisingly, it helps.

"What if what we had wasn't real?" I ask, loud enough for only him to hear.

"It was real. Trust me." Rookie shoots a wink to one of the

topless bartenders who hands him a baggie and some rolling papers. "Just give it a little time. Looks like she's gonna need some."

"No shit she's gonna need some. She's in the fucking Mafia, Rookie."

He shrugs, focused on his task at hand. "And you're an outlaw. But there is good news." He licks the blunt before rolling it tightly and handing it to me. "You can forget all that shit I said about it not working. Now she knows everything." He claps me on my back, striking a lighter. Maybe he's right. Maybe it can work. And three hits later, my problems with Diem are a distant memory.

Soon, the celebration that we're not only still alive, but now over the entire U.S., is in full swing. Monica was told to call in some extra help for the next few days, and chapter members from all around were pouring in by the minute.

It's an all-night party and in the early hours of the next morning, we're still going strong. The women are topless, the liquor is chilled, and the music is good. But my buzz is fading and Diem is resurfacing in my mind.

Aware that something is bothering me, Rookie attempts to snap me out of my depression. "Maybe you should call her."

"I'm not calling her," I snap, not intending to be a dick but acting like one.

"Fine," he says, giving me a few minutes of silence before coming up with another suggestion to ease my troubles. "Want me to get Monica to take you out back?"

"Fuck no," I groan.

Rookie laughs and slides me a shot. "Just offering."

Moments later, I notice that the noise has died down significantly. Rookie elbows me and I turn to see six men wearing suits standing just inside the door.

"Can I do anything for y'all?" Monica purrs in her fake southern accent.

"Yeah. Put a fucking shirt on." Diem emerges from the crowd of men and scans the room until she finds me. Her eyes narrow and I notice that another one of the topless girls is standing across from me with her natural DDs propped up on the counter. "Do you bitches not have clothes?"

Damn, I love when she's pissed. She looks so fucking sexy in that little red dress that I just want to rip to shreds. Then I want to throw her on this bar and fuck her in front of everybody and let them know that this one is mine. I'm sexually frustrated, hanging by a thin rope, and she's doing nothing but being the infuriating, delicious goddess she always is.

I want her more than ever. The look she's giving me tells me she wants me too. The electricity crackles between us. Everyone around us is forgotten. If they're looking, I don't notice. All I see is her. Fire blazes in her eyes. She exudes power. She's a walking, talking, bitching, underboss Mafia fucking queen. And until she tells me different, she's mine.

I hold her gaze as I stand, telling her I want to kiss her. Lick her. Fuck her until nothing else matters. Then I walk away from the crowd and toward the bedrooms at the back of the clubhouse—knowing damn well that she'll follow.

Over the noise, I can hear the click of her heels. She wants me. She wants this. She needs me and I fucking need her too. Standing just inside the door, I wait for her to appear. When she does, I jerk her in before slamming it shut and pushing her against the wall.

She grips the back of my neck, pulling my mouth down to hers. I groan at the feel of her warm tongue brushing over mine. My hands move up her hips, pulling her dress around her waist and ripping her panties from her body.

There are no words. No pleas, demands, games, deals, challenges . . . No Mafia, clubs, daddies, brothers, goons, or whores.

It's just me and her and the desire to fuck like crazy animals—just like we first did, and exactly how we want it.

The closest thing to us is a dresser. I lift her on it before pulling my dick from my jeans. She whimpers at the sight of it. I drag my fingers down my tongue, wetting them before rubbing them across her pussy that is already drenched.

"Fuck," I growl, lifting her from the dresser and sinking my cock inside her. Her breath catches in her throat as I fill her completely. Her eyes widen with shock and pleasure and before she can adapt, I'm pulling out and driving in again.

"Is this how you want me to fuck you?" I growl, knowing she won't be able to answer. Her moans are guttural. Her eyes roll back in her head. Those sexy heels are scarring my ass. And I fucking love it.

I fuck her against the wall, on the dresser, then throw her on the bed, roll her to her knees, slap her ass, and fuck her from behind. My hands grip her ass, opening her up completely so I can see every inch of her. I want to kiss her everywhere. I want to put my tongue on every inch of her body, starting with her pussy. I want to devour her until she is moaning and coming from every place I touch her with my mouth, my hands, and my cock.

Flipping her back, I lift her again in my arms, wanting to feel the weight of her on me. Slamming her back against the wall, I dig my fingers into her thighs—leaving my mark. Scarring her and reminding her I've been here. I fuck her like I hate her. Like I'm punishing her for lying to me. For not being who she said she was. And she gives it back to me tenfold.

She's pulling my hair, biting my neck, moving her hips with mine. Her nails claw at my skin—she's trying to hurt me. She wants me to fuck her like I hate her, because right now, she just wants to hate me too. She hates me for lying. Hates me for living. Hates me for giving her exactly what she needs. And hates herself for wanting it.

"I'm coming inside you," I growl. I have to do this. I want her pussy to smell like me. To taste like me. And every time she moves, I want her to feel me inside her, even when my cock is not.

"You're fucking right you are," she growls back.

Driving into her harder, I tilt my hips until I'm hitting that spot that has her eyes rolling back in her head. Her legs are locked around me. Her back is against the wall. And without breaking stride, I move my hand up her stomach and across her chest until my fingers are wrapped around her throat.

With a small squeeze, her voice catches as she comes all over my cock. I can feel the walls of her pussy throbbing with every beat of her heart. Then I'm filling her—burying my face in her neck to soften my roar. My cock pulsates as I release all my doubt, frustration, and tension inside her.

Relaxing my grip on her throat, she lets out a loud breath, panting in my ear, and her fingers knot in my hair. I lean into her, letting the wall support both our weight. When her ankles unlock at my back, I have to catch her to keep from falling. Slowly, I pull my face from her neck and meet her eyes. They're watery, red, heavy, and full of satisfaction.

She's panting in my face. I'm panting in hers. We'd just said everything we needed to without saying anything at all. This is our connection. This is our relationship. It's crazy, unpredictable, and totally fucked up. But it works for us.

"I have a meeting," she tells me, but I know it's hard for her to think about anything with my dick still inside her.

"I don't give a shit about your meeting," I say, my voice low and very, very serious.

"Tell me you'll see me tonight." Her demand isn't negotiable. And it's my pleasure.

"I'll see you tonight." I keep my eyes on hers as I pull out of her, then set her on her feet. I pull a bandana from my back pocket and slide it between her legs. The intimate gesture has her eyes softening as she lets out a small sigh. I take longer than I should, and wait until her breathing picks up before I pull away—stuffing the bandana back in my pocket along with what's left of the panties laying at her feet. Straightening, she starts to collect herself—adjusting her dress and taming her just-fucked hair. Walking to the dresser, I rummage around until I find some eye drops and a comb and hand them to her. Zipping up my jeans, I watch her in silence as she transforms from a sexy vixen back into the distant woman she was at the warehouse.

Looking devilishly fine, like she wasn't up against a wall getting her brains fucked out only minutes ago, she squares her shoulders. Pausing at the door, she turns and looks straight through me. "Wait ten minutes before you come out. No need to confirm everyone's suspicions."

There are plenty of things I want to say. But she's gone before I can answer. So to the closed door, I give a smirk and with amusement say, "Yes, ma'am."

Because I'm a piece of shit and I want to defy her, I only wait five minutes before I walk back to the bar. Rookie is still seated, and I scan the room but don't see Diem. "She's out back," he informs me, sliding a beer down the bar.

I take a long pull then light a cigarette—smelling Diem's pussy on my hand as I do. My dick stirs to life again and I have to remind him to behave. "Well," I start, turning to look at Rookie. "Go ahead and give me the gossip."

He shrugs. "No gossip. Either people are too scared to say anything or too stupid to notice." Well that's good news. "How'd it go?" I give him a crooked smile and he nods. "I thought as much."

"She's staying with me tonight. Not sure what's gonna go

down with me and her," I say, feeling my mood darken at the reminder.

"I'll keep my phone on," Rookie promises, sliding me another shot.

Holding up the glass, I offer him a toast. "To brothers."

Clinking his glass to mine, he gives me his signature shrug. "And the fucked-up women who love us."

A pleased smile crosses Diem's face when she walks in from the patio to find every woman fully dressed. I roll my eyes as she celebrates her small victory. I get her a Seven and Seven, and ask Monica to leave the bottle on the bar for me. Diem cuts me with a look but I ignore it.

Nationals followed her inside, probably wondering what in the hell is going on between us. Nosy fuckers. Diem's goons still stand at the door looking out of place and more like feds instead of Mafia guys.

"What's the deal with them?" I ask her, nodding my chin in their direction.

Diem follows my gaze and shrugs. "I'm kind of a package deal now." I shake my head. "What?" she asks, loud enough to draw the attention of several people nearby. Soon, the whole bar is quiet and listening to our conversation.

"You don't need them." I try to keep my voice low, but I'm sure everyone heard me.

She laughs. "So, all I need is you?" I look up to find Nationals watching us. Fuck it. I don't care who hears what I have to say.

"You know I'll take care of you," I say, reaching out to rub my thumb across her wrist.

She keeps her face impassive, appearing unaffected by my touch. To avoid me, she looks over at Rookie. "Hey, Joe."

"Diem," he says with a nod. "And it's Rookie, by the way." She quirks an eyebrow. "My name isn't Joe. It's Rookie."

"Ah," she says, finally catching on. "Rookie. Right."

I'm itching with anxiety—burning her with the intensity of my gaze until she finally sheds a little mercy on my sorry ass and turns to look at me. "I think we need to talk."

She appraises me a moment before looking at her goons. Just like her father, she uses the power of a chin tip to dismiss them. Turning back to me, she nods. "I'm ready when you are." Well, it's about fucking time.

I lead Diem out, throwing my hand up to Nationals on the way. I ignore their curious stares. If they want to know something, they'll ask. And knowing them, my phone will be blowing up by noon.

Dawn is breaking in the Nevada sky and it's the nicest time of day here in the west. It's my favorite time for riding too, and I can't help but feel a little excited at the thought of Diem riding with me. I'm smiling by the time I get to my bike, but it quickly fades when I notice she's stopped several feet away.

"I'm not riding that fucking thing," she says, looking at my bike like it's a camel.

"Those shoes comfortable?" I ask, jerking my chin toward her six-inch stilettos.

"Doesn't matter. I'm not riding it, shoes or no shoes."

"It does matter. Because if you don't ride, you walk."

She crosses her arms, glaring at me. "I could make you take me in a vehicle."

I laugh. So this was her game? Sucked for her. "Babe, I don't give a shit who you are. You want to kill me? Kill me. I figured I was going to die this morning, so I feel like every minute is a bonus. And I don't plan to spend one minute of it kissing your ass."

Her eyes widen a little at my words, but she covers it quick. "Still . . . I don't want to ride that thing. Especially in a dress."

"Look," I say, pulling her closer to the bike. "I'll go slow. Nobody will see what's beneath that little red dress. Trust me," I growl, already wanting to kill at just the thought of someone trying to sneak a peek. "You'll like it. I promise. And if it makes you feel better, this is Dirk's bike."

Hearing that, she observes the bike a little more closely. Her eyes move reverently over the recently rebuilt handlebars, motor, seat, and tires. Finally she nods. "Okay. I'll give it a try." I get on, then hold her hand while she clambers on the bike in a not-so-ladylike way. "I already feel like I'm going to fall off."

"Well, if you don't hold on, you will." She says something, but the sound of the pipes drowns her out as her arms tighten around me.

23

KEEPING GOOD ON my word, I ride slow, letting her take everything in. I feel her relax a little behind me, but she tenses every time I take a curve. I feel like I'm sitting still at fifty, but I slow down to forty just to ease her mind. The tension seems to leave her body the moment we turn down Dirk's driveway. The white, wood-frame house sits a good way back, but is still visible from the road. It really is a beautiful place, especially now that it's cleaned up.

I cut the engine and help her off. Her smile is big when she looks at me. She doesn't even know where we are, but it makes her happy. I smile back because this place makes me happy too. "This was Dirk's house," I say, watching her smile fade as the realization starts to sink in. I almost feel guilty that I didn't tell her it was mine now. Especially since she was so happy only moments ago.

We walk to the front of the house, both of us looking up at it and letting everything sink in. It seems different without Dirk and Saylor around. But still charming and welcoming. I walk up the stairs and take a seat on the porch.

"Who lives here now?" Diem asks, running her hand over the railing. She stays on the steps, almost like she's afraid to come any closer.

I light a cigarette, blowing out a large cloud of smoke before answering. "I do."

Her head jerks up and that smile she wore earlier returns. "Really? It's beautiful."

"Yeah it is. Dirk would have wanted you to feel at home here," I say, my voice thick. I clear my throat and take another drag, wishing I had something a little stronger.

Diem climbs the steps, taking a seat next to me. Reaching over, she grabs my cigarette. Her hand is shaky as she pulls it to her lips, taking a drag before handing it back to me. "I didn't know about Dirk until two days ago," she starts, fidgeting with her hands in her lap. She tries to fight through the emotion, but I can tell she's struggling.

"When Dorian told me, the first thing I felt was hate. I wanted to kill him for keeping my brother from me. But I knew I couldn't, so I saved my anger for Cyrus. I stayed up all day and night going over every detail of Dirk and Saylor's story, well, what I had of it. I didn't think I'd make it through that meeting. But then . . ." She looks at me, her eyes shining. "I saw you."

"Did you know about me?" I ask when she doesn't continue.

She shakes her head. "No. Not until I got there. And when I found out you were the infamous Shady, I didn't know what I was going to do." The flash of horror on her face at the reminder confuses me.

"What do you mean?" I ask, already knowing I'm not going to like the answer.

Unable to look at me, she stares out across the yard. "Because I was supposed to kill you."

Even though it's not funny, I can't help but laugh at the irony. She cuts her eyes, looking at me like I've lost my mind. "That's funny to you?"

"A little." I smirk, lighting another cigarette. For some reason, my adrenaline spikes and I feel anxious. "I woke up knowing I was going to die. But I didn't care. All I could think about was leaving you. So don't you find it the least bit humorous that you were actually the one who was going to kill me?"

"No. I don't find it humorous at all," she answers, deadpan. "Lucky for you, you don't know when to keep your mouth shut. The only thing that saved you was telling Dorian what nobody else had the guts to say. He appreciates a man with steel in his spine."

I'm still smiling, but then I realize what she's really saying. "So you would have killed me?"

"Oh like you haven't ever thought of killing me," she says, avoiding the question altogether. I decide I don't really want to know the answer. We all have to die sometime anyway. I guess yesterday just wasn't my day.

The silence drags on, both Diem and I lost in our own deep thoughts. We're both tired, but too anxious to sleep. There's something comforting about sitting on this porch with her by my side. I look over at her, for the first time really taking notice of the similarities between her and Dirk—the black hair, dark hazel eyes, olive complexion, and not to mention the shitty attitude. If he knew he had a sister, I'm sure he'd forbid me to even look at her. But I can't help but feel like he's looking down on both of us, proud that we found each other. In the most fucked-up kind of way, we worked.

"Would you like to see his grave?" I ask Diem, reaching out to take her hand and bring it to my lips. She nods, and I lead her to the backyard where the grass is beginning to grow over the two mounds of dirt. I watch her as she reads the hand-carved wooden crosses that mark the heads of Dirk's and Saylor's graves.

"I've never felt more joy than when I watched Cyrus take his last breath," she whispers. "I wanted him to suffer, but I couldn't stand the thought of him still being here, alive, when my brother was dead and gone. I never hesitated. Is something wrong with me?"

Her eyes search mine for some kind of understanding or truth. But I don't have it to tell. "I ask myself that question every day. You just have to find your own solution. It's the only way to keep you from going insane."

"What's your solution?" she asks, staring up at me with wide, patient eyes full of empathy.

"I love hard. Too hard. I tell myself I do it because I care. I wrong those who have wronged the ones I love. My club, my brothers, and my girl. I'll kill any and every motherfucker that hurts them. And I don't feel regret because in my fucked-up brain, I believe they deserve it." Looking down at Dirk's grave, I feel the same joy Diem does. I'm glad Cyrus is dead. I'm glad Death Mob is too. And if I had to do it all over again, I would.

Diem blows out a breath, moving her neck from side to side. "Okay," she says, slapping me on the arm. "Enough of this sappy shit. I'm hungry. And we're getting along too well. It's weird and you're getting boring." She walks toward the house, and I watch her ass sway from side to side, leaving me feeling guilty considering I'm standing at the foot of her brother's grave.

"Yeah," I call after her. "You need to change too. You look like a slut in that dress."

"Yeah?" she yells over her shoulder. "Well your breath smells like dog shit."

Damn it feels good to get back to normal.

———

The normalcy lasts all of one minute, which is the amount of time it takes to get back to the house. Now we're standing at the threshold waiting to walk in and our emotions are crashing through us like waves once again.

"Maybe a cigarette before we go in?" Diem suggests. I agree and light us a smoke. She doesn't ask, but I know she wants to know everything about her brother, so I start from the beginning.

"Your dad put Dirk in the care of a man who raised him until he was seven. He then called Roach, who was once Nationals president for Sinner's Creed. The man who owned this house and raised Dirk as his grandson owed a favor to Roach, so he took Dirk in. Roach thought it would help change him. It didn't." I take a seat in one of the chairs, and she sits in the other, fully invested in the story.

"What do you mean change him?"

"He was a real asshole. Treated Dirk like shit, but it made him strong. Black made him the man he was."

"Black?" she asks, confused.

"Yeah. Like death. Like nothing." I take a drag from my cigarette, hoping the nicotine will help calm my own emotions when I think about a life that might have been better for Dirk if his daddy wasn't such a chickenshit.

We sit and I know she's looking at me, but she isn't pushing, so I take my time. When I feel like I'm as ready as I'm gonna get, I stand and lead her inside. I watch her face as she takes it all in. By the surprised look, I'm guessing it's not what she expected. "Saylor knew Dirk had a lot of bad memories here, so she remodeled the house and they made new ones here together."

"What's all this?" she asks, pointing to all the covers and pillows on the floor.

"The Friday before Saylor died, she wanted to have a sleepover with her closest friends. Me, Rookie, Carrie, and two of Saylor's other friends stayed. We all slept here together." I don't look at her. I just stare at the spot I laid in and remembered the last time I looked at Saylor. She'd shot me a wink and told me she loved me.

"That's pretty amazing. I'm glad she had such good friends," Diem whispers, but her voice still sounds loud in the silence.

Moving on, I show her around the small kitchen and dining room, then down the hall to their bedroom. She walks in, but I stay outside the door. "I haven't moved anything. I've only been here a few times since it all happened. This is their sanctuary, you know? I feel like an intruder."

Nodding, she smiles. "I get it."

I point across the hall. "This is where I stay. It was Black's room, but Saylor gave it to me. For some reason, this place felt like home. She always made me feel welcome."

"Well, it's a lot better than your room at the cabin, that's for damn sure." She smirks and a little bit of the weight on my shoulders seems to lift.

I look at our reflection in the mirror, standing side by side in Dirk's house. I don't feel ashamed for being here with her. It feels right. Like this is truly what Dirk would have wanted. Even if he didn't, I know Saylor would've approved and Dirk would've done whatever in the hell she told him to.

"I'll tell you everything I know about him," I say, meeting her eyes in the mirror.

"I think I have enough to reflect on right now. I just need some time to let it all sink in." She pulls my duffel bag from the floor and digs around until she finds one of my shirts. "Mind if I shower?"

I shake my head, drawing my eyebrows together in confusion. "You're asking? What the fuck is wrong with you?"

She rolls her eyes and a disgusted look crosses her face. "I don't know," she whines, putting her hands on her hips. "I think it's all this emotional shit. I'm losing myself. I can feel it." She rambles on a little longer before closing her eyes and putting her hand out. "Forget I asked. I'm going to take a shower. Why don't you make yourself useful and order us a pizza or something." She spins on her heels, mumbling to herself.

"You know who makes a great pizza?" I call, just as the bathroom door closes.

"Who?"

"Monica," I say as I walk down the hall.

"I fucking hate you."

There's my girl.

"Monica didn't really make this pizza, did she?" Diem asks, three slices in. We're piled on the couch in the living room, in the same position Dirk and Saylor sat the last night they spent together. The memory doesn't ache like it used to, it actually makes me feel pretty damn good.

"No," I say, shaking my head. "Monica sucks at cooking. Remember the girl with the big tits that was in front of me when you walked in? She's the cook." Diem's pointy little elbow finds my ribs and I groan.

"I was married once," she says, just out of the fucking blue. I could stab her for ruining my good mood.

"What?"

"I didn't stutter. I was twenty-two. We were in love."

"Horseshit."

"We were!" She laughs, but I know that if any man ever had Diem's heart, she never would have let him go . . . unless she killed him, of course. Thinking back, she did tell me once that she was married. And that she'd killed her husband.

Now I'm curious. But I don't want her to know that. "Okay. I'll bite. What happened?" I ask, bored.

"It didn't work out. He was in it for my money. But what he didn't know was that I was in it for a different reason too."

"What reason was that?" If she says sex, I'll kill her.

"I needed to get close to his uncle. It was my first job. I had to make him fall in love with me, which wasn't hard by the way, get him to marry me, then convince him to take me to Paris to meet his uncle, who was hiding out from my father." She takes another bite of pizza. Clearly, she isn't upset at all about any of this.

"So, he didn't know who you were."

"No. He just knew I was rich."

"Well, how did you convince him?" She shoots me a look that has me wanting to growl. Sex. Of course. "That's very trashy of you."

She shrugs. "Call it what you want. But he did take me to Paris, and I did meet his uncle. He was even kind enough to take us on a fishing trip. Sadly, his uncle never made it back."

"What about him? How did you convince him not to tell?" She starts to say something, but I cut her off. "If you say sex, I'll shoot your left tit off."

She rolls her eyes. "I didn't have to convince him. He never made it back either." What an evil bitch.

"Why are you telling me this?" I ask, confused as hell. Is she trying to prove how badass she is? Or is she just trying to push me away?

Turning to face me, she puts the pizza box on the floor and stares at me long enough to make me uncomfortable. "This isn't the life I chose. I did what I did because I had no other option. I've never been asked if this is what I wanted. I don't want you to not know who I am. Like today," she starts, pulling her lip between her teeth and looking away from me. "I want you to know that who I was today is who I was trained to be. But it's not who I really am. I'm sorry you had to see it."

Pushing her hair back from her eyes, I run my fingers down her cheek before grabbing her chin. Forcing her to look at me, I offer her a smile. "Don't say you're sorry. I get it. Trust me."

Fidgeting with her hands, she lets out a breath that sags her shoulders. "I'm struggling, Zeke."

"With what?" I ask, ready to offer her any advice I can. I hate that she was forced down this path, but if she's going to do this, I want her to know what she's doing.

"People keep testing me. They undermine me and defy me and force me to do something I really don't want to."

"Like what?"

She looks up at me from under her lashes. "Like murder." Oh. That's impressive. My face shows it and she rolls her eyes. "I can't kill everybody. No matter what Dorian thinks," she adds.

She's confused, upset, and the guilt is quickly catching up to her. And she's just getting started. "You're right. You can't kill everybody. You have to be smarter than that, Diem. Smarter than your enemy."

Narrowing her eyes in confusion, she shifts to a more comfortable position—ready to absorb whatever knowledge I throw her way. "How?"

"People like me hold little value over their own life. So threatening them won't do any good. You have to dig deeper—find their weakness."

"What's your weakness?" she asks, and I don't hesitate to answer. "You."

I stand and grab the pizza box, an uneasy feeling coming over me. I don't like having a weakness. Good thing mine has the protection of the Mafia. If not, someone might be inclined to use Diem against me. The thought pisses me off and has fear—something I'm not used to feeling—settling in my gut.

She follows me to the kitchen, jumping up to sit on the counter while I busy myself cleaning. "You know you don't have to worry about that, right?" I don't answer her and completely avoid her gaze. I can't even look at her right now with the thought of someone hurting her running through my head. "Zeke," she begs. "Will you please just look at me?"

"What do you want from me, Diem?" I ask, giving her a tortured look. "What are we? What is this? Do I even have a right to feel the need to protect you?"

"What I want is for you to not worry about me."

"And what I want is a fucking answer," I bite back, my anger rising. I'm not even sure what I'm pissed about.

"This is complicated. It's always been complicated. Now that the truth is out, I don't know what to do." Suddenly, she looks exhausted. Drawing in a shaky breath, she looks out the kitchen window and I know she's looking at Dirk's grave. "I want us. I want this to work, but we have got to keep a low profile."

Hopping down from the counter, she walks up to me, taking my face in her hands. "This shit is bigger than me and you. We've both worked too hard to fuck everything up now. That feeling you have for your club? I have that same feeling for my family. I have to see this through. But I need to know you're on my side."

Her eyes move back and forth, searching for something in mine. "Okay," I whisper, knowing good and damn well what she's feeling right now. I loved her, but Sinner's Creed was my life. "And you don't have to ask, Diem. I'll always be on your side."

She smiles, shedding a little light on my shitty mood. "We can be like Bonnie and Clyde."

"As serial killers, I think we're a little more notorious than Bonnie and Clyde."

"We're not serial killers," she scoffs.

I raise my eyebrows. "Um, yeah we are."

"I don't believe that." She shakes her head, emphasizing that she doesn't agree. "I'm going with what you said earlier. We are simply righting those who wronged us. We're more like the angel of death."

"Great . . . I've created a fucking monster," I say, throwing my hands up and walking away.

"Takes one to know one," she says to my retreating back. "Hey! Where are you going?"

"To bed," I call over my shoulder. "Even monsters have to sleep."

And she joins me, because angels do too.

24

I WAKE UP to an empty bed. Stretching, I look over to find that it's after three in the afternoon. "Diem?" I call, but only silence answers me back. In the bathroom, I find a message written in lipstick on the mirror.

Duty calls. –D.

"Duty calls," I mock, in my best Diem voice.

After a shower and shave, I call Rookie to see where he is, and I'm not surprised to learn that he is still at the bar. Everyone else is either still partying or sleeping it off, so I decide to take the day and finally clean the house back to its original glory.

Memories come flooding back as I fold the covers in the living room. Saylor's scent still hangs heavy in the air and I swear I can feel her presence. I always thought she was some kind of angel. I start to ask for a sign from her, but then realize how ridiculous that sounds.

I don't know if it's because I'm bored, feeling lonely, or just reminiscing a little too hard, but I open Saylor's diary and scan the names on the front page until I find Jeffery's. He, along with his partner Donnawayne, were two of Saylor's best friends. I figure they'd like to know that they had a sister-in-law. But of the two, Jeffery is the least dramatic so it's his number I dial.

"Hello?" He answers on the second ring.

"Jeffery?" I ask, just to be sure it's him, although there is no mistaking his voice.

"You've got 'im. What can I do ya for, sugar?" At one time, his words would have weirded me out. Now I just smile.

"It's Shady."

"Shady! Ohmigod! Donnawayne! It's Shady!" I hold the phone away from my ear to prevent my eardrum from busting. So much for believing *he* wasn't the dramatic one.

"Put him on speaker right now," I hear Donnawayne command. He sounds excited and pissed at the same time—if that's even possible. "Did we or did we not promise to keep in touch?" he asks, and I visualize him standing with his hand on his hip and pointing his finger at the phone.

"I've been busy," I reply, thinking that maybe this wasn't such a good idea.

"We totally understand," Jeffery tells me, and I visualize him silencing Donnawayne with a look.

I take a deep breath, preparing myself for the overly dramatic cries I'm fixing to endure. Surely, it couldn't be worse than the time I'd told them Saylor had lost her mobility. I was still recovering from that one. "I have some good news," I start, but they're guessing it before I can finish.

"You're getting married!"

"Having a baby!"

"You're gay!"

"What?" I bark. "No! I'm not getting married or having a baby or . . . gay. Dirk has a sister," I spit out. A long silence. "Hello?"

"A sister?" Okay . . . not the answer I was expecting.

"Yes. A sister. I just thought y'all would like to know. And maybe we could arrange to get together sometime and I can introduce y'all." I hold my breath, listening to them whisper on the other end.

"Did he say sister? Yes he did! Ohmigod a sister! We have to meet her."

"We would love that, Shady."

I let out a sigh of relief and thank the ear gods for allowing me to keep my hearing. "Okay. Good. I'll be calling soon."

It takes them another five minutes just to say good-bye and by the time I hang up, I'm exhausted and need a drink.

I arrive at the bar just as Jimbo is walking out. He instructs me to pack a bag and tells me Rookie will be filling me in on where I'm going. I'm a little relieved to find out I'm flying back to Hillsborough. Our flight leaves within the hour and by dark I'm back in my cabin, feeling lonelier than ever. I hate that Diem isn't here and that she hasn't returned my texts or my calls.

Rookie grills us a burger and we watch reruns of westerns that just aren't the same without her sitting in my lap. My recliner feels too big. My house is too quiet. And I start to ask Rookie to initiate an argument just so I can pretend it's her.

At midnight my phone rings and Jimbo orders me and Rookie to go to Concord and shut down a Death Mob clubhouse that is still up and running. More than excited about the opportunity to do something to get my mind off Diem, my adrenaline is pumping before I even make it to my bike.

It's the first time we've ever been able to fly our colors on the East Coast. Even though the ride only lasts an hour, it feels fucking phenomenal as we pull into the clubhouse that will soon belong to us.

"Okay, boys, party's over," I announce to the group of men sitting around the card table inside.

My back stiffens and my smile widens when I recognize one of them as Fin, the chapter's SA. Good. I'll finally get to kill him.

He stands, knocking his chair over and glowering down at me. Damn, he's tall. "What the fuck are you doing here?"

Being the smart-ass I am, I turn and point to the patch on my back. "Sinner's Creed. I believe this is our territory now. Didn't you get the memo?"

"Yeah, we got the memo that some bitch came in and took out Cyrus. But her ass has yet to show up here."

I smirk. "Well, you're lucky she didn't. Instead, she sent me. Trust me; you don't want that bitch here. She's crazy."

"Sounds like Sinner's Creed still don't know how to put a bitch in their place. Maybe I'll teach you boys one day." He gives me an evil grin before his eyes swing to Rookie. I'm livid and suddenly can't wait to knock his teeth down his throat. One step in and I hear the sound of the safety being released on a gun. Shit. I should have counted them all. I turn slowly to see the old man behind the bar pointing a nine shakily at me.

"We don't want no trouble," he says, his voice quivering.

"Me either, old-timer. But—"

"Put the gun down." My eyes move to the door and I see one of Diem's goons standing there like a fucking Mack truck, holding a .44 Magnum that looks tiny in his hands. The bartender lowers his gun just as Diem walks through the door.

"Seven and Seven, please." I roll my eyes at her attempt to be polite. "Now, which one of you called me a bitch? Oh wait," she says, feigning shock. Her finger moves back and forth between me and Fin, who's still standing. "It was both of you."

She walks closer to me, her heels clicking on the concrete floor. How does she get to be so powerful, such a bitch, and fine as hell? It wasn't fair. "Did I upset you?" she asks, frowning. "The whole crazy bitch thing, isn't that a bit much?"

"In case you haven't noticed, sweetheart, I'm in the middle of conducting business," I tell her, my rage rolling in waves down my body. Fin was my problem. We had a history, and I owed him something. Nobody was going to take that away from me. I don't give a shit who they are.

Her cheeks redden with anger. "Don't do that," she snaps, giving me a deadly look.

"Do what?"

"Talk to me like I'm out of my league."

I shoot her a wink, hoping my charm will warn her off. "I just meant I have this one covered, babe."

She gives me a sardonic smile. "Well, *babe*. I can take it from here." She's beyond pissed. She's fucking livid. But so am I. And I don't like being put in my place by anyone, especially a woman. This woman. My woman.

"Seriously, Diem, back the fuck up. I don't know what your problem is and I don't care. This battle is mine," I say between my teeth.

"My problem is you speaking to me like I'm beneath you. I don't like it." She's close enough now I can smell the wine on her lips. I want to suck the taste right off her tongue, choke her out so I can handle my business, then fuck her back to consciousness.

"Well, I don't like you coming in here barking orders at me like I'm beneath you." She raises an eyebrow, reminding me that's exactly where I am. "Look *princess*," I drawl, and her nostrils flare at my choice of words. "If you're looking for a power trip, do it somewhere else. I've. Got. This."

She looks like she wants to slap me. I can almost see the steam boiling out of her ears. Her whole damn face is on fire and that death glare she's giving me is strong enough to have me considering backing down. But, I stand my ground.

"Leave. Now." Her tone is threatening, but I don't budge.

"I'm not leaving," I growl, letting her know I'm not in a negotiating mood.

She's not in the mood to negotiate either, and this is the maddest I've ever seen her. "Threatening your life is pointless. You've already made it very clear that you don't care whether you live or not. So, given our history, I'm going to allow you a second chance that I wouldn't anyone else. Leave now, or I'll put a bullet in Rookie's kneecap. And if that doesn't work, I'll be sending flowers to Carrie."

I conceal my heartache. I hide the shock. She'd just threatened the life of my brother and my friend. She was using my own advice against me. I'd told her she was my weakness, but she knew Rookie was a weakness for me too. And now, she was using him as leverage.

I'd lost too fucking much and I didn't need anybody who I couldn't trust. She'd just sealed her fate with me. What we had was good, but it's gone. This isn't the woman I fell in love with. This is a woman who's trying to prove something. And she just did.

I don't know if she's bluffing or not, but my brother's life isn't worth the gamble. My voice gravely low, I lean forward, growling in her face. "Don't ever threaten my family again."

I walk out with Rookie on my heels. I'd said I'd kill any motherfucker who wronged my family. And I meant it. I fully understand why she avoided my question when I asked if she would have killed me. Because now, I have the same dilemma.

If she ever threatens my family again—I'll kill her.

And like all the others, I'll have no fucking remorse.

"You know, she wouldn't have shot me," Rookie informs me. We're back at my place, passing a much-needed blunt on the front porch.

"Obviously, you don't know her like I do." I take a drag, hoping the weed will help to drown out the sound of her voice that keeps playing in my head. *"I'll be sending Carrie flowers."* What a coldhearted bitch.

"What did you expect her to do? You undermined her authority. You made her look weak. If people see you doing it, they'll do it too. I'd have shot your ass."

"Are you forgetting that she just threatened to kill you? Whose fucking side are you on? And why do I have to keep asking my brothers that question?" I kick at one of the boards on the railing and three fall. Great. Something else to fucking fix.

"She did what she had to do. You didn't see me shittin' in my pants and you don't see me holding a grudge. Why should you."

"Because you're my fucking family!" I yell, losing my temper. "I taught her to play on her enemies' weaknesses. *Me!* And like the bitch she is, she used it against me. But I'm not her enemy. I'm supposed to be her fucking man!" I'd been betrayed. My heart had been ripped from my chest. That speech about this world being bigger than us was just an excuse. This was for her. She was a selfish bitch who clearly wanted power more than she wanted me.

Rookie doesn't say anything until my breathing returns to normal. He's learned how far he can push me, and it's pretty obvious that I've reached my breaking point. "All I'm saying is to put yourself in her shoes. What would you have done?"

Even though I just want to be pissed, I consider his words. Reversing the roles, I know what I'd have done—the exact same thing she did. If I was her man, I should have acted like it instead of like all the other pieces of shit that had forced her to do something she didn't want to. I'd questioned her in front of the real enemy—Death Mob. I'd made her look weak in front of her own men. I was no better than the other men she'd killed and I deserved to die after how I'd treated her.

Fuck.

I hate my friend sometimes. He always has to be the voice of reason. Deep down, I know she wouldn't have hurt Rookie. I'm still pissed at her for making the threat. But already I'm finding the will to forgive her.

Handing Rookie a beer, I shake my head. "I should have just let her shoot you."

My phone rings around noon the next day and I nearly break my neck to answer it. I'm hoping it's her voice, but it's Jimbo's. And he's pissed. "Do you mind telling me why the fuck we have to ride halfway across the country for a meeting in the morning that was supposed to take place here tomorrow night?"

"I may or may not have pissed off my girlfriend." Ex-girlfriend. But he doesn't have to know that.

"Well, thanks a lot, asshole. And while Nationals fly, you'll be riding to Nebraska. Now get in the fucking wind."

What Jimbo failed to tell me was that part of my punishment wasn't just making me ride, but every other member within a five-hundred-mile radius had to ride too. I guess he learned that shit in the military—punish one by punishing them all. They're so pissed they won't even look at me. Even when we stop to fill up and smoke, they keep their distance. All because my man ego couldn't take a direct order from Diem.

If Dorian or Jimbo would have walked in and gave me that exact same order, I'd have listened and done what I was told with no questions asked. I was still pissed, but at least I understood her motive.

Before I can stop myself, I'm dialing her number. "What," she snaps, and I can hear the click of her heels as she walks.

"Hey, pretty girl," I say, the sound of her voice making me forget that we're in an argument.

"Zeke, don't," she says, but the fight isn't in her.

"Look . . ." I drag my hand down my face, trying to find the right words to say without the reminder of what happened pissing me off. When I realize I can't, I stick to business.

"Don't take your anger out on my club. If you got a problem with me, that's for me and you to work out. Don't make the club pay for my mistakes." Everyone is on their bikes, unable to leave until I do because I'm the highest-ranking officer here. I've smoked half a cigarette and been called every motherfucker in the book by my impatient brothers before she finally answers.

"It's clear that you're more upset over your club having to endure a schedule change than you are about hurting me." She pauses a moment, letting out a low breath. "I confided in you, Shady." The hurt in her voice has me closing my eyes and hating myself a little more.

"Diem," I try, but she cuts me off, her tone now cold and unforgiving like she just flipped a switch.

"I told you that I was struggling and you treated me with the same respect as the men I was forced to kill. I see where your priorities are, and I completely understand. Because like you, I know where mine are too." She hangs up and I roar loud enough to silence everyone in the parking lot. I've never been so angry with myself.

Of course the club was my priority. But Diem was too, even though I'd yet to make her feel like one. I kick at the air, mumbling obscenities while my club looks on like I've lost my mind. I straddle my bike, asking myself the same question I've asked over and over. What the *fuck* is wrong with me?

I'm at a hundred and twenty before I figure it out, but the reality hits me so hard, I nearly wreck with the impact. There's no answer other than the obvious—I'm just an insensitive, control-freak, anti-feminist prick.

By the time we make it to the warehouse, I'm fucking livid with myself. And exhausted. And running off of gas fumes and coffee. I light a cigarette and stand with my club as Diem steps out of the same SUV she arrived in last night. Damn, she's pretty. Even tired and overworked, she's exquisite. Just like the neatly pressed business suit she wears over that goddess body I know is hidden underneath.

"I need men on the ground on the East Coast right away," she starts. She's barking orders and calling shots without even as much as a "good afternoon" or a look in my direction. "We're expecting production to slow, and we will be patient with you. Don't get men you don't trust just to hurry the business along. We want good, dependable soldiers like you. How long do you think it will take?"

She directs her questions to Jimbo, who responds like a National president should. With the truth and no bullshit. "At least a year. We have several support club chapters we can Prospect, but it takes time. A one-percenter isn't born overnight."

Her small head nods as she purses her lips, just like she always does when she's thinking. "I suggest moving chapters you have now to fill in until you get some more guys ready. We'll make sure your territory isn't compromised." Jimbo agrees, and they discuss locations.

Meanwhile, Clark, the big man I recognize as the one from the Death Mob clubhouse, is burning holes into me, so I finally meet his gaze. He rolls his neck and I flex my fingers. It's an intimidation method that makes us both look like grade school kids.

"Do you have a problem?" Diem's voice rings out and I don't have to look at her to know she's talking to me. She only uses that tone when she's pissed at me. And I guess she's still pissed.

"Not at all," I say, not looking at her.

"What about you?" she says, and I know she's talking to the guy I'm sizing up. "Do you have a problem?"

"I don't like him," he growls, his voice low and gruff. He sounds mean, but he'll die just as quick as any other man who gets a bullet in his head.

"Yeah? Me either. But this is business. So if the two of you want to get in a pissing contest over whose dick is bigger, then do it when you're not on my time."

"Yes, ma'am," he answers, like a whooped puppy. I just smirk.

"Something funny to you?" This time, I turn to look at her.

"No, pretty girl. Nothing's funny." She's not embarrassed by my endearment, but she's not blushing about it either.

Her eyes narrow on me as she ignores everyone else in the room. The silence is uncomfortable, but not to us. "We're all on the same team here, Shady." She drawls my name out like it tastes bad in her mouth. It sounds bad too. I like when she calls me Zeke. Somehow, it means something different.

"And what team is that, Diem? Because right now it feels like you're on one side and I'm on the other." I'm over the whole keeping our relationship a secret shit. I don't give a damn who knows.

"These men are here for me. They're here to protect me," she argues, but her case is weak.

I offer her a smirk and shake my head. Her eyebrows rise in amusement. "You don't agree?"

"You don't need them."

"Why, because I have you?" She laughs, and it stings. Only because I've already answered this question once, and she still doesn't believe it.

"Yeah, babe, 'cause you got me. But even if you didn't, you can handle yourself. I always knew that, and I should have said it sooner."

"But you didn't," she cuts in. Her words are angry and laced with a hate I didn't know she had inside her. She takes a deep breath, crossing her arms over her chest. "You know how I love a challenge, so prove it to me. Prove that all I need is you." That creepy, evil smile crosses her lips and I narrow my eyes on her.

"How?"

She waves her hand across the room at the six men standing in a line with their arms clasped in front of them. "You think you're a wolf? Act like one."

I smile at her choice of words. I don't doubt myself in the least. I've always been good at fighting, but now, she's just given me something to fight for. "You want me to take on all of them?" I ask, flashing her the grin she once called irresistible.

"Well, there are only six. Surely a man like you can handle it. Don't worry. I'll stop them before they kill you." Damn, she really is pissed.

I take off my cut as my brothers move back and the six men move forward. I hand it to Chaps who just shakes his head at me. I know what he's thinking. *Dumb-ass.*

"You must really like to see me fight. What will this be? The third time?" I ask, knowing she gets off on this shit. Chances are I was fixing to get my ass kicked. But it wouldn't be the first time.

"I think so . . . Wait," she says, putting her finger on her chin. "Is this where I say this is going to hurt me worse than it hurts you?"

"Only if it makes you feel better, baby."

Her eyes narrow, the humor lost from her face. She's seething with rage. And she's going to enjoy the shit out of this. With a jerk of her chin, she gives the command. "Take him."

Naturally, they send the biggest guy first—Clark. He's the only one who's a real threat. The others are overweight, middle-aged men who are probably named Tony or Joe and are someone's uncle's cousin's brother's kid. Wasting no time, I throat punch Clark, and while he's distracted with the feeling of his throat closing up, I work on his temple until he falls like dead weight to the ground.

The next one comes at me, and it only takes two licks for me to take him down. After that, they keep coming. One by one I drop them. The only problem is that once they're down, they don't stay that way. Soon, I'm fighting off two at a time. Then three. Finally, they're kicking my ass. Diem is watching, and when I swing my gaze at her, I can tell that she's struggling with watching me bleed. I guess it does hurt her worse than it does me. Right now, I can't feel a fucking thing.

Finding what little energy I have left, I break free from their hold and reach for my gun that is hidden beneath my shirt. Knowing if I fire they'll kill me, I grab the man closest to me and use him as a shield while I keep my gun trained on his head. "I believe I've had enough," I announce breathlessly. I'm not ashamed of admitting it. I just took on six men for longer than any of them could have lasted one-on-one with me.

Guns are drawn, everyone is in a standoff, and Diem looks happier than a pig in shit. Clapping her hands, she walks toward me. "I'm impressed. I figured you would just shoot them."

I smirk. "Nah, I like to get a little sweaty. Keeps me in shape."

"Everyone, put your guns down. Like I said, we're all on the same team. Even you, Shady."

I give her a bloody smile that widens when she frowns at the sight of the blood running down my chin. "Does that mean I'm forgiven?" I ask, letting the man go and sticking my gun back in my pants.

Straightening her back, she purses her lips—that face of stone back in place. "That means you'll live long enough to try again tomorrow."

Bitch.

25

THE NEXT MORNING, Rookie walks in the living room wearing basketball shorts, flip-flops, a muscle shirt, and headphones. I've known him for years and this is the first time I've ever seen him not wearing jeans and boots.

"What's with that?" I ask, gesturing to his outfit that makes me feel a little uncomfortable. What the hell happened to my badass brother? He looks like a high school kid.

"Road trip clothes. I suggest you do the same," he says, throwing his duffel over his shoulder.

"You know where we're going?"

"Pennsylvania," he says with a shrug.

"How do you know that?" Nobody had told me anything. I was just told to pack.

"Diem told me last night."

I do the math in my head. We didn't see Diem last night. We saw her yesterday morning. Then it hits me. "She called you?"

"Yeah." He shoots me a look, then drops his eyes when I glare back at him. "I figured she told you too."

"Well she didn't," I snap, pushing past him out the door. "You're gonna look real fucking cute when you're the only one dressed like a Backstreet Boy." It's a pathetic comeback, but it's all I have. I grab my bag from the couch and open the front door to see an SUV pulling into the driveway.

The last thing I want to do is be in an enclosed space with Diem. I'd rather fucking walk. But when she steps out, a little piece of that ice around my heart chips off. She doesn't look like a contract killer, second in command Mafia guru this morning. She looks like Diem. And she's wearing road trip clothes—leggings, an oversized T-shirt, and no makeup. I look down at my boots and jeans. Then up at Rookie, who is smiling down at me from the porch steps.

"Rookie, can I have a minute?" Diem asks, her voice a lot softer than I've heard her lately.

"With all due respect, Diem, anything you say to me can be said in front of Shady," Rookie says. I want to stick my tongue out at her like a five-year-old, but I don't. I just avoid her gaze altogether and instead, look over the top of her head.

"I want to apologize for the other day. I was working on a tight deadline and had to handle some things quickly. It was the only way I knew how to get rid of . . . him." I feel her eyes on me, but I refuse to give her the benefit of meeting her gaze.

"I'm not worried about what you said to me. I get it." I think Rookie is finished, but then his voice drops and the air grows colder. "But don't ever mention Carrie's name again in front of people we don't know. And don't ever try to use us as leverage. Shady has every right to be pissed. He's a lot more forgiving than I would have been if you'd threatened me with his life."

I finally look at Diem, who nods, pulling her lip between her teeth. "I won't," she promises, and offers a smile. But Rookie doesn't return it. She turns around, but he calls to her again.

"And, Diem," he growls, his tone deadly. When she meets his eyes, something she sees makes her shrink a little in size. "I don't give second chances."

Rookie brushes past her, throwing his duffel in the car before getting in. I fight hard to contain my smile. I want to fist pump the air and announce to the world that he's my brother. But of course, I don't.

Diem looks at me, her face full of apology. "Can we talk?" she asks, hope ringing in her voice.

"Nope," I say, stepping past her. I hear her mumble something, but it's lost in my own laughter.

"Is this the road to Itta Bena?" I ask, thirty minutes into our drive south. Nobody answers, so I try again. "Are we there yet?" Nothing. "I gotta pee." Diem doesn't respond, but I can see her shift in aggravation.

Me and Rookie are in the backseat. He's wearing his headphones, so he can't hear me. Diem is up front with Clark, her personal driver and right-hand man, who is also listening to music. I'm guessing Diem isn't listening to anything in hopes that I will talk. I should probably sleep, but I'm too aware of her presence and I swear I can smell her from back here.

"Stop looking at me," she snaps, not bothering to turn around.

"I'm not looking at you. I'm looking out the windshield."

"Well, look out your window, asshole."

"Nah, I like to see where we're going. By the way, where the hell is that exactly?" I ask, and she turns around to give me a conniving smile.

"For me to know and you to find out."

"What are you, in fifth grade?"

"Says the guy who has been asking 'are we there yet' for the past fifteen minutes." She's got me there. Looking back out her window, she throws a dog a bone. "We're going to Pennsylvania."

"I know that. What part of Pennsylvania?" I lean forward, startling her when she turns and my face is inches from hers. She drags her eyes down my face with a disgusted look. I just smile.

"The middle part."

"Why?" I ask, moving closer. She pulls back, pretending like she's annoyed, but I can see her pulse throbbing in the side of her neck. She likes me this close.

"Business, Zeke. Everything is business."

My smile widens. "You called me Zeke."

She shakes her head in annoyance. "Yeah, well, it's gonna take a while for me to adjust to all your pet names." I burn holes into the back of her head until she finally lets out a breath and twists in her seat to face me. "You said you didn't want to talk."

"I didn't."

Her eyes narrow on the cut above my eye, then move to the one on my lip. Her face softens. "Does it hurt?" she whispers.

I laugh. "No, babe. It doesn't hurt. I'm not that fragile, you know." I shoot her a wink. "I can take a lick." A small smile plays on her lips. "What about you?" I ask. "Did it hurt you?"

"Hardly," she scoffs, but I can tell she's lying. "It's getting harder and harder to keep our secret when you continue to show your ass in front of everyone."

"So let's stop keeping us a secret. Everyone already knows something is going on." I shrug, looking over at Clark, who pretends he's not listening, even though I know the bastard is.

"First off," she begins, pointing her finger at me. "There is no us and nothing is going on. We broke up. Remember?"

I roll my eyes to the roof, twisting my lips in confusion. "Nope.

I don't remember that. The way I see it, we had a disagreement. Happens all the time with couples, from what I hear. You should know that. You were married once. Remember?"

"How can I forget?" she asks, her eyes taking on a dreamy state. "The honeymoon was the best part." My jaw tightens and she smiles at my reaction.

I lean back in my seat. If I've learned anything from being around women, it's that they hate to be ignored. Pulling my earbuds from my bag, I plug them into my iPod and put it on shuffle. She says something, so to drown her out, I cut the volume up and look out the window. Eventually, she gives up and turns back around.

I close my eyes, knowing I'm too pissed now to sleep, but trying like hell anyway. Time passes and just when I start to doze off, the universe fucks me once again and "Girl Crush" by Lady Antebellum plays, reminding me that I won't ever be able to forget what we had. And as long as I'm in this life, I'll never be able to escape her either.

My phone vibrating in my pocket wakes me. It takes a moment for me to remember where I am. I look around the car and Diem is asleep, Clark still has his headphones on, the car is completely silent, and Rookie is looking at me. His eyes move to the floorboard and I follow them to find a cell phone laying at his feet. His gaze shifts to the back of Diem's seat, then back to me. She must have dropped it.

He raises his eyebrows, silently suggesting that I pick the damn thing up. I don't know why he wants me to snoop around, but my curiosity is getting the better of me by the second. My hand in my lap, I turn my thumb up so he can see, and his foot pushes the phone over to me. Stretching, I can feel Clark's eyes on me in the rearview mirror and I yawn, then lean my head against the back of his seat like I'm napping.

I position the phone in my lap so that if Diem wakes, she won't see me with it. Sliding my finger across the screen, I find it locked and smile. Some days, it is good to be a nerd. I crack the code and scroll through her apps.

Candy Crush—predictable.

Menstrual Cycle Tracker—ugh.

MyFace—of course.

Fitness Pal—naturally.

I scroll through her contacts, smiling when I find two hearts, a knife, and a gun emoji next to Zeke's name. There is only one text that is still unread. I don't have to open it to read the small message displayed on the screen.

Do it.

Hopefully, whoever Tampa is, isn't giving her an order to kill me. I have two guns on me, one behind my back and the other strapped to my ankle. I make a note to keep them close even in my sleep.

The inbox in her email is empty and so is the trash file. Outgoing messages have been wiped too. If I knew I had the time, I could find anything that has ever been on her phone, but I don't. So, I go to her gallery and discover that Diem is a selfie queen. Duck faces, smiles, pissed-off looks, edited pictures, and bathroom pics go on for pages. Then I come to pictures of me.

They were all taken when I wasn't looking. I'm in the bar, at Dirk's house, on my bike, and even some from when she was staying with me at home. Did she have a phone the whole time? If so, where the hell did she hide it?

My temper spikes when I come across a photo of her with another guy. She's taking a selfie with him at what looks like a bar. His arm is around her waist. Her head is on his shoulder. And what pisses me off more than the fact that they look too comfortable, is the patch he's wearing—Death Mob. And what's worse than that is I recognize him.

It's Fin.

I shoot the picture to my phone, then delete the message. Diem is still asleep, so without drawing any attention to myself, I slide the phone under her seat. Leaning back, I study the picture from my own phone a minute before I send it to Rookie. The date was months ago, but she was alone with him only days ago. Was she playing us both?

Don't do anything stupid.

Rookie's text has me cutting my eyes at him. Then texting back.

I'm not an amateur . . . ROOKIE.

He smirks, putting his phone back in his pocket. The clock on the dash reads a quarter after eleven, and I'm ready for some lunch and to take a piss.

As if she could hear my thoughts, Diem wakes up seeming dazed and confused. Looking in the backseat, she raises an eyebrow at me, looks over at Rookie, then finally to Clark. "I'm fucking starving. Let's eat."

He nods. "We're almost to Allentown, ma'am," he says, his voice cool and level.

"Shit! Already?" she asks in a panic, looking around for her phone. She's searching the seat and the floor and her purse and I've never seen her like this. It's pretty comical. "I can't find my fucking phone!" she roars, and I wonder if it's the "Do it" message she's so anxious to read.

"Look between the console and your seat," I suggest, leaning forward in an attempt to help her. She's digging, her breathing coming in quick bursts. Damn, she really is in a panic. Feeling sorry for her, I grab the phone, pushing it toward her fingers.

"Wait," she says, concentrating hard while her arm is shoved down in the side of the seat. "I think I felt it." Pulling her arm out, she holds the phone in her hand, furiously punching in the code and retrieving the message. I lean back and watch her as she lets out a sigh of relief. Then turning to Clark she says, "We'll be staying in Allentown tonight."

"Babe," I whine. "Come on. We haven't been on the road for six hours. I thought this was a road trip." I catch Rookie's smile out of the corner of my eye at my dramatics.

"Look," she snaps, positioning herself so that Rookie and I both can see her. "This isn't a field trip. It's business. There are still a lot of people out there riding in your territory wearing Death Mob cuts. So I suggest you man up and jump on the kill Death Mob bandwagon."

Before I can stop myself, I'm putting my foot in my mouth. "Like Fin? Is he on that bandwagon too? Or are we handing out special privileges?"

"Do I look like an idiot to you?" she asks, not at all surprised at my assumptions about her and Fin. I don't answer because I don't think I could say the right thing in this moment. "Fin is my problem. But if there is something you want to know, why don't you just ask. Stop being . . ." She gestures her hand toward me, scrunching her face into a scowl. "So . . . Shady."

I guess the pun is intended. "Are you working with him? Because I didn't hear any gunshots after I walked out of the bar, so therefore, I'm assuming he isn't dead. That is, unless you cooked him something." I give her a sardonic smile, which she is kind enough to give back.

"Yes, I am. I needed a man on the inside. And he's my man."

I want to roar when she refers to someone else as her man. Someone that isn't me.

"You don't actually think you can trust him do you?" I ask incredulously.

She rolls her eyes. "Of course I don't trust him, you fuckwad. But money talks and bullshit walks and life is one hell of a bargaining tool for someone who's facing the death penalty. Do your job. Shut up. And let me do mine."

I look at Rookie, who gives me a shrug. So maybe she does know what she's doing. And in my eyes, she'd just earned herself some respect. But it means nothing if she isn't aware of it. So I say two words and then vow to never say them again. Although, I'm sure they'll bite me in the ass sooner or later.

"Yes, ma'am."

Diem instructs Clark to pull into a drive-through, and I try to prepare myself for the clusterfuck I'm sure is to come. Could we not go inside? Or eat somewhere a little nicer than fucking McDonalds? Thinking back to our one and only date, I think she chose this place on purpose.

"Just get four number ones with Cokes," Diem orders, and I'm leaning forward at her command. She might be the boss, but I can order my own food.

"Um, I want a number six," I say, ready to kill her if she deprives me of the white-meat chicken strips instead of the soybean patty. "What about you, Rookie? You want a number six?"

Diem glares at me as Rookie plays along and looks up to read the menu. "No, I think I want a number eight. But I want Sprite. Caffeine stunts my growth."

"He's a growing boy," I add, flashing her a smile. Even Clark's lip twitches, and I'm not the only one that notices.

Her eyes slide over to him, her tone sweet as honey but no less threatening when she speaks. "What about you, Clark? What would you like?"

"A number one will be fine with me, ma'am," he answers, like the puss he is.

I clap him on the shoulder and he tenses. "Come on, Clark. Live a little."

He clears his throat, then pushes the button, ordering a number six for me, an eight with a Sprite for Rookie, a one for Diem, and then a ten with coffee for himself. I beam at Diem, who turns in her seat, mumbling something about us all being fucking idiots.

While we wait, Clark fidgets with his phone, then lets Diem know the room is booked. What kind of outlaw books a room, over a phone, with a place that takes reservations? He probably used a credit card that's in his name too. Or one that's in Dorian's name with a little inscription below it that reads, *Underground Mafia LLC*.

The food comes and just the smell of it has my stomach growling. I didn't realize how hungry I was. Looking around at everyone else shoveling their food down, I guess we all were pretty damn hungry. Leave it to Diem to try and starve us out. Even though she's eating faster than everyone else.

"Do we have some ketchup?" I ask, just to be a dick. My answer is Diem wadding up the bag and throwing it at me. I narrow my eyes on the back of her head, then search the bag and come up empty. She turns to show me the delicious ketchup on the end of her fry before giving me a wink and taking a bite. Damn, I hate her.

At the hotel, I'm surprised to find that we all have separate rooms—not that I'm complaining. But I'm a little disappointed that I'm separated from Rookie. I don't completely trust Diem or the message on her phone, and I'd like to keep Rookie in my sights

at all times. I doubt she would kill him, but I'm not putting anything past her either.

"Be ready in an hour," she tells us, just before disappearing
in her room. Clark enters his own room, not bothering to speak
or even look our way.

"I think we should stay together," I tell Rookie, and he nods
in agreement. I shut my door twice, just in case someone was
listening. We remain silent inside, while I throw on a black hoodie
and add a couple more weapons to my body. Rookie changes into
an outfit similar to mine with a full arsenal beneath his clothes.
No sooner are we seated than I hear a knock on the door next
to mine. I keep Rookie in place with a look and go to the door.
Looking out the peephole, I can't see anyone so I put my hand
on my gun at my back and ease the door open.

Diem is standing in the hall, her eyes swinging to me in surprise.
"You looking for me?" I ask, keeping most of my body inside.

She gives me a smile that doesn't reach her eyes and walks
over, glancing nervously back at the other door. "Yeah," she says,
her voice a little too high. She'd once told me she never lied. No
fucking wonder . . . She sucked at it.

"What do you want, Diem?"

"I wanted to go over the plan. Can I come in?"

I shake my head. "You don't want to go in there. Trust me."
I give her a cocky grin and her back straightens.

"We've been here all of ten minutes and already you have
someone in your room? Who the fuck is she? The maid?" she
asks, her temper rising as she throws her hands on her hips. She's
so cute when she gets all jealous.

"No. I just took a shit," I say, deadpan. Relief floods her face
along with a little embarrassment. She crosses her arms over her
chest, pushing those perky little tits up for me to see.

"Okay. No biggie. I'll just fill you in when we're in the car."

Her brows draw together in confusion as she jerks her thumb toward the other door. "Have you seen Rookie?" she asks, trying to be nonchalant.

Damn. Could she be any more obvious? "Probably taking a shower. You need him?"

"No. I was just curious." Oh for fuck's sake.

"Cut the shit, Diem. What do you want with Rookie?" I ask, growing more impatient with every second that passes.

Her eyes widen. "Nothing!"

"Then why can't you look at me?" She continues to avoid my gaze and I step out into the hall, flipping the latch to catch the door before I do. "Let me give you a little advice, *ma'am*," I drawl. "If you want to try and play games or fuck with someone, make damn sure it ain't us. We didn't get where we are by being naïve. Now, I'll ask you one more time. What do you want with Rookie?"

"I need him for a job, okay?" she says, her body sagging with relief from finally telling the truth.

"Now, see there?" I coo, like I'm talking to a small child. "How hard was that?"

She gives me the finger and I close the distance between us until her body is a mere inch from mine. "That's strike one, Diem. Don't lie to me. At the end of the day, my brothers will choose me over you every time. I will pull the plug on this whole operation. Now that Death Mob is out of the picture, you need us as much as we need you. Don't fucking forget that."

I turn on my heels, pushing open the door and waving my hand for her to come in. Dragging her feet, she gives me the evil eye as she walks through, then looks to Rookie, who's standing on the other side of the room. "What is this? A sleepover?"

I shut the door, standing in front of it to block her escape. Rookie mirrors my position, his arms crossed and looking just as pissed as I feel. Taking a seat on the bed, Diem puts her head in her hands. We wait for her to speak, which she takes her precious fucking time doing.

"I need you to take out Clark," she says, meeting Rookie's eyes. He gives a one-shouldered shrug. "All right."

"And," Diem starts, pausing to bite her lip. She stands, lifting her chin high and finding her balls. "I need you to take his place." This time, Rookie looks to me and it's my turn to shrug. "We have a rat in our family. Until Dorian is sure who it is, you two are the only ones he trusts." She turns to level me with a look. "After hearing your speech about family, he thought you would protect me to no ends considering I'm Dirk's sister. I guess he sees me as part of that family you're willing to give your life to protect."

"So why not just ask Shady to step in as your second?" Rookie asks, clearly not comfortable with his new job title.

"Because it complicates things," she snaps, keeping her eyes on me.

"Complicates things how?" His words are deliberately slow, making sure she understands them.

She takes a deep breath, letting it out slowly. "Because some people already know about us. Word is spreading fast and if they think we're a couple, they'll look to him for guidance instead of me. I'm the first woman to ever hold this much power in the business. If things were like they used to be, I would have married and my husband would hold the power. Some people still see the Underground that way. It will take some time to adapt. Until then, the rumors about us will just have to stay rumors."

How fucking convenient for her. "Well the least you can let me do is handle Clark. I mean no sense in wasting all this talent for nothing," I say, flexing my arms for her.

She rolls her eyes. "Can't do that either."

"And just why the hell not?" I ask, a little offended.

Walking toward me, she smiles. A very pleased look crosses

her face when she reaches me. Standing on her toes, she whispers in my ear, "Because you're the bait."

Of course I am.

I let Rookie and Diem have their little private powwow, while I stay in my room and sulk. I don't know why she thinks they need privacy. He's just gonna tell me everything anyway. I'm not jealous that Rookie is getting what I consider a promotion; actually, I'm happy he is. I don't trust anyone with Diem as much as I trust him. I just hate being out of the loop.

When Rookie finally comes back, he fills me in on the plan. In a nutshell, Clark thinks that I'm the one who is supposed to die. Lucky for me, I get to ride with him tonight to "handle something," where he is supposed to shoot me in the back of the head and leave me. But Rookie will be there to take him out before he does, only after finding out who the leaks are. I'll also be packing just in case shit turns south. What makes me nervous is that if Diem wants Clark dead, it's because she or Dorian doesn't trust him. So what in the hell makes her think he will follow through with her plan, and not devise one of his own?

I'm skeptical about the whole ordeal, but I keep it to myself. I do, however, tell Rookie to watch his back and to not put too much trust into Diem. His response is a glare and a reminder that he isn't a rookie anymore. Still, I don't like it. So I decide it's time to devise a plan of my own.

26

DIEM

THINGS COULD NOT get any more fucked up for me than they already were. I finally make it to the top, which wasn't an easy task, only to be constantly pushed back down. I expected it, really I did. From everyone, even my own father. But not from him. Zeke, or Shady, whatever in the hell his name is, will never be able to look at me as his superior.

I'd gained a little respect from him today, but I was afraid with that, I was losing the love he once felt. But me? I can't get him out of my head. I've never loved this hard before. I've never needed something so bad. I can control the want—I'd done it for years. But this is a longing . . . a need that only he can suffice. I feel like I have to have him to breathe . . . to eat . . . to sleep . . . And sometimes I think he feels the same way. But mostly, I think he feels nothing.

My plan to take Clark out is nothing more than a distraction. I'm confident that Shady and Rookie will figure it out before things get ugly. Actually, I'm counting on it. There is no other way for me to escape them, and I have to do this alone. Two years of my life were spent preparing me for this one moment. If I succeeded, it would be my greatest accomplishment. If I failed, the blowback would be devastating to the entire organization.

A part of me is a little excited that I'll finally get to play that damsel in distress role I've read about in books. I've never been able to before—mostly because you can't fake weakness, or at least I can't. Sure, I'd love to just fall down, break a leg, and have Shady come running to my rescue. But that sickness inside me wants more. I want to push him to his limits and see just how far he's willing to go. Hopefully, he's as smart as I think he is.

Clark and Shady just left, and Rookie is waiting for them at their destination. Shady is smart enough to cover his own ass if Clark starts getting suspicious, so I'm not worried about things going south. I am, however, worried about things going south for me. I'm quick and skilled with a gun. I'm fast on my feet. But my size is my biggest disadvantage. And taking on Fin by myself might get a little ugly if things don't go as planned.

I meet Fin at a bar we've met at plenty of times before in downtown Allentown. My stomach rolls with disgust just at the sight of him. But I flash a smile and force my cheeks to heat by imagining Shady is talking dirty to me. Fuck, I love when he talks dirty.

"Damn, baby. You lookin' good." Fin whistles, making me want to claw my eyes out. Instead, I curtsy.

"Jeans okay? Am I underdressed?" I ask, batting my eyelashes like a teenage girl.

He shakes his head, pulling me down on his lap. "No fucking way. I love them jeans on you." I grab his drink, rolling my eyes when I turn away and replacing my smile after I down it.

"Did you bring it?" I whisper, contemplating biting his ear

but deciding against it. I think that would be considered cheating. Although the big boner pressing up against my ass might be considered cheating too.

"You know I did," he says, giving me a list of every Death Mob member who decided to go rogue right after Sinner's Creed refused to give up Texas. I take the jump drive from his fingers, sliding it into my back pocket.

This is supposed to be the part where I kill him and walk away. We're alone in the back room that I reserved without his knowledge for that particular reason. But what fun is that? Tonight, I want to be rescued. And I need to test Shady's loyalty. If he shows, he's my guy. If he doesn't, then he's not the man I think he is.

"I'm ready for the army. Imagine the look on Sinner's Creed's faces when we take over Texas. I hope that prick Shady is there. I plan to make him suffer." He stares off in the distance; the mere thought of killing Shady is enough to put him in lethal mode.

Fin is under the impression that I'm going to take out Dorian. Having no one else to take his place, the elders would be forced to put me in charge. During that time, I was going to give Death Mob Texas, and name him as the new leader. He'd gathered me a list of names and numbers so I could contact them. I made some bullshit excuse that I had to do extensive background research to ensure they weren't working with the feds or Sinner's Creed. Like the idiot he is, he fell right into my trap.

Sliding my hand across his face, I turn his head back to look at me. "Just remember. It's our little secret. At least until I can get rid of my daddy." I almost choke on the word. *Daddy*. I hadn't called him that in years. It was forbidden because I wasn't his daughter anymore . . . I was his employee.

"I'll keep your secret, baby. As long as you keep your promise."

I give him a wicked smile. "I always keep my word." Just not this time.

We've been here two hours and I can't put his invitation to go back to his place off any longer. The room is now filled with people thanks to a shitty hostess, and Shady has yet to show. Already my plan is turning to shit. And I've worked this motherfucker up so much I'm afraid his dick might explode.

With no other option, we leave and he keeps me pressed possessively into his side. The small .38 I carry in my purse is enough to do the trick. I'll just have to wait until we get back to his place to use it. I won't have the time to attach the silencer, so it will have to be a fast kill and an even faster getaway.

My heart sinks with every step I take toward his hotel. I can't blow this. I can't shoot him now, because the streets are crawling with witnesses. I can't just turn and run either. Then he'd know something was wrong. If he did, the past two years of my life will have been for nothing. He is a job. I have to see it through.

If I'd just stuck to my original plan to kill him here, I wouldn't be in this predicament. But I'd put my own selfish needs before my family. I wanted to prove to Dorian that Shady was the man I needed at my side. If he showed tonight and saved me, then both of my goals would be accomplished. But if I didn't succeed in killing Fin and escaping, then I'd be putting the whole Underground at risk. And I'd be losing Shady too.

As we pull away, a deep sadness comes over me. Zeke didn't come. Shady had left me alone. I loved both sides of him equally, and they were both gone. Either he was too stupid to figure out my plan, dead, or didn't really care. If I was a betting woman, I'd put my money on the latter.

27

SHADY

SOMETHING'S UP WITH Diem. The more I think about it, the more I think she's playing me. I don't know what she's really up to, but taking out Clark is just a distraction—I can feel it.

She knew Rookie wasn't in that room. But she wanted it to look like I forced her to add me into the conversation. As much as she wants respect, she would do everything in her power to get it. So to get inside her head, I think about what I would have done.

First, I'd have pulled the trigger on my right-hand man myself. I'd prove that no man was safe from my wrath. But she didn't. Instead she put it in the hands of Rookie—a man she doesn't trust near as much as she trusts me.

Second, Dorian wouldn't have sent her away with Clark if he felt like he was a threat. Diem wouldn't have allowed herself to fall asleep in the company of a man she couldn't trust either. Clark wasn't guilty of anything, he was just collateral damage.

Third, if he really wanted to kill me, he would have known I was smart enough to carry a weapon. A man in his position doesn't get where he is by underestimating guys like me. Plus, how could he get me in a vehicle without a gun? He knew I was packing, but just to be sure, I made it a point to show him.

We'd discussed guns. We'd compared holsters. He admitted to hearing a rumor that I was one of the best shots ever seen. He didn't want to kill me. He hadn't betrayed Diem either. And when I fake a call from her and inform him that she wants me to stay and let him and Rookie handle the problem, he doesn't question me. That's because he knows Dorian trusts me. So Diem's story wasn't a complete lie.

I fill Rookie in on what's happening, and he agrees to distract Clark by actually visiting a couple of Death Mob chapters in the area. Come to find out, that's what Clark was instructed by Diem to do all along. Now I just have to find her before she does something stupid or gets herself killed.

My only lead is Fin, who becomes my main suspect when I find that he booked a room in Allentown under his legal name. Fucking amateurs. I start there, but find his room empty. I could wait, but if Diem was going to meet him, she damn sure wouldn't do it here.

I drive around, my anxiety building. Fin is a big guy. She couldn't take him on by herself. If she shot him, she'd have to do it somewhere discreet, but somewhere she could make a quick getaway from. Pulling up a satellite image of Allentown on my phone, I notice a site just outside of downtown that looks like an old warehouse. I match it with the lists of Death Mob clubhouses in the area, and find that the address isn't exactly the same, but similar.

My emotions are everywhere, but fear takes precedence. I'm not used to the feeling. But where she is concerned, fear is all I feel.

Fear of losing her.

Fear of her hurting.

Fear of not being able to protect her.

But most of all, I fear that Sinner's Creed isn't my greatest love anymore.

28

DIEM

I'VE NEVER REALLY been scared in my entire life. Even when I was a little girl, I was fearless. I often pretended to be afraid because I got attention from it, but it was just an act. In this moment though, I'm terrified.

It's not my only life I'm scared for, it's everyone else who will be affected if I don't succeed. Dorian is a dick, but he is my father and he believes in the Underground. Hell, he lives for it. His life is absorbed by it. My grandparents, uncles, cousins . . . my entire family is at stake. If I fail, Dorian fails. And if Dorian fails, the Mafia will never forgive him. They will turn on him, and any who choose to stand beside him will be guilty of treason.

He'd put all his faith in me. The whole family had. Now I was so scared I would fuck it up that I couldn't even focus on my task at hand.

Fin's room is located at the very end of the hall, on the eighteenth floor, right next to the maintenance room that has to be opened with an electronic card. I count the seconds it takes to get there, and guess that I could get to the stairway in less than five.

I've been pretending to be intrigued by what Fin is telling me, but he's just rambling about his plans to buy a private island, so I don't pay him much attention. When he opens the door, I walk in and head straight to the minibar that has already been picked over.

"So you gonna wire the money now?" he asks, and I can tell by his voice that he's growing impatient.

Sitting on the edge of the desk, I sip from the whiskey bottle and try to look sexy in an attempt to distract him. "Is it just about the money with you, Fin? I thought you liked my company."

His eyes drag slowly up my body, taking in my tight jeans and sleeveless silk top that accents my cleavage. *There ya go, big boy. Think with your other head. I can control it better.*

Pulling my lip between my teeth, I widen my eyes, feigning innocence and lust. "How about I freshen up first, then we can talk money."

He walks closer, every step making my heart pound harder in my chest. But I appear unaffected. "No need to freshen up, baby. I like my bitches a little dirty." Without warning, he grabs my wrist, slinging me onto the bed. My purse falls to the floor, too far out of my reach.

The look of horror on my face doesn't go unnoticed, and for a minute I think he's going to leave me alone. But then, he grabs my purse, retrieving my gun and holding it up for me to see. "What's this for?" he growls, his face turning almost purple with anger.

I force a smile, trying to play it off, but my voice doesn't sound right. "I always carry a gun, baby. You know that."

"Baby, huh?" he huffs, shaking his head. "You ain't never called me baby." I stiffen the moment I see that lightbulb go off in his head. "You're fuckin' playin' me, ain't you?" I open my mouth to speak, but nothing comes out. "I'm going to fuck you up, but before I kill you, you're going to make that call and give me my money."

Narrowing my eyes, I dig deep and find the strength I know I have inside me somewhere. Love was for pussies and it had weakened me. I force myself to push thoughts of what will happen to Shady, to Dorian, and all of my family to the back of my mind. If I'm going to die today, I'm going to do it with my fucking dignity.

"I'm not giving you shit," I spit, feeling the sense of satisfaction spread through me like warm honey at the look on his face. "You think you're gonna accomplish something by killing me? Dorian has ten more in line to take my spot. Do your worst." I throw my arms out, inviting him over.

"Oh, I know your death will likely mean nothing. But I can guarantee that I will enjoy doing it. Don't be so quick to invite me over, sweetheart; it's gonna be a long night for you. But first, the drive."

He holds his hand out. Like hell I am going to give it back. I only have two options—lay here and die, or get up and fight. Unlucky for him, I'm a fighter. He moves quick, fisting his hand in my hair and backhanding me hard across my face. I spit back at him, which only earns me another slap that immediately has my eye swelling.

Like a switch, I turn it all off and feel nothing. I've been here before and this time is no different. Pain is weakness to me and I refuse to feel it in this moment.

Pulling back my leg, I kick him hard in the shin. He grunts, tossing me back on the bed. Straddling me, he rips open my blouse. I let him get all of two seconds with the bare breasts beneath it before putting my knee in his crotch. His face contorts and I waste no time gouging my thumbs into his eyes. It's enough of a distraction to get out from under him and I'm on my feet.

He's gathering his bearings by the time I make it to the door, and I can see the gleam of his pistol out of the corner of my eye. Knowing I won't be able to outrun his bullets, I rush into the hall and pray like hell the maintenance room is by some chance unlocked. Before I can twist the handle, it's opened and I'm jerked into the darkness as a hand covers my mouth.

"Shhh," I hear, and I whimper with relief as the smell of Shady engulfs me. His hand presses further into my mouth, silencing me as Fin shuffles around outside and tries the handle. Putting his back to the door, Shady's arm goes around my waist, holding me to him, and I know it's to protect me in case Fin is stupid enough to shoot.

Moments later, a door slams and Shady's phone illuminates the small room. The light blinds me as his eyes move swiftly over my face.

No sooner is his hand away from my mouth than I'm whisper-shouting at him. "It's about fucking time! I was two seconds from being ass raped before you showed up."

"Well now, we wouldn't want that, would we?" He's trying to be a smart-ass but I can see the flash of anger in his eyes. Softening his tone, he asks, "You okay?"

I nod. "I'm fine." But really, I'm anything but.

"How about you let me handle this one?" he suggests, tucking my hair behind my ear. The gesture is intimate and for some reason I feel like crying. But of course, I don't.

He doesn't wait for my answer; he just leans in and kisses my head, then bolts out of the room and across the hall. I stand in the darkness, waiting for him to return. Everything was going to be okay. I feel in my back pocket and smile when my fingers touch the jump drive. Soon, we wouldn't have to worry about hunting Death Mob. They would be coming to us.

Shady returns minutes later and I can tell by the look on his face that Fin is dead, but he didn't die the slow death Shady was hoping for. Pulling off his hoodie, he hands it to me and I slip it on over my torn blouse. Dammit. It was one of my favorites.

"We need to leave. Now." Grabbing my hand, he pulls me into the hall, keeping his head down as we walk to the elevators. "Rookie and Clark are waiting outside."

I smile beneath the hoodie, but he can't see it. I guess he was smart enough to figure out my plan. I just hope Clark doesn't hold any hard feelings against me. Business is business, after all.

"Clark doesn't know anything about this. Rookie doesn't know much either." I turn to look at him as we board the elevator, his hand tightening around mine as he clenches his teeth. That vein next to his temple bulges and I know he's pissed. And he has every reason to be. "What the fuck were you thinking, Diem?" he growls between his teeth, burning me with the intensity of his gaze.

When I don't answer, he reaches out and punches the stop button on the elevator. I guess he wants an answer now. "I had to do this alone. I figured turning each of you against the other was the only way for it to work."

"Why did you think you had to do this alone?"

When I take too long to answer, he lets out a growl of warning and suddenly I have diarrhea of the mouth. "Because I didn't want to risk getting caught. I've worked too hard and sacrificed too much for anybody to jeopardize this all because they thought I was too weak to handle it."

"You're the one in charge, Diem. Simply telling us to stay the fuck away would have worked." But even as he says the words, I can hear the doubt in them.

"Really? You'd have stayed away? What about Clark? His head is further up my ass than yours is."

A low rumble rips through his chest, and I can see him biting his tongue to keep from yelling at me. Or kissing me. Either wouldn't be very smart right now. Although I wouldn't mind being kissed out of anger. He has a way with his mouth when he's pissed.

"So the leak on the inside? Is that bullshit too?" he asks, seething.

"Not entirely. Dorian does think it's safer for me to have you around. In the event someone gets the idea to take me out. He's always been a little paranoid. You can never be too sure how people will react when someone new steps up."

"And Rookie being your second? What the fuck is that?" he barks, and I know he's trying to scare me, but I'm too relieved that he's here to be frightened.

"It went with the plan." I shrug. "If you really would've killed Clark, then that's exactly what would've happened. I needed you prepared just in case." Either he isn't pleased with my answer, or he's going over it in his head. But then I remember I have a question of my own. "How did you even find me?"

Digging in his back pocket, he grabs his phone. Holding it up, I see the picture of me and Fin in the bar displayed on the screen. I can't help it, I smile. "I knew you'd find that."

A little tension leaves his face, and eventually, he lets out a sigh. Looking to the ceiling, he mumbles a string of obscenities under his breath. I don't know if I do it in my shitty attempt to apologize or just because I need to feel his arms around me, but I bury my face in his chest and slide my hands around his waist.

Without hesitation, he engulfs me in a hug. "Please don't ever scare me like that again," he says, his voice deep. There is something comforting about having my ear against his chest as he speaks. The vibration soothing me and making me feel safe. "I'm only asking you to trust me, Diem. I know what you're fighting for. I'm fighting for it too. But I can't be here for you if you keep me in the dark."

I close my eyes, delighting in the only feeling of protection I've ever experienced. He makes me feel secure. Like I can conquer the world as long as I have him to lean on. I don't answer, because I refuse to make promises I can't keep—especially to him. Pulling away from his chest, I hit the button on the elevator and we're descending once again.

Rookie and Clark are waiting in the car at the front entrance. I slide in the backseat with Shady, keeping close to him because I can't bear the feeling of distance between us. I'd waited too long to be near him and I wasn't ready to let go just yet.

"Clark," Shady says, taking charge while I stay lost in my own thoughts. "I need a sweep of room 1859. Rookie, get Cleft on standby. We got some stuff coming his way." I meet Clark's eyes in the mirror, giving him a nod and confirming Shady's orders.

"You okay, ma'am?" Clark asks, refusing to move the car until I answer him.

"I'm fine," I say, but it doesn't appease him. "My head's still a little fuzzy from the hit. Shady's taking lead on this one until I can think straight. Do as he asks, please."

He nods. "Yes, ma'am. Should I call Dorian?"

I level him with a look, although I know he didn't mean any disrespect. But I hold tight to my authority, even though every minute that passes it feels more and more like a façade. "I might have taken a hit, but I'm still in fucking charge. Now, unless you want to call Dorian to ask for a promotion, I suggest you do the job that was given to you."

A sparkle of respect dances in his eyes as the corner of his mouth turns up slightly. "Yes, ma'am."

As we drive away, I pull the jump drive from my back pocket. "This is a list of every Death Mob member old and new along with all their information. Family, background history, addresses, phone numbers—everything you need. I've been working for two years to get this. Don't fuck it up." I hold it out to Shady, who offers me a smirk.

He's so much better at all of this than me. The more power I have, the more I want to give it away. Maybe I'm not cut out for this life. But Shady? He was made for it. Taking the drive from my fingers, there is a sadness in his eyes. He can see right through me. I've always been good at concealing my thoughts, but I've never been able to hide them from him.

He knows I don't want this. And he hates it for me. He doesn't have to tell me, but the promise is there. I can feel it. He'll do everything in his power to protect me. Whether it's from my father. From my family. Or even from myself.

29

SHADY

WE MAKE IT back to the hotel and I get busy sending the files straight to Cleft from my laptop. I'm not sure what Diem's plan is for it just yet, but I won't move forward on anything until I have a say-so from her. Two years of enduring who knows what is a long time for me to just take this from her without giving her the satisfying glory. Whether she wants it or not, I don't know. But it will be her who makes that decision.

She shows up to my room freshly showered, beaten, and looking completely exhausted. My blood boils at the sight of the bruise on her cheek. Fin deserved a hell of a lot worse than what he got. "I need sleep and it comes better with you." I couldn't agree more, and open the door further, inviting her in.

"I'm gonna shower," I tell her, while she helps herself to one of the bottles of whiskey at the minibar. She grabs a cigarette from my pack on the dresser, lighting it before giving me a nod.

I take my time, giving her some space. I know she feels more comfortable having me here, but she still needs to reflect on everything that happened tonight. I don't know what she endured in the moments before I got there, but the evidence on her face paints a picture that leaves me with a pretty good idea.

She doesn't seem to be struggling with that as much as she is something else. I just haven't figured out what it is. Maybe the responsibility is finally taking its toll on her. Maybe she is still feeling the impact of relief that her plan had been productive, even though it wasn't smooth. Or maybe it was the sight of me stepping up and taking charge that has her feeling inadequate or doubtful. Whatever it is, she has to figure it out on her own. I can't help her with that. All I can do is be here for her. Which is exactly what I plan to do from here on out.

Already tangled in my sheets, she flips the covers back, inviting me in. I crawl in beside her, and she curls her body around mine and I turn out the light, rubbing my hand up and down her back.

"Do you ever feel bad about some of the stuff you do?" she asks, her fingers rubbing circles across my stomach. "Like the killing," she adds, her tone softer.

"I've don't a lot of shit in my life. Eventually, you learn to block it out." I frown in the darkness, realizing how much of a monster I really am.

"So it gets easier?"

How can I lay here and tell her that killing people will soon be second nature? She's a lot of things, but she's not a lost cause. She's not me. "How did you feel when you killed Cyrus?"

"Euphoric," she whispers guiltily. "But I don't always feel that way. Sometimes I feel like I'm doing society a favor. Sometimes I assure myself that it was for the greater good. But, most of the time, I hate myself."

My heart clenches at her admission. I can relate to what she's feeling. "You remember that night at the cabin when I came to bed late and you asked if I was okay?"

"I remember," she says, her hand coming to rest on my stomach in the same position she kept it that night.

"I killed two Death Mob Prospects that night." My eyes close at the reminder, and that sickness returns to my gut. "They were innocent . . . just in the wrong place at the wrong time. I can't tell you that it gets easier, because it doesn't. But I can tell you that the only person who can make you pull that trigger is you. Don't live your life haunted by ghosts, Diem. If it doesn't feel right, don't do it. Don't try to force yourself to be a monster. It's not worth it. Take it from someone who knows."

I feel her hot tears on my chest. I don't know if she's crying for her, for me, or for the lives lost. But the effect of her sadness is still the same—it rips my fucking heart out. "I don't think you're a monster," she whispers, tightening her hold on me.

No matter how much evil I share with her, she chooses to only see the good in me. She has more faith in my humanity than I do. Even when I can't forgive myself, she finds the strength to defeat my demons. There are many different definitions of love—she is mine.

With our mission accomplished, there is nothing left for us to do here, so we head back to Hillsborough. The drive is long and silent. Back at my house, the only good-bye she offers me is a promising look that tells me she will see me again soon.

Rookie and I fly back to Jackpot, where Carrie meets us at the airport. They've been without each other for weeks, so I give Rookie and Carrie some time alone and tell them I'll catch a cab back to the bar. I feel envy at the way Carrie looks at him with a passion in her eyes that transforms Rookie from a one-percenter to nothing but her man.

What I would give to have that same kind of relationship with

Diem. But that's not possible for people like us. At least not in this life.

Two days later, I'm on the porch at Dirk's house when I receive a call from an unknown number. "Yeah?"

"It's Dorian," the gruff voice announces, and my heart kicks into overdrive as my mind immediately starts thinking the worst. The worst being, was something wrong with Diem? "From here on out, I don't want Diem going anywhere without you." The command is not negotiable. But I wasn't planning to argue.

"Done," I say, already walking inside to pack my bags.

"Keep her in your sights at all times. I don't have to tell you your fate if you defy me." His thick accent makes me think of a movie I saw once where the don told the man that he would be swimming with the fishes. I start to make a joke about it, but think better of it.

"I understand. Is there something I should be concerned about?" I shouldn't have asked. If he'd wanted me to know, he'd have told me.

"There are always concerns in this business." He hangs up, not offering me anything else.

I call Diem, and my heart rate spikes when she doesn't answer. Dialing again, she answers on the second ring, snapping in my ear. "What?"

"Why didn't you answer the first time?" I snap back, throwing shit in my bag with a little more force than necessary.

"Because I'm busy. What do you want, Shady?" She sounds aggravated. I can hear men around her talking, their accents thick and some even speaking in a different language.

"Business meeting stressing you out, pretty girl?" I ask, lowering my tone.

She sighs, a sure sign that she is overworked and exhausted. "You have no idea," she mumbles into the phone.

"Well, I got a call from your daddy. He wants me to come babysit."

"I know," she says, unaffected by my snarky comeback. "I had to endure his wrath because I didn't keep you with me after he told me to. I guess he figured he'd pull rank on me."

"He did. You okay with that?" I ask, not that her answer will matter either way. I don't want to swim with the fishes. And I miss her.

"Do I have a choice?"

"Nope."

I can feel her smile through the phone. "Well, when will you be here? I miss ordering you around." I know she misses me too, even though she refuses to admit it.

"I'm flying out in an hour. I'll be there by dark." Hanging up, I throw my bags over my shoulder, locking up Dirk's house behind me. Maybe one day, I'll be able to say it's mine. And I'll be able to share it with Diem. But as I mount my bike that rational side of my brain reminds me that will never happen.

Clark picks me up from the airport in Concord. If he's here to get me, then I know that wherever Diem is, she's safe. He greets me with a nod, and I waste no time picking his brain for information.

"How is she?"

He takes a moment to find the right words to say before answering my question. "She's fine."

I smirk. "Are those her words or yours?"

"Hers," he answers shortly.

"Do you believe her?" I ask, lighting a smoke. I offer one to him but he refuses.

"What I believe is irrelevant."

I shake my head, ready to cut through this Mafia loyalty bullshit. "It's relevant to me. I want the truth, Clark. Your truth. It goes no further than the two of us."

Cutting his eyes at me, he gives me a long hard look before glancing at the dash. I follow his gaze to the intercom system that is recording every word we say. With a push of a few buttons, I disable it. "There. Now talk."

"She's buckling under the pressure," he starts, throwing his sunglasses on the dash and dragging a hand down his face. Damn, he looks like he hasn't slept in weeks. "Ever since she took over, Dorian's been testing her. He wants her to appear ruthless so nobody questions her authority. And to do that, she's been doing nothing but killing since she got into this. Every time she pulls the trigger, I see a little piece of her die."

There is no denying the anger in his voice. He's pissed at how Dorian is handling things, and even more pissed that he can't do anything about it.

"You can't pull the trigger for her?" I ask, knowing that like me, killing comes second nature to a man like him.

He shakes his head. "He wants her to do it. Like she has something to prove. She doesn't have shit to prove. She is Diem Demopolous. The *Mafiusa*. Daughter of Dorian. The underboss. That is proof in itself." His Greek accent thickens with the rise of his temper. "I do not agree with Dorian, but he is my don and I stand behind him. But Diem." He lets out a breath. "She is better than this. Better than us." He looks over at me, letting me know that I'm in that category.

"How are you tied into Dorian?" I ask, and he's reluctant to answer.

"I am his brother." His voice is low, almost a whisper. He keeps his eyes on the road, ignoring my curious stare.

"But he said his brothers were murdered."

"So he said. Like Dirk, I was protected. But Diem is the future in his eyes. She is the one who will change the face of the Mafia. I am nothing more than a soldier." His lips curl as he says the words. "But at least I get to watch over the one I still see as a little girl. She needs someone to count on. I know she has me." He glances over, trying to read me. "Does she have you too?"

With conviction and promise, I give him my answer. "You're fucking right she does."

On the top floor of the Concord Skyrise Building, Diem is seated at the head of the table surrounded by the Mafia hierarchy. The walls are glass, giving you a full view of the entire lobby and the outside world. After all her hard work, she'd finally made it to the top. But I believe it's the last place she wants to be.

I'd slipped my cut on in the elevator. It was my name tag—letting everyone know who I am. Diem wears a name tag too—a white business suit that separates her from the black ties in the room. But it also gives her an angelic appearance.

I watch her stand, placing her hands on the table and leaning forward. I can see her tone, tanned legs beneath the glass. Fucking skirts . . . they do something to me. She's portraying her role as *Mafiusa*, and living up to its name.

The steel in her spine . . . the grit in her tone . . . the ice in her eyes . . . She's every bit of the underboss Clark said she was. I look over at him and see pride sparkling in his dark eyes. He's a big man. Around forty years old. Now that I know the truth, I can see the avuncular role he plays where Diem is concerned.

"Come on, Clark. Let's bust up this party." I move forward with determination. I don't give a shit how important these men think they are. The woman at the head of the table belongs to me. And I'm the motherfucker who will now and forever be standing to her right.

I push open the glass doors, drawing the attention of everyone in the room. They look down their noses at me. To them, I'm nothing more than biker trash. I'm beneath them. But to her, I'm the only man in the room.

Walking directly up to her, I ignore everyone as I slide my hand around her waist and pull her in so I can whisper in her ear. "You look fucking delicious in that skirt." My teeth graze her earlobe before I release her and focus my attention on the men at the table. Their eyes move from me to her and back.

She has her lip between her teeth, fighting a smile. She can pretend to be unaffected all she wants. But I know she's turned on, and dammit if I am too.

Clearing her throat, she addresses the room. "Gentlemen, this is Shady. He'll be serving as my head of security and our enforcer."

"Does Dorian know about this?" one of the older men asks. He looks like a character from *The Godfather*, and I have to bite my cheek to keep from smiling.

"Actually, it was Dorian who sent me," I answer, taking the heat from Diem and putting it on myself.

The old man stands, buttoning his suit jacket as he does. "It's hard to believe he would send . . ." His eyes appraise me with disgust. ". . . You . . . for such an important job."

"My only job is to protect Diem, which I will do at any cost." I give him a challenging look, but still try to remain respectful. Even though he doesn't share the same courtesy. I'm sure at one time, he was a very powerful man, and I never underestimate an OG like him.

"You know Diem personally?" he quips, giving me a smile that suggests he knows something about our love life.

I offer him a smile of my own—a cutting one that suggests he mind his own fucking business. "I knew *Dirk* personally." The air thickens with tension and the windows frost with the iciness in my tone.

"I see," he says, taking his seat. *Told that motherfucker.*

Clapping her hands together, Diem absorbs everyone's attention once again. "Now that we're through measuring dicks, can we get back to business?"

The room returns to talk of production and distribution. I stand tall and proud beside Diem, who handles the meeting with the knowledge and sense of someone far beyond her years. She's skilled in this department. Every argument that approaches the table is won in her favor. For every possible problem, she has a solution. By the time the meeting is adjourned, there is no question that she is in charge. And there isn't one man in this room who doesn't have her respect.

Every day this week is the same thing. Meetings last all day and sometimes into the night. The fall of Death Mob was inevitable, but with it came a stall in distribution. Sinner's Creed chapters were sent from all over to occupy the East Coast, leaving our territory vulnerable to outsiders. Diem assured Nationals that we would not be compromised, and I knew she would stand firm on her word.

At the end of every day, Diem and I drive back to the cabin, which serves as our escape from reality. After an entire day of talking, we enjoy the silence in each other's company. Mostly, we sleep, but sometimes I just hold her in my recliner. Or we sit out on the porch and get lost in the peacefulness. But tonight, Diem feels like talking.

We're in bed, me sitting against the headboard with her head in my lap while I rub her hair. She hadn't even bothered getting undressed, so I didn't either. "My whole life I thought I wanted to be like him." She doesn't have to say Dorian's name for me to know who she's referring to. "But since you came into my life, I'm not so sure anymore."

She flips to her stomach, turning her head to face me. My hand moves from her hair to slide up and down her back. "So what do you want?" I ask, brushing my thumb across her lip.

"I want this." She looks down at my cut—her eyebrows narrowing slightly in confusion. "Tell me what they mean." My eyes fall to the thick, dirty threads she's touching.

"This one." My finger follows hers as it moves over the stitches of the *SFFS* patch. "Sinners forever forever sinners. It means I'm in this for life."

"And *SCMC*?"

"Sinner's Creed Motorcycle Club." She traces the *Pas 2 Las* patch and she shoots me a questioning look. I smirk. "It means 'can't get right.'"

"Ain't that the damn truth," she mumbles, before glancing over the other patches. Without her having to ask, I find myself telling her the meaning of every patch on my cut. And what's more surprising is I want to.

"*Night Crew* is the name of my Houston chapter. The number thirteen inside the diamond is a reminder to never lie to my brothers. One-percenter defines my commitment to my club. *FTW*—"

"Fuck the world." Diem cuts me off, and my lip turns up at the confidence in her words. I shake my head. Frowning, she looks back at the patch, then up at me.

"Common misconception. It means forever together wherever. There's no amount of miles that can keep me from my brothers if they ever need me." I point to the *I am my brother's keeper* patch. "That's how I earned this." She studies my cut a moment, letting my words and the true meaning of my brotherhood sink in. Her eyes land on the one I've yet to explain and she quirks an eyebrow.

"Nasty bastard?"

"You don't want to know." She looks like she wants to argue. But really, she doesn't. "That's an earned patch, babe. Trust me. You don't want to know." Either she's smart enough to heed my warning, or she's too tired to press further, but her head lays back in my lap and that lost look crosses her face again.

"You know." She lets out a breath. "I used to wake up every morning, ready to conquer the day and earn my stripes. Now I can't wait for the sun to set so I can come here with you. And when I get here, I never want to leave."

"Then don't," I offer. Dropping my voice, I add, "Walk away."

She rolls her eyes as she stands. "You know it's not that easy." I watch her undress, wishing I could do something to ease her mind. Visions of her naked give me an idea, but I'm sure her mind is too preoccupied to be in the mood.

"This is your life, Diem. You only get one," I say, preaching as much to myself as I am to her.

"It's not the meetings," she starts in frustration. Ripping her bra over her head, her pretty, olive-toned tits come into view and I bite back a groan. "I feel like I'm accomplishing something when I'm there."

"You do," I tell her as she slips one of my T-shirts over her head. For some reason, that's sexier than her being naked.

"But it's everything else that I hate." I know she's talking about the killing. How can any man subject their daughter to such a life of darkness?

"I promise that as long as I'm around, you won't have to do it anymore."

She smiles the saddest smile I've ever seen. It's worse than seeing her cry. "You're too good to me. I don't deserve you." The words only hurt because she believes them.

"Come here," I order, pulling her down so that she's straddling my lap. Taking her face in my hands, I kiss her head. "You deserve to have everything your heart desires." She looks like she's fixing to break, so I kiss her. Soon, her hands are fisting in my hair and her body is asking for everything I want to give her.

Wrapping my arm around her waist, I move her beneath me, trying my best to kiss away any doubt that she has about herself.

I push my cut off my shoulders, then break the kiss long enough to pull my shirt over my head. Finding her mouth again, I devour her. Kissing her until she's breathless and panting. My lips trail down her neck as my hands move slowly up her sides, pushing her shirt up her body, and then ridding her of it completely.

"You're beautiful," I whisper, running my hands up her arms and holding them above her head. My tongue traces a pattern down her neck and across her chest. Her breasts are just the right size for me to wrap my hand around, and I massage one while my mouth massages the other.

Her body contracts with every breath, and I move my tongue down to her navel, my hands all over her. The lower I dip my head, the more breathless she becomes in anticipation. Finally, I make it to my happiest place on earth.

I drag my nose up the length of her pussy, inhaling the scent of her that has my dick hardening to its fullest. With the tiniest touch of my tongue, her body jerks. Figuring she's been deprived long enough, my mouth covers her, my tongue not leaving one spot untouched.

Pushing my finger inside her, I curl the tip, feeling that small area of velvety flesh that craves to be touched. Then, adding another, I finger fuck her while my mouth sucks at her clit, my tongue swirling around it as she comes on my fingers.

She smells like fucking sunshine. She tastes like heaven. And where she wants to spend every moment with me, I want to spend every moment right here—my face buried in her pussy while she screams my name. A place where there is no Mafia. No rules. No pressure. Just me and her and the beauty of coming.

Pulling my fingers from inside her, I drag them back up her body and into her mouth. She greedily sucks my fingers, proving to me what she can do with her mouth. I'd love to let her test it on my cock, but I'd rather be inside her pussy.

Leaning over her, I kiss her as I kick my boots off. Her feet push at my jeans, sliding them down my legs. I keep my hands in her hair, lifting my hips and positioning my cock at the entrance of her pussy. Slowly, I push into her. Letting her feel the full effect of me as I stretch her walls until I'm completely buried inside.

I fuck her slow, keeping my mouth on her mouth. My hands on her hands. My fingers threaded through hers as I make love to her in a way that makes her feel special. Because she is. She doesn't rush me. She doesn't talk. She just lets me give her exactly what I know she wants. Her trust in me is overwhelming. It goes far beyond the bed. She trusts me with her entire life. She is my queen, and I will always be the one she can count on.

"I love you, Diem," I whisper to her as she comes. "I love you so fucking much."

She moans at the feel of me bursting inside her. The rock of my hips slows as I drag out our orgasm as long as I can. "I love you, Shady," she whispers back to me. My heart swells at her words. She loved Zeke. He was her man. But the sound of my name, my real fucking name on her lips as she tells me she loves me, makes me feel like more than her man. It makes me feel like a king.

Her fucking king.

The next night, Dorian calls Diem for a meet. I know she's nervous, but on the outside, she's the woman he trained her to be. The killer he wants her to be. And the person she is not.

We ride to an abandoned building just south of Hillsborough, in the small town of Deering. Bikes are lined up and down the dirt driveway, and I don't recognize any of them as Sinner's Creed. I keep my face impassive, but my eyes move to Clark's in the rearview. After a moment, he senses my glare and meets my gaze. Frowning, he gives me a small shake of his head, and I know I'm not going to like what is fixing to go down.

Inside, there are over fifty members of Death Mob standing in a huddle in the center of the room. The building is concrete with all the windows missing and nothing but concrete pillars scattered across the bottom level. Dorian is here, surrounded by men who have their guns trained on Death Mob.

"She's here," I hear one of the men say to Dorian, and his eyes move to focus on Diem and then me, who stays right by her side. He offers her a smile that holds no warmth. She gives him a nod as we close the distance.

"I figured since you were the one who put in all the effort, that you should be here for this," Dorian says, a cold look in his dark eyes.

"Be here for what?" Diem asks, her voice strong.

Dorian leans in, keeping his voice low enough for only us to hear. "The slaughter." Turning away, he walks toward the group of bikers, addressing them as if they were his friends.

Diem's breathing is coming in short, fast pants, and I see horror in her eyes even though she's fighting like hell to conceal it. Reaching out, I squeeze her hand. "Calm down, pretty girl. I got you," I say when she turns those big frightened eyes on me. I offer her a wink and an encouraging smile. She focuses on my face a minute while she controls her breathing. Then nods.

I let go of her hand, and place mine on the small of her back, guiding her forward. Straightening her spine with her chin held high, she joins the crowd of her father's men.

"I don't like rebels," he's saying, speaking to the members of Death Mob who were under the impression they were joining an army that he wasn't leading. I see the hate forming in their eyes when they notice Diem. Soon, they're all looking at her with betrayal.

I want to protect her, but this is something that Dorian will insist she face. So all I can do is stand next to her and glare back, promising them a slow death if they so much as take one step in her direction. The leader of the group is champing at the bit to say something. He just better hope like hell it doesn't involve Diem.

"That bitch betrayed us, and she'll probably betray you too," he says to Dorian. And I'm already on my way over.

Dorian catches movement out of the corner of his eye and turns to me. His gaze follows me the thirty steps it takes to be nose to nose with the motherfucker who'd just called my woman a bitch. Pulling my gun from my back, I use the butt to break his nose, then shoot both of his kneecaps. His brothers, like the cowards they are, stand back in horror as their brother screams in pain. They don't even attempt to rush me.

"Shut up," I growl, pointing my gun down at his head as he lays on the floor. Since he can't control his screams, I put a bullet in the man next to him. "Shut up or I'll smother your screams with the bodies of your brothers." He puts his fist in his mouth, biting hard to keep from crying out.

"Does anyone else have something to say about her?" I ask to the entire room, spinning around so that I address not only Death Mob, but the Underground too. "I have plenty of bullets for everybody." The only sound is the rush of adrenaline I hear in my veins and the heavy beat of my heart.

My eyes move to Dorian, who gives nothing away. I don't need his approval or respect. My offer of bullets was extended to his ass too. Placing my gun in the back of my jeans, I give Death Mob one last look of warning before reclaiming my spot next to Diem. Her hands are clasped so tightly in front of her that her knuckles are white. Her arms tremble slightly and I hope like hell it's not from fear of me. When she looks up, a hint of a smile crosses her lips as her big brown eyes thank me. Shooting her a wink, I let her know it's all good.

Dorian goes on about respect and knowing your place. About how each of them could have been saved if they would have just disappeared. How their greed had finally caught up to them and their desire for power had sealed their fate. What was it with him and this power trip? He was the most powerful man in these parts. Was that not enough? Did he really have to make this big speech?

When his men move to form a line in front of Death Mob, I know he's wrapping it up. I look down at Diem, who is white with fear at what her eyes are fixing to witness. Taking a gun from his back, Dorian stands in the center of the men. When he says the words, "This is for Dirk," I move my body in front of Diem, blocking her view.

The sounds of gunshots surround us, as the men fire round after round into the bodies that continue to fall. I keep my eyes on Dorian, watching his every move. When the last body falls, I move back beside Diem. A tear runs down her cheek as she squeezes her eyes shut. With my thumb, I reach out and wipe it, and she jumps at my touch.

"It's me, baby," I whisper. "You're okay, but I need you to hold it together until we get out of here." Her eyes dance in her head, trying to find something to focus on that isn't the pile of dead bodies. "Look at me, Diem," I command, a little sterner. She does, and I know she's fixing to break. "Keep it together. Don't let him see you weak."

Slowly, she comes back to reality. I can almost see the shield as it creeps down her face, concealing her feelings. Brushing the backs of her hands across her face, she stands a little taller and nods. "I'm okay."

I turn just as Dorian approaches, giving her another couple of seconds to get her shit together. By the time he has her in his sights, she's back to the trained killer he raised her to be. "This is your glory to have, Diem. Your hard work paid off and I won't forget it."

I clench my jaw, wanting nothing more than to slap him like the bitch he is and tell him to eat shit. But when he looks at me, I just look right through him. "Shady," he says, nodding his good-bye.

Two men leave with him as the others stay to clean up the bloodbath. Clark comes over and instructs me to get Diem out of here, and I waste no time leading her to the car with my hand on her back once again. I call Rookie on the way, telling him we're leaving. I'd let him know where we'd be as soon as I found out, and he was waiting only a few minutes away.

I usher Diem into the backseat. Like a puppet, she follows my every command. I'm not even sure she hears me. I'm anxious to get to Rookie so I can be with her. The closer I get to him, the harder she breathes. Then her eyes start to blink rapidly, trying to control the floodgates I know are coming.

Finally, I spot Rookie's bike on the side of the road. I pull over, and get out to see Diem getting out too. "I need some air," she says to no one in particular. Crossing her arms over her chest, she starts walking down the narrow road toward nowhere.

"What happened?" Rookie asks, keeping his eyes on Diem.

Unable to peel my eyes away from her either, I answer. "A fucking slaughter."

"Damn," he breathes, shaking his head. He knew Diem was on the verge of breaking just like I did. "She have to do it?"

"No. I didn't let her watch either."

Diem finally stops walking about twenty yards out. Even from a distance, I can see that what we all knew was coming, was finally here. "I need you to drive us," I tell Rookie as I jog toward her. I slow down a few yards away, not wanting to startle her. "Diem," I say cautiously.

Turning to face me, she shakes her head. Tears rain from her eyes as her body jerks with sobs. "I don't want to be a monster anymore," she cries, and my heart breaks. She walks into my arms, her weight crashing against me.

"Shh," I soothe, placing my lips on top of her head. My hands rub her hair, her back, up her sides, and back down, trying to let her know that I'm here.

"I don't want this, Shady. Please don't make me do this anymore," she cries harder, the sound of her broken voice echoing around me.

"Shh. Okay, baby. No more." I lift her up, wrapping one arm around her legs while the other holds her to my chest. In my arms, I carry her back to the car. "I got you. I promise. I got you." Seeing her this hurt devastates me. It's a feeling of heartache I've never endured until now. Even losing Dirk wasn't as painful as watching the woman I love beg me for a better life.

In the car, I hold her in my lap. Letting her cry out everything she's been feeling her whole life. I absorb her small body, her tears, and all of her problems. I'm her man and it is my duty to be the one to carry the weight. I want her burdens, her fears, her heartache, and her doubt. It belongs on my shoulders. Not hers.

Several days ago, I feared that my love for Sinner's Creed was fading—being replaced with something else. Someone else. In this moment, I realize it's no longer a fear—it's a fact.

I'm ready to live for her.

I'm ready to give it all up.

I'm going to get her out of this life and away from this pain.

Like many of my brothers, the club has always been the sole purpose of my existence. But now she's my purpose. I can't live in a world where both her and Sinner's Creed exists. And for the first time in my life, I'm okay with that. Because now, I only want to live in a world with her.

30

DIEM CRIES IN my arms all the way back home. I carry her inside and she cries in my arms while we lay in my bed. Then she cries all through the night and into the morning. I just hold her and rub her and tell her over and over that I love her. That I'll protect her. And I promise that this life is over, and I'll spend the rest of my days building her a new one.

Eventually, she cries herself to sleep. When she does, the only comfort I find is in the peace that is her slow, steady breathing. It calms my heart and my racing mind to know that as long as she's asleep, she can escape from reality.

I refuse sleep even though my body begs for it. I won't waste one moment of her needing me and me not being here for her. If she sleeps for days, I'll still be awake—waiting for her to open her eyes so I can promise her again that I'm going to take care of everything.

It's after nine in the morning when she stirs. It's takes a minute to remember where she is and how she got here, but I can tell the minute realization dawns on her. As the memories come flooding back, I see them weighing heavy on her with every new one her mind processes.

Laying her head back on my chest, she sighs. "Do you think I'm weak?"

I almost laugh. "No. You're the strongest person I know." She has the strength of Dirk.

"Are you disappointed in me?"

"I'm proud of you. It takes a helluva lot more strength to walk away than it does to stay." Tilting her head so she looks up at me, I give her a sad smile. "I was too weak to do it myself."

"Walk away?"

I nod. "We all have a choice, Diem. I chose power and evil over a life that could have been a fuck of a lot more than the one I've made."

"It's never too late," she whispers, begging me with her eyes to give up something I've already decided to let go of.

"I know." I refuse to say anything else until I'm sure I can deliver on my promise. Sinner's Creed wasn't something you just walked away from. But for her, I was going to do everything in my power to make it happen.

"I've got to pee," she says, breaking the thick tension in the room. I've never been so grateful for her bladder or her bluntness. Getting up, she drags her feet to the bathroom, and I take the moment to go outside and piss too before I explode.

The shower is running when I return. Opening the bathroom door, I see her clothes strewn across the floor. "You okay?" I ask, rolling my eyes at my own stupid question.

"I'd be better if you were in here." At her answer I'm stripping. Moments later, I'm lathering her body with soap. "Did you mean what you said? About finding me a way out?" she asks, keeping her eyes closed as my fingers massage shampoo into her scalp.

"Every word." I reassure her by pressing my lips against her forehead—a gesture I know makes her feel wanted and safe.

I'm shampooing her hair for the second time, her request, when she asks, "How?"

"Do you trust me?" Cracking one eye open, she tells me she does without hesitation. "Then let me worry about that. I promised I'd take care of you and I will."

"What about you?" She looks down at our feet, mindlessly washing the same part of my stomach over and over. "Who's going to take care of you?" This time, she meets my eyes, searching for an answer.

"Rookie," I shrug, smirking.

She cocks her head to the side, a concerned look on her face. "Seriously, Shady."

Pushing the wet strands of hair back from her head, I grab the back of her neck. Staring into her eyes, I tell her the truth. "I can take care of both of us. So promise me that you'll let me handle this." It takes her a minute, but finally she finds something in my eyes that makes her believe that what I'm saying is the truth.

"Okay. I promise."

I smile. "Good. Now, unless you're trying to remove my skin, try washing me somewhere else."

While Diem attempts to cook something that I swear I'm not going to bitch about, I sneak away to call Rookie. "I need you to come over and stay with Diem while I handle a few things," I tell him as soon as he answers.

"Want me to bring Carrie?" I think about that a moment. Either way, it had its pros and cons. But four eyes on Diem were better than two.

"Yeah. But Rookie," I say, lowering my tone with warning. "Do not let her out of your sight. I mean it. I'm trusting you."

"Who the hell has you so paranoid? I'll shoot her in the foot if I have to, but I give you my word she won't leave my sight." The sad part about that is he's telling the truth. I am paranoid. And he would shoot her if he had to. I just hope it doesn't come to that.

"Something smells good," I lie, walking back into the kitchen.

"It's a fucking sandwich, Shady." Good to see she hasn't lost her attitude.

I scan the counter looking for mine. "You make me one?" I ask, my eyes still searching.

"One time. One time I lose my shit." She glares at me. "I had an emotional breakdown. Not amnesia. I still remember who I am, and the last time I checked I didn't make you sandwiches."

I can't take my eyes off her. I can't wipe this smile from my face either. I love her so fucking much. Just like this. This is my Diem— bitchy, self-centered, and bossy. I think it's the cabin. Almost every good memory we have was shared here. I was going to miss this place.

"Stop looking at me like that. It's creepy." She grabs her sandwich and her milk, heading straight for my recliner. Dressed in my shirt, she pulls it down over her legs, using her knees as a table. I hear the opening credits of *Gunsmoke* and capture this moment. Then I remember all the other moments we've had together. Like so many times before, I'm prepared to give my life for the ones I love. Today might be my final day, but it would be just the beginning for Diem.

Rookie and Carrie arrive, and judging by the smile on Diem's face, the decision to bring Carrie was the right one. I jerk my head toward the bedroom and Rookie follows. Closing the door behind me, he starts before I have a chance to say what I need to.

"Carrie will not let Diem out of her sight." The finality in his tone has me shaking my head. He just ignores me. "I trust her. You should too. But I'm coming with you."

"No," I say firmly. "I need you here. If this shit goes south, this will be the first place they come. I won't leave our girls to fend for themselves. I need you here. They need you here." He doesn't like it, but finally he agrees.

"Fine. But if I don't hear from you by morning, I'm coming to get you."

I nod. "Call Cleft. Get him to arrange for her to have a passport in a different name. Have him meet her at the airport in Houston along with a one-way ticket out of the country. There is some money in my safe along with the information for my accounts overseas. If I'm not back by morning, put her ass on a plane and get her out of here. If you don't, she will die."

Removing his hat, he rubs his hand over his head. "I'm not so sure about this, Shady. Dorian's not the kind of guy you just walk up to and demand shit from."

"I'm not demanding anything. I'm just going to talk to him. Her leaving is just a precaution. Trust me."

"It's him I don't trust," he snaps, cutting me off. "He will kill you."

"Then guess what, I'll die and Diem will be free." Stepping closer, I wrap my hand around the back of his neck, bringing his face an inch from mine. "I would give my life for you. For my club. For Carrie. I am not scared to offer up the same thing for Diem. I will not be intimidated by any man. I don't care who that motherfucker is."

Taking a deep breath, he nods, grabbing my shoulder. "Okay," he says, his eyes burning with respect and pride. "Do what you got to do. I'll take care of everything else." Pulling him in, I hug my brother. My best friend. The one person I trust with the one thing that I hold close to my heart—my Diem. He will do this for me because he loves me. And because he knows I'd sure as fuck do it for him.

My bag is packed, slung over my shoulder as I prop up against the wall and stare at Diem, who wears a genuine smile for the first time in weeks. She already looks free . . . happy. Her eyes move to me and I give her a smirk. Her face falls as she takes me in, fully dressed and packed to leave. "A minute?" I ask, nodding my head toward the kitchen.

She follows me in, her hands fidgeting nervously. "You're leaving?" she asks, once we're alone.

"Yeah." I smile, caressing her cheek with the back of my hand. "Remember when I told you I would handle everything? Well, some things can't be done over the phone."

She nods. "I know."

"Look," I start, framing her face with my hands. "I made some arrangements for you. Rookie is going to handle everything. But I need you to do exactly what he says when the time comes."

She pulls away, shaking her head. "He will kill you, Shady."

I roll my eyes. "So I've been told," I say, bored. "What he will do is listen to what I have to say. Trust me, babe. I'm pretty good at this. I know what I'm doing, I just don't know how long it will take. So I need you to do as I ask."

"I'm not gonna sit back and let you deal with this shit yourself," she snaps, her eyes flashing with anger.

"What happened to letting me handle shit, huh? Where's that Diem from the shower this morning?"

"She found her nuts in a sandwich," she spits back at me. And I almost smile.

"I made you a promise. I plan to make good on that promise too. Now it's time for you to keep your word. I've never asked you for anything, Diem. I'm asking you for this. And if I remember correctly, you owe me one." It's a shitty hand to play, but it's the only one I have. But it doesn't hurt her.

Coming closer, she reaches out, fisting her hands in my shirt. "My life will be worth nothing if the rest of it is spent grieving you. I can deal with anything this shitty life throws at me because I know I'll have you to come home to. But if you leave, I lose everything."

Her words are the most beautiful thing I've ever heard. She's what I've spent my whole life searching for. She's the only thing that can fill that void in my chest. And for that reason alone, is why I'm doing this. "I will come back to you. I swear on *your* life, Diem—the most precious thing I value. I'm not asking anymore. I'm telling you." Cradling her neck in my hands, I run my thumb across her cheek and whisper my final plea. "Let me go."

Her brown eyes well with tears. I can see the resolve in them even before she speaks. "Then go."

Closing my eyes, I breathe a sigh of relief. It's not that she's letting me do this; it's that she trusts me enough to. "I love you," I tell her, planting a soft kiss on her trembling lips.

"If you die, I'm going to kill you," she says against my mouth, and I smile.

"Deal." Allowing myself to drown in that sea of brown, I gaze into her eyes one last time. "See you around, pretty girl."

I turn and walk out, promising myself that this is the last time I will ever leave her again.

Dorian is currently staying at his mansion in Boston—one of the many he has in the U.S. It makes my cabin look like a shack and Fort Knox look like a playground. A sixteen-foot wrought-iron fence wired with motion detectors surrounds the property that sits on a corner lot. The yard is guarded by numerous pit bulls that I'm sure live off of human flesh. Men are at every corner, constantly on watch for any suspicious activity. It's a little much if you ask me, but whatever lets him sleep at night.

I park on the street, and I'm still getting out when I'm shoved to the ground. My guns are taken from me, which I predicted would happen anyway. "Who are you?" one of the men asks. He sounds excited and I'm guessing that they don't get much action around here.

"Shady," I say, the side of my face pressed against the sidewalk. "I'm here to see Dorian." I'm pulled to my feet while someone speaks into an earpiece. Whoever responds on the other end must have told them who I was. Now they're brushing off my clothes and offering me a cigarette. But they don't offer me my gun.

"I'm good. But, I'll be expecting that back when I leave," I tell them, pointing to my gun that one of the other guards is already admiring.

"Sure thing, Shady." Fucking goons. They were worse than Prospects.

I'm ushered through the gates, and up the stone steps of the palace. A heavy wooden door opens once I reach the top and an old man greets me, offering me a glass of wine, which I decline. When he offers whiskey, I accept.

Another goon holding a machine gun leads me into a parlor that smells like cigar smoke and money. My eyes scan the room, appraising all the fine artwork and expensive decor I should probably give a shit about. But I don't. The one thing that does capture my attention is a mural on the wall of a woman in red. Diem had the same portrait.

"My wife." I turn to see Dorian walking in. His white dress shirt is untucked with his sleeves rolled up to his elbows. He holds a glass of scotch in one hand and a cigar in the other. "She reminds me that love is a dangerous thing." He stands beside me, looking up at the beautiful woman that resembles Diem, but there is still no comparison.

"No man has ever loved a woman as much as I loved my Dia. She was my world." He pauses, turning to look at me. I can still see the hate sparkling in his eyes. "Then she fucked me. Both literally and figuratively."

The old man appears with my whiskey and I take it, thanking him kindly. "Do you mind if I smoke?" I ask, needing the nicotine to help calm my nerves.

"Smoke," Dorian says with a wave of his hand. "What brings you here on this beautiful evening, Shady? It has to be important considering you disobeyed my direct order to not leave Diem's side. So, are you here for business or pleasure?"

I light the cigarette, letting the smoke fill my lungs before answering. "Both."

"Both." He nods his head, gesturing for me to take the seat across from him. I'd rather stand, but considering his position, I sit out of respect. "Go ahead, the floor is yours."

"I'm here to discuss Diem."

At the mention of her name, a spark of concern flashes in his eyes, but he doesn't ask about her well-being. I wasn't expecting the show of weakness, but it gives me a little more confidence than I had a moment ago.

"She wants out," I say, cutting through the bullshit. This isn't a man who cares to hear it, so I don't waste his time.

"Out? There is only one way out." His voice remains calm, but I can see the disappointment written all over his face.

"That's why I'm here. To help find another way out."

He shifts, not liking my tone. Unfortunately for him, I don't give a shit. "I don't take kindly to threats, Shady. You'll do well to remember that."

"I'm not threatening you. I simply want to make you an offer. Someone to step in and take Diem's place."

He laughs, finding humor in my suggestion. "Who? You? This isn't your bike club, Shady. This is the Mafia. Blood matters in this business. You have to be made to be a part of my family. And even if your tanned skin and dark eyes make you appear to be from our bloodline, my people will know the difference. You look more Mexican than Greek, my friend."

Now it's my turn to laugh. "*Sí, señor.*" I take a sip of my whiskey, letting him recover from his fit of laugher. Damn, he's easily amused. "But I wasn't talking about me." My smile drops, and I watch as his fades too.

"There is no one else," he says, a warning in his tone.

I lean forward. "But you know that I know better than that, don't you, Dorian."

He shakes his head, a look of disgust on his face. "You come into my house and tell me what I know? What's to keep me from killing you where you sit? Other than my expensive Persian rug that your filthy blood will stain."

"Diem is falling apart. She's not made for this. No amount of training can force her to become someone she isn't. You and me," I say, gesturing between the two of us. "We were born for this life. Dirk, he was born for this life." At the mention of his name, Dorian's eyes narrow. "She's a woman, Dorian. I'm not saying that makes her any less of a human, but I'm saying that she needs more than just death, and money, and power. She needs love, nurturing, and knowledge that there is a man in this world that will always protect her."

"And that man is you?" Dorian growls, using his best death glare to intimidate me. It might be working. Just a little.

"No." I shake my head, feeling my body heat with anger. "That man is you."

"I gave her everything!" Dorian suddenly yells, jumping to his feet. I stand too, not willing to be talked down to. "I gave her the opportunity to have whatever she wanted."

"All she wanted was you," I say between my teeth. If he kills me now, at least he'll have my words to haunt him for the rest of his life. "You never gave her an opportunity because you never gave her a choice. You forced her into becoming a monster. Your own fucking daughter!"

Now I'm yelling, and out of the corner of my eye, I can see we've drawn a crowd. Dorian jerks his head toward the door and they all disperse. Looking back at me, a lethal gleam flashes in his eyes. This time, there is no respect to mask it. He's pure evil. But a part of me is too.

"She is the future," he says, pointing his finger at me.

I shake my head, giving him an incredulous half smile. "She was your future. But not anymore. You're killing her. Not physically, but her spirit is breaking. Her will to live is dying. I saw it in Dirk. He searched his whole life for something, trying to fill that void that was you."

"Dirk was fine," he argues, but his own voice is doubtful.

"Dirk was lost. The club helped, but the only time he really lived was when he was with Saylor. And when she died, nobody had to put a bullet in him. Her death was enough to kill him." Straightening my spine, I try to look through his eyes and into his soul. Hoping that, maybe, a small piece of it still lives.

"I've never begged any man for anything. My life is of no value to me compared to my family. So I have nothing to lose. But you once told me that being a coward was sometimes worth more than your pride. And I'm standing here before you, begging you to offer her the choice that you never offered Dirk. Please."

The silence is deafening as he stares at me. I don't know if he's trying to read me, or figuring out how to kill me. What I do know is that I've done everything in my power. And that very soon, no matter if I'm breathing or not, Diem will be out of his life forever. But a small part of me still hopes that he will give her freedom to live her life wherever she wants.

"You are no coward, Shady. But you are a very stupid man." He walks over to his desk, shaking his head the entire time. "Like I said, love is a dangerous thing. It is your weakness. I will give Diem the choice, but blood is thicker than water. And she will always choose me."

A small part of me believes him. As much as I want to believe that Diem meant what she said, I'm not sure if I can. She was loyal to him all these years. She hasn't known me near as long. Was I wrong to have that much faith in her? Would she really give it all up? For me? Power was her kryptonite. Without it, she would just be normal. And Diem didn't do normal.

"Let's call her, shall we?" Dorian says smugly. He can see the wheels turning in my head.

"No need. I'm already here." At the sound of her voice, my eyes roll. *Motherfucker.* Why am I not surprised?

31

"**TELL ME YOU** killed Rookie," I say as a form of greeting to my intruding little pain-in-the-ass woman.

She walks in, dressed like she's ready to take on the world in pajama pants and flip-flops. Confused, she looks at me. "No. I wouldn't do that." She sounds defensive, but what she doesn't know is that the only way she could possibly be here is if he was dead. Now that he's not, I'm going to kill him.

"Diem," Dorian greets her, appraising her outfit with the same disgust he'd been looking at me with. "I can see your new surroundings have rubbed off on you."

"And I see that someone can't move on from the past." Her eyes glance up at the mural, and Dorian's face grows red with anger.

Now I guess we're all pissed. I had this shit under control. But leave it to Diem's infuriating fucking tactics to outsmart Rookie, crash my party, and insult the don of the Underground Mafia. I think she deserves a round of fucking applause.

"I'm out, Dorian. And I'm not asking."

I throw my hands up in surrender and take a seat, lighting a smoke that will likely be my last and enjoying the show.

"Do not come in here and demand anything of me," Dorian threatens, grinding his fists into the desk as he leans forward. I wish she would look at me for help. If she does, I'll shoot her myself.

"The family rules state that I'm allowed a decision in the matter. Especially considering that one of your brothers still lives." I have to hand it to Diem. She looks more powerful in pajamas than she ever has in a business suit. Maybe even sexier too.

"You are under a blood oath." My eyes swing to Dorian, who I'm sure has a gun strapped under his desk. Two shots—boom, boom—and Diem and I are both dead. But either she has a better plan, or she's just stupid.

"I'm under nothing," she says, her own accent shining through. "You forced me into this."

"And I will force you to stay. You want a choice? Here it is. Who dies first, you or him?" He points to me, just as his hand leaves the desk.

I'm on my feet, blocking Diem's body with my own just as the shots ring out. My right shoulder jerks, but the rush of my adrenaline keeps me from feeling the pain. I look down at Diem, who is blinking up at me. She's fine. Uninjured. Alive—for now.

I look up to see Clark holding a gun in his hands. Looking behind me, blood is spattered on the wall where Dorian once stood. I slowly get to my feet, helping Diem up, I try to push her behind me, but she moves out of my grip.

"Find the seal," she orders, walking quickly to the desk. She rummages through the files on top, then glances down at what must be Dorian's body before stepping over it and opening the drawers. Her eyes are cold and unfeeling. She doesn't look the least bit concerned that her father is lying dead at her feet. I guess when someone tries to kill you, you tend to lose the love you once had for them.

"Would somebody please tell me what the fuck is going on?" I ask, feeling helpless as I just stand here with my hands on my hips.

"Remember that whole trust talk we had a few hours ago?" Knocking books from a shelf, she pauses long enough to look at me expectantly.

"I do. But, obviously you didn't," I snap.

"Well, now it's your turn to trust me. Rookie is outside. I need you to leave with him. I'll be back at your place in two hours."

I want to laugh at her suggestion. "Yeah. That's gonna fuckin' happen. How about this. Somebody tell me what the hell is going on, or I'm gonna start breaking shit. Starting with your fingers."

"Got it," Clark says, grabbing a silver box from a shelf. Inside is an antique seal that dates back for centuries, engraved with the family crest.

Diem pulls some papers out of the back of her pants, laying them out on the desk. Clark scribbles his signature while Diem grabs a letter opener and slices her palm. My eyes widen. "Holy shit. Y'all really believe in this whole blood thing, don't you?"

Ignoring me, Diem commands that I find Harry, whoever the fuck that is, and bring him back. "Harry!" I yell, causing her to nearly jump out of her skin. She shoots me a look and I shrug. The old man with the whiskey walks in, looking at me like I shouldn't be alive.

"Don?" he asks, searching the room for Dorian. I couldn't kill this poor man, I'd just have to hit him in the head with a book or something.

"He's dead, Harry," Diem informs him, and he looks to me for confirmation.

"Sorry, Harry."

He closes his eyes, drawing a cross over his chest before kissing his fingers and looking up. I don't know if he's mourning Dorian's death, or thanking God for taking him. He walks up to the desk, signing his name to the paper before handing it back to Diem. Patting her cheek, he gives her a smile. She holds his hand to her face a minute before turning her lips to give it a quick kiss.

I watch him shuffle out, then look back at Diem, who is doing some kind of chant with Clark. Then it hits me; she's swearing him in. Then I start realizing that there is no one else here. That all is quiet. That Diem and Clark seem to be in a hurry and my shoulder hurts like a son of a bitch.

"Um," I say, staring at the blood that rolls down my fingertips onto Dorian's rug. *Fucker.* "Where the hell is everybody?"

"They left before the elders got here," Diem says.

"Elders?"

"The old guys from the meeting room. If they get pissed about this, nobody wants to be around to feel the wrath." She moves the mural on the wall to reveal a safe.

"So should we be around?" I ask as the hair on the back of my neck stands up. I don't even have a gun.

"Nope. That's why we're leaving. Don't worry. Clark will handle it."

To confirm, Clark gives me a nod. "Everything will be fine, Shady. Trust me."

I laugh at the irony. Trust. I didn't trust anybody anymore. Except for Harry. He walks in, handing me another glass of whiskey. "Thanks, Harry." He smiles proudly up at me, patting my arm. So maybe Harry is a little crazy.

He walks out, and I whisper to Diem, "How long has he worked here?"

She looks over her shoulder at me. "Who, Harry?" I nod. "His whole life. He built this place."

I can't conceal my shock. "What?"

"That's why I needed his signature. He's the oldest living elder."

"What, is he your uncle or something?"

Slinging a bag over her shoulder, she shakes her head. Grabbing my whiskey, she finishes it off before shooting me a wink. "He's my grandfather." This is one seriously fucked-up family.

True to Diem's word, Rookie is waiting in the car outside. The first thing I do when I slide in the front seat next to him is hit him right in the jaw. "That's for fucking up. And I'm pulling your patch for lying to me. Good luck Prospecting for the next year."

He moves his jaw with his hand, trying to line it back up. "Do what you want. I heard a plan B and went with it. If I have to Prospect another five years, it'll be worth it. At least you're still alive."

"Don't throw that guilt trip shit on me. You gave me your word. That's worth more than fucking plan B."

Diem's hand comes to rest on my shoulder from the backseat as Rookie pulls out. "It's not his fault," she says, but her words fade out as she switches on the light and looks at her hand. "Ohmigod! You've been shot!" she screams in my ear.

Rookie glances over. Looking at my face, he doesn't like what he sees. "Shit," he says under his breath, pressing harder on the accelerator.

Suddenly I feel weak. Removing my hoodie, I see that the sleeve is soaked in blood. "It's just a shoulder wound," I say, then clear my throat in an attempt to speak louder. "It's nothing."

"Put pressure on it. He's lost a lot of blood," Rookie instructs Diem.

"Why didn't you tell me you'd been shot?" she asks, and the only pain I feel is at the sound of her voice that's full of worry.

"I'm fine, pretty girl."

"Don't you die on me, you bastard," she chokes out.

"I can't. If I did, you wouldn't be able to kill me like you promised." Leaning my head against the back of the seat, I smirk at her.

She smiles through her tears. "How can you hate someone that you love so much?"

I start to answer her, but everything goes black.

I wake up in my bed. Rookie is asleep in a chair across from me. Diem is curled into my side and Carrie is lying next to her. There is a sling on my arm and gauze covering my shoulder. The only thing I'm wearing is my boxers, and for the life of me I can't remember how I got here.

Then it starts coming back. I look over at Diem, who sleeps peacefully, finally free from her father's hands. I guess a bullet in the shoulder was worth it. I move my arm and something pulls at my skin. There is an IV hooked into my arm, and an empty blood bag hanging from the post. Damn. Good thing Carrie was around.

"I'm not dead," I announce to the room. Rookie jerks awake at my words, but Diem and Carrie both remain asleep.

"How you feeling?" Rookie asks, wiping the sleep from his eyes.

"I'm good. Hand me my smokes."

He grabs my cigarettes from the dresser, lighting one before passing it to me. "You still pissed at me?"

I look up at him, remembering that the last thing I said was that I was going to pull his patch. "Nah, just disappointed." No need in lying about it now.

Pulling his chair next to me, he takes a seat. "Clark came by right after you left. He'd been working on a plan of his own to get Diem out." Dropping his eyes to the floor, he continues. "Dorian thought you were overshadowing Diem's power. He already had plans to kill you. I figured I didn't have anything to lose."

"Diem's life, Rookie. You had that to lose," I say, flicking my ashes into his open palm.

He shakes his head. "She'd have never got on that plane, Shady. You know that as well as I do. Even if I drove her there myself, she'd have found a way to escape. That's real love, man. I know because I got it myself." His eyes move to Carrie. I watch him as he looks at her with the same burning love I have for Diem.

"You could have called me," I say, pulling his attention back to me.

"Your phone's bugged." Fuck. Of course it is. "You didn't take a prepaid and I knew you'd rather me stay with Diem than go after you. So, that's what I did."

Knowing he'll answer truthfully, I ask, "What would you do if you were in my shoes?"

"I'd be pissed, but I'd know where your heart was. And I'd trust that you did what you truly thought was right." The sincerity in his eyes can't be faked. My brother is telling the truth. So I give him the same courtesy he would have shown me.

"Then that's where we stand." I give him a knowing nod that he returns.

"Now isn't that sweet." Diem's sleepy voice fills the room. Looking up at me with tired, swollen eyes, she smiles. "Of the two shoulders you have, could you not have gotten shot in the other one? How in the hell am I supposed to sleep? This," she says, waving her finger over my shoulder, "is my favorite pillow in the world. And you just had to go and fuck it up."

"Well pardon me, ma'am," I drawl, letting my southern accent shine through. "Maybe we can find another body part for the little lady to lay her head on."

Smacking me on the stomach, she smiles. "I missed you."

"How long have I been out?"

"Two days," she and Rookie both announce.

At the reminder, I close my eyes. "I'm wearing a catheter, ain't I?"

Diem nods. "That is aaaaall Carrie."

I look over at Rookie, who tightens his jaw. "Aw, come on. She'll probably still love you anyway."

"I have no problem shooting the head of it off," he growls.

I laugh, but he finds no humor in my joke. "I get it. No jokes about Carrie. He gets so sensitive," I say to Diem, who frowns up at me.

"Do you get that defensive when people talk about me?" Oh, for fuck's sake.

"Of course I do," I lie, knowing that I'd find it hilarious if Diem had to put a catheter in Rookie. "Remember the guy with no kneecaps?" I ask, and her frown deepens at the reminder.

"You hungry?" Rookie's ability to change the subject has me forgiving him completely, if there was any doubt that I hadn't already.

I'm catheter-free thirty minutes later and I still can't meet Carrie's eyes. It's just fucking weird. She's unaffected though, proud to see that I didn't die on her makeshift operating table that was actually my kitchen floor.

We're eating pizza, everyone reliving the two days I was out. I'm surprised to find that Carrie had to slap Diem to calm her down. I hope like hell she sleeps with a gun. But the news is good for me. I guess Diem really does love me.

It's the most normal my life has ever been up until the moment

Rookie's phone rings. He walks outside, shooting me a look on the way. I already know it's Nationals. Following him out on the front porch, I hear the words "I understand" before he hangs up.

"They want us in Jackpot. Tomorrow." I drop down on the steps. "Shady," he says, and I glance up at him, getting a sick feeling in my gut at the look on his face. "That ain't the only problem we have."

"Shit. What is it?" I ask, waiting for him to walk around so we're facing each other.

"Diem has to leave the country." My face falls at his words. "Clark says it isn't safe for her here. She needs to be gone in a week, tops."

"How long does she have to stay gone?" He takes a moment to answer, and in his silence, I already know.

"Forever."

"Forever?" Diem asks, even though I've already told her twice. We're in my room while I try to break the news to her as gently as possible. "I'm no coward, Shady. I'm not scared of any of them."

Grabbing her face with my good hand, I meet her eyes. "I know that. But it's the only way. If you stay, you'll spend the rest of your life looking over your shoulder."

"I'm not leaving you," she says through her teeth, her voice shaky but determined.

I offer her a sad smile. "It's only for a little while. I'll come as soon as I sort some things out here."

"They won't let you leave. I know it. There is no out for you." I didn't know who she'd been talking to, but I would kill them if I ever found out.

"Let me worry about Sinner's Creed," I try, but she shakes her head. Not listening.

"I'm not leaving unless you come with me. That's final." Giving me a look that confirms it, she adds, "It's my word."

Later that night, Rookie and I leave Diem and Carrie inside while he helps me pack up my shit in the shed. No matter the outcome, I wouldn't be coming back here. If Diem had to leave, then I was leaving too. And if the club wouldn't grant me my freedom, they'd have to kill me. Either way, my home in Hillsborough would only be a memory.

When the announcement is made that I want out, I know he is the one who will take it the hardest. I dread telling him, but he deserves to be the first to know.

"I'm out, Rookie," I say, taking a seat on my bike and lighting a cigarette.

He straightens, forgetting the box he'd been packing and narrowing his eyes on me. "What?"

"I want out," I repeat, dropping my eyes. "I love Sinner's Creed, but I love Diem more. She needs me and damn if I don't need her too."

"Shady," he starts, but I cut him off.

"When Dirk died, I lost something. The club couldn't fill that void. I tried, but the emptiness was there. Every day I woke up, all I could think about was how incomplete I felt." I shake my head, remembering the feeling. "Then I found her." I smile. "From the first moment I saw her, something inside me changed. I still grieved for Dirk, but the pain was bearable. Now the only pain I feel is when she hurts."

I finally meet his eyes, feeling guilty at the disappointment I see. But if anybody gets me, it's Rookie. "I'm truly happy for the first time in my life. I want to live without the power and greed and killing. I want something better."

He nods with understanding. But he'd be a shitty brother if he didn't at least try to get me to stay. So when he speaks, I'm expecting an alternate solution. But what I get is something else. "I had Carrie before I had the club. For a long time, I thought she was all I needed. But the club gives me something she can't." With eyes that beg me to understand, he tells me something I haven't considered.

"I want you to be happy, Shady. I swear I do. But I'm scared that one day you'll look back and realize that your new life isn't everything you thought it would be. Men like us can't live on love alone. We're just not made that way."

I consider his words. Hell, I don't doubt them. But I have to try, because I owe it to Diem. I've said many times that I'd give my life for her, and that's exactly what I plan to do.

Standing out of respect, I enforce my decision that I know he'll support. "I'm leaving Sinner's Creed. I'm gonna give Diem that life I promised. I might miss the club. One day I might hate myself for leaving it. And I'll have to live with that. But just the thought of living one more fucking day on this earth without her hurts more than anything I've ever felt. And that's a pain I just can't live with."

He studies me, knowing he'd do the same if he ever had to choose. His jaw clenches, fighting against the same emotions I feel in my chest for this man. Next to Dirk, he's the greatest brother I've ever had. I was his teacher, his leader. He felt like he owed me his life, but he owed me nothing. It was an honor to ride with him, and I know he feels the same.

With my one good arm, I pull him in. There is no pride when it comes to loving my brother. There is nothing I wouldn't do for him. He's looked to me for guidance for years. He's depended on me to carry him through the dark times. This moment is no different. So I stand strong and bear the weight of his grief. I'll miss all my brothers, but I'll miss him most. Losing him is the only regret I have in my decision to leave Sinner's Creed.

Placing my lips against his, I kiss this man—my brother. It's not a romantic gesture or a passionate kiss like I'd give Diem. This is a show of love, loyalty, honor, and respect. Where Diem was my greatest love, Rookie was my greatest accomplishment. Like Dirk, he expresses the true meaning of Sinner's Creed by just existing. Even though I'm saying good-bye to the club, I'm leaving my mark with Rookie.

Because he isn't just another member with a patch—he's my fucking legacy.

32

I TAKE EVERYTHING from the cabin I can carry on my back—the important things that I just can't live without. Standing at the door, I give one last look at the only place other than Dirk and Saylor's that has ever felt like home. And I'm reminded that the feeling existed because Diem was there.

The four of us climb into my truck, and Carrie drives us to the airport for our flight to Jackpot. Rookie once told me that he keeps things from her. Judging by the look on her face, she's about tired of being kept in the dark.

I give her a one-armed hug, kissing her cheek as we say our good-byes. "Till next time," I say, giving her a wink.

She smiles. "Take care of that shoulder . . . and Diem. I kinda like her." I smirk. I guess Diem does have a friend.

We head inside, leaving Rookie to say his good-byes that don't go as smoothly as he probably planned. I should probably tell him that keeping her in the dark is a bad move on his part. But I wasn't much on giving relationship advice. He'd figure it out soon enough on his own.

Diem is shocked that we're flying first class. I guess she thinks we're poor. She even offers to pay for her ticket, but quickly shuts up when Rookie and I both level her with a look. I keep her close to me and my eyes open. I don't want to be caught off guard if one of Dorian's men shows up. Diem doesn't look the least bit worried. Rookie assured me we had a week. So did Clark and Diem. Obviously, I'm not as trusting as them.

We're drinking Bloody Marys on the plane waiting for the final passengers to board, when a familiar face catches my attention. I look over at Rookie, who's sitting across the aisle from me, but his eyes are closed and he's wearing headphones.

I try to clear my throat, but he doesn't budge. So I just let Carrie stand in front of him, with her hands on her hips while she wears a look that makes me think she's devising a plan to kill him. I feel Diem's hand wrap around my arm as she shifts in her seat to get a better view of the shit that's fixing to hit the fan.

Eventually, I guess Rookie feels eyes on him and looks up. He takes Carrie in, blinking a few times to make sure he isn't dreaming. Then he looks over at me. Knowing he'd do the same, I just give him a shrug. Turning back to Carrie, he slowly lowers his headphones.

"Carrie," he says cautiously. I've never seen her this pissed. I'm guessing he hasn't either.

"You've walked out on me for the last time, Rookie," she starts, her voice shaky with anger. "I hate it has to come to this, but I'm giving you an ultimatum. Either I'm in this or I'm out. Your choice. But I'm tired of the lies. The secrets. The lonely nights. I can't do it anymore." Her voice breaks as she struggles to hold it together.

Rookie just stares up at her, his face unreadable. I want to kick him, then demand he say something. The girl is dangling by a thin rope. And that motherfucker is holding the other end. He needs to just let her go, or grab her by the arms and pull her in. There's no other option at this point. She'd said her piece.

Without taking his eyes off her, he grabs his bag from the seat and stands. My eyes narrow, wondering what in the hell he is doing. Then, lifting the compartment above his head, he shoves the bag inside and motions for her to take a seat.

"I may or may not have had something to do with this," Diem whispers to me. I turn to look at her, raising my eyebrows. "What?" she asks, feigning innocence. "I like her. She deserves to know the truth."

I shake my head. "See, this is why most of the brothers don't have girlfriends. Y'all are like a pack of bloodsuckers. Y'all stick together and try to pick our brains for info and drain us dry."

"That's about the shittiest thing I've ever heard you say." She leans back in her seat, jerking her hand from my arm.

Great. Now my woman is pissed too. Fuck girl power. "I'm just saying that their business is not our business. Maybe Rookie thought she couldn't handle it. And that's for him to decide."

She whirls back around to face me. I can tell by her look, I'm fixing to be subjected to her wrath. "No, it's for her to decide. But she can't decide shit if she doesn't know what she's deciding." Now I'm confused. "I know what it's like to be kept in the dark." She quirks an eyebrow at me, but really? It's not like she was Mother Teresa.

I roll my eyes, knowing this is a fight I cannot win. "Whatever you say, Diem. But if this shit comes back to bite me in the ass, I'm biting yours." Downing my drink, I motion for the flight attendant to bring me another. When she hands it to me, I shoot her a smile of thanks, and because Diem is already pissed, she takes it out of context.

"I saw that," she mumbles, just as the same flight attendant starts speaking over the intercom. "I'll choke that bitch with the phone cord."

"What happened to you not wanting to be a monster?" I ask, keeping my voice low enough for only her to hear.

"Just because I don't like slaughtering hundreds of men doesn't mean I don't get satisfaction out of killing a few deserving ones. Especially women who hit on my man."

"Oh, for fuck's sake. Calm down." Damn, she's exasperating.

"You calm down," she says, poking me in the ribs.

I groan, holding my side and eyeing the phone cord. Maybe I could choke her just long enough for her to pass out. I look over at Rookie, who is holding Carrie's hand, kissing it reverently while she leans her head on his shoulder.

"Why can't you be more like that?" I ask Diem, jerking my thumb toward the two lovebirds across the aisle.

"Because that would only make you like me." I look at her expectantly, waiting for her to continue. Taking my drink from my hand, she downs it and smiles. "And what I'm looking for is love."

She's right—love for her is exactly what I have.

By the time we get to Jackpot, the sun is setting in the Nevada sky. It's a beautiful September day that will likely turn ugly in a matter of minutes. A Prospect is there to pick us up, and the ride is silent back to the clubhouse.

Rookie keeps Carrie pressed tightly against his side. Even though we're among family, he warns off every man we pass with a look. I don't even hold Diem's hand. Nobody but me is stupid enough to get involved with a crazy bitch like her. But I smile with pride knowing that she's mine.

"Monica," I greet, flashing a smile to her across the bar. I can feel Diem stiffen and my smile widens. "You remember Diem?" Looking down at Diem, I give her a look of warning. "Play nice."

She walks past me, sliding on one of the barstools and reaching her hand out to Monica, who takes it, shooting me an uneasy look. Not knowing what else to do, I look back at Diem. Damn, I hope she doesn't do anything stupid. "Nice to officially meet you, Monica. Although I think we spoke one time on the phone." Shooting daggers at me, Diem drops her smile, gives me the finger, then turns back to Monica. "I'll take a Seven and Seven."

"Okay. What can I get for you, sweetie?" Monica asks Carrie, who takes the seat next to Diem. I notice Diem cringe at the endearment, and pray that Monica doesn't use that sweetie talk on her.

"Surprise me," Carrie says, clutching her purse a little tighter in her lap. Poor thing.

"This isn't gonna end well, is it?" Rookie asks from beside me. Shaking my head, I give him the truth. "Nope. Not at all."

We leave the girls and join Nationals on the back patio. We stand, hug, shake hands, then I grab the blunt from between Chaps's finger before taking a seat. "How's the shoulder?" he asks, pointing toward my ridiculous sling that Carrie insisted I wear.

"It's good. I'm a little stiff, but this helps." I hold up the blunt with a smile.

"Got a call from Clark," Jimbo starts, getting right down to business. "Says Diem is out. That true?"

I nod. "It's true."

"And Dorian?"

"That's true too."

"Well, that's good news for us," Chaps says, sitting back in his chair. "Heard form a source that he wasn't taking much of a likin' to Sinner's Creed. I guess the more he thought about Cyrus's speech, the more he thought Dirk's death was our fault."

"Your girl, she think like that too?" Jimbo leans forward, taking the blunt from my fingers.

"She's out. Doesn't matter what she thinks. But the answer is no. She holds no ill feelings toward Sinner's Creed," I tell them, making sure I look all of them in the eye so they can feel the full impact of what I'm saying. Diem's name didn't need to be brought up anymore. She wasn't anybody's business but mine.

Jimbo gives Chaps a look, and he nods. Leaning forward in his seat, he clasps his hands together, taking a moment before finally dragging his eyes up to meet mine. "We know you want out." I keep my face impassive, not giving anything away. But what I really want to do is punch Rookie in the jaw. Again.

"And we get it," Chaps continues, giving me a look of understanding—the same look all my brothers wear. "But you're never just out, Shady. You know that."

Of course I know that. I was just hoping my brothers would give a little fucking credit where credit was due. I'd earned my right to be in this club. And I'd earned the right to walk away. I'd done everything for them. This was their chance to do something for me.

I light a cigarette, giving each one of them the same look of disappointment I feel in my heart. "I've never asked this club for anything," I start, remembering that Dirk had given this same group of men that same line a little over a year ago. "I'm not saying you owe me anything, because you don't. But ever since Dirk left, things haven't been the same for me. I feel like I've been living a lie for months. It's not fair to y'all for me to be a part of this if my heart just ain't in it. I've found something else to live for. And now that I have, I'll never be able to give this club the dedication it deserves."

They listen to my argument that I'm sure is falling on deaf ears. It doesn't matter what I say. Their minds are already made up. They know what they're going to do, and I'll have to accept my fate in whichever form they deliver it.

"I can't let you just walk away, Shady. And for that I apologize," Jimbo says, narrowing his eyes on me. "But, however . . ." He offers me a smile, looking around the circle at the other members. "I can put you on an undetermined, extended medical leave." Leaning closer, he grabs my good shoulder, bringing his face level with mine. "This is my gift to you, brother."

I bite my lip, drawing my eyebrows together in an attempt to control my emotions. My eyes burn, begging me to allow the tears building in them to release. This is family. This is brotherhood. This is Sinner's Creed.

Standing, I embrace Jimbo in a hug, silently thanking him for giving me a chance at a life most of us only dream of. A life Dirk dreamed of. One by one, my brothers hug me, kiss me, tell me how much I'll be missed and how proud they were to serve beside me. I brush the tears from my cheeks with the back of my hand, finally losing the battle with my emotions.

There are no words to describe the feeling I have. I'm happy and sad at the same time. I'm excited and scared. I'm saying good-bye to the only thing I've ever known, and walking into a world that I never thought I'd see. I turn to Rookie, knowing that I have him to thank for all of this. He'd planted the seed. He was the one who fought the battle with Nationals so I didn't have to. I'd once told Diem that Rookie was the one who'd look out for me. And today, he'd proved it.

"I need you on one final ride, Shady," Chaps informs me, his hand on the back of my neck pulling me closer. "Houston needs their bottom rockers. And you're the only man that can give it back to them."

I nod, my heart breaking a little knowing that this will be the last time I'll ever ride with a patch. The last time I'll ever be a part of the greatest brotherhood I've ever known. The last ride with Sinner's Creed—and the first ride of the rest of my life.

I decline the offer of a farewell party in fear of me changing my mind if I stayed any longer. Right now, I need to be with the reason I'm leaving all this behind. I need to be with Diem.

She's laughing when I approach her, but immediately stops when she notices me. Her eyes search my face for a clue. Then my body for more bullet holes. Then they widen with excitement when I smirk. I hold her face in my hand, kissing her deep as the bar erupts in applause, whistles, and catcalls. My heart beats—for her. My blood pumps—for her. I breathe—for her. My reason. My purpose. My Diem. To me, she is worth it all. And I'll spend every day loving her like it was my last.

There would always be a special place in my heart for Sinner's Creed—but there would never be a void. She captivated me. She owned me. And everything I've been searching for, I finally have. Leaving the club wasn't a loss—because with her, I had so much more to gain.

My bike is at Dirk's, so Rookie, Carrie, Diem, and I take a car to his house. Soon, the place is alive with laughter and talk just like it was on the last night Dirk and Saylor were here. The mood isn't melancholy, and there isn't ache in my chest at the lack of his presence. Somehow, I feel like he's here with us.

"I have to make one last run before we leave," I tell Diem, knowing I can't keep it from her any longer. We're all in the living room, which grows completely silent at my announcement. "Just down to Houston. I'll be back in a few days."

"How long will it take once you get there?" she asks, her mood a cross between pissy and sad. I'm hoping she stays pissy. Between her tears and mine, we could fill the Mississippi.

"An hour, tops."

"So just fly there and I'll wait in the car."

I smile at her solution. "I think this is one ride I want to take." I look in her eyes, begging her to understand how much I need this.

"Okay, fine." She shrugs, crossing her arms over her chest. "I'm going with you." Hell, no.

"I don't think so, princess. We're talking a twenty-five-hour trip. Tell her, Rookie." I look over at him, already nodding my head in agreement with what he says.

"I choose my battles, Shady. And this ain't one of 'em." He holds his hands up in surrender.

"Well if Diem goes, I'm going," Carrie adds, straightening her spine and looking at Rookie. I give him the finger. Serves the fucker right. He looks at the ceiling, shaking his head.

"Having visions of choking Diem?" I ask. "Don't worry, I get them aaaall the time."

"We're fucking going. And that's final." Diem gives me a challenging look. One that tells me I won't be winning this fight. Fucking women. And here I was throwing my life away for one. And not even a nice one. A vindictive, bossy, bitchy one.

I look to Rookie one last time, hoping he has something. But of course, he gives me that *fuck it* look and shrugs. There is no reasoning with her. Even if I try to tell her how dangerous it is for her to still be in the country, she won't listen. She'd told me that her life without me was meaningless. I know I'd never leave her, so I can't fault her for having the same feelings about me. She is my ride or die. My heart swells with the knowledge that what Diem and I have is true love—even if it infuriates the fuck out of me.

I drag my hand over my face, knowing the next three days will likely be the worst in my entire life. With women's power in mind, I pump my fist in the air. And with zero enthusiasm in my tone, I mumble, "Go team."

The sound of bikes wakes me early the next morning. It sounds like a fucking parade and I open the blinds in my room to find that there is one. Bike after bike, they roll down the driveway, parking on either side. There are at least thirty and more are pouring in by the minute.

I pull my jeans on, walking outside to find Rookie, Carrie, and Diem already on the porch. "What's going on?" I ask to no one in particular.

Diem comes to stand next to me, wrapping her arm around my waist. Looking up, she smiles. "They're here for you."

Less than an hour later, I'm dressed, our bag is packed, and the Prospects have my bike clean and polished. I look at myself in the mirror, dressed like the Johnny Cash of MCs—all in black. Grabbing my cut from the bed, I look down at the dirty patches and remember when they were white and new. Years of riding, blood, sweat, and tears are in these threads. And I'd earned every damn one of them.

Slipping it on over my shirt, I fasten the chains across my stomach and take a deep breath. This is it. Pulling my riding cap over my head, I grab my full face, turning one last time to look at my bedroom. I'll come back to it one day. Even if it is just for a visit. This was my home, and even though I'll miss it, I'm ready to make a new one.

I walk outside, hearing a silence come over the crowd of men here to see me off. I don't have words for them. The loyalty I've shown them over the last eight years is enough. Words are not needed for me on their behalf either. Just having them here is more than I ever could have asked for. So I just look out at all of them, and offer them a nod of respect.

Diem is standing next to my bike, looking every bit the biker-bitch part. She and Carrie had done some shopping yesterday, and I remind myself to thank her for it later. Black leather pants cover her legs, accenting her toned thighs. Knee-high riding boots with a six-inch heel have never looked more sexy on a woman. And the black shirt she wears shows off her perfect tits and molds to her tiny body.

Damn.

She walks over to me, crossing her ankles on every step like she's on a runway—one of the first things I noticed about her. "What is it about a bad boy in leather?" she asks, dragging her eyes up and down my body.

"Nobody does leather better than you, pretty girl." Wanting nothing more than to squeeze her ass in those tight little pants, I clench my fists, knowing if I get started, I won't stop. "We need to go over a few things," I start, but she shakes her head.

"I've been lectured for the past thirty minutes. Trust me, I know the rules." To emphasize, she starts calling them off on her fingers. "No bitching, no whining, no complaining, and no fucking tears." Her voice deepens on the last one, and I know that Chaps is here somewhere. He can't stand to see a woman cry. I guess that's why he sticks to the whores—not that I blame him.

Jimbo comes over, eyeing Diem a little too appreciatively, but I decide to let it go. "We'll follow you out of town, but then we gotta get back. Someone has to run shit now that I'm losing my best man."

"Thanks, Jimbo. For everything." I shake his hand respectfully, remembering the sacrifices he's made for me. Not only is he letting me go, but he gave me the time I needed to do right by Dirk. And I'd never forget it.

"A little something for the lady," he says, pulling a vest from his bag. "I believe any woman that can capture your heart, deserves to wear your patch."

I get nervous, wondering how Diem will react when she sees the *Property of* words on the back of her cut. If she shows her ass, I'll have to kill her. But she stands proud, a sparkle of pride in her eyes to wear something that means so much to me.

"I'd be honored," she whispers, holding her arms out for me

to slip the patch on her back. She looks down at her name, running her fingers over the threads. She starts to get a little teary eyed, but laughs and fans herself. "Does it look good on me?" Her laughter fills my ears, clenches my heart, and touches my soul.

Taking her chin in my fingers, I lean down and give her a soft kiss. "It looks perfect." And it fucking feels perfect too.

"One final ride," Rookie says from the seat of his Harley that stands next to mine. I stretch my arms, my adrenaline serving as a painkiller to my shoulder.

Pushing my fist against his, I nod. "One final ride."

Diem clings tightly to my waist as I fire up my engine. Closing my eyes, I listen as one by one, every motor rumbles to life. The sound of pipes racking off echoes in my ears. The gravel beneath my feet shakes. My song of choice blares through my speakers, "Bartholomew" by The Silent Comedy.

I say my good-byes today. I start my new life tomorrow. I finally have what I want. Love is not my weakness—it is my strength. I don't know if I'll be a better person with her. But I'm the best person for her. And she's the best person for me. She's my sunshine. My promise. My tomorrow. My everything.

She gave me hope when I thought all was lost. With her, I found my way. I owe her my life. And soon, she'll have it.

Until then, I have to live this life. *My* life. For what will be the last time, my club needs me. So I give them the greatest part of me—my respect, which they more than deserve. Pulling my shades over my eyes, I close the visor on my full face. This might be my final ride, but in this moment, I remember who I am.

I am a one-percenter.

I am Sinner's Creed.

I am fucking Shady.

EPILOGUE

Three Months Later

"I SAW THAT."

I roll my eyes at Diem's words. Could she be any more of a jealous bitch?

"What, Diem? What did you see?" I turn on my sun lounger to face her. She hides her eyes behind her sunglasses, but I know they're blazing with fury.

"You've been checking that girl out for weeks. I'll kill her, Shady. I swear I'll drown that bitch in the Caribbean."

"If you don't stop acting so fucking crazy, I'm gonna drown you." Upon my threat, I scan the beach for any witnesses. Lucky for her, this girl I allegedly want to fuck is too close for me to commit the crime and not be seen.

Sitting up, she pushes her glasses on top of her head and glares at me. "Why do you do this?"

Closing my eyes, I take a deep breath before answering. "Do what, Diem?"

"Act all innocent. Why else would you want to come to the beach at the same time every day?"

Over her shit, I sit up. My knees touch hers as I lean on my elbows and push my shades up on my head so I can match her death glare with one of my own. "I get up every morning at six," I start, fighting my temper and losing. "I go for a run. I come back and eat cereal because my girlfriend can't cook for shit."

Her eyes narrow, but I don't let it stop me. "Then, I watch the Spanish soap operas like the house-trained, lovestruck, domesticated pussy I've become until noon. And guess what happens then?" I give her a second to answer, knowing good and damn well she won't. "I eat another shitty meal consisting of either a sandwich or chips and salsa.

"After that, I take a nap like a fucking fifty-year-old man because in my sleep is the only time I don't have to hear your bitching. When I wake up at three o'clock, I like to come to the beach and relax. Now." I clap my hands together to keep from choking her.

"At any time during my pathetic day, if I had even one moment to be out from under your watchful eye, I'd spend it doing something other than burying my dick inside some random bitch who isn't nearly as hot as you."

Pushing my shades back down, I lay back on my lounger. My pulse is racing. I'm trying to catch my breath. My adrenaline is pumping through my body—exposing my veins with every pulse.

"You pissed?" she asks, hope in her voice.

I smile in satisfaction. "Finally."

"See, honey, I knew you still had it in you." Diem straddles my waist, and my hands come to rest on her warm thighs. Nobody does a bikini quite like Diem.

"It's been so long," I say, rubbing my hands up and down her smooth legs. "I need to get mean before Rookie comes to visit. He's gonna think I've completely lost my balls."

"Oh, I can assure him you still have your balls." Diem smiles, and I can't help it. I have to kiss her. Sitting up, I wrap my hand around the back of her neck, pulling her in for a deep kiss. She tastes like coconut rum—her newest addiction.

My life here isn't pathetic in the least. It's the greatest fucking decision I ever made aside from Diem. There are no worries, no stress, and no problems. The only time I don't feel pure elation is when she won't let me have the remote.

Pulling my lips from hers, Diem holds my face in her hands. "Did you see him today?" I shake my head, and she offers me an encouraging smile. "Maybe tomorrow then."

My mind drifts back to our first night here. We'd chose Barbados for a reason that neither of us could determine. No sooner did we walk into the real-estate agent's office, than we were ushered out the door to see a new property that went on the market that morning.

Because I'd never been to the beach, Diem insisted we find a place on it. The small villa was perfect for the two of us. The location was great. But it was the scent of citrus that sold me. I ignored it at first, but then shit started getting weird.

We stayed in a hotel for two days while the paperwork was being processed. On the day we moved in, a welcome home present was waiting for us on the bedside table. A bouquet of fresh flowers, a bottle of champagne and . . . Skittles.

That night, I laid down, and on the ceiling above our bed was a scripture. *I have found the one whom my soul loves.* And at the end, where there should have been a chapter and verse number, there was something else.

D&S

By the time I got Diem's attention, the words had disappeared.

I snap back to reality, and give Diem a shrug. "Maybe it's all in my head. I mean the supernatural? I think I'm losing my shit."

"You're not losing your shit," she says, pulling my hair and forcing me to look up at her. "We all have to believe in something."

Smirking, I ask, "What do you believe in, pretty girl?"

"You."

Damn, she's perfect. Maybe not in anyone else's eyes, but in mine, she's the ideal mixture of everything I've ever wanted.

"Okay." Grabbing my shoulders, she pushes herself off my lap. "I'm going to get a drink. You want one?"

What kind of question is that? Three months with me all to herself and she's still asking? Then again, the fact that she's actually asking is progress. I'd better not fuck this up. "Yeah, babe."

"Don't call me babe," she snaps.

Picking up her cup, she turns to leave but her eyes focus on something down the beach. Lowering her shades, I watch her squint in the sun. "I'm so jealous."

I roll my eyes. "Let me guess. Her ass is bigger than yours? Her tits are nicer? When are you going to stop worrying about what everyone else looks like and start appreciating me a little more for loving you the way you are?"

"It isn't always about you, Shady." She spits my name. Great. Now I've pissed her off. "And I wasn't talking about her body, you perv. I was talking about her hair."

She stomps off, mumbling to herself. I just shake my head. Turning to see this fabulous hair, my heart stops and my breath catches at the sight.

And there they are.

Walking hand in hand.

I can't see their faces, but there's no mistaking who they are. Saylor's hair is just as wild and untamed as ever. Dirk's big body looms huge beside her. Even if I wasn't able to identify him from behind, I know it's him. He's the only motherfucker on the beach in jeans.

There appears to be a halo of light surrounding them. I blink a couple of times to make sure I'm not just imagining them. But when I open my eyes, they're still there. No one else is paying attention to them, and a part of me knows that it's because only I can see them.

I watch Dirk as his arm wraps around Saylor's shoulders—pulling her in to kiss her hair. Then, with a glimpse that only lasts a second, his dark eyes narrow on me. They're not filled with hate or pain or pride. There's no steel or distance or coldness in them either. He's Dirk like I've never seen him. For the first time ever, he's happy. And even death couldn't stop him from getting the one thing he's always wanted—love.

I look back over my shoulder for Diem, but she's already inside. When I turn back to Dirk and Saylor, they've disappeared. I wait for my heart to plummet. For my hopes to die. But all I can do is smile. I saw him. He lives. And finally, he is at peace.

My heart swells with joy for my brother.

With pride for knowing him.

With honor for serving with him.

With serenity . . . the one feeling he finally has.

We were two brothers born into a life full of nothing. It was a long, hard, uphill battle, but we'd finally found something worth living for. Our lives were measured in miles. Our paths determined by our next mission. But somewhere along the way, God had decided to shed a little mercy on two of the darkest souls he'd ever created. And today, I witnessed what I've really known all along.

Dirk had found his happily ever after.

And finally, I've found mine too.